"I DISCOVERED THIS CAVE MY FIRST YEAR IN BERMUDA. I WANT IT TO BE THE FIRST PLACE YOU LEARN TO LOVE."

She wondered at his words. They echoed in her ears above the sound of the rising surf and the call of wild birds circling overhead. Learn to love. He loved her. He truly loved her. God knows, she had adored him as long as she could remember.

They arrived at a ledge in front of a small opening in the cliff. He scrambled up beside her and guided her into the aperture.

She had expected darkness, but was suddenly dazzled by a pink crystalline light that left her gasping in surprise and awe. "Braden," she whispered at last. "It's not of this world. It's the middle of a star—it's—it's a magician's lair."

He reached for her and held her against him. "Amanda—Mandy, my darling girl, this will always be our world of magic. Let me take you—here—now—we'll seal our love as man and wife."

Looking up at him, she knew she wanted nothing more in this life than to belong to him. "Yes, my love," she whispered. . . .

"FIVE STARS . . . HIGHEST RATING! *WIND ROSE* is an excellent colonial-romance novel. . . . A good writer just keeps getting better!"

—Affaire de Coeur

"PASSION, ROMANCE, EXCITEMENT, ADVENTURE—*WIND ROSE* HAS IT ALL. KRISTA JANSSEN IS A STAR ON THE RISE."

—Romantic Times

Books by Krista Janssen

Ride the Wind
Wind Rose

2-14-'94

To Sue,
Best wishes. Hope
you enjoy

KRISTA JANSSEN

Krista Janssen

POCKET BOOKS
New York   London   Toronto   Sydney   Tokyo   Singapore

This book is a work of fiction. Names, characters, places and incidents are either products of the author's imagination or are used fictitiously. Any resemblance to actual events or locales or persons, living or dead, is entirely coincidental.

An *Original* Publication of POCKET BOOKS

POCKET BOOKS, a division of Simon & Schuster Inc.
1230 Avenue of the Americas, New York, NY 10020

Copyright © 1994 by Rhoda Poole

All rights reserved, including the right to reproduce this book or portions thereof in any form whatsoever. For information address Pocket Books, 1230 Avenue of the Americas, New York, NY 10020

ISBN: 0-671-74499-2

First Pocket Books printing February 1994

10 9 8 7 6 5 4 3 2 1

POCKET and colophon are registered trademarks of Simon & Schuster Inc.

Cover art by Alessandro Biffignandi

Printed in the U.S.A.

To the memory of my parents,

Billie and Pete Grady

For your enormous love and joyful sharing. For inspiring me always to succeed. I feel your presence every day. Thank you, Mother and Dad, for being the best.

With special thanks to Persephone for agreeing to appear in this book—and to her guardians, Brent and Angela, for allowing her to do so.

AUTHOR'S NOTE

One of the joys of writing historical novels is finding real-life people who led fascinating lives, then bringing them to life along with their time period. My research of the late seventeeth century, which included the Salem witch trials, proved extraordinarily engrossing. After a visit to Salem, Massachusetts, during which I viewed a wonderful documentary film at one of the original "witch houses," I knew I had a great setting for a book. What I didn't expect when I delved into my local library was to find such an intriguing and controversial figure as Reverend Cotton Mather, a third-generation Puritan minister who was heavily involved in the trials in 1692. In New England, as in the British Isles and Europe, witches and their dark power were regarded as very real threats to the Godly souls traveling life's path toward Heaven. The eradication of witches was considered necessary for the protection of the community.

Though well known for his hell-and-brimstone sermons, Mather was also devoted to the study of medicine. He was a Harvard graduate of 1678, and in the early 1700s he made inquiries regarding the technique of inoculation against smallpox—the dreaded plague of the time—among slaves. After great soul-searching, he was himself inoculated along with his own family. I couldn't resist developing Reverend Mather as an important character in *Wind Rose.*

During this time, events in England continued to strongly influence the young British colonies of the New World. "Cavaliers," dashing second sons of landed English gentlemen, arrived in Virginia to claim land and establish plantations modeled on the great estates of their ancestors, while simultaneously escaping the Puritanical rule of Cromwell in their homeland. The rich Virginia soil was ideal for growing fine tobacco, and farms flourished. These settlers brought with them ambition, an aristocratic society based on land holdings, and their Anglican religion.

Englishmen of a different sort were populating the northern colony of Massachusetts Bay: settlers from the industrious middle class engaged in fishing, shipbuilding and managing small farms and villages. After Cromwell's downfall, the Puritans found refuge from royalist reprisal in Boston and its environs.

On the island of Bermuda, as in Virginia, investors hoped to establish a successful settlement and grow the highly profitable tobacco crop. Although the soil proved unequal to the task, the excellent climate and convenient location to sea-lanes brought a diverse group of settlers to the lovely island. Anglicans, Puritans, privateers, shipbuilders, a handful of Spaniards, Africans and American Indians coexisted in the benign sun, six hundred miles from the American coast.

Look to the Rose that blows about us—"Lo,
Laughing," she says, "into the World I blow."

Come fill the Cup, and in the Fire of Spring
The Winter Garment of Repentance fling:

And then and then came Spring, and Rose-in-hand
My thread-bare Penitence apieces tore.

—*Rubaiyat* by Omar Khayyám

PROLOGUE

Virginia—October 1685

Amanda saw it all—from the first puffs of smoke drifting above the village, to the terrible sight that would haunt her forever. If it had not been for Lord Braden Hamilton turning her face against his ripped, bloodstained shirt, she would surely have fainted dead away.

It was a soft Indian summer morning. Gentle breezes were tinged with melancholy, aware of summer's passing and the certain approach of winter. Honeybees still buzzed around the hollyhocks lining the breezeway between the house and the summer kitchen. Overhead, the sky arched cerulean blue, and the air was as still and toasty warm as a lazy day in August. Beyond the fields, the James River sparkled in the sun's tawny glow as it moved sluggishly toward its final destiny in Chesapeake Bay.

On that benign morning, heavy with humid sunshine, eleven-year-old Mandy headed for the grove of oaks separating the river from the tobacco fields of Briarfield Plantation, her family's home for two generations. In one hand she carried a fishing rod, in the other, a cherry tart.

Because of Briarfield's distance from the settlement at

Jamestown, she had few friends to play with and few diversions other than riding her pony and lessons at her mother's knee. Her half brother, Philip, was much too old to provide companionship. Now nineteen, he was a full-grown man and spent much of his time helping their father oversee the thirty-thousand-acre estate—that is, when he wasn't away at the fledgling college at Williamsburg.

She didn't want her brother's company anyway, she thought, settling into a shady spot on the riverbank. She pulled off her shoes and stockings and reclined in the tall grass. Though Philip was her only sibling, he had always made it quite clear that he found her a nuisance and far beneath his interest. It was his habit to avoid her whenever possible, unless of course, he could use her as a scapegoat for his own frequent misdeeds. Now that she was excelling at reading and numbers, as well as horsemanship, he took every opportunity to disparage her efforts and belittle her in their parents' eyes. "Just a silly girl," he often said with a sneer. "A clumsy chit of no use till she's breeding age," he added with disdain.

Philip's mother had been their father's first wife, a grand English lady who had died shortly after childbirth during her first year in Virginia. Amanda's mother was a Jamestown girl of sturdy pioneer stock, descended from a middle-class family of Suffolk.

Amanda deftly placed a wiggling worm on her hook. It was a feat she'd learned from one of the darkies and it gave her a pleasant sense of accomplishment. Philip would never have touched the squirmy thing, even had he been inclined to help her. No matter, she concluded, dropping the hook with a plop into the shimmering water. Briarfield Plantation was large enough for the two of them to occupy without stepping on each other's toes. Her grandfather Sheffield's first crude home on the river had long ago been abandoned for the spacious brick house on the hill. With the lush Virginia soil producing the finest tobacco in the world, the farm had prospered beyond the Virginia Company's wildest expectations.

Sitting there under the emerald green canopy dappled with swaying golden light from above, Amanda was completely content. She would live forever in this secure and gracious environment. If Philip was so anxious to marry her off so she could produce some stranger's offspring in some far place, he was doomed to disappointment. When the time came, she would marry one of the boys she knew from Jamestown, one of those strapping youths attending school in the village. She would bring her husband to live at Briarfield, and he would be her partner in the work of the plantation. Together they would build their own house and be at peace with her brother. When Philip married (if any lady would have him), she would enjoy having a sister-in-law, and their children would play along this very riverbank.

Leaning back on her elbows, she breathed deeply of the moist, earthy fragrance. She bit into the juicy tart and let its pink sweetness cover her lips while crumbs fell unheeded to her cotton shift. With a sigh, she pushed one foot into the ooze along the streambed and squished the cool mud between her toes.

Dreamily, she allowed her thoughts to turn to the elegant young man who had arrived just yesterday on the ship from England. Why, he wasn't much older than Philip, around twenty or so, she guessed. Her parents had fussed over him as if he were King William himself. Last evening, they had laid a feast in the dining room the likes of which she'd never seen. Fresh trout had preceded succulent mutton chops; spoon bread and baked sweet potatoes had been followed by rich rum-cream pie and cherry tarts (the last of which she now enjoyed.)

She, of course, had occupied a seat at the far end of the table, where she was expected to be seen and not heard. The mayor and his wife had been present, and several town council members and Reverend Trask.

But her attention had been focused on their guest—as indeed had that of all those present. The man was Lord Braden Hamilton, second son of the Earl of Wentworth, and she'd never encountered a more fascinating and wonderful man in all her days. A true English lord, a captain, at her very own table, and as handsome as a make-believe prince in her books of English legends and fairy tales. His eyes were as blue as a jay's wing, and his skin sun-bronzed after his long sea voyage. His nose was straight and his chin clean-shaven with a slight depression in the center. His hair was dark, and it curled thickly about his forehead and ears before being drawn back and tied at the nape of his neck. During the lengthy meal, she had studied his profile above his crisp ruffled white collar; it seemed to be masculine perfection. And he was tall—taller than Philip, taller even than her father. But best of all was his smile, which lacked any artifice and exuded warmth and a sense of humor, as if all of life were an amusing game—one which he was enjoying very much. For one brief moment, his smile had included her. She had dropped her eyes at once to stare at her plate, but his look was etched in her memory.

Never had she dreamed such a man could exist in the real world. And how disappointing that his visit would be so brief. Yesterday and today he was inspecting the fields with her father and Philip. After all, Lord Braden was an officer of the Virginia Company, which sponsored so much that was happening in the colonies. It was his duty to make certain the company's interests were being properly served. Tomorrow, he was off to that northern city of Boston, there to meet with her father's brother, Hugh, another major stockholder in the Virginia Company. Too bad, she sighed. If she could have a noble husband like Lord Braden, she might even consider leaving Briarfield entirely to Philip.

She had just finished the last of the tart and was sucking the juice from her fingers when she saw the pillars of smoke in the distance. Not the usual white plumes from cooking fires, but swirling black towers.

She dropped her pole and stood on tiptoe, straining her eyes toward the northwestern horizon. This was no small fire.

The sound of distant clanging reached her ears: the

alarm—the bell from the church steeple by Jamestown Commons.

Quickly, she pulled on her stockings and shoes and ran toward home. She plunged through the tobacco fields and crossed the wooden footbridge over the ditch which brought water from the river.

She neared the house at a run, then stopped in her tracks and gaped in horror.

Indians. Dozens of them. They were swarming through the fenced enclosure around the main house and dashing into the servants' huts and smoke sheds. Their war whoops erupted as they urged each other to the attack. Some carried hatchets and spears, but many were armed with English pistols. Where was her father? Where was Philip? Where were the men from the fields?

Suddenly she saw one of the painted savages drag her mother onto the porch of the house. She heard her mother's frantic screams as the Indians' knife blades flashed in the sun. She covered her ears but couldn't tear her eyes from the horrible sight. When the screams stopped, the Indians tossed aside the body and ran from the porch.

Amanda sank to her knees in the dirt. She watched in shock, her eyes wide, her heart pounding, her stomach sending bile into her throat. It was a scene from some hideous nightmare. What had turned the normally peaceful Powhatans into killers?

Shots filled the air. Several field hands were firing from inside the huts, but these cottages were quickly torched, and the fleeing men and their families were cut down without mercy. It was a massacre.

From across the pasture, a single white-shirted rider approached at a gallop. He fired a brace of pistols into the howling savages, then brandished his sword.

The Indians began an organized retreat. Apparently they had accomplished all they had planned and had their booty. One waved a silver candlestick, another whirled a black satin cape, a third held high the scalp of the mistress of Briarfield Plantation. Their victory cries pierced the quiet afternoon as they ran toward the woods.

The white-shirted rider rode in pursuit. One last shot rang out. The man was thrown back in his saddle, almost losing his seat. Then he recovered and reined in his frantic stallion.

Amanda jumped up and ran to him. "Lord . . . Lord Braden," she shouted, "My mother . . . oh, please . . . help!"

Another rider approached at a fast clip, jerked his horse to a halt and dismounted.

"Philip!" Amanda screamed. "Mother . . . on the porch!"

Amanda reached the front steps simultaneously with her brother and Braden Hamilton.

Philip turned to Lord Braden. "My father's dead. Mother . . . oh, my God."

She heard these words but was frozen in place at the sight of her mother's bloody, half-naked corpse stretched on the porch near the open front door. Oddly, she also saw the colorful nodding heads of the hollyhocks juxtaposed near the body, hollyhocks her mother had tended so lovingly during the Virginia summer.

"No, don't look," came a commanding voice from above her. Strong hands turned her away from the sight, forcing her to bury her head in a broad, damp chest. She was gasping, fear jolting through her, shaking her, engulfing her in spasms of sobbing. She clung to the man, trying desperately to erase the nightmarish vision from her eyes.

"I'll take the girl inside," Philip said. "You're hurt, Hamilton. We'll send for the physician from the village . . . if he's been spared. There's . . . nothing to be done for my parents . . . Holy Jesus," he croaked.

Amanda was faint, her head spinning, as she was torn from the comforting arms and half dragged past her mother's corpse and into the house. Philip hauled her up the stairs and thrust her into her room.

"Stay there, girl," he ordered. "Don't come out until I

give you permission. You can count your blessings you're not scalped like your mother."

After he left, she sank onto her bed and stared at the closed door. The wind outside in the cottonwoods lulled her into a trancelike state—beyond fear, beyond coherent thought, beyond feeling. After what seemed an eternity, she lay across the bedspread and covered her eyes. Then the tears came, slowly at first and then a torrent of weeping. Hours passed and she slipped into a state of semiconsciousness, finally waking after dark, shivering with shock and uncertainty. Apparently Philip had forgotten all about her.

She dozed fitfully until shortly after dawn. Her door eased open and the wife of Reverend Trask entered carrying a bowl of steaming porridge.

"Poor baby," the lady crooned. "I daresay you haven't had a bite since before . . . the awful massacre."

Amanda sat up. Her head ached horribly and the thought of food was nauseating. "I . . . can't . . ." she began.

"Now, child, you must eat. You're the lady of the house now, and must find strength in food and in God."

"But . . . Mother . . . Father . . ."

"Gone, dear . . . as you know. They'll be buried today along with twenty other poor souls from the village."

"What . . . what happened to Father?" she asked just above a whisper.

"Shot off his horse. It was a miracle your brother and Lord Braden escaped. It was a renegade band. The Powhatan chief assures us they'll be punished."

Mandy forced a few bites of the gruel down her tight throat. Then feeling a bit stronger, she asked, "Is Lord Braden all right? He tried to help."

"He was wounded, but not too seriously. He left on the ship for Boston late yesterday."

Mandy replaced the spoon in the bowl and stared into space. Her grief was overwhelming and a new sense of loneliness added to her misery. Philip was all she had left and he cared nothing for her. What would she do . . .

how would she manage? To grow up without her parents, with only her indifferent, if not completely hostile, half brother as her guardian, was a frightening thought. She would have to avoid him as much as possible, otherwise he would surely use his authority to dominate her life and destroy all her dreams. Taking a deep breath, she summoned all her courage. She would somehow survive the next few days, and then bide her time until she was old enough to make her own decisions. She would learn to depend only on herself. Philip might now own Briarfield . . . but he would never own Mary Amanda Sheffield.

CHAPTER

1

Briarfield Plantation—April 1692

Amanda turned her chestnut mare toward home, relishing the feel of the brisk spring wind at her back. Swirling across the fields from Chesapeake Bay, it carried the scent of the sea and the pungent fragrance of freshly plowed earth.

She loosened the reins and leaned close to the thrashing mane of flaxen silk. The animal, so long confined to the stable area, sprang forward, muscles rolling, nostrils flaring, its pleasure in the freedom of the gallop equal to Amanda's own delight.

"Fly, Lucy, fly," Amanda called above the sound of the rhythmic thuds on the packed earth lane. On either side, the shrubs melted away; the ground beneath the pounding hooves was a dark blur.

Finally, reluctantly, she eased in the mare and sat upright. She jogged into the grassy plot surrounding the veranda of the manor house and lifted a gloved hand to acknowledge Philip, who was watching her approach. She made no attempt to straighten her honey-colored hair, which floated in lush disarray around her face. Her bonnet hung behind her back and her riding skirt was bunched around her knees. It was only at the last moment that she noticed the scowl on Philip's face and the paper clutched in his hand.

"You ride like a wild Mohican, Amanda. Come in at once. We have business to discuss." Philip was his usual authoritative self.

By the time Amanda dismounted and gave Lucy to the groom for a cool-down walk, Philip had disappeared inside the house. Her mood shifted from exhilaration to annoyance as she followed him into the cool interior. Philip hadn't changed a mite in the two years she had been in London. He had a way of destroying her happiest moments with his black, piercing demands. As a child, she'd been forced to accept his authority, especially after the death of their parents. But now, at eighteen, having lived with adoring Sheffield relatives in the enlightened society of London, she would no longer tolerate his haughty officiousness. With determined steps, she marched into the first-floor library.

"What now, Philip?" she asked. "I've been home a week and all you've done is order me here and there—do this, do that, don't rise early, don't sleep late. Really, Brother, we must discuss your attitude."

Philip's brow furrowed as he glared at her from his position by his ornately carved oak desk. "It's easy to see you've been spoiled aplenty, missy. Remember, while you've been wined and dined, hobnobbing with the upper crust and living a life of easy affluence, I've been struggling here at Briarfield to keep the place from going to ruin. I've got the tobacco crop to sweat over, fifty cantankerous slaves to instruct, unsuitable weather, demanding investors, restless savages, and I alone responsible for all. So climb off your high horse, milady. You're in the Virginia Colony, not the salons of English bluebloods."

Taken aback by his ferocity, she hesitated. Philip did have a point, after all. Though she knew how eager he'd been to see her off to England, he had in fact been bearing the burden of Briarfield in her absence. "I'm sorry," she murmured. "It's just that I'm used to being treated . . . with a bit more respect. I do want to be of any help I can. What business do you have with me?"

He gave her a condescending look. He wasn't an unattractive man at twenty-eight, but where Amanda had a certain happy glow that kept her face alight and turned her lips upward, Philip's manner was heavy and somber and totally lacking in warmth. It was no wonder he was still a bachelor, she thought. What lady would enjoy living with such a glum and pessimistic soul? Or bringing children into the world who might inherit his same miserly spirit?

"I have received a letter today which concerns you," he stated. "It's from Lord Braden Hamilton."

The very name stopped her breath. Lord Braden's image rose before her, the image she had etched into her mind so many years ago. Never had she forgotten the dashing young nobleman who had fulfilled her ideal of princely perfection when she was just a girl. Nor would she forget his heroic effort to revenge the death of her parents, or especially that brief moment of comfort when, though injured and certainly in pain, he'd held her to him, taking her horror-stricken gaze away from the sight of her mother's body. She'd not seen him since. But she had carried him in the deepest part of her heart as one would lock away the most precious of treasures for safekeeping and occasional private worship.

"Lord Braden? I've heard nothing of him for years. How does he fare?"

"Extremely well," Philip answered caustically. "Far better than I, in fact. For several years, he was away fighting the Turks or some such. But now he resides in Bermuda at a small plantation. His family has always been a primary investor in the Virginia and Bermuda Companies. Lately, he's been more than a little high-handed—nosy, if you will, prying into the private affairs of Briarwood."

"I would think he's entitled to pry." She hurried to his

defense. "We here in the colonies owe much to the English investors. After all, they risked a great deal in those early years."

"They risked money. We risked our lives. We paid for our land one way or the other. And we've broken our backs to repay them for their investment."

"Yes, but we've personally made a fortune selling our tobacco overseas by using their connections and their ships. It's good business. And they have a right to know how the enterprise is doing."

"You've adopted superior airs, I see, mistress. It's unbecoming a woman to discuss business matters. But I will tell you this: Briarfield is in a sorry state—through no fault of mine. The fortune you mention so casually is nonexistent. We've had five lean years and lost half our slaves to the fever. In short, my dear, we need money. If Briarfield is to survive, we need a new investment, a large sum, and before next spring's planting."

Stunned by this news, Amanda shook her head in disbelief. "But . . . but how can this be? Virginia tobacco is the best in the world. Prices are high. The slaves should be replaced with indentured servants. It's far more efficient and—"

"Don't accuse me of lying!" he bellowed. "I'm telling you we are deeply in debt. We must do something at once if Briarfield is to be salvaged."

Dark thoughts entered her mind: Philip had always been lazy and prone to gambling and living beyond his means. As few luxuries as there were in Virginia, he had always managed to obtain the best of everything, purchased locally or imported from abroad. Never had she dared question his business acumen. She had assumed he had learned all that was necessary from their father, a fine businessman, tireless and dedicated. Looking at Philip now, she had to remember his singular lack of friends in Jamestown, and yes, his variety of women in lieu of a proper wife.

"I see," she said quietly. "It's disturbing news. But what has Lord Braden's letter to do with all this?"

Philip looked down at her, then answered, "I offered him your hand in marriage."

Instantly her heart leaped in a wild somersault. She was speechless. Was it possible her brother had inadvertently made her most secret dream come true? Finally she managed to whisper, "I-I'm to marry Braden Hamilton?"

Without changing his expression, Philip said, "Oh no, my dear, Lord Braden politely refused. Nothing personal, of course. He explained he was not in a position to take a wife at this time. He spends much time at sea. Rumors have it, he . . . ah . . . does some privateering along with his shipping business. It's probably just as well he refused my offer."

As quickly as her heart had soared, it plunged to the very depths. She took a deep breath to steady herself.

"You look disappointed," Philip continued, "but I do have excellent news. You needn't despair. Hamilton has arranged a match for you—one he says is far more suitable. An acquaintance of his, the Marquess of Staffordshire, who is an extremely wealthy widower with a title above that of Hamilton's, has formally accepted your hand. He saw you in London, so he says, and was captivated by your charms. So everything is settled, after all."

"What?" Amanda's shock turned to fury. "You mean Braden Hamilton refused me, then tossed me aside like a leftover bone to a waiting hound? No, I'll have none of this. I absolutely refuse!"

"Calm yourself, mistress. You will *not* refuse. Lord Braden has long been a friend of this family. He has acted in your best interests and I have accepted his choice."

Amanda was now shaking with anger. "So now Lord Braden is a dear and trusted friend. A moment ago he was nosy and prying. Suddenly he's a man trustworthy enough to choose your sister's husband. I won't marry a stranger. I swear it on our father's grave!"

"Hush, girl. You blaspheme. You *will* marry the marquess and that's an end to it. His first deposit accompanied this letter."

"Deposit!" she shouted. "How dare you sell me to some . . . some old lecher I don't even know!" Hands on hips, she faced Philip's blazing look. "How old is this widower?"

"Oh . . . sixty or so. But quite robust, Hamilton assures me," Philip added hastily. "The nobleman has a great estate not far from London. You can indulge your passion for horse breeding. As for other passions . . . to put it bluntly, the marquess has assured Hamilton that he is still quite potent, if you understand my meaning. He will give you children—as many as you like. In fact, one of the reasons he seeks a wife is to replace his only heir, who died a year ago. The child you bear him will be the next Marquess of Staffordshire."

Amanda fairly shouted, "I won't do it! I won't leave Briarfield no matter what great sum you're required to refund to the marquess."

Philip stepped toward her and gripped her shoulders, almost shaking her. He had never been physically cruel to her, but now his fingers dug into her flesh beneath her thin cotton sleeves. "I sent you to England to find a husband, and you returned to me a single woman with age advancing. I have no money left to support you. There are few prospects in the colonies—certainly none to equal a landed nobleman. I offered you first to Hamilton because you've often mentioned your admiration of the man. He refused. You have no choice. A girl does as she's told by the head of the family. And in case you've forgotten, *I* am that head."

"But . . . surely . . . surely there must be—"

"No other way," he stormed. "No way to save Briarfield but through a prosperous marriage. I know how much this place means to you. Now you can save it for future generations. Keep in mind you'll outlive the marquess by many years. You can visit Briarfield as often as you like, though naturally your primary residence will be in England."

Her throat tightened as she felt herself succumbing, like a leaf thrust into a rushing stream by a fierce wind. "I . . . I will consider it," she murmured.

"That's better." He released her and stepped behind his desk. "You'll have a few weeks here before you sail to Boston. The marquess has generously included funds for your trousseau. You'll stay with our uncle Hugh Sheffield and his wife, Sara, in Boston and do your shopping there. Lord Braden will come for you before the end of May. He'll take you to Bermuda for the wedding. Then you'll return to England with your new husband." He averted his eyes. "The . . . ah . . . marquess's wedding gift will arrive in my hands by September. It is more than generous, I assure you. I must compliment you on making at least one conquest during your visit to foreign shores."

Numb to her core, she could only stare at her brother. It did indeed seem settled. How happy she had been to leave the coldness of England, the stuffiness of drawing rooms, the inane conversations of empty-headed matrons. She had dreamed of home, of freedom, of a time of relaxing amid the beauties of Virginia, a chance to consider the course of her life. She had expected to help in the management of the plantation, to work beside Philip, perhaps someday to marry a gentleman farmer from the area. But now she must return to a place she found uncomfortable as the wife of a stranger who had bought her in the same manner as he would buy darkies to work the fields. And she had Braden Hamilton to thank for her fate.

Sudden loathing filled her. She felt betrayed by her brother and especially by the princely lord of her dreams. Facing Philip with uplifted chin, she said, "I'll go to Boston and to Bermuda. But if the man is repulsive when we meet, I will not go through with the marriage. I'll . . . I'll run away . . . take a position as a barmaid . . . enter a convent . . . something . . . anything . . . starve if I must. But I won't spend my life with a man I abhor."

"You're young. Before you know it, you'll be a rich

widow and can do what you please." He shook his finger close to her nose. "But you *will* marry the marquess. Now go to your room and settle your nerves. I'll send Coco to tend you. Dinner will be at the usual hour. Tonight we'll open the bottle of vintage Madeira I've saved for a special occasion. We'll celebrate—toast your good fortune . . . and Briarfield's."

Amanda tossed her riding ensemble into a heap in the corner of her room. Since she could not direct her anger toward the guilty parties, her clothes would have to take the brunt of her temper. And though she was terribly annoyed with Philip, her real fury fell on the head of Braden Hamilton.

With unseeing eyes, she stood before the mirror, picked up a brush and began pulling it roughly through her tangled hair. She should have expected such a ruthless plot from her brother . . . but Lord Braden . . . he had been her idol for so long, her hero, her gentle and handsome nobleman who had once risked his life for her safety. How could he have become so callous, so unfeeling, so cruel? Perhaps he had also become ugly and fat and besotted. And privateer was only a more polite term for pirate. She tried to envision him as he must now be at age twenty-nine. Yes, she thought, he must surely be showing the wear and tear of years of hard living. She pictured him on the deck of his ship: paunchy, his skin ruddy and lined from the sun's rays, perhaps a ragged beard and beady, squinting eyes. He probably lived in a rustic shack on the beach in that remote possession of England founded by the Bermuda Company at the same time the Virginia Company established its colony on the mainland. By the time she had given her hair its usual hundred strokes, she had an entirely new picture of Braden Hamilton—and it was not pleasant.

A tap came at the door and Coco entered the bedchamber. The young mixed-blood servant wore her traditional brightly colored skirt, creamy muslin blouse, and a fuchsia length of fabric wrapped around her raven curls. Her wide smile displayed even white teeth; her figure was ample but not rotund and her skin was the color of amber glass in the sunlight.

Coco's smile faded when she saw her mistress's bleak face reflected in the mirror. "Oh my, what's wrong? You look as if you've seen the Devil hisself."

Her lips pursed, Amanda continued to stare at her unhappy visage. Then she spat, "My dear brother has *sold* me to an English lord. For the first time, Coco, I understand how your people must feel in similar circumstances. I've always opposed the slave trade. And now, more than ever."

"My goodness, how came this to be?" Coco questioned as she poured fresh water from a porcelain pitcher into a waiting bowl. "Surely Master Philip wouldn't sell his own flesh and blood."

"He would and he has," Amanda replied sharply. "Though he doesn't call it a sale. I'm to leave in a fortnight for Boston. There my . . . my once dear friend, Braden Hamilton, will pick up the goods and deliver them to the purchaser in Bermuda. In return, a large sum will appear in the coffers at Briarfield." Her voice was laced with bitterness. "Then I'm off to England to warm the bed of some aging gent who fancies reproducing himself several more times before he wings his way to Heaven."

"Boston! England! But you jus' got here from there!" Coco cried. "I've sorely missed you these past two years, and now you're off again."

Amanda's look softened and she turned from the mirror. "I missed you too, Coco. You and I grew up together. You've been my dearest friend and closest confidant."

"Con . . . confi . . ."

"Confidant. A person who shares your deepest, most important secrets."

"Yes, miss, 'tis true. Like the time we poured rum in master's punch when the reverend and his missus come to tea. Or the time you skipped school in the village and came to a singin' in the darkies' cabins. And the time I accidently let the ram in with that she-goat and caused such a fuss. I'd had a beating for sure 'cept you kept my secret . . . you being my . . . confidant, like you say."

"That's exactly right, Coco. And I intend for you to continue as my companion. I'll need a lady's maid when I go to Boston and for my wedding in Bermuda. I'll insist you go with me . . . if you want to, that is."

"Oh, yes, ma'am! I'd surely be pleased to go with you to see all those places. Oh, yes, ma'am."

"Then it's settled. But in the meantime, if you can think of any way to prevent my marriage to the marquess, you'd be a friend indeed."

Coco's dark eyes narrowed to slits. "Is that so? Since you've asked, there might be something I could do."

Amanda cocked an eyebrow. "Oh, really? Why . . . what would that be?"

A sly smile crossed the girl's full lips. "Oh, we darkies have ways you white folks have never known about, ways of doin' things we learned from our old people, passed down in deepest secret, whispered about on stormy nights, powerful magic known only to a few. Since you and me is confidants, I can tell you sometimes things can be changed, if you know jus' how to do it."

Fascinated, Amanda plopped on the side of her feather bed. "Really? Magic? Like the magic of fairies and elves and . . . and witches?"

"Better than those," Coco said breathlessly. "My people brought it from the islands and before that, it was carried from Africa by my people's people. It's magic all right. Powerful magic."

Awed by the prospect, Amanda leaned forward. "You know I'm a good Christian, Coco. I've attended Reverend Trask's Anglican Church all my life. I wouldn't offend our Lord Jesus, but everyone knows there's magic all around. Some good, some bad. I talked to an Indian slave girl in Jamestown once. She told me about the shaman, the medicine man of her tribe. It's all very mysterious . . . and even frightening."

"The Lord looks after slaves," Coco said. "And He must surely look after white believers too, especially a nice young lady like you, mistress. Jus' leave it to me. There's a mamba here at Briarfield. That's a black woman who holds the power. I'll talk to her about your English bridegroom. We'll see if she has enough magic to reach across the sea."

"But I want no harm to come to him," Amanda said quickly. "I just . . . I just wish there was some way to save Briarfield other than my marriage to a stranger."

"We'll see . . . we'll see," said Coco. "Now time to wash up for dinner."

CHAPTER

2

Bermuda

Braden hopped on one foot across the beach, stumbling through the shallow waves, cursing loudly with every awkward step. The foot he held aloft began to drip blood onto the white sand before he reached the boulder and sat heavily on its flat surface.

"Goddamnit to bloody hell," he hissed between clenched teeth.

The girl, clad only in loose-fitting brown cotton breeches, dropped the shells she was gathering and ran to kneel beside him. Her skin was the color of fresh cream and her hair hung in dark waves around her bare breasts and down her supple back as she studied the damaged foot.

"Brae, it's deep. It needs cleaning and binding," she said gently. "But it's on the side so you should be able to walk without too much pain."

Bare to the waist, soaking wet with salty seawater, Braden grimaced and leaned forward to inspect the cut. Already the blood was drying, but the salt seeping into the wound burned like a hot poker.

"Holy—" he sucked in his breath.

"Ahhh . . . I know," she crooned as if to a child.

"Wait, I'll fetch some fresh water and some cloth to bind the cut."

"There are clean rags in the boat," Braden said, collecting himself. "I don't know what in hell I scraped. Probably a sharp rock. There aren't any ship bones resting in this shallow cove."

Seated on the bleached boulder, he watched her run through the surf to the small open boat they had shoved onto the beach. She was a delightful creature—and quite devoted to him, he knew. A stab of guilt almost made him forget the aching foot. Not that she'd been a virgin when he had carried her unconscious body from the sultan's harem three years ago. She'd offered herself with such love and trust—such unabashed passion. He would have been a saint or a eunuch to have resisted such a willing and desirable companion. Aye, he'd taken the girl, tenderly and with true affection. But this past year, he'd made it plain he didn't love her, at least, not in the way a man must love to make a woman his wife. He would honor her and provide for her, even protect her with his life, but he could not give her his heart nor his hand. He adored her, but he had no intention of settling down to the life of a married man.

She returned now, running barefoot across the deserted beach, her young breasts bobbing with every stride and her face set into a reassuring smile. She dropped again beside him and began to tend the wound.

He reached out to stroke her hair, sparkling now with drops of moisture from the sea. "What would I do without you, Tamara? You have the magic touch of a healer."

Smiling up at him, her delicate features glowing with his praise, she spoke with confidence. "As you know, my lord, my people are much experienced in the healing art. We have studied this for many hundreds of years in the Arab world."

"So I've heard . . . and fortunate for me this day to have an expert by my side."

"There. Is that better now? When we return home, I'll

put a salve on it that will protect it and speed the healing."

"Aye. 'Tis much improved. Come sit beside me for a moment. Perhaps this is a good time to share my news."

She scooted next to him and rested her head against his shoulder. "What news, my lord Brae?" she queried, closing her eyes and lifting her face to the warm Bermuda sun.

"I must sail next week to the mainland—to Boston, actually."

"Oh?" She popped open her eyes to look up at him. "Am I to go this time?"

"No, my dear. You know I count on you to look after the house while I'm away. You must be my eyes and ears and strong right hand. Rodriquez, of course, will continue to oversee the fields and make sure the hands do their jobs and are properly paid."

Her look was one of disappointment, but held no surprise or rancor. "Very well. But if you kept slaves . . ."

"Nay, love. I'll never own a human being. You know how I feel about that."

"I know. It's just that in my world . . . and yours, as well, slavery is not an uncommon practice."

"Tamara, you were once a slave. You, of all people, should appreciate freedom."

"I do, I do," she hastened to answer. "Except . . ." she said, smiling invitingly, "to be your slave would be a great honor."

He slipped his arm around her. "No, my lass, you must be free . . . free as that snow-white petrel over there in the cedar tree. Free to fly as high as your pretty wings will carry you. Free to find your destiny . . . as I find mine."

"Freedom is a good thing," she agreed, "but love is better."

He gave her a serious look. "Love is a fragile breeze. It comes at will, and then leaves when it must."

She shook her head. "You've never known love, my lord. Forgive me for saying so. If you had, you'd not speak so lightly of its powerful force."

His lips crooked upward. "Ah, the wisdom of the ages from the oriental world of mystery and enlightenment. We shall see, little one. I'm nearly thirty and have yet to be overcome by this power you describe. Perhaps I never shall."

She pouted. "You should love *me.*"

He smoothed back her hair. How could he explain his feelings without hurting hers? "But I do love thee . . . in a very special way. I love thee as I would a darling child."

She reached out to rest her hand on his knee. "You speak not the truth. I know how you love me . . . or used to. It's *not* as you love a child."

Gently he removed her hand. "Very well, then. I love you like any normal man loves a beautiful woman. But I also care deeply for your happiness. As I've explained before, I won't possess your body when I can't give you my heart."

"But, Brae, I want you to. I don't understand. Why?"

"Because, my sweet, I won't bind you to me; therefore I must free your love to one day belong to another. You deserve a man who will give you his love and his name—a man who will make you his wife and give you children."

She clasped her hands and stared at her toes dangling above the sand. "But you took me from Karim. You saved me from his cruelty and I owe you my life. I would rather belong to you above all others."

"Tamara, listen to my words. They also hold wisdom. You do not—must not—belong to me. You are not a possession. You're a lovely girl, a human being, a newly converted Christian. Continue your lessons with the reverend. And, by the way, he'd not approve of your . . . ah . . . less-than-modest attire."

She giggled, but made no attempt to conceal her bosom.

"Humph," she said and lifted her hair with both arms, thereby lifting her enticing breasts at the same moment. "I may be a new Christian, but I was a woman first."

He couldn't help grinning. "A woman . . . at age sixteen."

"Seventeen," she answered quickly.

His laugh disappeared into a frown. "Seventeen? So soon? Then I stand corrected. And 'tis all the more reason for proper modesty. Come, we'll start for home."

Keeping his arm around her, he hobbled along the shore.

"Tell me, Brae, why must you go to Boston?" she asked.

"To take possession of my new ship at Salem Shipyard. Hugh Sheffield promised me t'would be finished in late May. And, I've decided to name it *The Tamara*. Would you like that?"

"Oh!" Her eyes danced. *"The Tamara.* Yes, yes! Surely this means you care for me."

"Of course, my girl," he answered, feeling a bit of his guilt slip away. "I will always care for you. Haven't I promised you that?" Looking down at her, he prayed his forthcoming absence of nearly two months would open a wider gulf between them. "And while I'm away, you can talk to the reverend about plans for a gala celebration. I'll be bringing the young Sheffield girl here to marry an English marquess."

"Marquess?"

"Aye. The Marquess of Staffordshire. He's no young duck, but he is one of the wealthiest lords in England. Actually quite a robust old fossil, if I remember correctly. Amanda's brother asked me to find a rich husband for her, so the marquess is ideal."

"We'll be having a wedding feast?" she asked, assisting him into the rocking skiff.

"With all the trimmings," he replied. "A quiet ceremony at the church in the settlement, then a feast at the plantation. Make the arrangements while I'm gone. There won't be many guests, but I want a grand show for the marquess. He's already spent a tidy sum to obtain his bride. Mayhap we can jolt him out of a bit more here on

Bermuda. Hamilton Plantation could use some extra funds just now."

Tamara pulled on a smock and hopped aboard. "Then I'll go right to work on the plans," she said brightly.

Braden leaned against the oars, pulling the boat out of the sand and into the incoming tide. He thought of little Mary Amanda Sheffield. How well he remembered the pudgy, sunny-cheeked lass with the tangle of near-white curls dancing around a freckled face full of youthful adoration. Lord Pickering said she had been quite the rage in London, but as elusive as a silk thread in the wind. Said she was comely, with a healthy body ripe for bearing his heir. How could the old boy know that, he wondered. Perhaps he'd already sampled a bit of her tempting fruit. More than one ambitious lady had used her body to obtain an old man's fortune. The girl was no doubt still plump, though probably sans freckles by now, and undoubtedly spoiled and indolent after a life of leisure in Virginia and England. Her brother was certainly a no-good sort; Philip Sheffield had frittered away the income from the largest and best tobacco plantation in the Virginias. But the marquess had guaranteed to cover all the Sheffield debts, repay the Virginia Company its initial investment and even fatten the pocket of Philip Sheffield—all in exchange for the hand of the fully blossomed Mary Amanda. Picturing her in his mind, Braden congratulated himself on escaping the marriage proposal offered by Philip Sheffield. One thing he didn't want was a pale and demanding English wife—a woman to confine him to the traditional ways of British society—a woman to glower from beneath her bonnet at his loose way of living and zest for adventure. No, if he did marry someday (and he might in order to have an offspring or two of his own), it would never be to one of the colonial dames he'd met in polite salons on the mainland. Whether Puritan or Anglican, Catholic or Reformed, they all had one thing in common: They wanted to tie their husbands to the bedpost and use their wiles to clip his wings.

He strained against the oars and ignored the throbbing in his foot. No, he'd sail with the trades, capture the occasional wandering Spanish caravel when he had the chance, and take a willing woman now and then when it suited his fancy. Now that Bermuda was a Crown Colony, his only official duties were as member of the General Assembly and as consultant in building the new Bermuda sloops, the fastest and most beautiful small sailing ships plying the ocean-sea.

A week later, his foot healed satisfactorily, Braden stood on the St. George's wharf on the eastern side of the island and bade Tamara farewell. Resting at anchor behind him, the aging carrack was laden with Turk's Island salt to sell to the Bostonians. When he returned, he would be captain of a new frigate of thirty guns—a modern vessel, sturdy enough to sail with ease to England and beyond, and more importantly, equipped with enough cannon to deter any Spanish pirate's ambitions to capture her.

Oddly enough, the man who stood next to Tamara, awaiting last-minute instructions for the running of Hamilton Plantation, was as Spanish as any buccaneer on the Main.

Braden shook the swarthy man's hand. "Stay alert, Rodriquez. I should be back by the end of May."

"Bueno, señor. We'll expect you then."

Braden gave Rodriquez an appraising look. Handsome bastard, he thought. He could catch any woman's eye with those smoldering, intelligent black eyes and auburn mop of curling hair. In his early twenties, Manuel Rodriquez's body was muscled like a fighting bull's. He was a devout Catholic, hardworking and trustworthy. Manuel and his father had been survivors of a Spanish shipwreck just off the island ten years ago. Since then, the lad had risen from stable boy to second-in-command at the prosperous plantation. Braden studied him until the young man appeared uncomfortable under his scrutiny.

"Rodriquez," Braden said abruptly, "I want you to take special care of Tamara in my absence. 'Tis time she learned to sit on a horse like a lady."

"But, my lord, I can ride—" Tamara began.

"Adequately," Braden finished. "But in Virginia, and in the Spanish Indies," he added, "ladies ride with a certain style that is quite special . . . a pretty sight. We'll bring one of the amblers from Hispaniola, eh, Rodriquez? What do you think?" The Spaniard warmed to his employer's ploy.

Manuel's face was now alight. "Yes, señor. There's no horse on Bermuda to equal that Spanish line. And now with peace between our countries, one could be obtained without much risk."

Braden guffawed at the thought of the highly tenuous peace between Spain and England, but he was pleased that Rodriquez understood and eagerly accepted his invitation to spend more time with Tamara. "Fine, fine," he said, still grinning. "Then start daily lessons while I'm away. And while you're at it, give Tamara some . . . ah . . . instructions in your faith. I've encouraged her to attend Reverend Miller's church, with a certain success. She may as well have a full range of religious education."

Tamara gave Braden a saucy look. "I'm content with my own beliefs, as I've often told you, Lord Braden. I've only added affection for the dear little Jesus."

"Aye . . . and that seems a good beginning. Knowledge of beliefs other than your Muslim faith could be enlightening. At least promise to listen politely to Manuel's lessons. Both riding and ritual. Agreed?"

Her eyes now softly adoring, she nodded. "If you ask it, my lord."

Braden smiled and drew her into his arms for a parting embrace. He had planted the seeds that could lead to his loss of the girl's devotion, but 'twas only fair to her, and from the look in Rodriquez's eyes, the boy was more than pleased. Before he could regret his decision, he kissed her lightly on the cheek—as brotherly a peck as possible—and tossed his cloak over his shoulder.

"Good-bye, little one. Adios, Rodriquez. *Buena suerte.*"

He boarded the ship and climbed to the captain's deck. "Weigh anchor," he shouted to his first mate. "The winds are high toward the mainland."

CHAPTER
3

Amanda took one last lingering look at the deck of the *Mary B,* then made her way along the gangplank leading to the dock. Not far behind came Coco carrying a carpetbag and hatbox.

Amanda regretted the end of the pleasant voyage from Virginia. Not only did she love the sea, but she felt certain that her arrival in Boston boded ill for her future happiness.

I'd have been a sea captain, she thought, stopping on the dock to wait for Coco to catch up. Yes, if born a man, I'd have spent my days exploring the seas of the world.

"Amanda . . . Amanda, my dear!" came a masculine voice from behind her.

Turning, she held on to her hat as a fresh breeze threatened to send it spinning. "Uncle Hugh?" she inquired of the man approaching at a brisk pace. But her questioning tone was unnecessary as soon as she looked closely at the paunchy gentleman's face. His visage was a mirror image of her father's; the familiar features brought sudden tears near the surface of her eyes.

"What a lovely girl, I must say," he effused. "Why, I'd

have recognized you anywhere. You have your mother's fair good looks, but I see my own brother looking from those golden eyes. Come, child, I've brought a carriage to take you home. Sara is most eager to welcome you to the house."

The brief ride from the wharf, down the length of King Street, then left to Milk Street and the Sheffield home, was so absolutely fascinating that Amanda's melancholy was soon overcome and her lively curious nature back in place.

Boston was a miniature of London, lifted and transported to the New World to become the pride of the Massachusetts Bay Colony.

Uncle Hugh pointed out the sights with great enthusiasm as they rolled along the cobbled streets in the open conveyance beneath a bright noontime sun.

The predominance of black-frocked citizens indicated an austere life-style, but there was no denying the prosperous and energetic atmosphere of the community. The broad thoroughfare leading away from the docks and shipyards was bursting with shoppers and business-folk.

The carriage halted before a two-story brick house with a high attic and a row of dormer windows. It was a freestanding structure set in the midst of a small, but nicely landscaped plot. Compared to the gracious mansion at Briarfield, it was not overly impressive, but it had an air of solid, no-nonsense permanence, as if the builder's message were "Here is a house to shelter and sustain a family throughout the years—with no intent to glorify the owner's economic accomplishments."

A houseboy hurried outside to take charge of the trunk and baggage.

Hugh offered Amanda his hand as she stepped down and then climbed the four steps to the porch.

"Why, it's lovely, Uncle Hugh," she said sincerely. "Father often spoke of his visits to Boston and your home."

Hugh led her into the front hall, which was cool and sparsely furnished.

"I'll call Sara," he said, removing Amanda's traveling cloak. He hesitated when he saw her exquisitely tailored emerald velvet suit, its full sleeves embroidered in an elaborate black design which was repeated near the hem of the flowing skirt. It was high-necked and entirely modest, but something in his eyes reflected concern.

"I'm eager to meet my aunt," said Amanda.

Hugh's expression brightened. "Of course . . . ah . . . come into the parlor. I expect she'll have laid tea. We weren't exactly certain of the time of your ship's docking."

She entered the parlor, a relatively diminutive room dominated by a huge fireplace banked by two high-backed wooden chairs of simple design. Indeed, the room was furnished so plainly that Amanda wondered if it was ever used. But the wide-planked floors shone with polish, and white linen panels graced the windows. The flicker from four fat candles competed with the sunlight filtering through the shuttered windows. On a square oak table in the center of the room, a plain porcelain tea set offered refreshment, but there was as yet no hostess to serve.

For a few moments, the only sound was the ticking of the hall clock.

Amanda turned to her uncle as he reentered the room. "You do have a strong resemblance to my father. He said you were very close as boys."

"Ah, indeed we were." Hugh smiled in remembrance. "He was but a year my senior when we left the Sheffield clan and took off on our grand adventure. Cavaliers, they called us, but we weren't as dashing as all that. Ambitious would be a better word."

"And hardworking as well," she added. "And of course, each of you successful in different corners of the colonies."

"We did go our separate ways. Your father was born to the land, a farmer who was happiest riding his horse across field and fen. But I was drawn to the sea. The English Sheffields have built fine vessels for centuries and

I soon found myself a niche in the seafaring commerce of New England."

Feeling instant rapport with her uncle, Amanda smiled and drew off her gloves. "I understand that attraction," she said. "I do love the sea myself."

"Good. Good," he effused. "Tomorrow I'll show you my shipyards. I've a new frigate almost ready and . . ."

At that moment, a tall, slender woman, clad in a black dress, its plainness relieved only by a round white collar, entered the room. Her graying hair was pulled tight under a white cap and her face was as stiff and drab as her attire. Her gray eyes and eyebrows matched the pallor of her fish-belly complexion, and most unsettling was the aloof, icy expression she laid upon her newly arrived guest.

Before greeting her niece, she took a moment to speak to Coco, who was standing quietly near the door. "Girl, this is the parlor. Go at once to the servants' quarters behind the house."

"Yes, ma'am, but if you please, my mistress's wardrobe needs—"

"Go at once. We'll fetch you by and by, if need be. Everyone here addresses his or her own needs." Turning now from a retreating Coco, Sara Sheffield gazed coolly at Amanda. "This is not Virginia, daughter. Servants are free and stay in their place. You are welcome, of course."

Amanda was speechless at her aunt's rude greeting. Her earlier pleasure created by her uncle's warmth evaporated like water droplets on steaming coals. "Thank you, Aunt Sara." She matched Sara's look and tone. "It's good of you to have me for a brief visit. Naturally I and my servant Coco—a free woman from Jamaica—will abide by your rules. We wouldn't think of upsetting the household."

Hugh stepped forward and rested an arm around Amanda. A head shorter than his wife, he was as stout as Sara was thin. "The girl has had a long journey, Sara. Please serve refreshment and we can discuss *rules* later."

Amanda relaxed and smiled gratefully at her uncle.

She couldn't help wondering how this kindly, charming gentleman could have married such a sour crone. Perhaps the choice had been limited in those early days in Boston. And, in fairness, she'd only just met the two. More than once, she'd been accused of hasty judgment. It was a fault she would try to correct.

"Yes, I would appreciate that," she said, giving Sara her best smile. "And . . . and Philip sends his love to you both."

Sara sat at the tea table and began to pour.

Hugh drew up a chair for Amanda and patted her shoulder reassuringly before he sat.

Amanda had the distinct feeling that a conspiracy was born at that moment—a conspiracy between the two of them against the haughty Sara.

"Is Philip as spoiled as ever?" Sara asked, handing her a steaming mug.

Despite her own difficulties with Philip, Amanda rushed to his defense. "He is doing his best, I believe, to manage Briarfield. It's a difficult task for one man alone."

"Especially one with such a frivolous view of life," Sara snapped.

"Then you know Philip well?" Amanda asked brittlely. She was certain it had been years since Philip had visited Boston. And, as far as she knew, her aunt had never been south of Massachusetts.

"Not well. But reports of his mismanagement and lack of maturity have reached us with regularity."

"Sara," Hugh interrupted. "This is not the time—"

"Why not?" said Sara briskly. "We have a financial interest in Briarfield ourselves. You and your brother invested a good deal of money in those early years. And we've never seen a farthing in return."

"James worked diligently . . . sweated in the fields himself. We made an agreement the day I sailed from Jamestown. If the plantation thrived, he would repay my original investment, nothing more. I took to the sea to make my fortune. I left him with the work and responsibility of building Briarfield and repaying the Virginia Company. I did what I pleased and I prospered. As far as I'm concerned, Philip owes me nothing."

Sara's scowl deepened. "You prospered because of my father's more-than-generous dowry."

Hugh nodded. "I admit it was the beginning of Sheffield Shipyards. But I've never slacked in my efforts, Sara. Even you must agree to that."

Her eyebrows lifted contemptuously. "You are devoted to your work, I agree. Now if you were equally devoted to the Church . . ."

Hugh groaned softly. "Aye, as you point out unfailingly. I accepted the Puritan cloak long ago, but religion interests me little. I did it to please you but failed even at that."

Amanda squirmed in her chair and hid her lips behind her cup. It was quite apparent she had come into a household with no love lost between its members. Remembering the happiness among the English Sheffields, she wondered how the two American branches had managed to find so little contentment. Had it been a mistake for the brothers to leave hearth and home in search of a better life? James now lay in his grave, slaughtered by Indians; Hugh had a childless marriage with this stiff-necked wraith of a woman, though at least he did seem to love his work.

Hoping to lighten the mood, Amanda asked, "Uncle, tell me about your new ship . . . the frigate you mentioned earlier."

"Aye, 'tis a bold ship and beautiful," he said, his face brightening. "I built it for your sponsor, Braden Hamilton. He has accumulated a small fortune working in Bermuda, though some of his enterprises have required more brash than brain." He winked.

Momentarily stunned, she gaped at him. "Captain . . . Hamilton?" she finally stammered.

"Aye. Two days ago he arrived in Salem aboard his lumbering carrack. He's off-loading a supply of Turk's Island salt and will dry-dock the ship for repairs. Tomorrow we may take his new ship on a short cruise. I must say, he'll love the vessel," he said proudly.

"He-he's already here? I didn't expect to leave for Bermuda so soon."

"Oh, I don't suppose he'll sail for a few weeks. We still have some spit and polish to apply to the frigate and a shakedown cruise to test for seaworthiness. No, I wouldn't expect we'll be off for the wedding right away," he said, eyes twinkling, "though I understand your impatience."

Sara looked appalled at Hugh's suggestive remark, and Amanda was equally appalled at the sudden reality of her approaching marriage. No matter how strained and difficult a time she might have under the roof of Sara Sheffield, she was hardly eager for the journey taking her to her unknown bridegroom.

Hugh ignored both women and smiled pleasantly, his gaze drifting toward the window and the lowering sunlight. "Aye, on the morrow I'll take you to the shipyards, lass. If you're truly a Sheffield, you'll love what you see there. I'll show you everything. We'll—"

"Mister Sheffield," came Sara's cutting voice. "Tomorrow is the Sabbath. We'll sit in Reverend Mather's congregation as always. Amanda will accompany us . . . *if* by tomorrow, she can find a more suitable garment among her extensive wardrobe. Suitable, at least, for a proper girl in Boston Town."

Amanda tossed for hours on the hard, narrow bed of her tiny, upstairs room. The knowledge of Braden Hamilton's arrival in New England brought home the imminence of her fate. Suddenly her sacrifice to save Briarfield seemed more than she could bear. Given half a chance, she would have slipped back aboard the ship and stowed away back to Virginia—or anywhere the ship was headed. At the top of her list of people she most despised was the mighty Lord Braden himself. He had traded her as if she were a goose. She would be forced to spend her years bedded by the lecherous marquess in return for money to benefit Hamilton's various investments. She pounded her pillow in anger. Why, she was less free than Coco.

Shortly after dawn, Coco appeared with two cups of coffee. "I'm sorry, Miss Amanda. I felt like a thief slippin' up the stairs. I even left my shoes down below. I don't think they want me to tend you at all."

Groggily, Amanda sat on the bed and began pulling on long black stockings. "Don't worry." She sighed. "We probably won't be here long. Braden Hamilton is already in Salem. His ship will be ready soon; then we'll sail for Bermuda . . . and the wedding," she added bitterly.

Setting the tray on the bed table, Coco glanced furtively behind her, then quietly closed the bedroom door. She put one finger over her full lips. "Shh, mistress. Don't make a sound and I'll show you what I brought. I have something with very special magic—magic strong enough to delay . . . or stop the wedding."

Startled, Amanda looked up, leaving her hose pulled only to her knee. "Really? Not . . . not black magic, Coco. Certainly not here in Boston under the roof of my pious Aunt Sara."

Coco leaned near and rolled her eyes. She whispered, "Some say white, some say black, some say *voodoo* like the mamba back in Virginia. Whatever 'tis, mistress, 'tis powerful and does mysterious work. Look here now, but don't make a sound."

From the folds of her flowing skirt, Coco removed a small, doll-like figure dressed in ragged pants and blue linen shirt. Its arms and legs extended like four sticks, and it had no face on the white fabric lump of its head. But black hair, which looked altogether real, was fastened in untidy strings around its head. A large pin protruded from its left side.

Staring at the doll, Amanda felt a chill along her spine. She knew the natives from the islands had brought to the New World ancient pagan beliefs from their African roots. But all the slaves at Briarfield had been instructed in Christianity as soon as they were purchased. They had church meetings attended by Reverend Trask himself, and sang their spiritual songs with fervor that brought tears to her eyes when she heard them. Where had Coco found such an evil-looking figure, this doll that more resembled a faceless corpse than a child's plaything?

"Coco," she breathed softly, "what is that thing? It looks like . . . like . . ."

"A man," Coco said, her eyes wide with excitement. "Captain Braden Hamilton is who 'tis. He was last seen at Briarfield wearin' a blue shirt—and his hair was black and thick, so they say."

"Who says? That was years ago," Amanda observed with horrified fascination.

"Some of the older slaves. The mamba . . . she remembers the day of the murders . . . the day your mother was killed and Lord Braden was near shot off his horse."

Still gaping at the cloth doll, Amanda murmured, "No one who saw it could forget it. But Lord Braden left soon afterward. And of course, this . . . this doll has no face. It could be any man . . . any man at all," she said shakily.

"Oh, 'tis Hamilton, all right. It's got something of his inside."

"It . . . does? But what?"

"Sewed up in the belly. A gold button . . . and the scrap of cloth for the shirt is his'n too." Coco's eyes seemed about to pop. "You see, the day he was shot, he was tended by a native woman from the quarters till the town doctor come. Captain Hamilton took off his fine blue coat and shirt, then gave it to the woman to keep—as a gift, you understand, which made the woman mighty proud. She kept them all these years—wore the coat sometimes, but never washed the shirt."

"Didn't wash . . . I don't understand."

"Blood," Coco hissed between her teeth. "The blood of an English lord spilt on the shirt. Powerful magic, even if the mamba never made the doll. There's a drop of Hamilton's blood inside too."

Amanda bit her lip and looked closely at the figure. She

was horrified, but at the same time, fascinated. "And what does the pin mean?" she asked, already fearing the answer.

"Pain . . . misfortune . . . or maybe even death," Coco answered dramatically. "'Tis up to the magic to decide."

"Oh." Amanda covered her mouth. This was shocking, much worse than anything she'd imagined. She stared at Coco. "You must take it out—the pin. I'm extremely angry at Lord Braden. He must be greedy and cruel, but I would never wish such harm to a human being. This . . . this magic probably won't work, but you must try to stop it just in case."

Coco's forehead creased. Disappointment swept over her face. "But you said . . ."

"I know what I said, but I didn't mean he should be badly hurt, or for God's sake . . . killed! He's only a manipulative schemer. I, on the other hand, have agreed to his plan. Hurting him won't change anything. I'm surprised you didn't make some magic against the marquess."

Coco shook her head. "I thought of it, but we had nothing of his to use in a potion. No, all we had was from Captain Hamilton." Her face drooped sadly. "I'm sorry, Mistress Amanda. I wanted to help . . . that's all."

Amanda swallowed hard and patted Coco's arm. "I understand. But you should have consulted me first. Can you undo the magic? Remove the pin?"

Coco stared at the figure. "Don't know. I'm not the mamba, but I guess I can try." She pulled out the needle and looked at the doll for several seconds. "Don't know. We'll see by and by, I s'pose."

Talking a deep breath, Amanda calmed herself. "I'm sure it will be all right. Maybe I can undo the harm by sitting in Aunt Sara's church half the day. We'd better hurry. I'm expected downstairs any moment . . . with my hair bound tightly and wearing the black silk dress I wear for funerals. I do hope my aunt will be satisfied."

Coco stuffed the masculine figure back into the recesses of her skirt. With a resigned look, she opened the trunk to search for the dreary garment Amanda would wear to Sunday service.

Amanda had expected to doze her way through tedious hours of a boring Puritan sermon, but within minutes of taking a seat on the hard wooden bench, she was not only wide-awake, but rigid with attention. Furthermore, she was more than a little uneasy.

The young minister giving today's sermon was none other than Cotton Mather himself—a man duly elected to his high position, a third-generation religious firebrand, a man described as the most brilliant young member of the Massachusetts clergy, and without doubt, the most dynamic speaker Amanda had ever heard. As his bright eyes roamed the congregation, they seemed to fall directly on her—and his words thrust deeply into her non-Puritan soul.

"Today we speak of witchcraft," boomed his voice. "That it exists, we have no doubt. We read Exodus, which says, 'Thou shalt not suffer a witch to live.' Where there is Heaven, there is Hell." His voice intensified, sweeping the listeners into awe, leaving no room for doubt. "And, my good people of Boston, where there are unwary souls treading life's path in innocence, there are demons waiting to ensnare them into the fires of eternal damnation."

Amanda felt her heartbeat quicken when, for one instant, Mather pinned her with a condemning look. She had the wild impulse to stand up and defend her moral character, but she continued to sit straightbacked in her seat, flanked by Aunt Sara on her left and Uncle Hugh on her right. The moment passed and Mather looked away and continued his sermon.

"The evil is here, even as I speak," he intoned. "It touches our brethren in Salem Town, and it must be torn out and destroyed before it spreads disease more horrible than the plague! For the plague defiles the body, while the evil of Satan claims our very souls!"

Mather's fist crashed on the pulpit, pounding home his terrible warning.

He then elaborated. "In Salem, innocent young women now show evidence of having their minds and bodies possessed by the specter—that is, the spirit—of the Devil's servants. The entire matter is being studied by the clergy and by the courts. The trials will soon begin. It is an awesome task, a responsibility requiring the most sincere prayer of every Godly soul assembled here this morning. Mistakes can be made by men trying to do their best. And much controversy surrounds the means of interrogation of the accused."

He spoke with absolute authority. "As you know, I studied medicine before God called me to His service. I attended Harvard College and learned the importance of carefully scrutinizing every fact to arrive at undeniable truth." His voice rose. "And I tell you it is certain that the Devil can take the shape of virtuous persons, occupy their bodies and possess their minds. I myself have dealt with such unhappy victims, taken them into my own home, rendered the Devil's specter begone by using prayer and the power of the Almighty."

He pounded the pulpit twice. "Heed me, citizens of Boston! Pray for the poor wretches of Salem Town! Pray for divine guidance for the court's judges!" He pounded thrice. His voice soared. "And pray God's mighty sword will cut a lightning path, destroying the diabolical evils that swirl heavily over that suffering community!"

A long prayer followed before the sermon continued. By the close of the service, Amanda was stiff from sitting, but she had to admit, she was overwhelmed by the enthralling magnetism of Reverend Cotton Mather. And the news of the witch trials commencing in nearby Salem was morbidly fascinating.

At the church door, Aunt Sara introduced her to Reverend Mather. "My niece, Mistress Amanda Sheffield. She is visiting us from Virginia, Reverend. She is not one of the chosen of our flock, I fear, but she is still very young. Perhaps the Lord will yet bring her into His fold."

Having had her lack of God's grace pointed out, Amanda was at a loss for words, but she extended her gloved hand.

Mather caught it at once and gave her a completely disarming smile. Neither condescending nor bold, it carried a look of sincere interest, even friendliness that put her at once at ease. No one who smiled like that could be simultaneously condemning her to Hell.

"My pleasure, young lady. There is always room in God's kingdom for one more newly converted soul. You were very attentive today. I appreciate that."

"You . . . you noticed?" she asked in a small voice.

"The presence of a stranger in church is always of notice. Had Goodwife Sheffield not introduced you, I would have called to make your acquaintance. I would like to invite you to visit my home one day—meet my wife and children. Virginia is a very distant and mysterious frontier to my youngsters. Indeed, even to me. I've traveled to England but never to the colony of Virginia."

"I'd be happy to describe it," she responded. "And I'd be delighted to meet your family."

"Fine. Excellent. But for now, farewell," he said as Uncle Hugh guided her on through the door.

After a short stroll across the Commons, Amanda accompanied her aunt and uncle home to partake of the main meal of the day, then the afternoon's rest, followed by prayer and Bible study. Tedium set in and she was enormously relieved when she was given a taper to light her way to bed.

To her surprise, Uncle Hugh followed her upstairs and paused at the door of her cubicle.

"Rise early tomorrow, lass," he whispered after glancing below. "We'll slip away to the wharf before Sara knows you're about. My hunch is you'd like to see the new frigate I've built. Of course, you'll miss morning prayer and wash day."

She could have hugged him. "Oh, I'd love it, Uncle. Is it . . . Lord Braden's ship?"

"Aye. But I don't expect his lordship aboard for a day or two. According to his message of yesterday he's taken rooms in Salem and has pressing business."

She lifted her chin. "I'm in no hurry to confront Captain Hamilton," she announced. "But the ship—and your construction office—now that I'd enjoy seeing very much."

He smiled warmly and patted her shoulder. "Then rest well, child. I'll tap on your door at dawn. Be ready. We'll have coffee and scones in my cluttered little office at the shipyards."

CHAPTER
4

The fog-shrouded chill of early morning dissipated under a brightening sun as Amanda allowed Uncle Hugh to assist her aboard his new frigate of thirty guns. Riding at anchor beside the Sheffield docks, the ship gleamed proudly with fresh paint and polished brass.

Amanda gathered up her buttercup-yellow skirt and climbed down the ladder to the deck. She had worn the dress, with its creamy ruffles and scooped neckline, in defiance of Aunt Sara's pointed suggestion to wear only demure attire. She also wore a short cape, but with the sudden rise in temperature, she tossed it back over her shoulders.

"Ah, you make a pretty sight, lass," Hugh said, leading her across the deck. "'Tis most refreshing to see a young girl dressed so smartly, especially one with such natural beauty. I've never supported the theory that a woman's God-given gifts of fairness and grace should be hidden as if they were objects of shame."

"Thank you, Uncle, though you flatter me far too much. Now tell me about your ship. *It* is what I would call beautiful."

"I copied the design of the old Arab fregata. It was a

superbly maneuverable craft, but without sufficient fire-power. *The Tamara* carries thirty cannon in a single battery, and she's full-rigged to add to her speed."

Amanda covered her eyes to gaze up at the rigging and the three masts piercing the sky. Yards of snowy canvas billowed from the foremast in the cool breeze from the bay. Overhead, sea gulls turned and cried as they began their daily search for sustenance.

"We hoisted the foresails to check their balance. The ropes are tied loosely at the moment. Would you like to see below?" Hugh asked with animation.

"Of course."

"Follow me, my dear."

She grasped the handrail and descended the steep steps. It was cool down below and the smells of polish and paint overpowered those of salt air and fish.

Hugh pointed out the latest in technical advances and explained in layman's terms how they worked. The ship was so clean and well designed, Amanda envied the seamen who would soon be clambering through these decks, working hard, but heading for the high seas in pursuit of fortune and adventure.

After a tour of the spacious and elegant captain's quarters, with its tasteful mahogany furnishings, Hugh suddenly stopped. "What's that?" he grunted. "Foot-steps above. My workers aren't due for half an hour. Wait here, Mandy. I'll see who's trespassing."

She waited several minutes, strolling about the cabin, then opened a diamond-paned window to peer astern. When her uncle didn't return, she decided to follow him to the upper deck.

As her head emerged, she saw Hugh talking with a tall man whose back was toward her. The conversation sounded friendly and animated, so she decided to approach.

As she neared the two, both turned to face her. Her breath stopped in her throat. Her smile froze on her lips. Braden Hamilton stood an arm's length away. An older

Braden Hamilton, to be sure, but more devastatingly attractive than she remembered.

The moment stretched into eternity. Braden's expression was cool, his blue eyes slightly questioning, his lips relaxed with no hint of surprise or welcome.

The urge to flee, combined with the need to observe the proper amenities, kept her momentarily fixed in place. Then she took two steps backward, wishing desperately to escape the scene.

But in her awkward haste, her heel caught a coil of rope and she tripped to one side, grabbing a length of suspended rope to keep from falling.

But the second rope gave way and snapped upward, its flying tail wrapping tightly around her wrist.

She screamed and grabbed the rope with her free hand, clinging to it to keep from being hoisted above.

A strong arm encircled her waist and a knife blade flashed. She was free and falling against the man who firmly held her.

From a distance, she heard her uncle shout a warning. Suddenly, as if all the angels in Heaven were converging from above, she and her rescuer were engulfed in an enormous white cloud. Heavy and smothering, it bore them to the wooden deck.

Braden Hamilton's arms were around her, his body protectively covering hers. The canvas sail enveloped them both—and across Hamilton's back lay a large piece of the splintered mast.

Amanda lay very still. Her shoulder ached and her breath was short and labored, but beyond discomfort, she seemed all right. She tried to move, but Hamilton's weight pressed against her.

"Please . . . I'm not hurt," she managed to gasp. "Could you . . . move, please?"

Braden stirred, but his arm stayed across her. "It's my fondest wish to do so, dear lady," came his voice quite near her ear, "but there is some weight upon me. I expect help will soon arrive to free us."

With the pain in her shoulder abating, she now felt her cheeks begin to flush with embarrassment. Here she lay, intimately entwined with the man she hated most in the world, hidden from view by an enormous white shroud, her dignity and her modesty forever destroyed.

She wiggled.

He moaned as if in pain.

She lay still. "Are you hurt?"

"A . . . something is not quite right."

His body was hard against her, his legs across hers and one arm covering her breasts. She kept her head turned away but felt his breath soft along her neck. Oh, this was intolerable.

"I suppose I should thank you," she said stiffly, "but I do wish you could move just a bit."

"Your thanks might be appropriate—and I cannot move, as I've already explained."

"You know, of course, who I am," she continued.

"No, forgive me. There was no time for introductions, if you recall."

"I know you're Braden Hamilton. I, sir, am Amanda Sheffield."

There was a moment of silence. Then he chuckled. "Well, I'll be damned. Perhaps we should stay where we are till the ship sails. I find it a rather intriguing position."

"Oh . . . how dare you!" She squirmed again.

Again he groaned.

"What's the matter?" she demanded. "Can't you unhand me?"

He made an effort to lift away from her and finally succeeded. One end of the mast that lay across him clunked on the deck.

"That's much better, thank you," she said. "Surely we'll soon be freed from the sail."

No sooner had she spoken these words than the sailcloth was pulled upward and the mast rolled away. Her first thought was of her skirts wrapped around her knees, revealing her stockinged legs to curious eyes.

She sat up and lowered the petticoats and yellow layers of cotton skirt until her ankles were well covered. Then she dared to look at the man prone beside her.

"Oh, my goodness!" Her hand flew to her mouth. Braden Hamilton was flat on his back, his legs outstretched and his hands grasping a large wooden splinter that emerged from his left side.

"Dear God, Hamilton," said Hugh, bending over him. "You've been stabbed by a piece of the foremast."

"'Tis only through the flesh, I think. But it does pain me a bit. Pull it out, if you will."

"No," cried Amanda.

Braden looked up at her. "And why not, my lady? Surely you'd not have me spend my days with this stake protruding from my chest."

"No . . . no, it's just that . . . the pain . . . I can't stand to see—"

"Damnation, woman!" Braden snapped. "If I can stand it, *you* can. If you faint at the sight of my blood, you're a fragile thing, indeed." He looked back at Hugh. "Pull it out, Mister Sheffield, and we'll both have a drink."

"Yes, I'll do it," Hugh said. He removed his handkerchief, gripped the splinter and pulled it from Braden's side. Then he shoved the handkerchief against the red flow that followed.

Braden flinched and cursed under his breath, as he slowly sat up, keeping the handkerchief tightly in place. Blood oozed between his fingers, but he rose to his feet and stood shakily.

It was all Amanda could do to keep from fainting. She still hated the man, of course, but some other powerful emotion was turning her heart into a battleground.

Unable to speak, she continued to sit on the deck, her knees hiked before her, her shoe-tips peaking from the ruffles of her skirt.

"There now," Hugh said, grasping Braden's arm. "And oh yes, let me introduce my niece, Amanda Sheffield. But then, I suppose you remember her from your visit to Virginia. You probably just saved her life, you know. I'm deeply grateful, Captain."

Braden gazed down at her for a long moment. "Lady Sheffield has just introduced herself. Despite our . . . ah . . . close proximity, I hadn't recognized her as the child I once knew."

She knew she should be grateful, but she had no wish to be obligated to a man she despised. He looked ten feet tall, and she was annoyingly aware of his muscular thighs encased in form-hugging pants tucked into black knee-boots. His white linen shirt was, of course, ruined beyond recovery, but his black coat covered most of the damage. The hat he'd been wearing a moment ago was gone, and the dark hair she'd once so admired was loosened from its binding and curled around his neck. Perspiration, no doubt caused by pain, dappled his forehead and clean-shaven upper lip. But, to her utter amazement, he was smiling now and his eyes held a merriment that completely unnerved her.

Pursing her lips, she fought the urge to return his smile. She wouldn't be captivated again. She'd fallen once under the spell of his charms, but she'd been a mere child. Now she was a woman—one he'd rejected without a second thought and sold to another man.

She rose to her feet and smoothed back her rumpled hair. Her cloak had fallen away and she was certain her appearance was a complete disaster. Still, she tilted her chin and said haughtily, "Yes, Uncle, we first met so long ago, I'd nearly forgotten. I appreciate the captain's assistance just now, but I doubt my danger was as great as you described. We should go, however. Lord Braden may need to see a physician. As for me, I plan to go riding this afternoon."

She scooped up her cape and walked toward the gangplank. Her shoulder and wrist still ached, but she ignored them. If Braden Hamilton expected her to fall at his feet in gratitude for having rescued her from the coils of the rope, he would wait till Judgment Day. Behind her, she heard her uncle's muttered apology for her rude behavior. But then, he didn't know how Hamilton had misused her.

She climbed into Hugh's carriage and popped open her parasol, but she couldn't resist peaking under its lacy edge. Captain Hamilton was mounting his horse and leaning forward to speak to her uncle. He laughed and put the horse into a slow canter heading toward Ship Street.

At that instant, the blood rushed from her head and her heart turned in a wild somersault. She suddenly remembered Coco's doll . . . the figure stuffed with Braden Hamilton's gold button beneath a coat made from his own blue fabric. And the silver needle jammed into the doll's left side. The vision of the captain, stretched on the ship's deck with a piece of splintered wood in his side, was a near duplicate of Coco's magic doll. The eerie coincidence made chills run along her spine. Or was it mere coincidence? If the magic had truly brought about today's accident, she was the cause of it all. Guilt, remorse and fear raced through her in one overwhelming surge. She had much to answer for—to Captain Braden—and even to God.

CHAPTER
5

Braden entered the waterfront pub and walked straight to the bar. "A shot of rye, Flint. Quickly, if you please. Nay, make it a double."

The rotund, bug-eyed Flint reached for a glass. "What's this, milord? Ye ne'er touch the stuff this early."

Braden held his hand against the rag at his side. "For pain, Flint. I had a slight accident this morning. Nothing serious, but hurts like an axe through my ribs."

Flint served the brimming glass and leaned across the counter. "Let's have a look." The bandage was soaked and fresh blood coated Braden's palm. Flint's eyes popped even farther. "My God, sir, ye're bleeding your life away. What happened to ye?"

Before answering, Braden downed a large swallow. "Piece of splintered wood. Stuck in the flesh, that's all. I doubt the ride from Boston did me any good, though."

Flint left his place behind the bar and reached for Braden's coat. "Take this off and come out back to the kitchen. I've a cot there. Ye can lie down while I fetch Goody Walcott."

"No, I'm fine," Braden said and snapped down the remaining whiskey. He started to turn when lights suddenly danced behind his eyes. The next thing he knew, he was seated in a chair in the center of the pub, with two of Flint's early-day customers gaping down at him.

As his head cleared, he tried to stand, but the weakness returned. "Goddamn," he cursed under his breath. "If someone will help me to my room upstairs, I'll soon be fit."

"I'll help ye to the kitchen," Flint said from near his side. "Goody is at the courthouse—the witch trials, ye know. But her daughter Mary, and Mary's friend Elizabeth, are waiting for ye out back. The girls aren't allowed in the pub, o'course, nor will any Puritan cross my threshold."

Braden stood and grasped Flint's arm. "Why do you think I chose your establishment, my friend. 'Tis the only place in Salem Town with decent refreshment."

In minutes, he was lying on the kitchen cot, silently cursing the burning pain while waiting for the swooshing between his ears to subside.

Two young ladies proceeded to open his shirt and clean the caked blood from his side. Even in his fuzzy-headed state, he could see that the girls were in their late teens and unfortunately as plain as yesterday's raisin pudding. With thin pale hair pulled tightly behind their heads in secure knots, the two displayed no youthful charm at all. Still, as the one called Mary probed and bathed his wound, he was grateful for her gentleness. Her fingers felt cool on his forehead and his chest. He wondered idly why she took so long exploring his upper torso; then he heard her say she was checking for additional damage.

"That's enough," he said, turning restlessly. "I'll go upstairs now."

"We'll help you, sir," Mary said. "One on each side. You don't want to start the bleeding again."

He was further disgruntled when he found it necessary to accept Mary's offer in order to climb the narrow steps. Once in his room, he collapsed on the bed.

His head was spinning and the room grew dark. He

heard the two girls whisper and giggle, but they sounded so far away. He felt suspended, floating in a cloudlike vapor. The sensation was not entirely unpleasant, as he drifted into an odd dreamlike state. It could be loss of blood, he thought, or the whiskey, or the draft the girls had given him to ward off the fever. Whatever it was, he was feeling very peculiar.

He found himself beneath the heavy, white sailcloth, his body tight against Amanda Sheffield. He had done well to conceal his initial shock at the girl's loveliness— her petite waist, her golden hair and blushing cheeks, her large amber-green eyes looking at him like a cat startled by a sudden intruder. He had felt her warmth as he cut her free from the rope. Together they had dropped to the deck as he tried to cushion her fall. For a moment, she clung to him, but then, as they lay trapped, she had stiffened and let her temper flare. What in hell had caused her to dislike him so quickly? He hadn't seen her in years and believed he had always acted in the best interest of the Sheffields. Hadn't he arranged an excellent match for her? Secured her a fortune and a title? She should be a bit more appreciative. Not to mention, he had probably saved her life, at the cost of considerable pain to himself. Women were impossible to understand. That's why he'd wisely steered a course away from serious entanglement.

The voices continued from far away. He saw Amanda's face. She was so near. He moved close to her and touched his lips against tendrils of flaxen silk. He wanted to stroke her, to caress the mounds he felt against his forearm, but he couldn't seem to move. He was very hot. Sweat ran in tiny rivulets along his spine.

He saw the outline of Amanda's body encased in filmy yellow cotton. Her breasts rose and fell in rapid rhythm. He was aroused and tense as he reached for her. Through a veil of swirling silver mist and the sound of throbbing like the ocean's surf, he again heard girlish giggles.

He blinked, forcing himself into conscious thought, moving on his bed despite the return of pain.

"He's waking up," came a small voice from some distance. "He'll know we're still here."

"Do you think he'll be angry?" was the response from a second feminine voice.

"No, no. He's been completely out of his head. Didn't you hear all that talk about falling and someone called Amanda?"

"Yes, but—"

"Hurry up, goose. Put the sheet over him and we'll be on our way."

"Very well, but . . . oh, Mary . . . just look at him. He's so . . . so magnificent. I've never seen any man so handsome."

"Shut up, Elizabeth. He may hear you. Besides, when have you ever seen a strange man asleep in only his breeches?"

"Never. But it is exciting, isn't it."

"It shouldn't be. After all, we *are* nurses."

"Not . . . not exactly."

"But we soon will be. Mother's been teaching us, hasn't she? Now come on. We'll return later with some porridge."

He listened to this chatter with his eyes closed and suppressing a grin. At least he had passed inspection by the young scamps. No need to let them know he'd overheard their comments; that would only frighten or embarrass them. Besides, what chance did a young Puritan lass have to learn anything about men before her wedding night? A little healthy curiosity was certainly no sin.

He was feeling better. A cool sheet lay across him and the pain was easing. He could sleep. And if his little angels of mercy returned with soup, he'd relish the nourishment.

CHAPTER
6

"Would you care for sugar in your tea, Reverend Mather?" inquired Sara Sheffield.

"Yes, if you please, madam," the reverend replied.

Sara ladled a spoonful into the white porcelain cup and handed the steaming brew to the minister.

"And you, Amanda dear?"

"No, thank you, Aunt Sara." Amanda reached for her cup, glad to see her hands were steady despite her nerves. Just the presence of the renowned Cotton Mather was enough to make a body jittery, but in addition, she knew at any moment Captain Braden Hamilton would be arriving at the Sheffield house.

It had been two weeks since that horrible misadventure on board the captain's frigate. Since then, she had found it impossible to erase the enigmatic Hamilton from her mind. Uncle Hugh had reported that for a week the captain had been abed fighting a fever caused by the wound made that calamitous morning. Then, once recovered, Hamilton had visited the ship daily to oversee the final work and to begin provisioning it for the upcoming voyage. Summer squalls swirling in from the Atlantic had caused some delay, but now the frigate was almost ready to leave for Bermuda. Uncle Hugh said the name *Tamara* had been painted in golden letters on its bow, though he didn't know the inspiration behind that unusual name.

A knock sounded and in a few moments, the houseboy escorted Captain Hamilton into the parlor. Both Hugh and Reverend Mather rose in greeting.

Amanda sat quietly, her cup and saucer resting in her lap.

Braden bowed first to his hostess, then to her, his expression coolly polite with just a trace of a smile. He drew up a chair and sat between Amanda and Reverend Mather.

Keeping her eyes lowered, she listened to the men's conversation on such varied topics as the price of salt and the threat of Spanish conquest in the New World. Braden was as worldly as she had expected, but Cotton Mather was also surprisingly sophisticated for a man of the Church. Only occasionally did Uncle Hugh interject his opinion, and not once did Aunt Sara part her lips except to sip tea or nibble a biscuit.

Amanda followed her aunt's example of silence for quite some time, and she kept her eyes averted from Braden Hamilton. But suddenly Reverend Mather turned and addressed her, "My dear Mistress Sheffield, you must be quite excited about your coming nuptials. It's unfortunate they're to take place in Bermuda rather than here in Boston. I would have been pleased to attend."

"Not excited, Reverend. In fact, I'm not entirely happy about the match."

"Amanda!" came Aunt Sara's shocked voice. "It is quite improper of you to make such a remark."

"But no, Mrs. Sheffield," Mather responded. "It's one I hear often from young and sheltered maidens in my flock. Marriage must not be undertaken lightly. And in your niece's case, I understand she's never met her future husband. Any proper young woman would have qualms, whether she is Puritan or Anglican."

Uncle Hugh leaned forward. "Amanda, girl, you never mentioned this to us before. Are you truly unhappy about the marriage?"

Amanda felt Braden's eyes on her, but she refused to look his way. Instead she concentrated on her uncle. "Reverend Mather is quite correct. To become the wife of a stranger, especially a man three times my age, causes me a good deal of concern."

"Oh!" gasped Aunt Sara, her mouth dropping in shock.

Amanda continued. "Of course, everything has been arranged by my brother and by Captain Hamilton. And, as you know, my fiancé is a man of title and great wealth. It wouldn't do for me to refuse such an opportunity to . . . to bring this wealth into the Sheffield coffers."

Aunt Sara found her voice. "You needn't include Hugh Sheffield in that description, Amanda. To desire material goods—wealth, if you will—is a sin against God. Is it not, Reverend?"

Cotton Mather was watching Amanda closely. "Greed is a sin, madam," he said, without looking at Sara, "but I wouldn't think an arranged marriage to a man of distinction could necessarily be called materialistic. What do you think, Captain Hamilton?"

Now Amanda turned toward Braden. His face was solemn, and she saw deep concern in his blue gaze.

"Yes, Captain, what *do* you think?" Amanda asked sharply.

"I think you and I should have a private conversation —with your family's permission, of course. This is a matter of serious import."

"No need for private conver—" Sara began.

"Private. I must insist," snapped Braden. He rose and reached for Amanda's hand. "Is there some other room to which we can briefly adjourn. I have extremely important questions to put to Mistress Sheffield."

For once, Hugh ignored his wife. "By all means, Hamilton. Just across the entryway. My office. You have been a close confidant of the Sheffields for many years.

My brother trusted you completely. And so do I. I'm sure Reverend Mather will understand this divergence from strict decorum."

The reverend rose. "Of course. In fact, while you discuss this urgent matter with Mistress Sheffield, we will bow our heads in prayer for divine guidance that God's will be done."

Amanda's throat was dry and her hands clammy. She hadn't expected her remark to create such a fuss. Still, she had hoped for a moment of private conversation with Braden Hamilton. And what she wanted to say had nothing to do with her coming marriage.

Braden escorted her into Hugh's small study, its one tiny window heavily curtained and its only decoration a watercolor of an English warship in full sail on a rough sea.

Keeping as much distance as possible between them, Amanda revolved slowly to look at him. The way he was studying her—his eyes narrowed, a slow smile beginning to crook one corner of his mouth—she wondered if he read her thoughts. Could he hear her heart racing or detect the confusion he created in her emotions?

Why didn't he speak? Good heavens, he'd asked for this meeting, hadn't he? And at this very moment, wasn't the most illustrious minister in New England praying for some divine good to come from this conversation? And still the captain stood there, looking like the most dashing prince in Christendom, staring at her with as seductive a smile as she'd ever seen, waiting for her to tell him if she would accept his arrangement for her marriage to the marquess—and if she said she would not, what then?

The silence was agonizing, and Amanda felt compelled to speak. "I . . . I must apologize for the unfortunate accident on your ship. It was my fault and I didn't thank you properly for your help."

His smile deepened. "You didn't thank me at all, Mistress Sheffield."

"Also . . . also . . ." Drat, why couldn't she stop stuttering? "Also I wanted you to know I've been quite concerned about your injury. It must have been more serious than I realized."

He took a step toward her. "Not serious at all. Painful, but quickly healed."

She held her ground, though she felt the urge to move away. She had to tell him—tell him how she had caused his wound—about the voodoo magic. After all, the doll still existed. Something must be done with it. "You . . . you . . ." Drat. She must sound like a complete fool. "You are quite well now?"

"Quite." He opened his coat and his snowy linen shirt showed a slight bulge along his left side. "A thin bandage. 'Tis all that's needed over the spot. Now, mistress, perhaps we should discuss your future. My ship will soon be ready to sail. But naturally I have no intention of abducting you against your will or forcing you into a life of subjugation to a husband you don't love. It is best you tell me now. What is it to be?"

He was standing close, close enough for her to see him breathing beneath the soft white linen, close enough for her to see the tiny lines etched in the golden skin around his eyes. His scent was some masculine fragrance, or a residue of fine, sweet tobacco.

"You hesitate," he said. "Perhaps you blame me for this uncomfortable set of circumstances. To be honest, I thought you would be pleased with the match. Philip said you would be delighted. If I've caused you unhappiness, I will rescind the betrothal as soon as possible. I will sail to Bermuda without you, and face Lord Pickering myself."

She couldn't think clearly. She didn't know what she wanted, except she was suddenly positive that she didn't want this man to disappear forever from her life. "I . . . I need more time. I thought there was no other choice for me. If I knew more about the marquess, perhaps I could make a decision."

"You could meet him first, if you like. It would be more awkward for you to refuse him after that, but at least you could make a more enlightened decision."

"You mean if I went with you to Bermuda—properly chaperoned, of course—I could still reconsider the match?"

"Certainly. We would say nothing to your family, but if, when you reached Bermuda and met Lord Pickering, you decided to decline his offer, I'd return you home at once."

She took a deep breath. It appeared Cotton Mather's prayers had borne some fruit indeed. "Very well. I'll consider it for a day or two."

"Perhaps I could have your answer by tomorrow. If the weather is fair, I would like to take you riding—climb to the hill where the beacon stands. It's quite a nice view of the town and harbor."

Amanda felt her heart skip a beat. Hiding her delight, she answered casually, "Tomorrow? I suppose I could interrupt my sewing a few hours. My trousseau, you know."

His grin told her she hadn't fooled him for a minute.

"Your trousseau is most important," he said, "but if you decide not to marry, it may no longer be of such urgency."

Flustered, she shook her head. "I . . . I haven't made my decision yet, Captain. After all, a rich lord doesn't sue for one's hand every day."

Before she could move, he took her hand and raised it to his lips. The kiss was feather-light, but his grasp was firm and warm. Still holding her hand in his, he said softly, "'Tis a hand I've learned to admire more than I expected."

She withdrew it and said crisply, "A hand you will also respect, Captain Hamilton. What time will you call for me tomorrow?"

"At two, if that is convenient," he answered with twitching lips. "And now, we should return to the parlor and see if the good reverend has completed his prayers."

She slipped her hand through his arm. She was pleased —no, much more than pleased—thrilled to the tips of her toes. She had little experience with men, but she would swear Braden Hamilton was attracted to her. And her fury at him was fast disappearing. Tomorrow could be a most important day. She would lay aside her dreary black attire and wear her most attractive riding suit. And horsemanship was her forte. It was hard to keep from laughing with pleasure as she reentered the parlor to face the dour stare of her aunt, and the questioning appraisals of her uncle and Cotton Mather.

CHAPTER
7

Wearing a crisp, jade-green riding ensemble, complete with matching bonnet, chocolate-brown riding boots and brown kid gloves, Amanda walked with measured steps to the nearby riding stable. Behind her, she left a fuming Aunt Sara, scandalized over Amanda's insistence on riding alone with the captain; a victorious Uncle Hugh, who had for the second time in twenty-four hours defied his wife on behalf of Amanda; and a smug Coco waving an encouraging good-bye from the kitchen window.

Amanda had spent the morning trying on and discarding a number of outfits before she and Coco agreed on the green. And she had counted every minute until the time for her rendezvous with Captain Hamilton. It was ten past two, and she walked as slowly as she could. It was important to arrive just a bit late so she wouldn't appear too eager for the meeting. On the other hand, she didn't want to risk his becoming sufficiently annoyed to abandon the outing. She still had to explain to him the problem of the voodoo doll. Even now, she felt its weight where she had concealed it in an inner skirt pocket.

Nearing the stable, she set her expression into one of serene nonchalance. She recognized Captain Hamilton's broad-chested bay stallion standing in the shade beside the barn door. She entered the musty, straw-scented enclosure and blinked in the dim sunlight.

"Good afternoon, Mistress Sheffield," came a masculine voice. "Your horse is ready—waiting as impatiently as I."

Braden Hamilton stood by the mounting block holding the reins of a dark gray mare.

Amanda was satisfied that her timing was perfect. "Good afternoon, sir. I'm sorry to be late, but I became so absorbed in my sewing, I lost all account of time. I barely had time to change into riding clothes."

"Yes, I can imagine that sewing must be totally absorbing for a young woman of high spirits."

He was teasing, she thought. Still, sun-blinded, she couldn't see his expression. Without further ado, she stepped onto the block and eased onto the sidesaddle.

The captain led her horse outside and handed her the reins. The sight of his broad shoulders encased in midnight-blue linen, his broad-brimmed felt hat, his glove-less hands sporting a massive gold ring with onyx center, reminded her that she dealt with a man of wealth and power. While his words were flattering, his manner revealed his enormous self-confidence. This was no simpering English drawing room dandy.

He swung atop his stallion and smiled pleasantly. "We'll ride toward the Commons, then cut across Beacon till we pass Cotton Hill."

"Cotton Hill? Named after the reverend?"

"Named after his grandfather, who settled on its slope years ago."

"You seem to know a great deal about Boston," she said, joining him on the bridle path. Her animal plodded in droop-eared resignation beside Hamilton's steed.

"It's a port I frequent when sailing from Bermuda. Actually I prefer the quiet of Salem Town as a rule. I stay at a favorite inn owned by an old sea dog. 'Tis something of a refuge from the Puritan stronghold of the area."

"And what persuasion are you, Captain?" Her mare continued to plod despite her nudging its ribs with her heels. She was beginning to suspect the creature was dozing as it walked.

Reining left onto School Street and putting his bay into a jog-trot, Braden answered, "Somewhat of a loose spirit, I fear, my lady. Born an Anglican and a royalist, I escaped Cromwell's influence. Bermuda is a Crown Colony and primarily Anglican now, though we've a smattering of other beliefs among the settlers. We all get along there, whether Reformed or Roman. Rather a new and refreshing idea, in my opinion."

"Yes, most interesting," she answered vaguely while concentrating on her sluggish mount. Even a tap of her crop barely stirred the beast. And its trot was like four rods pounding the cobbles at once. Bouncing in the saddle, she felt the pins loosening in her hair despite Coco's best efforts to secure them.

Hamilton increased the pace. His horse's flowing black tail flashed near the nose of her mare as if in haughty disdain.

She kicked hard against the animal's sides, but only turned the slow, jarring trot into a faster trot that bounced her teeth in her mouth. She grabbed her hat before it could fly off, and in the process, almost lost her seat entirely. Gripping the reins, she steadied herself. She had always been fearless in the saddle, and her horsemanship was outstanding, but with such a beast beneath her, she was making a complete fool of herself.

At the edge of the Commons, Hamilton drew in and spun his horse in a controlled circle to watch her approach. His smile held both sympathy and condescension. "Your first time on the mare, I assume. I asked the stable hand for a lady's gentle mount, but I did expect it to be half alive."

"A gentle . . . " she sputtered. "No wonder the mare can barely be coaxed to go forward. I ride quite well, Captain Hamilton. After all, I grew up in Virginia. I was racing my father's excellent stock on country lanes before I was five. I fear you've done me a disfavor, sir, by placing me on this . . . this plodder."

He threw back his head and laughed heartily.

Watching him, she was at first annoyed, then couldn't resist his contagious amusement. As if by plan, the mare abruptly broke into a canter, nearly tossing her backward over its rump. Her hat flew off to land like a stricken green bird in the middle of the road, while her hair was blown into uneven clumps and stringlets.

"Oh," she cried, collecting the reins and regaining control. "My hat!"

Still grinning, Braden wheeled his horse and with great flourish scooped up the stray hat. "My lady," he said dramatically. "You are now further in my debt."

Knowing her dignity was in shambles, she dimpled shyly and hooked the hat onto her saddle. "Indeed, you continue to play my hero," she said. "I scarcely know how to express my thanks."

"No need. Now, how are you at climbing?" he asked.

"Climbing? A tree or a mountain, Captain?"

"Nothing so risky. We can leave the horses in the shade and walk to the top of yonder hill. It's the largest of the three dominating the peninsula. There's a beacon there to guide ships to the bay."

"Yes. I'd like that. Anything is better than continuing to sit aboard this uncooperative beast."

In the shade of spreading oaks, he lifted her to the ground. Standing before him, with his hands around her waist, she felt a tingle of pleasure in his overpowering presence.

"It's a perfect afternoon," she said, moving quickly away. "So nice after the rain."

"It is, indeed," he agreed. Then for a time, they made their way silently up the slope of the hill. The path was well-worn and easy to maneuver. As they climbed upward, the panorama of the village and the sea became even more breathtaking. At the top sat the beacon tower and several cannon facing the bay.

"It's amazing," Amanda said, truly awed by the sight spread beneath them. "The houses look like toys, and the wharf and the ships are so small. There—I see Reverend Mather's church—and how green the Commons appears."

She didn't realize until she looked up that Captain Hamilton was gazing at her with far more interest than at the view.

Without taking his eyes from her, he said, "Look closely and you can see Milk Street and your uncle's home. Next door is Josiah Franklin's, and toward the north end is Revere's house, built after the fire fifteen years ago. It was built on the property belonging to Cotton Mather's father, Increase . . ." His voice trailed. He stepped close enough for her to see the moisture brought on by the sun's harsh heat dotting his forehead.

"Could you tell me, Mistress Sheffield, if you've reached a decision regarding your betrothal?"

"I . . . I thought you said I could decide later . . . when I reached Bermuda."

"Then you will sail with me to the island?"

He was very close, his eyes holding hers in their depths. Her knees felt weak from the climb—or from something else.

"I will sail to Bermuda. I will meet the marquess, then decide."

"And will you have some means of comparison, my charming little mistress? On what will you base your decision?"

He must be teasing again, she thought. What comparison could there be? The marquess was a man like any other, only richer and with an important title. If he treated her nicely and wasn't entirely too old . . .

Braden gripped her shoulder. "I want you to be sure," he said in a low tone. "My bet is you know little of men and their ways—what to avoid and what to desire. Money isn't the only criteria in choosing a husband, little one."

He drew her to him, pressed her against the length of

his body and tipped her chin upward. Before she could protest, he covered her lips in a kiss of tender restraint. Her senses stirred, then swirled in a burst of emotion. Her hands flew to his shoulders, and though she didn't embrace him, neither did she push him away.

His lips stayed, more insistent now, while his hands moved along her spine. Tingling shafts of delight spread through her body and a strange new sensation warmed her deepest recesses. Her eyes popped open, and regaining her senses, she started to slap him, but he caught her wrist.

For a long moment, he held her, studying her in silence. She thought she saw a shadow cross his face before it was replaced by a crooked smile of amused indifference. Abruptly, he turned and walked to the cannon, keeping his back toward her.

Amanda was thrown into complete confusion. He must surely have known a kiss was far too intimate, and she would have to respond with some reprimand. No man had dared to kiss her lips before—though a few had asked permission and been promptly refused. And why had her body reacted to his touch in such an outrageous manner? The entire episode was quite disturbing, most especially the way he'd turned coldly away from her.

She was suddenly annoyed at his treatment. She would pretend nothing had happened and proceed to the point of her meeting. From the folds of her skirt, she withdrew the fabric doll.

"Captain Hamilton, I forgive your impertinence just now, if you will forgive me a grave harm I have done you."

When he turned, his face was once again friendly. His eyes twinkled. "I haven't asked for your forgiveness, Mistress Sheffield. The kiss, as I explained beforehand, was for your benefit—a test to help you in the momentous decision you must soon make. You may find one kiss is not quite enough. If you need additional information, you may ask at any time between now and . . . the moment you take your vows."

The audacity of the man, she thought, almost forgetting the doll she held. So he was doing her a favor to crush her in his arms and tantalize her beyond all rules of decency. "You amuse yourself at my expense, sir. I'm certain I can make a decision when the time comes based on many considerations other than your kiss."

His lips crooked in a sideways grin, but his eyes again clouded. "Yes, there are other matters. Such as money and a title, a great estate in England, power and influence at court, hobnobbing with royalty—yes, many factors to consider, after all."

She wanted to stamp her foot as she'd done as a child. Braden Hamilton was the most exasperating person she'd ever met. "If I'm not mistaken," she snapped, "the marquess's wealth was a primary reason you and my brother arranged the match in the first place."

"You accepted readily enough."

"How do you know that?"

"Your brother said you were delighted."

"He exaggerated. I did accept, but only after you—" She stopped. She would not give him the satisfaction of knowing the pain of his rejection had been a catalyst in her decision. That, and saving Briarfield. He would not know how desperately the money was needed for the plantation. And he would never know how she had worshipped him since she was a child. His ego was already far too lofty to be further inflated.

"Yes? Continue," he suggested.

"—after carefully considering the other offers from gentlemen in Virginia and England. Lord Pickering's does seem the most promising."

"I see. Of course."

He didn't sound convinced. No matter. She must regain her composure and change the subject. "Excuse me, Captain Hamilton, but I came today with a specific purpose, not just to see the view, though it's quite wonderful."

He lounged against the cannon. "Then state that purpose, my lady."

"It's . . . it's this." She handed him the blank-faced doll.

He looked at it quizzically, then chuckled. "Rather a crude toy," he observed. "Is it a gift?"

"No. Yes. In a way."

"Hmm. Should I be overjoyed?"

"The gift is not the doll itself, but its power. You see, this is a magic doll. It's a likeness of you, and contains some of your clothing, which gives it power over you." She suddenly felt incredibly foolish. Standing here in the bright afternoon, looking at this sophisticated, self-assured man-of-the-world, having just had her senses shattered by the thrill of his kiss—how dare she suggest the silly puppet could be a threat to him.

But he didn't laugh. He just turned it around for closer inspection. "My clothing?" he inquired.

"Yes. Cloth from an old jacket—and inside, there's a brass button."

He depressed the chest. "Yes. I feel it. Well now, lass, this must be a voodoo doll." It was a simple statement, made without a trace of fear.

"You . . . know about . . . voodoo?"

"Certainly. I travel often in the Indies and have soldiered in Africa. My question is how did *you* come by such a token?"

She lowered her eyes. "My servant girl got it from a . . . a mamba at Briarfield. She thought I was very angry with you because of the betrothal. She . . . she stabbed it with a pin—the day before you . . ."

Now he laughed. It was a belly laugh born of true merriment. When he regained control, he captured her eyes. "My dear Mistress Sheffield. I don't understand all the mysteries of life, or death, but I do believe I control my own destiny. No servant, no witch, no preacher and certainly no lovely young girl can bring about my demise with a doll and a pin." He placed his hand beneath her chin. "Don't apologize," he said gently. "You have no guilt."

"You're not frightened?"

"Frightened?" He chuckled again. "I'll show you how frightened I am." He dropped the doll to the ground. Then with the heel of his boot, he ground it into the rocky soil.

She emitted a tiny scream. "No, don't do that. No, Braden," she choked. "What if you're wrong?"

He put his arm around her and held her to him. "Aha," he murmured. "Already the doll has brought me good luck. For the first time, I hear my Christian name from your lips. And, little Amanda, it pleases me very much."

She was trembling—from alarm or from nerves or from his nearness, she had no idea. She moved slowly out of his grasp. "You do tempt fate, don't you, Captain Hamilton. If you know about these dolls you call voodoo, you know what power they might have."

"Only if you believe in that power—or at least, that's my personal conclusion. You mustn't worry over the coincidence of the doll and my injury. Come along now," he said, smiling. "We'll return to our mounts. I have cider in a jar on my saddle."

Shaken to her depths, she was quite happy to walk back down the hill. She only glanced once over her shoulder at the figure of the cloth captain lying crushed beside the cannon.

The morning following the outing to Beacon Hill, Braden awoke early. While he shaved and dressed, he mulled over his meeting with the delightful Amanda Sheffield. He had expected to test her determination to marry Pickering, but he had surprisingly put his own feelings into sudden turmoil.

His initial reaction to the grown-up Amanda had been correct. She was the most fascinating woman he had met in years—not just a beauty, but a woman of intelligence and spirit. And behind those feline eyes, he had sensed an undercurrent of passion of which she was blithely unaware.

The kiss had proven him right. Though she had attempted to display righteous indignation, he knew she had enjoyed his forceful touch, the sensation of his lips covering hers, the awareness of his attraction to her charms. Aye, she had liked it well enough. If he decided to stop her marriage to Pickering, he was sure he could do it.

An early morning fog still swirled through the narrow lanes as he strolled to a coffeehouse which opened early and where he hoped to find time to be alone with his thoughts. There was little talk these days of anything except the witch trials, a subject he preferred to avoid. He'd heard tales of witches in England, in Africa, in the Indies and now New England. The war between the powers of good and evil had a long and violent history and there seemed no end to it. He believed in God—and Heaven and Hell—but he found life more peaceful when people kept their noses out of other folks' business.

The inn had four small tables. It was deserted this morning except for a sleepy-eyed servant who managed to deliver the mug of hot brew with a minimum of comment.

As he relaxed and sipped the stimulating drink, Braden luxuriated in the memory of Amanda in his arms. She stirred him like no other woman ever had. Was it possible he had made a terrible mistake when he rejected Philip's offer so quickly? Had Amanda known about the offer before it had been made? He wished to hell he knew. If so, it would explain why she was so cool toward him that day on the ship. But if her kiss was any indication of what she felt in her heart, then surely that animosity was long forgotten. Still, if he decided to pursue the lady, he must court her with great finesse. And he must be sure that if he won in the end, he was ready to take her to wife. He had assumed his own marriage to be far in the future—until he kissed Amanda Sheffield.

The door to the inn swung open and a girl entered carrying a straw basket. Without hesitating, she crossed to Braden's table, placed the basket before him and sat down.

"Why, 'tis Mary Walcott, abroad so early. Would you like some tea or coffee, Mary?"

The girl gazed at him from beneath her crisp white bonnet. "Nay, Captain Hamilton. I just thought you might be here, and I wanted to inquire about your wound."

"Oh, it's healing nicely, dear. As I told you last week, you and your friend were very helpful. You'll both make fine nurses when you grow up."

"But we're already grown-up—at least, *I* am," she said glibly. She leaned forward to whisper, "Haven't you been keeping up with the witch trials? We've been in Judge Corwin's chamber several times already. We . . . we're going to be famous once the witches are put to death."

He considered this a moment. "Famous? No, I guess I hadn't heard about it—your involvement, that is."

"Why, I've been suffering terribly, Captain," she said, rolling her eyes. "No one knows what it's like to be tortured by the Devil—to be the victim of his evil ways."

"Tortured?"

"Well, possessed. You know, taken over by the spirit of someone else. Why, it's beyond my control, and so very awful. And Lizzie, too. Our families are desperate. They've asked Reverend Cotton Mather to help. I . . . I do wish you would come to the courthouse, Captain. You would surely have great sympathy for my ordeal."

Her eyes roved his face, as if to absorb him into her inner soul. "Would you come, Captain Hamilton? Your presence would lend me great strength—maybe enough to resist the witches' specter possessing my mind and body."

God in Heaven, this was the last thing he wanted. As gently as possible he said, "Nay, child. I'm sure if anyone can help, it would be Reverend Mather. He's far more expert in such matters. In fact, I'm preparing to sail soon to my home in Bermuda, where urgent business awaits."

"Oh, sir," she pleaded, "don't forget how I saved your life. I risked my family's wrath to come to your room to aid you. Could you not help me in my hour of need?"

He hid his growing exasperation. "Mistress Walcott, I expressed my deep appreciation as soon as I gained my strength. I also paid you and Mistress Hubbard a more than ample sum for your soup and ministrations. The fact is, I wasn't anywhere near death, my dear. Though you did relieve my pain."

"Then you're leaving?" she said, her face longer than usual.

"Aye, within the week. Naturally, I'll pray for right to prevail at the trials."

Her chin trembled as she pushed the basket toward him. "I . . . I brought you a gift. Even if you don't wish to help me, you may still have it."

Heaving a sigh, he lifted the lid of the basket. Peering up at him were two enormous orange eyes set in a demure bewhiskered face.

"Oh. A kitten," he said without enthusiasm. "How . . . a . . . nice of you, Mary. Yes . . . yes, indeed, just what I've been wanting." Already an idea was forming in his mind. He reached in and lifted the delicate creature from its container. "Well, well, calico, isn't it? Distinctly marked, and a female. Yes, I like the black mask and tail."

The kitten meowed softly, but appeared unafraid.

"I have another one at home," Mary ventured.

"No doubt."

"As long as you have this cat, we'll have something in common—a bond, you see. She's two months old and very healthy."

He put the kitten away. "Yes, thank you very much, Mary. Now I must go. I have a busy day ahead. My new ship will leave the bay for a test cruise." He tucked the basket under his arm and headed for the door.

Mary scooted out ahead of him. "I hope I see you again, Captain. I'll think of you all the time after you've gone. You must come back to Salem. Promise you won't forget me."

"No, of course I won't forget you," he said, patting her shoulder.

Her eyes narrowed. "And pray for me. Pray hard, Captain Hamilton, that I escape the Devil's clutches."

"Yes, indeed I will, my dear. I'm sure your goodness and innocence will triumph over Satan's wiles." Leaving her gazing at his back, he walked toward his room. He knew exactly what he would do with the kitten; the pretty creature would surely melt a certain lady's heart.

CHAPTER
8

As June progressed, each day became hotter and more humid than the day before. Amanda tried to contain her impatience as the time crept by at a maddening, sluggish pace. There was no word from the captain though work progressed without interruption on the new sailing vessel.

For three days Hugh was away from home while testing the frigate in Atlantic waters. When he returned, he reported the ship had performed beautifully, even in heavy seas. But still, another week passed with no word from Captain Hamilton.

Though she found the daytime hours spent under Aunt Sara's close scrutiny an excruciating bore, she made no complaint. She told herself there was no real harm in learning to polish silver, dip candles and cross-stitch pillowcases. Someday, as the marchioness of Staffordshire, she would have need to instruct a household of servants in those and many other tasks. After her present experience, she would be able to properly judge their work; she tried to imagine how surprised they'd be when she demonstrated personally how things should be done.

No, it was not the long days of work in the summer

heat that drove her to distraction. It was the nights when she lay abed in the stifling room, her sheets thrown aside and her body damp with sweat, that she was most miserable. Sleep was impossible in the early hours, and with nothing to do but lie on the pillows and suffer, she couldn't stop thinking about the decision she soon must make.

Some nights she would leave her bed and go to the open dormer window and gaze out across the rooftops of the town. Most of the village lay in darkness, but if the moon was up, she could make out the coastline and the shadowy outline of ships' masts above the wharf. There Captain Hamilton's ship lay at anchor. Uncle Hugh had said the captain named it *The Tamara;* the letters were being painted in gold on the bow.

Soon *The Tamara* would carry her to her destiny. It was a mystery why Braden was challenging her decision to marry Lord Pickering now when everything was already arranged. She admitted, as she rested her chin in her hands and gazed at the moon-splashed panorama, that she was both confused and extremely unhappy.

Before that afternoon on Beacon Hill, she had been resigned to her fate. She had convinced herself she was most fortunate to have secured a wealthy husband who could give her every luxury and provide her with estates and children. Love? What did she know of that strange emotion described in fairy tales and books of poetry? Whatever it was, it had nothing to do with real life and the security of an arranged marriage to a suitable partner; the kind of marriage Philip had chosen for her.

Then why, pray tell, had Braden Hamilton's kiss sent her spirits to the depths of despair? Why did the thought of his smile, half teasing, half inviting, torment her every waking hour and deep into the night? And when she finally slept, why did his image rise before her, his arms holding her, crushing her, protecting her from any harm that might befall her. Always in the deepest of her dreams, she clung to him in desperation, but in the end he drifted into the sea mist, leaving her breathless and frightened and unfulfilled. When she suddenly awoke, she was invariably filled with a dull ache often laced with anger; the cause of the anger was just beyond her comprehension—perhaps it was Philip, perhaps Braden, even, perhaps, herself.

Of one thing she was certain, however. She would hold Braden Hamilton to his promise not to force her to marry against her will. Once she was in Bermuda, once she had met Lord Pickering, she would then decide what to do. She would go on with her life, with or without the marquess—and without any further assistance from the captain. If she returned in disgrace to Briarfield, without wealth or title, she would face Philip unflinchingly. After all, she was James Sheffield's offspring, the same as Philip. And she had suspected for some time that she was the stronger-willed of James's children.

On the first day of July, Hugh brought home the news that they would embark on *The Tamara* within twenty-four hours. Amanda and Coco went into a flurry of final preparations and packing.

At dawn, on July 3, Amanda bade Aunt Sara a polite farewell. At last she was escaping the suffocating atmosphere of the Puritan woman's home—and off to what could prove to be the adventure of a lifetime. Her heart leaped as she rode with Hugh and Coco to the Sheffield docks.

Her uncle had volunteered to act as chaperone and give away the bride in Philip's absence. Amanda was sure, though, that Hugh's primary attraction was the maiden voyage of his beautiful new frigate. Hugh would return to Boston following the wedding on the captain's fast sloop, a new design which piqued his curiosity beyond measure.

As she stepped on deck, Amanda received a passing nod of greeting from Lord Braden, who was busy on the captain's bridge. As casually as possible, she returned his acknowledgment. But to her private annoyance, she felt a thousand butterflies dancing in excitement beneath her ribs. He was as handsome as she'd remembered in all her recent thoughts of him. And she was boarding his ship and placing her safety and her future in his keeping. He was, after all, her guardian as well as the ship's captain.

Admonishing herself to control her girlish emotions, she went directly to her cabin and began to arrange her belongings while Coco bustled at her side. But when the call came to weigh anchor, she hurried above deck to watch the activity—and to steal glances at Lord Hamilton.

The captain was issuing commands from the helm. Seamen were in position to cast off and man the rigging. The morning was perfect, with the sun shattering the haze with its brilliance. Dressed in flowing blouse and full skirt bound at the waist by a wide sash, Amanda shaded her eyes and watched the sails billow into the wind. With ease, she adjusted her stance to the increasing roll and waved her encouragement to Hugh. It was, indeed, a magnificent ship, the finest vessel Sheffield Shipyards had ever produced. As the ship eased into the bay, Captain Hamilton called for the flag of England to be hoisted on the mainmast.

Amanda crossed to the railing to take one last look at Boston and its expansive and scenic harbor. The village looked small now, dominated by its three hills, with Beacon the most prominent. Feeling a thrill of joy and release from confinement, she crossed to the starboard bow to gaze down at the blue-green swells of the beckoning Atlantic. The roll was gentle, but she knew how quickly the sea could turn into a churning cauldron. Still, she had no fear at all. Hadn't her own uncle built this wonderful ship? And the captain at the helm was vastly experienced.

Overhead came the snap from the square sails as the wind caught the canvas on all three masts. The air was brisk and fresh with salty tang as *The Tamara* left behind the heavy atmosphere of the land.

Amanda grasped the rail, lifted her head and breathed deeply. With closed eyes, she lost herself in the sensation of flying through wind and mist, all her senses alive and tingling in delight.

"Excuse me, Mistress Sheffield. By necessity, I had to delay my personal welcome aboard."

She turned to look up at Braden Hamilton, who was gazing at her with eyes she could swear were the same color as the sea. "No need to apologize, Captain. I've crossed the Atlantic before, and I know what duties are required of a ship's master. In fact, you needn't concern yourself with my well-being at all during the voyage."

"Then you have no worries about sailing?"

"Worries?" She laughed merrily. "Why, I have more concern about strolling to the market in the village. Nay, sir, I should have been born a seaman—or perhaps a pirate. 'Tis a life I would have relished."

His look held open admiration. "My compliments. I've known some ladies who shun the sea like the plague."

"Not I," she asserted.

"Still, I won't have much time to spend entertaining guests. Though, of course, tonight we'll have a special dinner served in my cabin, if all is going smoothly."

"I'll look forward to that. In the meantime, I'd like your permission to watch the crew at their work—quite out of the way, of course."

He gave her a slow, enigmatic smile. "Of course. They're good men with a high moral code. Mostly Bermudians with wives and children awaiting their return. However . . ." A teasing grin tugged at his lips. ". . . you may attract an occasional glance or two from one of the lads. They have been away from home a good while—and in a Puritan stronghold. And, if I may add, you're a winsome lass with the wind lifting your curls and swirling your skirts."

She was momentarily tongue-tied. The man had all the charm in the world. His flattery along with his rare good looks just took her breath away. Braden stood there, a fist on one hip, and the other hand tucked inside the deep open V of his soft shirt. Despite herself, she felt heat rising in her cheeks. He didn't need to tell her he found her attractive. The thought was written plainly in his eyes. And, my goodness, how much pleasure she found in his silent tribute.

When she found her voice, she said softly, "I'll behave, Captain. That I promise."

His grin broke forth. "Unless, of course, you have my permission to do otherwise."

She dropped her eyes. His implication was far too bold and she had no response.

"My dear Mistress Sheffield, I have something here to amuse you during the voyage—if you like it, that is."

Surprised, she looked up to see him draw a living creature from inside his shirt.

"Oh, how adorable!" she cried, reaching for the kitten. "And so sweet to stay hidden for so long." She held up the tortoiseshell orange and black cat for inspection. It was quite calm under her gaze and settled happily into her arms.

"Why, she's a darling," Amanda effused. "How did you find her?"

"She was given to me by a friend in Salem a few weeks ago. She's very young—about three months now. I thought of you right away. She'll need a name, of course."

"Yes, I'll think of one. Thank you so much, Captain Hamilton."

"Why not address me as Braden. After all, we've been acquainted for many years."

"Very well. Thank you, Braden." She freed a hand to clasp his. "I'll take very good care of her."

"I felt sure you would. Now I must get back to work. I expect fair sailing for the next few days. But there's a great deal to do. With luck, we'll be in Bermuda within a fortnight."

She stroked the soft fur as Braden strode away and disappeared below deck. Was it possible a man of such power and responsibility could also be so caring and thoughtful? Surely she could forgive him for merely cooperating with Philip's plan to arrange her marriage. After all, Braden Hamilton hadn't laid eyes on her since she was eleven. She had misjudged his motives, she was certain. Yes, it would be easy to forgive him, but more difficult to control her growing attraction to the fascinating captain.

The captain's dinner was not to take place. By midafternoon, the sea had changed its tranquil mood and become blue-black and angry.

Amanda was no stranger to the squalls of the sea. She threw on a cape and found a sheltered area on the main deck from where she could watch the changing colors of sky and water, and the well-trained crew working with ropes and winches. Tucked under her arm beneath the cape snuggled the nervous kitten. Unfortunately Coco was showing signs of seasickness. It would certainly be unpleasant for the girl if she were ill the entire voyage.

Amanda scanned the deck for Hugh, but he was nowhere in sight. Nor did she see Braden—as she now liked to address him. In fact, she discovered herself repeating his name with great frequency, even if only inside her head. She had hummed to herself all day while unpacking her belongings and writing in a journal, and found visions of the captain constantly intruding on her thoughts.

Now, as she watched the prow of the ship dipping and rising in the swells, she smiled at the memory of Braden's deep-throated laughter and the gentleness of his touch.

A sudden lurch threw her off balance. She regained herself quickly, but the kitten meowed loudly and squirmed from her arms. She grabbed for it, but the little creature raced across the damp planking and entered the first opening it came to.

"Oh, no," Amanda muttered, running after the terrified kitten. "Come back," she called, knowing her pleas were wasted.

The animal's black tail disappeared down the steps leading below.

Without a second thought, Amanda followed. She glimpsed it jump from the lower deck level to the second flight of stairs going farther into the hold.

"Oh, dash it all," she swore under her breath and continued her downward climb.

Another rapidly descending section of stairway took her to the dimly lit ship's storage hold. A single lantern hanging from the low ceiling cast swaying light and shadows across the floor and walls. There was the mingled scent of fresh-cut tobacco and musty hay. The room dipped from side to side and from below came the sound of waves thunking against exterior timbers.

She gripped the handrail and searched the area with increased alarm. Crates and barrels were stacked in all corners of the room. If the kitten chose to hide behind the storage goods, she might not be found till the voyage's conclusion—and what state would the poor little thing be in by then? Was there a mouse or two already in residence? Would the frightened kitty know how to stalk and kill to survive? Was there any water for it to drink?

She thought she heard a meow behind the bales of hay.

"Here, kitty, here, kitty," she called. She listened, but heard no response above the clunking and creaking and distant sound of thunder.

Dropping to her knees, she bunched her skirts and began to crawl across the pitching wooden floor. A sudden lurch sent her bumping hard onto her forearms and elbows.

"Ouch," she whispered and squatted on her heels, frustrated and upset.

"Hello there," came a voice from the dark stairway. "Have you invented a new pastime?" Wearing a rain-splattered cape, Braden ducked into the hold.

Her emotions were mixed as she sat on the floor beside the hay, holding her bruised elbow. As foolish as she felt in this position, she was happy to have help in finding her pet. "Braden, the kitten scurried down here. I hadn't meant to let her escape, but—"

"Don't worry," he said. "She can't get away. We'll find her soon enough."

"If . . . if you have a moment, maybe we could move these bales a bit. I thought I heard her cry just now."

"I have a moment," he said. "I left the helm in good hands for a while to have coffee." He removed his wet cape. "Now, where do you think the scamp is hiding?"

She pushed against a bale, but it didn't budge.

A tiny meow came from behind it.

"Aha," said Braden. "She's in there and wanting to be rescued, I'll wager." He shoved against the hay bale, but only succeeded in breaking the twine and scattering the straw across the floor.

"Damnation," he muttered. "Wait a moment, I'll crawl behind." He dropped to his hands and knees and squeezed between two large bales.

Sitting there watching his efforts, Amanda couldn't help but think how few men, especially titled lords and ship's captains, would take time for such a chore.

"Ah, I can just reach her. Be still, little one; there, I've got you. Don't shake so—you're safe now," he said softly.

Braden emerged from the bales, clutching the ball of orange and black fur. Straw clung to his damp hair and shoulders, but his grin was triumphant. He sat beside Amanda and handed her the cat.

She stroked it in silence for a minute until it stopped trembling and began to purr.

Braden seemed content to sit cross-legged beside her, watching her pet the kitten.

"That's it, baby, purr. 'Tis a good sign," she murmured.

"Have you named it yet?" Braden inquired.

"No. I've been thinking, but . . . I have it. I could call it Persephone. *Purr*sephone. What do you think?"

"Wasn't the original Persephone a goddess of the underworld?"

"Yes. She was Greek and abducted by Pluto."

"Then the name seems downright appropriate. Especially after the kitten scurried down here. If it had gotten any lower, it would be swimming," he observed while scratching the creature behind its ear.

"It's Persephone, then. Maybe I'll simply call her Perci."

"Perfect," he agreed, then held her eyes for a long moment, until she nervously looked away and began to fuss with the sleeping kitten in her lap.

"Amanda," he said in a low voice, "you are a remarkable woman. Part child, part lady, saucy and innocent at the same moment. I admit I'm irresistibly drawn to you." He leaned near and slipped his arm over her shoulders. His eyes were narrowed and his lips tauntingly close. Gently he pulled her to him and covered her lips, at first softly, then with growing force.

Flames of pleasure erupted through her as she tasted him and inhaled his masculine scent tinged with sea air and moist ocean brine. One hand cupped the back of her head, the other bent her to him. His lips parted hers and his tongue explored her mouth.

Forgetting the kitten, Amanda gripped his shoulders and responded to the kiss with a sudden passion she had never known existed.

His mouth dropped to her throat and then to the swell of her bare skin revealed above the neckline of her simple blouse.

Carefully he untied the drawstring of her cape and let it slip off her shoulders and onto the floor. His tongue tickled her flesh, sending spikes of delight to her deepest recesses.

"Braden," she whispered. "No . . ."

He laid her across his knees and cradled her in his arms. "'Tis all right, little one. I won't even awaken Persephone. But for one moment, let me hold you—luxuriate in your extraordinary beauty—give you some pleasure in return."

She looked up at him and knew without doubt she had nothing to fear. The swaying of the ship rocked them both; the dancing light played around them, the sound of the storm drew them together. All reality fled, leaving them in a strange and beautiful dream.

"Braden," she said again, loving the sound of his name. She reached up to touch his cheek and found it rough with the beginning of a day's growth.

His hand covered hers and moved it to his lips, where he tickled her fingers with the tip of his tongue before placing a kiss gently on her palm. In her lap, the kitten stirred, but quickly settled.

Braden stroked her cheek and again his touch fired her beyond her wildest imaginings. Without a thought of shyness or remorse, she slipped her hand behind his neck and pulled him down to join their lips in a kiss of surging passion, heavy with desire.

This time, when he drew away, he rested her head against his chest and stoked her arm for a time. "Amanda Sheffield," he said, his voice husky with emotion, "this is a new beginning for me. You've touched my heart like no other woman in my entire life."

"I . . . I do find you extremely attractive, Braden. But you surely know that already—after the liberties I've permitted."

He leaned forward to lightly brush her temple with his lips. "And *you* must surely know how much I rejoice in the privilege." He gave her an enigmatic smile. "But now, my lady, I fear I must abandon our straw nest and return to my duties." He stood and raised her to her feet, then brushed wisps of hay from her hair.

She couldn't resist a shy giggle. "I feel rather wicked, Captain."

"Aye." He grinned back. "Completely wanton behavior. Imagine, tumbling in the hay while my ship tosses on storm-ravaged seas. But I pledge you this, if *The Tamara* founders, I'll pay full price by sinking with her to the bottom."

"Oh no," she said, suddenly alarmed. "Don't say that. If I—and Perci—should cause such a tragedy—"

He interrupted her with a swift kiss, then guided her toward the steps. "No, lass, as I said, we're in no danger.

Your uncle constructed a superb vessel. Now take your pet and go to your quarters. I'll make sure some sort of meal is sent to you from the galley."

Her head still spinning from his kisses, she pulled the cloak around her and started upward. Something profound had happened to her in the hold. But exactly what—and how it would affect her future—she wasn't yet sure. Cuddling the kit, she made her way to her cabin.

Later that night, after a dinner that tended to slide from one edge of the small table to the other, Amanda lay in bed thinking of the events of the afternoon. Finally she propped herself on one elbow to face Coco, who slept on a nearby cot.

"Coco, are you awake?"

"Yes, miss. My supper won't quite settle."

"I'm sorry. But Captain Hamilton said the storm should pass soon."

"Oh, I'll be all right."

"Coco . . ."

"Yes, mistress?"

"I don't believe I'll marry the Marquess of Staffordshire."

"What's this? But I thought that was the reason for this journey."

"Yes. I thought so too. But I believe I've changed my mind."

For a moment there was silence. "I do swear, mistress, I wish you had decided a bit sooner. Is there any likelihood of turning back?"

Amanda lay back on her pillow. "Oh no, not at all," she said firmly. "A visit to Bermuda is something I wouldn't miss for the world."

CHAPTER

9

For three days, Amanda had no further conversation with Braden and only saw him working at a distance. Though the storm abated, the seas remained rough and the winds unpredictable. The sky was overcast and spitting rain both day and night.

A week out from Boston, the sun at last reasserted itself and the temperature soared. The crew doffed their shirts and wrapped bandannas around their heads, giving them the distinct appearance of pirates. Spirits were high after the leaden grayness, and the ship was put under full sail to make the most of the light breezes.

Amanda decided to venture to the lower deck in search of Uncle Hugh. Each morning since their departure, he had visited her in her cabin, but then he disappeared below and was not seen again until the following day. She wondered what he did to amuse himself for so many hours. He had assured her he felt quite well and was extremely pleased with the ship's performance. She wondered if he could offer some diversion from the long, hot afternoon tedium.

Before she reached the campionway, she was hailed by an approaching Braden.

"Excuse me, my lady, but I must ask you where you're going."

"To find my uncle, if that's permitted," she said, not wanting to break any rules of the ship.

Standing before her, bare-chested, bronzed and damp with sweat, wearing a dark blue bandanna around his unruly hair, he exuded a primitive, almost threatening power. Nothing about him today resembled the cultured English gentleman she had known before.

He frowned. "Your uncle is . . . quite busy. I don't think he'd care to be disturbed."

"Disturbed?" Something in Braden's manner bothered her. Certainly he was captain of the ship, but her uncle was its builder. She hadn't expected to be denied reasonable freedom of movement. "My uncle always makes me welcome. Is he all right?"

"He's not ill. He's . . . just busy. He asked not to be disturbed."

"Oh, posh," she said saucily, "Uncle Hugh is always quite happy to see me. I'll find him, if you'll allow me."

"Nay," he said sharply. "Leave him be."

Startled at his tone, she shrugged her shoulders. "If that's an order, Captain."

He didn't smile. "Not exactly an order. But a firm request, Mistress Sheffield."

So the captain could be officious, she thought. Very well, she would have to oblige him. "Then I'll return to my cabin at once," she announced. She started to move past him when he gripped her arm. Facing him, she cocked an eyebrow. "I'm going to my cabin, sir, as you requested."

His look softened perceptibly. "Amanda, trust me. I've just left Hugh and he . . . doesn't want visitors."

She relaxed a bit. "Then another time, perhaps."

"Thank you. And the belated captain's dinner will take place tonight at eight, if you will promise to attend."

Looking up at his ruggedly handsome face, his wide shoulders and well-muscled chest so near, she decided she could forgive his touch of rudeness. Besides, she had a plan of her own. "Of course," she answered, granting him a sweet smile. "I look forward to the occasion."

He returned her smile. "Good. Then go to your cabin and tend to your sewing. Don't worry about Hugh. No doubt he'll join us at dinner." She held her tongue and walked back toward her quarters. Tend her sewing, indeed. Is that how all men thought a woman should spend every waking hour? Not only did she despise sewing, but she had lost all interest in preparing her trousseau. No, something was afoot with Uncle Hugh, and she would discover what.

She entered her cabin, where Coco was in the midst of an afternoon nap. Standing just inside the door, she waited until Braden disappeared from sight. Then crouching, she hurried out along the walkway and scrambled down the steps to the lower deck. Hugh's cabin was close by and she tapped lightly on the closed door. There was no response.

"Uncle Hugh?" she called. "Are you there?" The silence continued.

"Uncle Hugh," she called again. "Are you ill?" Still no reply.

She chewed her lip in indecision. Perhaps her uncle was elsewhere—or perhaps he was indeed ill and needed her help. Braden may have thought her too delicate to administer to a sick person, but she had done it before and would do it now for her uncle.

After a backward glance, she cracked open the door and peeked in. Her uncle lay on his cot in the tiny shuttered cabin; his loud snoring now reached her ears.

For a moment, she was relieved—and then she smelled it. Whiskey. So strong it took her breath away.

Slipping into the room, she closed the door behind her. Her hand over her face, she looked down at her uncle. His mouth was open and he slept heavily.

Drunk. This kindly old Puritan was as dead drunk as a barfly. She shook her head in dismay. The poor man must be carrying a heavy load of sorrow, and she had an idea who was responsible. She backed toward the door. Well, the gent was in his cups and Braden was right. Her uncle wouldn't want to be seen in such a state. She'd leave him in peace and he'd never know she had been in his room.

Feeling a trifle guilty, she hurried back up the steps and crept toward her cabin. A stealthy glance showed Braden busy helping his men lower the spritsail. She prayed he hadn't seen her. After all, his request had been most emphatic, and he was the *captain* of *The Tamara*.

Braden watched the lengthening twilight drift across the sky, pink light dancing atop the silvery peaks of the sea, shades of shimmering blue becoming an opaque lavender glow.

Behind him in his cabin, the table was laid with heavy silver and four place settings of fine china brought from the Orient. A candelabra holding eight slender tapers graced the linen-covered table, and gilded Spanish flatwear rested beside each plate. With great care, he had transported his personal belongings from the old carrack to *The Tamara*. Though he rarely put the silver and china to use, he liked to keep it handy for an occasional special dinner—and tonight could be very special indeed.

Amanda Sheffield was an enchantress, no question about it. A lady with the looks of an angel, the spirit of a tigress and the mischievous nature of a leprechaun. He had seen her slip back to Hugh's cabin against his most emphatic orders. He had only wanted to spare her the sight of her uncle sprawled in a drunken stupor on his bunk, at least until he could have the room tidied up a bit. He could tell she adored the man and depended on him for security and guidance. It was Braden's guess that Amanda had more courage and determination than the rest of the Sheffields combined. It was downright disturbing to meet such a woman, he thought, especially when the same lady had both heart-stopping beauty and the manner of a lively child.

He peered out at the light fading over the sea. Should he scold her for disobeying him? Or should he pretend he didn't know of her escapade? The temptation to embrace her, to seek again a forbidden kiss, to awaken desire within her as he knew well how to do, was nearly overpowering when in her presence. The tilt of her head, the latent passion in her eyes, the invitation of her full lips, drove him to consider seduction. If action followed thought, it could create a problem of enormous proportion. Now, while he was in command of his emotions, he should consider the consequences with a cool and pragmatic mind. Later, when looking across the table into those haunting amber eyes, he might not think clearly at all.

He had ordered table settings for four, knowing full well that both Hugh and Coco would not be attending. Coco was not yet able to face a laden table, and Hugh was unconscious below. But it would appear to Amanda that he had attempted to observe proper etiquette; he couldn't be blamed if the two of them found themselves totally alone in his cabin. Except, of course, she now knew of her uncle's condition.

A tap interrupted his thoughts. His first mate announced that Mistress Sheffield had arrived at the door.

"Admit her, please, Mister Stiles," he said, turning slowly.

Amanda entered the room and was struck at once by the elegant table occupying much of the cabin. The captain seemed a shadow near the open windows, silhouetted by the last deep purple of the waning light. Amanda noticed the four table settings and was amused by the captain's attempted subterfuge. Apparently he didn't know she had discovered Uncle Hugh's unpleasant state. Though Braden's plot was painfully obvious, she found it delightfully intriguing.

He stepped into the candle glow; at the sight of him, her confidence slipped. Dressed in midnight-blue satin of the latest French cut, his smooth-shaven face tanned, his curling hair sculptured neatly around his ears and neck, a massive gold ring set with a bloodred ruby adorning his finger, he radiated sophistication, wealth and self-assurance. The sweating pirate had disappeared, and in his place was a man of commanding presence with eyes as absorbing and all-knowing as if they could read her mind. Words momentarily failed her.

"Welcome, Amanda." His voice was low and cool. It was as if he were daring her to enter his private niche of potent power.

Attempting a casual air, she moved to place the table between them. Her heart was thudding furiously beneath the fitted, low-cut bodice of her mist-green satin gown.

"You set an exquisite table, Captain," she observed, relieved to hear the steady sound of her voice. "I suppose Uncle Hugh will soon join us, though I must report that Coco is not yet able to eat at the table."

"Is that so? Most unfortunate, as Hugh is also indisposed, or so I've just been told."

"Oh my." She lifted her eyebrows in feigned surprise. "One would think such an old sea dog would fare better."

"Aye, one would," he said, moving around the table.

"I . . . suppose I should excuse myself and return to my cabin."

He faced her, his look mildly amused. "If you wish," he agreed lightly. "On the other hand, my chef has prepared quite a feast, and we're at sea in disputed waters—so perhaps some rules could be relaxed for a time. Who would blame us for the absence of our . . . less sturdy traveling companions?" Without waiting for her response, he pulled out a chair and reached for the wine decanter.

Since her acquiescence was assumed, she quietly took a seat. Their little game ended, she would now enjoy her dinner.

He poured wine into their goblets before sitting in the chair opposite her. Almost at once a cabin boy entered bearing pewter serving platters. A word of instruction from Braden, and the boy uncovered capons baked in honey-brandy sauce, steaming corn bisque and puffed potato dumplings in a thick cream sauce. Glazed grapes sat in a separate silver compote, and a selection of cheeses completed the offering.

Amanda's unease grew as Braden ate without speaking except to offer more wine. She had expected witty conversation or even a discussion of seafaring matters. Their earlier intimacy during the hunt for Persephone seemed merely a dream, and she began to suspect he knew of her defiance of his orders. As she nibbled at her meal, her appetite vanished, and her sense of discomfort overtook her formerly bright mood. She drank a third goblet of wine, then sipped on a fourth. Still, he said nothing and she matched his stony silence with her own quiet demeanor.

Just as the awkwardness was becoming unbearable, he took notice that she no longer ate.

"You barely touched your food, my lady. I hope you're not ill."

"Not at all," she snapped. "The roughness of the sea only heightens my enjoyment of sailing. My stomach is indifferent to the wildest tossing, but tonight my appetite isn't great."

He stood, laid aside his napkin and walked around the table. As he pulled back her chair, he said wryly, "Nor do you have stomach for obeying my orders."

Her throat constricted, but she faced him squarely. "So you saw me. I suspected as much from your . . . your aloof manner over dinner. After all, you were hiding my uncle's condition and I only went to investigate. If that is a crime, how would you punish me, sir—have me flogged at the yardarm?"

"My God," he said, staring at her with heated eyes. "You're a sassy wench, Mistress Sheffield. Sassy and too spunky, by half. I saw you creeping along the deck, saw your head bobbing and those furtive glances. At that moment, I'd have turned you over my knee."

"Like a naughty child, I suppose. I was a child when

you met me in Virginia, Captain, but now I'm quite grown-up and inclined to do as I please."

His lip twitched in controlled amusement. "My orders are obeyed on my ship—always without question. In this instance, I was trying to protect you from heartache. At least for the moment. Instead you search it out like a determined hound pursuing a skunk."

Laughing, she moved away from the table. "Curiosity is a woman's privilege, Captain Hamilton. I must claim it as my only excuse for . . . misbehaving."

"No, 'tis more than that," he said, grasping her bare shoulder and turning her gently toward him. "'Tis your nature to walk the sword's edge of danger and defiance. Had I not given the order, you'd have forgotten your uncle unless further alarmed, I'll wager. I'm amazed . . . nay, astounded, when I consider that you obeyed your brother's order to marry Lord Pickering."

His hand seared into her skin. He wasn't pressing, but the feel of it spread along her shoulder and sent arrows of fire through her body.

"My brother is . . . my brother. And the decision to marry has not been made with certainty. Though I'm quite inclined to accept the offer."

"And if *I* order you not to do it, what then, Amanda?"

"You? *You* order *me*? You have no authority over me, Captain."

"Captain, aye, and lord, as well. You desire a title? Wealth? I have these and more."

"What . . . what are you suggesting?" Her head was spinning. The wine—his nearness—the warmth and vigor of his body.

His other hand went around her waist and he pulled her to him. His arms entrapped her, his lips found hers in a kiss that forced her head backward and her breasts against the hardness of his chest.

Her hands lifted to his shoulders, but the effort to resist was scant.

A new hunger tore into her loins, a need as desperate as taking her next breath. Her hands found the back of his neck and she clung to him, wanting more and more—of what she wasn't exactly sure and didn't care. *He* must know, and he would lead the way.

He swept her into his arms, not taking his tongue from her mouth, then laid her across the bed.

Reason fled and she felt wave after wave of pleasure as he loosened her bodice and lifted one breast to touch his tongue on its swollen tip. "Now the other one," he whispered. "So sweet, so lovely a pair."

His mouth traced a fiery path between the soft, fleshy mounds and upward to her throat. Nothing mattered, nothing in the world but that he continue the inflaming exploration of her body.

The buttons of her bodice, the ties of her chemise were opened and he pinned her hands above her head and found the sensitive flesh with his lips. Vaguely she was aware of the slight rocking of the ship, the splash and thunk of midnight waves beyond the open window, the salty scent and caress of the night breeze on her bare skin. She moaned and with an instinct as old as womankind arched her body against his.

Only then did he hesitate. She heard his breathing become ragged and felt his weight lift away from her.

"Oh, dear God," he muttered.

"Braden . . . Braden." She sighed. This wasn't all. It couldn't be all.

He grasped her hands and carefully pulled her up to stand before him. He crossed her arms over her breasts as if shutting a forbidden gate. "No, my little one," he said hoarsely. "Not now. Not you. Others perhaps, but not you."

Confused, her mind whirling without comprehension, she looked up at him. "Braden, I trust you. You've always, always been my lord and prince."

"I know," he answered, stroking her cheek. "But that is why we can't continue. I thought I could—God, I want you more than I've ever wanted any woman, but . . ."

"I don't understand."

"I know you don't. And that's why I can't take

you—make you mine. You would share your exquisite body, but amazingly I find I want more of you, my lady Amanda. You're a woman of intelligence and rare spirit. I must take care if I'm to reach for the greatest prize of all."

His words made no sense. Tears filled her eyes. He must want to be her friend—nothing more—and she had wantonly thrown herself into his arms, permitted every liberty. Embarrassment engulfed her and she turned away, then with trembling fingers, began securing her bodice. He had only dallied with her and finally found her either unattractive or even boring. Intelligent? Spirited? How could she feel complimented when she'd failed as a woman. Her cheeks were aflame with mortification.

He put his hands on her shoulders, but she stepped away.

"Amanda . . . Mandy, my darling girl. We need more time. Decisions must be made—so it will be right between us."

She crossed to the door, then spoke coolly without turning. "When do we make landfall?"

"Within the week, with favorable winds."

"That is plenty of time," she said. "Until then, stay busy, Captain. Tend your ship, and I'll give much more attention to . . . to sewing the beads on my wedding gown."

CHAPTER
10

"I don't understand it, mistress. You hate beadin'—or so you always say—and for five days you've sewed those pearls and baubles without scarcely lookin' up except to play with Perci now and then. Besides, you told me you didn't plan to marry the old lord, after all. Now you jus' sit and poke at that hem with somethin' akin to anger and scowl until your pretty face is certain to suffer damage. Why don't you tell me what's wrong, missy. Are you going to marry or not?"

Amanda rested her hands but didn't look up. "I . . . suppose I'll marry Lord Pickering, after all. I was just a bit confused for a time. It's true I dislike beading, but it's something to pass the time, though I do think the dress looked better before I started." She held up the liquid-white satin to inspect her work. "Honestly, Coco, a turkey could sew better than I. Just look at that row of crystals. No doubt they'll go clunking to the floor as I approach the altar. Oh, well," she said, sighing, "it might liven up the dreadful affair a bit."

Coco, who had been busy with her own needlework, shook her head. "If you feel that way, you'd best call it off is my advice. Even if he's old and bound to die soon, he'll still demand his pleasure with you plenty before he goes. I know you well, Miss Amanda. You're not one to . . . to lie quietly and take what your master demands."

"Coco . . ." Amanda's eyes came to life. "Coco, what is it like . . . really? Have you . . . well, I don't suppose you have, since you've no husband. I mean, my mother died so long ago . . . and . . ."

Coco chuckled deep in her throat. "Poor little lady," she said. "Poor little innocent. Never knowin' a man's intimate touch."

Amanda felt her cheeks turn to flame. "No . . . yes . . . well, once I allowed a certain privilege, but only a bit, you understand."

Coco leaned forward. "Only a bit? What's this? You'd better tell Coco if any man is makin' unseemly advances. After all, I'm here to chaperone, so Master Philip told me."

"It . . . it wasn't his fault, really. I . . . I just had a good deal of wine; he did too, I believe. He . . . touched me." She touched her blouse. "Here."

"Ohhh. Now tell me the truth. He touched you upon the fabric, or within?"

Amanda lowered her eyes to stare at her lap. "Within. I made no resistance, and . . ." She looked up. "I liked it, Coco. I liked it very much. Too much. It was brazen, I know, and the . . . gentleman . . . closed my blouse and sent me packing. That's the truth of it."

"He did? My glory above. How come? What did the *gentleman* say?"

"He said, 'I do it with others, but not you.' Those were his words. Obviously my body held no further interest for him."

"Well—glory above."

"So, that's the last of him," she snapped. "Maybe Lord Pickering will at least appreciate my offering myself to *him*. If only . . . if only I hadn't known the other . . . feeling."

"The feelin' you tell of is quite a natural thing, mistress. It's a good sign that you're fit and ready to be a woman. But it also tells me you have strong feelin's for another man. Beware, my girl. I have no husband, but I had love once. A man in the quarters who was the most beautiful man I ever did see. He took my innocence when I was twelve and I liked it plenty—even then."

"Oh, Coco. How exciting. Then tell me what it's like. I do so want it to be wonderful. I want to feel again the way I did with Bra—with my gentleman."

"Braden Hamilton, eh? I thought as much." She shook one brown finger near Amanda's nose. "If the captain touched you thus, and then backed away, it could be a very good sign. Or maybe not. But if it's him you want, you must be very careful. Don't let it be too easy. Play the game a bit. It's my guess he's got his mind on you this very minute. He's had a samplin' and that's never enough for a man like he."

"I'm not very good at playing the coquette, I'm afraid."

"Don't you worry none. I can promise you, Amanda my girl, you're as lovely to behold as any woman alive. Use your charms to get what you want. Every woman since creation has done jus' that."

Amanda was nibbling at the supper Coco had brought to their cabin when she heard the shout of "Land ho!" She dropped her spoon and hurried outside; it was the first time she'd ventured forth since the evening in Braden's quarters.

The ship was rolling in gentle swells of deep crystalline blue. On the eastern horizon an opaque moon lifted in shy splendor from a watery womb, while to the west, the sun had disappeared, leaving purple light shimmering behind a curving speck of green earth that was the isle of Bermuda.

"Land ho!" came the shout again from above the rigging. "East, southeast, she lies."

Amanda leaned against the rail of the main deck and stared toward the island. Yes, it was land, but small and alone in the vast reaches of the ocean-sea. It would grow larger, of course, as they approached, but there was no denying that Captain Hamilton's homeland was incredibly small—smaller than Massachusetts, smaller than Virginia, in fact, even smaller than Briarfield.

She was studying it thoughtfully when she felt a presence at her side. She stiffened but didn't turn.

"My lady," came Braden's low voice. "'Tis good to see you abroad on this momentous occasion. We've made landfall. As you requested I've kept my distance until now. I've brought us safely to our destination, and I've also made a decision. I would like to speak with you privately—if I may."

She grasped the rail. A light breeze ruffled her lace collar and cooled her fevered cheeks. Keeping her eyes on the green speck, she answered, "I will grant such an interview. Perhaps it can wait until we're ashore."

"If you prefer. Tomorrow we'll weigh anchor at Deep Bay," he explained. "The following day, we'll pick our way through the reefs around Spanish Point and make harbor at my wharf at Hamilton."

Relaxing a bit, she turned to face him. "I'm looking forward to setting my feet on land," she said. "And I must say, your island looks quite inviting, even from this distance."

"It does indeed," he said with a slow smile. "Now it's quite peaceful, but occasionally we have one hell of a storm. Maybe you saw *The Tempest* at the Globe Theatre in London. A Bermuda hurricane inspired Shakespeare's play."

"Why, yes, I did see it. How interesting," she observed, though her concentration was held by his half smile and the glitter of his eyes.

"Bermuda is like that—like a wind rose."

"Wind rose?"

"A term applied to a compass point in a mariner's map where winds converge from all directions. The pattern resembles a rose."

"A pretty name."

"Aye. Quite serene considering the powerful and uncontrollable forces it represents. As a matter of fact, I have a new racing sloop under construction I've christened the *Wind Rose*."

She smiled up at him. How could she stay angry with such a fascinating man? she chided herself.

He lifted her hand to his lips. "Have a good evening, Amanda. Tomorrow I'll welcome you properly to Bermuda and to Hamilton Plantation."

Watching him walk away—the easy confident gait, the masculine grace—she admitted her resistance to the captain was extremely low.

The following morning was occupied with preparations for leaving the ship. Amanda supervised Coco, but her mind was on only one thing—Lord Braden Hamilton. Occasionally she went outside to check *The Tamara*'s progress toward land. The tiny speck of yesterday soon became a series of green and verdant hills, loosely connected like jewels of an emerald necklace.

By noon, the ship had maneuvered near a deserted shore a hundred yards away. Never had Amanda seen a sight as serenely beautiful as the one that lay before her. The water was so clear she could see myriads of sparkling fish darting through its silky depths. Rolling in soft azure swells, the sea led to a curving shoreline where a stand of twisted cedars guarded the interior of the island. Perhaps those were the "devils" that ancient mariners had spotted when Bermuda was first named "Isle of the Devils." In the distance, cliffs jutted up from the beach.

She was gazing shoreward when Braden arrived at her side.

"Inviting, isn't it," he said when she turned to him.

"I'm dying to see it . . . the island, your home . . . everything."

"Would you like a tour of those cliffs? I've ordered a boat."

"You mean . . . now? Only you and I?"

"Your uncle is . . . indisposed. Your maid wouldn't betray your brief absence, would she?"

"No . . . I'm sure Coco wouldn't tell anyone."

"Good. Be ready in a quarter of an hour. We'll explore the cliffs and have a small picnic. But we'll be back well before dark."

Though she knew she was misbehaving, she was eager for the adventure. She'd been cooped up for so long on the ship, and in truth, she had longed for Braden's company. She put on her simplest muslin skirt and blouse, comfortable slippers, delicate white stockings and a plain straw hat borrowed from Coco. She laughed at her reflection in the mirror, but decided comfort in the hot and humid atmosphere should take priority over elegance.

Standing in the longboat, Braden reached up for her. His strong hands encircled her waist as he eased her into the boat, then guided her to a plank seat. A breeze lifted the brim of her hat as she smiled at him before turning to face the bow of the craft.

He took up the stern paddles. "You appear to have made good your escape," he quipped when they were a distance from the ship.

Clutching her hat, Amanda glanced back at him. "Are you able to row this craft alone? I could help, if you'd show me how."

He grinned at her suggestion. "You *are* a delightful lass. Nay, just sit and enjoy the ride. It's a bit slower with just one buc plying the oars, but we'll arrive eventually."

For a time, they bobbed and rocked in silence, drifting along the shore and then inching around a steep bluff created from sea-sculptured limestone. The expanse of sand and the magnificent forest of cedar appeared untouched by humankind, and the only sounds in the late, steamy afternoon were the cry of gulls and petrels and the sloshing of the blades as Braden dipped them into the shimmering brine.

"Over there," he called at last. "We'll beach her there and walk around to the back side of the cliffs. You'll find a bundle under the seat—brandy and a few scones and two apples. That should nourish us till we return to the ship." With a gallant air, Braden hopped into the surf and pulled the boat securely onto the sand.

Amanda noticed he was barefoot, having stowed his boots under the stern seat. She looked with concern at her own slippers.

"Take them off," he recommended. "The water is warm and I see no sea varmints here."

"Well . . ." She hesitated.

He cocked one eyebrow. "Or else I'll have to carry you like a sack of corn."

Thinking she would enjoy that immensely, she nevertheless pulled off her slippers and swung her legs over the side.

"Wait. Your stockings," he said quickly. "They'll be ruined."

"Don't worry. They'll dry in the sun."

The water did feel wonderful as she sank to her ankles in the sand. The wet sand was soft and tickled her toes, sending a fleeting memory of days long past at her favorite fishing spot on the James River. She held Braden's hand as they waded ashore like two children out for an hour of play.

"Over there," he said. "We'll sit in the shade of that overhanging rock and have our snack before we climb the steps."

"Steps? What steps?"

"Ah, that's my surprise."

"Very well," she said, grinning. "But I may become very impatient."

They sat on the sand, their backs against a cool, moist boulder. Braden uncorked the flask of brandy. Amanda was so thirsty she took a large mouthful before she could stop herself. She coughed, but swallowed the heady liquid.

After he offered her a scone, he took his turn drinking from the flask.

She found the biscuit tasty but dry and soon she needed another drink. Water would have been welcome, she thought, but it would be quite rude to complain. She drank again, more slowly; the brandy warmed and relaxed her.

"Tell me, Braden," she said, feeling quite at home in his company, "tell me why you left England."

"I fear I was more or less expelled," he replied wryly. "The Hamiltons of Scotland lost their land when Cromwell took power. Later when Charles restored the monarchy, my father, Lord Richard Hamilton, was created Earl of Wentworth. My older brother inherited the title fifteen years ago when our father died; soon after, my mother went into seclusion."

"You must have been a lonely boy."

"Not terribly, though I did grow up alone at the family estates. I found books to be great companions and soon went off to school. My heroes became the likes of John Smith and Walter Ralegh, not to mention that scalawag Francis Drake."

"All adventurers with questionable reputations," she noted lightly.

"After a voyage to the Indies, I decided it was time to fight the Spaniards and the Moors—either or both—in the pay of the king. I joined the Royals and sailed to Tangiers. When I returned to England, I found my brother less than willing to share the duties at Wentworth. Don't blame him, really. I . . . uh, had an escapade or two and . . . a few companions who didn't suit his standards. I went to work for my family's investment company, then seven years ago came to Bermuda to develop Hamilton Plantation, founded by my great-uncle. So there you have it, my lady, the tale of a rascally and wandering soul."

She took another sip of brandy. "Rascally to be sure." She stretched her stockinged toes into a patch of sun. The fact that her ankles and lower calves were quite exposed bothered her not at all.

"'Tis a shame we didn't meet in England during your visit there," he observed, his mood becoming more intimate. "Things might have been . . . less complicated."

Looking into his eyes, noticing the way his dusky skin accented their blueness, she wondered why his nearness invariably caused her mind to work like a sluggish millstone. "Complicated? What do you mean?"

"This marriage thing—this betrothal to Lord Pickering. All that could have been avoided if only I'd known . . ."

"Known what?"

"How easy it would be to love you. How I've been searching for you without even knowing it. How you would capture my heart in spite of my best defenses."

She gazed at him, almost without comprehension. "You . . . love me? You? Braden Hamilton? Is this possible?"

He set aside the flask and took her hand. "I'm getting ahead of myself. I wanted to talk—there." He pointed to a spot in the cliff above. "Come," he said gently. "Follow me."

Her head still reeling from his declaration, and perhaps a bit from the brandy, she let him lead her to the cliff, where rough steps had been scraped in the limestone.

"Take my hand. It's steep here, but easier later. I discovered this place my first year in Bermuda. I want it to be the first place you learn to love."

As she climbed, gripping the uneven rocks and stepping carefully, knowing he was just below her, she wondered at his words. They echoed in her ears above the sound of the rising surf and the call of wild birds circling above. Learn to love. He loved her. He truly loved her. God knows, she had adored him as long as she could remember.

They arrived at a ledge in front of a small opening in the cliff. He scrambled up beside her and guided her into the aperture.

She had expected darkness, but was suddenly dazzled by a pink crystalline light that left her gasping in surprise and awe.

The spacious cave was carved out of stark limestone. The floor was a grainy powder of pink and blue and pearl-white sand. The walls were opaque white, reflecting rays of rainbow color throughout the lofty, damp interior. From above, spikes of solidified liquid jutted down from the ceiling like streams of diamond droplets, frozen as they slid toward earth.

Overwhelmed by the shimmering, dreamlike beauty, she revolved slowly, looking all around and upward, seeing the blue-green reflection of the sea drifting through the angular openings in the sides of the cave.

"Braden," she whispered at last. "It's not of this world. It's the middle of a star . . . it's a magician's enchanted lair."

He reached for her and held her against him. Cupping her chin with his hand, he murmured, "I do love you, little Mandy. I brought you here to ask you to marry me. Cancel your betrothal to Pickering. I can't give you everything he can offer, but I can give you this." He kissed her softly, then with a moan crushed her against him and sought her mouth with his tongue.

She responded joyfully, clinging to him, delighting in his strength and fire, standing on tiptoe to return his embrace.

Lifting her in his arms, he sank slowly to the sand and rested her across his lap. "You will be my wife," he whispered. "In less than a fortnight, I do swear. Amanda —Mandy, my darling girl, this will always be our world of magic. Let me take you . . . here . . . now. We'll seal our love as man and wife."

Looking up at him, she knew she wanted nothing more in this life than to belong to him. "Yes, my love," she whispered. She ran her hand along the back of his neck, fingering the thick, dark hair, then moving down to his shoulder. "I will be your wife," she murmured. "I've loved you—dreamed of you for so long. You're everything I've ever wanted."

He was so close, his eyes as blue as the depths of the sea, absorbing her, challenging her to prove the truth of her words. He traced the curve of her cheek, then outlined her ear and finally lifted stray tendrils from her forehead. Bending near, he placed a kiss where the curls had lain.

He began to untie the ribbons of her blouse.

"Let me." She slipped her blouse over her head and opened her chemise. For a moment, her hand rested lightly over her breasts. Her cheeks felt feverish as she struggled with sudden modesty.

"You're perfect, my darling—exquisite. I will always adore your body and honor it as was intended by God. Have no fear, sweet Mandy." His voice soothed and reassured her. She moved her hand away.

Leaning down, he feather-kissed each pink tip in turn, then nuzzled between the soft mounds before moving his lips up to the hollow of her throat.

Her eyes closed; she rested against his arm and gave up all inhibitions to an increasing sense of tingling pleasure.

Gently he eased her onto the sand and pulled off his shirt. When she raised her arms to embrace him, he moved across her.

His heated chest pressed against her breasts. Flesh meeting flesh, slowly he rotated, sending spasms of sensuous waves racing through her body and a sudden tugging deep within her being.

She felt him release the buttons of her skirt. He lifted her hips just enough to slide away the filmy skirt and petticoat, then he crooked his leg across her lower body and rested his head on his elbow to gaze down at her.

"Open your eyes, my love."

Keeping them closed, she answered, "I'm . . . almost naked."

"Yes. Look at me." He took her hand and held it over his heart.

When she obeyed him, she saw the half smile she so adored. His eyes were friendly and his manner relaxed. "I'm so nervous. I . . ."

He nodded. "I know. There isn't any hurry. If you wish we'll just rest here awhile, then go."

Moving her hand across his shoulder and forearm, she

felt the sinewy muscles beneath the taut skin. She traced a white jagged scar with one finger. "What happened?" she asked, peering through lowered eyelids, her thoughts half on her question and half on the pleasurable sensations caused by his stroking of her breasts.

"Long ago. An Indian's misplaced musket ball."

"Briarfield?"

"Aye."

"Oh, I saw it then. You were very brave."

"You too, little Mandy." He scooped up a handful of crystal sand and dribbled it along her waist.

"Oh, that tickles," she said lightly.

Quickly he kissed her where the sand had fallen.

Catching her breath, she gripped his arms. "Braden, I love you," she whispered, moving under his caress. "Show me how to please you."

"Good lord, Amanda," he murmured, "you already please me beyond imagining." He bent to kiss her, teasing open her lips with his tongue, then forcefully possessing her mouth.

While holding the kiss, he shifted his leg and splayed his fingers across her bare stomach; his palm kneaded her sensitive skin from hipbone to hipbone. Ranging downward, he guided her thighs apart and cupped her softness.

An explosion of feeling engulfed her as she instinctively responded to his exploration by pressing against his palm. His continued fondling turned her senses into liquid fire, sending her writhing into the curl of his arm.

He moved across her and placed his knees against her inner thighs. She felt his leg muscles contract. A stronger force replaced his hand.

"Now, my love. Hold me. Accept me," he whispered huskily.

His power was there, teasing, hesitating, pressing forward, then thrusting. The sudden sting startled her. She gasped and her eyes flew open.

"That's all—the only time I'll ever cause you pain."

Already she had forgotten it, aware now of the pulsing heat filling her, the shimmering surge of awakened passion sweeping her into the tide that awaited.

He rocked against her, his hands supporting her hips as he moved within her in a sensual, pulsating rhythm as old as time.

Now she felt what it was like to be one, body and soul, with a man she desired beyond reason or thought.

Again and again. He filled her moist recesses with swelling power, deeper and demanding, making her whimper in unabashed, unexpected delight.

"My darling, my love," she heard him say hoarsely.

She desired him beyond enduring. Reality fled before the onslaught of her desperate longing.

He pulled back but did not quite leave her.

"No," she whispered, finding the sudden emptiness unbearable.

As she arched her hips, he clasped his hands behind her head and thrust once again, filling her need with his hungry maleness.

Bonding. On the edge of awareness, she knew she gave him great pleasure and her own was intensified.

"Now, my lovely girl," came his voice like an anguished sigh.

She hovered for one exquisite, agonizing moment, then cried out at the shattering instant of release. Damp with perspiration, she clung to him while his love flooded them both, drowning the heat and the fire.

Her breath returned in ragged gasps; she drifted like a gull's lost feather, wafting downward on an errant breeze to fall at last onto the serene surface of the sea. Braden's waiting arms gathered her close; he rocked her as gently as he would a child waking from a heavy sleep. He stroked her, rubbed her tense thighs, her calves, even her feet encased in tattered stockings. He pulled her dress across her like a gossamer sheet to protect her from the cooling sea breeze.

After a time, he murmured, "You're a wonder, my

little Amanda. My God, how could such a rogue as I be so blessed. Are you all right?"

She rested against his length and let her body melt into softness. She was so sleepy. She heard the ocean pounding, but was content in the safety of his arms. He belonged to her—and she to him. She would think later of a wedding, a home, children, the future. For now, she was happy to be in his arms, to know for certain he would love her forever.

She dozed awhile, but then awoke at his kiss.

"Forgive me, little one. We must go. The sun is low and we're expected back at the ship. The outgoing tide will help speed our return, but still, it will take time. Your Coco will have me keelhauled if we arrive after dark."

She put on her clothes. The light was fading from the cave and the wind was brisk and chill. She noticed her ruined stockings and said ruefully, "Yes, keelhauling is in order, I fear. My stockings are quite beyond repair."

He placed his finger on the tip of her nose. "Ah, but I warned you, so you must lighten the sentence. Flogging, perhaps. Or a night without you beside me."

She gave him a hug and looked up with her chin against his chest. With an impish smile, she said, "More than *one* night, my darling buccaneer. We have a wedding to plan, and a certain lord to disappoint before we can spend our nights together."

"How well I know," he responded with mock agitation. "Like all bridegrooms, I must wait patiently and appear stupidly benign." Suddenly he threw an arm around her waist and leaned to kiss her firmly and soundly. Without further conversation, he assisted her down the cliff and into the waiting longboat.

She rode facing him on the return trip, oblivious to her surroundings, but floating in a euphoria of happiness and deep satisfaction. She watched him as he leaned against the oars, shirtless still, the muscles in his arms and chest tanned and straining, gleaming with sweat and spray from the sea.

She was startled when he stopped rowing suddenly and for several seconds gazed intently over the side of the boat.

"What is it?" she asked after her curiosity overcame her patience.

"I saw a glint—the slanted sunlight reflecting on some object in the sand below."

She looked over the side. "Yes, I see it too. I think you can reach it. It's right there."

He chuckled and began removing his boots. "The clear water is deceiving. It's not as shallow as it looks. But there's one way to find out what it is. I'll go down and have a look."

"Down? You're going after it?"

"Aye. This reef is well-known for its wreck of a Spanish caravel ten years ago. I've found dozens of doubloons washed ashore, but there's been no sign of the ship except a half-buried cannon a bit farther out."

"How exciting!" she said, truly fascinated. "Dive then, and I'll steady the boat."

With a nod and a grin, he arched over the side and sliced downward, leaving a trail of bubbles in his wake.

She could see him dive like a sleek brown fish, cutting downward toward the shining object till a rush of sand obscured him. Within seconds he was returning, and the sight of his ascent was as crystal clear as if he drifted with extended arms through pristine air.

Splashing and sputtering, he emerged at her side and tossed back his hair from his forehead.

Gaily she laughed and shielded herself from the spray. "What did you find, or was it only a sea nymph's ploy?"

He hauled himself dripping over the gunwale and sat on the bottom of the boat. His grin told her his quest had not been in vain.

"For you, my love, to mark our new beginning." He laid in her hands a silver cross, two inches in length and crudely made, but inlaid with strands of pure gold.

She held it against her heart. "It's so lovely. Do you think the Spaniards who lost it will willingly give it up?"

He laughed again and the sight of his merry brown face, his wet hair curled around his ears while rivulets of water streaked his temples and cheeks, made her throat grow tight with desire.

"Rarely have the Spaniards given *anything* willingly to the English. But I claim this prize for my beloved. 'Tis a Christian symbol which spans nations and dogmas. It is my betrothal gift for thee—plucked from the sea—and from ages past."

Leaning forward, she placed one hand on his cheek. "I do believe you've a bit of the poet in your soul, my lord. I accept your gift and give you my heart." Her lips met his and the taste of salt and love mingled to add to her ultimate moment of joy.

CHAPTER
11

For the next few hours, Amanda drifted in a euphoria of purest joy and newborn love. When she returned to the ship, she said nothing to Coco except that she'd had an exceptionally pleasant outing and the island was lovely and fascinating. She showed Coco the cross and secured her aid in selecting the perfect silver chain from which to suspend it.

Later in the long twilight, they snacked on baked fresh fish, biscuits and the last of the dried apples brought from Boston. Amanda relayed Braden's description of the abundant fruit they would enjoy on his island: bananas, oranges, grapes, peaches and even the mysterious avocado.

The two were enjoying their meal when a pounding came on the door, followed immediately by the entry of Hugh Sheffield.

"Why, Uncle, how—" Amanda began.

"My dear niece, I've just learned of your excursion this afternoon. It is my duty as your guardian on this journey to give you a severe reprimand."

She pushed back her chair and faced him. "Now,

Uncle Hugh, you've been ill. Please don't upset yourself."

"Aye, ill I've been. And I fear you've taken advantage of my incapacity," he blustered.

With hands on hips, she replied firmly, "If you're speaking of my outing today, I was with Captain Hamilton—who is also considered to be my guardian while I'm on his ship and in Bermuda."

Hugh swayed a bit. "The point is, lass, you went without my permission. Nor did the captain ask for it. I intend to speak to him as soon as I'm a bit stronger."

She reached for his arm. "You'll be feeling fine now that we're in calm water. Go to bed now and stop worrying."

Hugh appeared willing to take her advice. He had turned to leave when he looked back and scowled. "It's improper for an unmarried woman to traipse abroad with a bachelor. Improper and . . . dangerous. Some men would take advantage of such an opportunity. Not that I don't admire Hamilton, but there are plenty of stories about his . . . his escapades. I'm sure your morals are sound, Amanda, but I'll have no more of such behavior. Is that understood?"

For a moment, she couldn't respond. Her pink cloud turned into gray reality. Dear heaven, if her uncle knew the truth, he would kill Braden. She squared her shoulders. "We climbed the cliffs and had a picnic. Don't worry, Uncle, the captain is a fine man."

"No doubt, no doubt," Hugh grumbled as he hurried out.

She returned to her chair, but avoided Coco's eyes. She tried to reassure herself, but the seeds of guilt and doubt were planted. She had indeed succumbed quickly and completely to Braden's undeniable charms.

Coco retired early, but Amanda was far too agitated to think about sleep. She stayed on deck as the ship skirted the island near Spanish Point, where a beacon had been lighted to welcome them home. Braden was busy guiding the frigate around the dangerous reefs and through hidden shallows as he maneuvered expertly toward his harbor at Hamilton Plantation. She forced herself to forget Hugh's tongue-lashing and feel only pride in the man who would soon become her husband.

It was nearly midnight when Braden called the order to drop anchor. A crescent moon hung low over the dark land. Not wanting to be in the way, Amanda found a secluded spot from which she could watch the seamen furl the sails and prepare the ship for docking.

Leaning on the rail, she strained her eyes toward the wooden platform extending from the vessel's side to a rise of land not too distant. At the crest of the hill, she could just make out the silhouette of a one-story structure set among tall trees. Was that to be her new home after the wedding? If it was Braden's home, it would certainly be hers. She would love every inch of it and do her best to make him happy there. Oh, she had so much to learn about her new love. She wanted to know everything: what he liked to eat, what pleased him most, and even—or perhaps especially—what made him angry. She wanted to fill every moment of his life with joy and love and peace.

Ropes were thrown to the dock and husky men jumped down to secure the ship to its moorings. They laughed and called loudly to each other in their excitement at the successful completion of the voyage. She must get to bed, she thought. She should try to sleep a little so she would be refreshed for the events of tomorrow.

At that moment, she heard the surprising sound of a woman's voice. Looking down at the dock, she saw a slight figure running alongside the ship waving at some unseen person on board.

"Brae, Brae!" came the cry. "Come down!"

To her astonishment, Braden obeyed at once, jumping from the deck to the dock without waiting for the gangplank to be lowered into place. He embraced the girl tightly and stroked her waist-length raven hair.

Amanda couldn't hear their conversation, but the girl

was laughing gaily and clinging to Braden as if she'd never let him go. The name *Tamara* came from Braden's lips seconds before the girl pulled his head down to give him a kiss of obvious passion.

Braden moved away after the kiss, and Amanda thought he briefly glanced her way. She shrunk against the exterior wall of her cabin and prayed the slice of moon would not reveal her presence. Her emotions zigzagged in quick succession from confusion to dismay to stabbing heartache. *Tamara.* Of course, a woman's name—the exotic foreign name of an equally exotic and sensuous girl. Braden's ship carried the lady's name in golden letters on its prow. She had seen it from the beginning. And now she had seen the living Tamara, inspiration for Braden's beautiful ship.

Why hadn't he mentioned the girl? Why had he chosen to dock so late at night, then hurry immediately to enfold his love in a fierce embrace? Just hours ago he had held Amanda in his arms and promised *her* his love. Or had he? He had said the words; she was sure of it. And he'd taken her love—her body—so completely and asked her to marry him. She hadn't dreamed it. She touched the cross suspended from her neck. No, she had given herself totally, without hesitation, without considering that she could be making a fool of herself over a man she barely knew. She had always worshipped him, placed him above all others, thought of him as a prince in a picture book. But he was a man, after all. Flesh and blood with a man's hungers and schemes. And he had a past—one in which she'd played no part. Now that she considered it, he was really a stranger to her. His proposal could have been a trick to seduce her, to satisfy needs held in check since he'd left the woman he truly loved in Bermuda.

Shaking with an inner chill, she leaned against the cabin wall. What could she do? In a few hours, it would be dawn and she would have to face Braden, go to his plantation, and no doubt, meet Tamara as well.

Another glance showed Braden and Tamara walking

arm-in-arm along the dock. The girl's simple garment didn't even conceal her calves and bare feet. Her excited laughter drifted on the night breeze. In moments they disappeared into the woods near the shoreline.

Amanda scurried into her cabin and closed the door silently against the moonlight and the scene it had revealed. Her uncle must have been right. He had hinted at Braden's questionable morals. And now . . .

Tossing aside her clothes, she lay on her bed. Braden had told her to stay on board the ship till morning, when he would escort her ashore. It was plain why he had not wanted her to disembark tonight. She had no thought of sleep. She would lie awake during all the dark hours wondering where Braden was sleeping, and if he held the sultry girl for whom he'd named his ship locked in his arms.

After one more kiss of welcome, Braden disengaged himself from the clinging Tamara and went back to secure the ship. He was disappointed that apparently Rodriquez had made little headway stealing the girl's affection. As soon as he was finished at the ship, he walked to the manor house and entered his study. He was exhausted, but determined to settle things with Tamara before another hour passed. The girl had surprised him by rushing into his arms despite the lateness of his docking. He couldn't risk another such display tomorrow. No, he'd have to delay getting rest this night until he spoke to her.

In the light of a single lantern he paced the room, paying no attention to the disarray: the cluttered desk, the boxes stacked in corners, the maps and charts rolled haphazardly on the shelves behind a globe on a baroque Italian base. This was going to be difficult, but it was better to get it over with before he brought his fiancée to the house.

Tamara entered in a rush and once again flung her arms around his neck. She forced a kiss while pressing her lithe body against him.

As gently as possible, he eased her away.

"Brae-Braden," she said breathlessly. "You're back, safe at last. We expected you last week. I was worried."

"No need for worry. We had fair seas and an easy crossing. Tomorrow you'll see the ship named for you, my dear. But now I must speak seriously with you, Tamara. Something important has taken place."

"Oh, I can't wait to see my ship. Why don't we explore it now. It must be beautiful in the moonlight and most of the crew will have gone ashore. We . . . we could spend the night aboard in your cabin."

"Tamara, we must talk. Tomorrow we'll see the ship. First, how have you done with your lessons with Manuel?"

"Oh." She tossed her head. "That. I spent every afternoon with Manuel—either riding or learning about his Catholic faith."

"Good. He's a good man, don't you agree? And handsome as well."

"Hmm. I suppose so."

"And he is very fond of you—perhaps even in love with you, so I've gathered."

"He does seem to be. But why talk of this now? You know it's *you* I love. You needn't be jealous of Manuel."

Braden took a deep breath. So Manuel had done what he could, but failed to win the girl. Well, he'd just have to do what must be done, say what must be said. "Tamara, I've brought a woman from Boston. She's on the ship."

"Oh, I know. The lady who will marry the marquess. I've planned a celebration, a fiesta for tomorrow night to welcome her. And the wedding feast will be prepared as soon as the date is set."

Bloody hell, thought Braden. This was more difficult than he expected. "Tamara dear, I've always been honest with you. I told you long ago I loved you like a daughter, not as a woman whom I would take to wife."

She shrugged her shoulders. "Yes, you said that, my lord. But I'm sure you care deeply for me. I want to belong to you always."

"I know what you want, or think you want. But you must now consider my wishes. I've brought a lady to Bermuda whom I intend to marry."

Her expression froze. "To . . . marry?"

"Aye. Mistress Sheffield has decided not to marry the marquess, but to become my wife instead."

She stared in disbelief, then her deep brown eyes flashed hotly. "You would marry a fragile lady from the mainland? It's a thing you swore never to do."

"I know what I swore. But I've changed my mind. And the lady is not at all fragile, though at first she appears so."

"I don't believe you. You'll change your mind, I know. She . . . she can't love you as I do. I will show you, and I will show her!" She flung from the room and slammed the door.

"Holy Christ," Braden muttered. He should have known Tamara's Turkish blood would boil at the news. Well, tomorrow he would deal with the problem. Perhaps when he brought the beautiful Amanda into the house, Tamara would accept the inevitable. He didn't want to hurt Tamara, but he would have to be firm. And it might become necessary to find her different quarters. If only she'd fallen for Manuel, he yawned. He'd talk to the man tomorrow. Maybe there was still some way to ease the girl into the Spaniard's keeping.

After a restless night, Amanda had dozed off at daybreak but was soon awakened by voices just outside her cabin. At first she thought she was dreaming, but then she recognized Tamara's tinkling laughter. Instantly alert, she sat up and strained her ears. The girl was talking to one of the seamen and obviously she didn't care who heard her conversation.

"I'm so happy the ship is named for me," Tamara said gaily. *The Tamara*—oh, it's lovely. And it proves how much the captain loves me, don't you think so, Mister Stiles?"

A man mumbled something unintelligible.

Tamara continued loudly, "Oh, he missed me so much. Last night (high-pitched giggle) we could hardly tear ourselves apart—I'm sure you understand (another giggle). Braden is *sooo* wonderful. Just think of it, he named his best and most beautiful vessel after me. No other woman would have such an honor." She was practically squealing. "I must go now to see about the celebration. I'm his hostess as usual. He always depends completely on me to see things are done properly." Her laughter faded as she hurried away.

Amanda flopped backward and pulled the sheet over her head. So it was true. There were no more doubts. She had given her heart—and her body—to an adventurous lecher. She wanted to cry and scream, but instead she hardened her emotions like tempered steel and prepared to face the day. If Braden Hamilton thought she was nothing but a simpleminded Virginia tulip, he was in for quite a surprise.

Braden slept later than usual, waking at midmorning in the high feather bed of the master's suite. A soft breeze billowed the sheer white curtains of the open doors leading to the enclosed patio.

After washing with tepid water from the lavabo, he dressed in a white ruffled shirt, snug white satin pants and black boots. He felt refreshed and ready for the challenges of the day. After all, he was master of Hamilton Plantation. He had helped build the gracious limestone house in the grove of tall cedars with his own hands. He had plowed the fields in the early days, putting his own back to the yoke. He'd struggled with a mediocre tobacco crop and searched for the elusive ambergris rumored to be near the island. In the end, he'd pirated Spanish ships in the name of the English king, and poured his wealth into his property in Bermuda. The Hamiltons had roots on this island—and now he had developed the sleek Bermuda sloop built from the native trees. No, he wouldn't let two females disrupt the peace and prosperity of his existence. He would marry Amanda Sheffield within a fortnight. Tamara could accept the new mistress of Hamilton Plantation, or she could move elsewhere and begin a new life. He would see that she was always cared for, but she must acquiesce to his wishes and stop acting like a spoiled, jealous child.

After a quick cup of coffee and a sugar-sweetened scone, he walked to the dock. Surely Amanda would be packed and ready by now to disembark.

Halfway up the gangplank, he stopped and stared in amazement. Waiting for him on the deck, with Coco at her side, stood Amanda. But she was almost unrecognizable in a garb of black, her hair severely bound, and a Puritan-style cap securing a black veil that suggested deep mourning. Around her neck hung the silver cross he'd given her. What on earth had possessed her to dress like this on such a warm and festive morning, a morning when he planned to show her off to his staff, his friends—and Tamara?

Nevertheless he smiled pleasantly as he arrived at her side. "Good morning, mistress. Did you sleep well?"

He could barely see her profile as she swished past him and marched down the gangplank to the dock. Coco's raised eyebrows indicated she was as bewildered as he.

He reached Amanda and tried again. "My dear lady, welcome to Hamilton Plantation. I've arranged for your apartments. I've—"

"I do hope you haven't gone to a great deal of trouble, Captain. I won't occupy them for long. I expect the marquess to arrive soon and we'll be married at once." Her voice sliced like a Toledo sword.

Stunned, he put his hand on her shoulder, but she stiffened under his touch.

"My God, Amanda, what's wrong? Yesterday you agreed to marry *me*. I thought it was settled."

She didn't look at him. "I fear I don't know you, Lord Hamilton. Nor can I trust you. If you'll show me to my rooms, I'll retire with my maid to assist me until the marquess arrives."

"Hell, woman, that could be days or weeks. I don't know what's caused this . . . this sudden change of heart, but I assure you I intend to find out. If you want to dress like a popish martyr on the way to her doom, that's your business—though you may truly expire from heat and discomfort—but I intend to present you to my household as my fiancée. Tonight there is a gala in your honor and you *will* attend. I understand your uncle is already settled in and doing his own private celebrating."

"Uncle Hugh?" She lifted her eyes to his for the first time.

"Oh, hell, leave him be. He likes his whiskey and you'll not reform him. But you're my guest and we're officially betrothed. I've already announced it. For the moment, I expect you to act the part properly." His tone softened. "Amanda, if somehow I've offended you, I'm sorry. But after yesterday, I think you owe me an honest explanation of your peculiar behavior."

"Honesty is not *your* strongest quality, Captain. You failed to mention your . . . other woman. I'll meet your staff, of course, and if necessary put in a brief appearance at your reception this evening. But don't expect me to take second place to your Tamara—the Tamara for whom you named your magnificent new vessel. I'll not come between a man and the mistress of his heart."

His brow furrowed as he absorbed this speech. Then he pursed his lips and took her elbow to escort her along the bower of palmetto trees lining the path to the house. So that was it. She must have seen Tamara's enthusiastic greeting last night. What a stroke of bad luck. He couldn't blame her for being furious, and yet, it could be she was also jealous. And jealousy was as powerful an emotion as love. This was something he could handle, he was sure. At least she had worn the cross he'd given her. She had not rejected him entirely. He would give her a day or two to calm her ruffled feathers. She was sure to abandon the heavy clothing as the temperature soared, and he would have baskets of tropical flowers and bowls of fresh fruit delivered to her quarters right away. He was sure he could melt her coldness in the balmy beauty and abundant pleasures of his island homeland.

CHAPTER
12

Amanda stripped off her heavy black garments and threw herself across the brightly colored quilt of her bed. Its cool softness soothed her heated flesh.

Coco gathered up the dress and hat, hose and slippers, all the while clucking her disapproval.

"I know, I know," Amanda said, her face half buried in the spread. "I made a complete fool of myself. But, Coco, I had good reason."

"I do think you treated Captain Hamilton mighty bad, mistress, and I don't mind sayin' so. Jus' look at this beautiful room he provided and look at the flowers. Why, I never seen such blossoms, such colors in all my days."

"I'm tired, Coco. And sweating like a pig on the spit. I really think I'd like to take a nap."

"It's all these bunches of clothes, missy. You looked ready for Sunday meeting in a Boston snowstorm. Why, those nice folk who lined up to greet you at the door must think you're a bit touched."

"No doubt they do. Now go along and let me sleep. I'm so awfully tired."

"I can see that, all right. Your eyes looked like two

burnt coals when you got up this morning. Could it be you'd been weeping all night? Why don't you tell me what's wrong, Miss Amanda."

"Maybe later. Right now I need to rest—and think."

"Yes'm. I'll take these to your dressin' room and hang them up. They're still damp."

"Thank you, Coco," she said drowsily.

The door closed and Amanda rolled to her back. It felt so good to lie there in her shift, letting the breeze from the wide windows wash over her. She knew her childish impulse to dress in the black had been a mistake. But she had been as miserable as if she were going to her own funeral. The Spanish cross had seemed just the right touch; it would remind Braden of his pledge of yesterday, so soon forgotten.

Even now, more tears threatened to fill her eyes. She had given herself so willingly, so completely. She had not questioned his love, nor considered the consequences of her actions. One thing was certain, she was no longer a virgin. If she and Braden married, as he still seemed willing to do, she would wonder if his code as a gentleman was his reason for making her his wife. But if she married Lord Pickering and disappointed him on their wedding night, her life could become a living nightmare. Why, it wasn't long ago that great lords had their brides tested for virginity before the ceremony could take place.

With her eyes closed, she was haunted by the sight of Braden holding the mysterious Tamara in his arms. Why hadn't the girl come with the other members of the household to meet her? Braden had said Tamara had been with him for several years as the head of his house staff. Housekeeper, indeed. She'd never seen a master more willing to embrace his cleaning lady, or more reluctant to explain his shocking behavior. In fact, he seemed annoyed and defensive about the entire matter. Maybe if he'd been more upset, more humbly apologetic, more inclined to offer explanations, maybe eventually she'd be willing to forgive him. "Oh, drat," she said aloud in frustration. "Braden Hamilton, you're impossible."

The celebration, or "fiesta" as it was being called, was scheduled to begin at dusk. It would take place in the expansive grassy area that lay between the main house and the sand beach of Hamilton's Cove. All day servants in high spirits had set up long plank tables under towering cedars and palmetto trees and decorated the tables with lavish bouquets of English roses and delphiniums intertwined with the native blue-flowered Bermudiana and red and yellow hibiscus. Swagged from tree branches were long vines of blooming morning glory. The area resembled a banquet hall created in the midst of a floral garden. A bonfire was laid in the center of the grounds and for extra lighting, kerosene torches on long bamboo poles were placed around the perimeter.

Having had a long nap and a refreshing bath, Amanda was in a much better mood. It was hard not to feel good when surrounded with so much man-made and natural beauty. Never in England or America had she found an ambience that so pleasured all the senses. As the heat of the day subsided, her energy returned and she enjoyed touring her colorful, airy apartment, with its white stone walls and floors and charming mix of furnishings made from English oak and native cedar and bamboo. Every table was graced with baskets of fresh fruit and flowers. The vista from her sitting room of the tall, spreading trees framing the more distant curve of beach and azure water was absolutely breathtaking. Double doors in each room stood open to receive the soft, floral-scented breeze drifting from the bay.

Amanda took Coco's advice and wore a rose-pink organdy gown with rounded bodice and short puffed sleeves. It was a dress she'd had made two years ago by a London seamstress adept at copying the Paris designs now becoming the rage of Europe. Amanda felt the need to compensate for her appearance that morning, when

she certainly made a poor first impression on the staff of
Hamilton Plantation.

Braden called for her just as the sun's last glow painted
the sky a dazzling pink as its farewell to the day. He was
quiet, almost introspective as he guided her through the
great-room of the house, and along the gravel path to the
site of the fiesta.

She was awestruck by the exquisite setting, whose
atmosphere was now further enhanced by the music of
five Spanish guitars strumming softly in the gathering
twilight.

"Uncle Hugh," she said happily when guided to her
seat at the head table.

Hugh stood and gave her a warm embrace. "Ah, how
lovely is the bride-to-be," he said. "When the pink of the
sunset is gone, we'll still have the glow of your beauty to
delight us."

Laughing, she removed one of the three pink rosebuds
Coco had intertwined in her hair and tucked it into the
buttonhole of his jacket. "Now," she said gaily, "you
look more like you're attending a fiesta rather than
Sunday meeting."

He winked. "And I feel more like a fiesta—whatever
this Spanish celebration may provide."

Braden took the seat next to her and called for drinks.
Amanda tried to keep her attention on her uncle at her
left, though Braden's appearance in snug white breeches
and flowing belted shirt of India silk was a sight that set
her pulses racing.

"Taste this, love," suggested Hugh. "'Tis a local drink
made from palmetto sap. They call it 'bibby' and it's
potent enough to bring tears to your eyes. Just a sip
now."

She tasted the heady liquid and as promised, tears
sprang to her eyes and she nearly choked. A sidelong
glance showed Braden grinning slyly at her uncle.

Course followed course as the evening progressed. At
each of four long tables forming a large square sat
approximately ten or twelve guests: couples and bache-

lors with a variety of national origins. There were no single women. That observation gave rise to Amanda's first direct question to Braden.

"Where is the famous and lovely Tamara tonight? Such an exotic name and such a beautiful girl." If her voice was slightly cutting, Braden took no notice.

"Yes, she is lovely, a true Turkish beauty."

"Turkish? How interesting. How did she arrive at Hamilton Plantation?" Amanda could see her questions were amusing Braden. Though this annoyed her, her curiosity was longing to be satisfied.

"I brought her here from Turkey when she was fourteen. Since then she has learned to run my home with great expertise. I had no one else, you understand. She was quite willing and her work has been more than satisfactory. When I marry, however," he added with twinkling eyes, "my wife will oversee the household—I hope with Tamara's assistance."

Amanda was aghast. It was worse than she'd thought. Why, Braden Hamilton must expect to house both Tamara and his wife under the same roof—two women to adore him and—my goodness—to see to his needs! It was scandalous and of course out of the question if she were to become Braden's wife.

Braden's eyes widened with innocent questioning. "Is this not a fair arrangement, at least until the girl chooses a husband and goes to make her own home? After all, I am her only guardian and responsible for her welfare."

"Is that why you brought her here in the first place? To be your . . . your housekeeper?"

"I brought her here because she was a lovely young girl in a dire predicament." He paused and in the background the guitars sang out a throbbing Moorish rhythm.

"May I inquire what sort of predicament?"

"Amanda . . ." Braden's voice lowered. "I will reveal the secret to you because I have asked you to marry me. If you accept, we'll have only honesty between us. I must ask your pledge not to ever speak again, to me or anyone, of what I'm about to tell you."

"Why . . . yes. Of course."

"I was fighting the Turks in Tangiers. I barreled through the sultan's palace and entered the innermost room where he kept his harem."

"Harem!" she whispered tensely. "You mean his collection of ladies?"

"Yes, but in this case, only one lady was present. Tamara. And she was stripped and bound to a whipping post and torture had begun."

"Oh my!"

"She was nearly unconscious, but I cut her free and started to leave. Some guards popped up and a fight ensued. By the time I fought my way out, I was covered with blood and Tamara was screaming in terror. I got to my ship and returned to England, then later to Bermuda."

"Oh! What a story! So you are more a hero to Tamara than even to me."

"She feels she owes me a debt, though I've assured her she does not."

"But she must love you."

"In a way. The way of a young girl for a man who saved her from a dreadful fate."

"And you must have feelings for her."

"Naturally."

A long silence lay between them. All around them was music and laughter, but Amanda's unspoken question hung in the air, closing out everything else.

"I'm not in love with her, Amanda. But, in truth, I made love to her during the voyage to England when she was so eager, so willing, and I was so desperately hungry for a woman's passion. Later I was sorry and did what I could to compensate—to treat her like my own daughter."

Braden's honest admission tore through her heart like a searing knife. Of course she had known he'd made love to others. But to hear him say it and to be asked to share her home with the object of his early love was almost too painful to bear. She turned away to hide her unhappiness.

He took her hand. "I know I've hurt you and I'm sorry. I love you, Amanda, and I want you to marry me. But I can't send Tamara away. I had hoped you would understand."

She fought to keep her lips from trembling. Softly she said, "You . . . you should have told me about her . . . before."

"I know. But how could I? We were there by the sea. We wanted to make love to each other. It happened before we could have this talk. I don't regret it for a moment, my darling girl. I hope you don't either."

She bit her lips, but the trembling continued and tears spilled onto her cheeks. How could she not regret it when she had such doubts about the wisdom of becoming his wife? Could she really believe he loved her after she had seen him with Tamara? Could she marry him and live here, sharing a home with another woman who plainly desired him? And what about Briarfield—her own ancestral home that might be lost if she didn't marry the marquess? She wanted to believe Braden was a man of goodness and character, but the doubts were there. She needed more time to make a decision.

The music changed as deep-throated drums began a new rhythm and were joined by the plaintive wailing of a flute.

Through misty eyes, Amanda watched a man setting a torch to the central bonfire amid wild cheers and applause. Her festive mood was gone, but she would have to see the evening through.

"Good lord," she heard Braden mutter.

A barefoot woman clad from head to foot in shimmering veils emerged into the firelight. Slowly she revolved while the bells on her ankles tinkled in counterrhythm to the drums. She lifted her arms in a graceful arc; her fingers snapped and she turned more rapidly and the veils lifted in a filmy cloud around her.

She wore diaphanous pantaloons and a wide gilded leather belt. Above that, it appeared her voluptuous tawny breasts were left uncovered.

Amanda was now attentive. She stared at the exotic creature engaged in the most sensuous dance imaginable, her hips undulating in a most bizarre manner, her body tilted, her upper body laid back, her long dusky hair almost touching the ground while her arms reached skyward.

The men watching began to clap in time, but at least two of the women left their seats and melted into the darkness.

Amanda didn't know whether to stay or go. She looked at Hugh, but her uncle was well into his cups and clapping with the others. It crossed her mind that Aunt Sara would collapse from apoplexy on the spot.

Well, she wasn't Sara. And the music was exciting and the girl well trained in her Moorish dance. Braden had said all ethnic groups lived here in friendship. She would prove she could be openminded too. To help herself to that end, she picked up Hugh's cup of bibby and took a large swallow.

Gracefully the dancer removed a veil from her shoulders.

Amanda was relieved to see she had a piece of cloth covering her ample bosom.

The girl faced Braden. With hips lifting invitingly from side to side in staccato rhythm, she moved toward him.

At this moment, with the lamplight illuminating the girl, Amanda recognized her. The dancer was Tamara. Her heart skipped a beat. Her senses froze. Tamara. Braden's Tamara.

"Tamara," Braden said under his breath. He stood to accept the veil she offered. "You've never—you shouldn't—Jesus Christ!"

Flashing a dazzling smile, Tamara stepped backward. She snapped her fingers and a dark-skinned boy ran forward carrying a small iron pot containing three wooden rods.

The boy knelt at her feet and with a flourish she took a rod in each hand. The rods were tipped with a wad of knotted fiber. Tamara walked to the head table and fired the knots by touching each to the kerosene lamp.

It was then that Amanda heard Braden chuckle. She tore her eyes from Tamara long enough to see he was grinning and shaking his head. Obviously he found this whole episode highly amusing. She looked back at the girl.

Tamara was staring directly at her, holding both burning rods at arm's length. Her eyes caught the firelight and were as heated as the flames. Slowly she spread her feet and leaned back, making an arch of her body. The top of her head touched the ground. Her belly was fully revealed; her hips, covered by the delicate cloth, tipped upward.

The music grew to a crescendo of drum and flute. Her belly began to throb, to undulate, to have its own magic life, to dance in time to the whine and throb. The girl raised up, but kept her head lowered and her lips parted. As gasps sounded from the onlookers, she lowered first one, then the other flaming tow of fiber into her open mouth, extinguishing each with a sucking motion of her lips.

Amanda gripped the table. She hadn't realized until now that she was standing along with everyone else. But she didn't applaud. She was too frozen with shock and amazement to move one finger.

To her horror, she saw Tamara now draw the third rod from the pot and walk toward her. The girl lighted the tip and offered it to her in obvious challenge. Amanda could only stare wide-eyed, stunned, unable to speak or move.

"God's blood, Tamara!" Braden interjected. "You've gone too far. She doesn't know how . . . Give me that." He took the rod and left his seat to stand beside Tamara.

Tamara threw a victorious look over her shoulder at Amanda, then dropped to her knees before Braden.

The audience yelled its encouragement. "Hamilton ... Lordship ... We dare you, Captain," came the shouts.

Braden threw back his head and lowered the flaming tow into his own mouth, holding it close to his lips for one moment before he popped it in and extinguished it.

The applause was thunderous.

Braden was laughing, enjoying himself thoroughly. He walked to Amanda and called, "Watch this." He paused a few seconds at the table, took something from a servant nearby, then returned to the center and stretched his hand to touch the kerosene torch. Flames darted from the bare flesh of his fingertips. He pivoted in place, his arm extended, fire erupting wherever he pointed his fingers.

Amanda sank into her chair. Her heart was beating so hard, she thought it must overpower the drums. Was the man truly magic? He and his exotic handmaiden appeared to exist in a mystical world of their own creation. Confusion and dismay enveloped her as she watched the two laughing together in the glow of the flames.

Smiling, the fire gone from his fingers, Braden accepted accolades from the crowd. Like a matador he turned in a slow circle. Then he threw an arm around Tamara's waist and hustled her into the trees. A moment later he reappeared and made the rounds of the tables to visit and laugh with his friends.

"Uncle Hugh ... Uncle, take me to my room," Amanda pleaded between clenched teeth. But her uncle's head rested heavily in his arms and he could not be sufficiently roused to accommodate her.

With tight lips, she flung down her napkin and marched up the path to the house. It was all she could do to keep from running. The display of pagan dance and devil's trickery was beyond her comprehension. Yes, she had better marry the marquess and find safety among Christian souls on England's shores. If Braden's Turkish harem girl had plotted to be rid of her, she had achieved her goal.

CHAPTER
13

At midmorning, an English merchantman fired its cannon from off Spanish Point to announce the arrival of Lord Dudley Pickering, Marquess of Staffordshire.

Coco dropped her mending and jumped to her feet, but Amanda remained at her writing desk, where she was penning her description of last night's terrible experience. After that nightmare, she wouldn't be surprised if the island was attacked by pirates or suddenly sank into the middle of an erupting volcano. In the clear, peaceful light of morning, her fear was gone. In its place was the absolute certainty she would marry the marquess and proceed with her life as Philip had planned.

Last night and again this morning, she had stayed in her room and firmly refused Braden's request for a meeting. Now, however, she allowed his houseboy to enter to announce the arrival of the marquess. Her presence was requested at high tea at four o'clock.

So today she would meet her husband-to-be. She would be glad to get it over with, have the wedding, and travel to England. She wrote in her journal *Today I will meet my future husband. I pray he will be kind and not too disagreeable to look at. I will do everything in my power to forget Lord Braden Hamilton, though I fear he'll haunt my dreams forever. He says he loves me, but will not give up his woman, Tamara. Last night she displayed her hatred of me. And she and Braden exhibited magic power which I don't understand. It is best I leave Bermuda as soon as possible.*

Braden stared out the window of his office, but took no pleasure in the lovely view: the vegetable gardens, the fields stretching toward the barn and stables, and beyond all, the hazy blue of the sea meeting the sky. This afternoon his thoughts were deeply troubled with what seemed a hopeless situation.

Tamara had gone too far. If he'd had any idea of the stunt she had planned, he'd have certainly forbidden it. Normally she preferred to forget her experiences while a captive in the harem of the sultan. But her dance last night was obviously learned under the instruction of the harem women and was never intended to be viewed by polite society. Not that the high-spirited atmosphere of the fiesta had been a formal affair. Few of the Bermudians had been terribly shocked by the display, though it was the talk of Hamilton Plantation this morning.

But for Tamara to have created such a scene in front of the delicately bred Amanda Sheffield was an affront to the lady, and it more than complicated his efforts to win Amanda's hand. The fact that she had adamantly refused to see him today was cause for concern. And for the marquess to have arrived just at this time was no help at all.

If only he had stopped Tamara at once and resisted the temptation to join in the fire trick. The trick she did with the flames was utterly simple and harmless. They had both learned the art of fire-biting and flame-tossing from an English chemist who had learned it from the Italian physician, Sementini. All it took was sugar and soap and careful timing. Anyone could do it. He had thought by participating in the show, he would distract attention from Tamara's sensuous performance and put everyone in a relaxed, fun-loving spirit. But when he returned to his seat, Amanda had disappeared, and today she wouldn't even give him a chance to explain.

But in a few minutes he would see her. It was an occasion he feared and dreaded. If she appeared at tea and pleased the marquess—which of course she would —she might accept the man's proposal on the spot. Then there would be no turning back. He knew he would lose the woman he loved—all because of one evening of careless frivolity.

"Lord Pickering is in the salon, milord," came the announcement from the doorway. "The lady is expected at any moment."

He left the study and strode down the hallway to the great-room. It seemed there was no choice but to play this out to the end.

"Lord Pickering, welcome to Hamilton Plantation," said Braden after a slight bow.

"Y-y-y-es indeed," stuttered the marquess. "T-t-'tis quite good to set foot on land after t-t-the long voyage and to meet y-y-you at last, Captain Hamilton."

Braden took a good look at Amanda's betrothed. If he hadn't been in such a sour mood, he would have laughed aloud. The marquess was squat and paunchy and reminded him of a goose egg with toothpicks for appendages. His remarkable attire emphasized his odd shape. He wore a crimson and gold satin waistcoat above ballooning pantaloons, red satin hose and gold high-heeled shoes. His face was round as a cranberry and nearly the same color. He wore a full powdered wig, the latest fashion of the day, and a red and gold satin cap with dangling gold tassel.

He did, however, have some redeeming features. His smile was as bright and merry and free of guile as a child's. And despite his age, he appeared vigorous and energetic.

"I hope you've been comfortable since your arrival,

your lordship," said Braden. "We didn't know exactly when to expect you."

"Ah, y-y-yes indeed-indeed yes. Aye, quite comfortable."

He seemed a bit tongue-tied, or maybe just nervous, Braden thought. "Lady Amanda Sheffield will soon join us for tea. Actually we just arrived from New England yesterday. Excellent timing, don't you agree?"

"Y-y-yes . . . quite . . . indeed quite," managed Pickering.

At that moment, Amanda entered the salon on the arm of Hugh Sheffield. In her free hand, she carried the calico kitten.

Braden's heart plummeted at the sight of her. Her proud bearing, her youthful innocence, her golden beauty stopped his breath. She had been his in the fullest sense of the word, and now he was losing her. She was exquisitely gowned, a vision in floating amber organdy embroidered with a lavish design of silver thread. Her flaxen hair was arranged atop her head and a few loose curls fell about her ears. But what tore at Braden was her eyes, as golden as the dress and framed in thick ash-brown lashes, but sunken and anguished and underlined with dark smudges despite artful powdering. Though *he* had worried the night away, *she* was suffering too. Why hadn't she let him speak to her before now—apologize, explain, somehow prevent what was certain to happen next?

Almost speechless with misery, Braden mumbled some inane compliment and bowed before her. He greeted Hugh and introduced them to the marquess.

Amanda relinquished Persephone to Coco, who trailed behind. Then, as regally as a queen, she extended a hand toward the marquess.

The poor man appeared flabbergasted. Twice he tried to speak, but only stammered unintelligible garble. Finally he took her hand, bowed low and touched her fingertips to his lips.

Quickly she withdrew her hand. By the time Lord Pickering pulled his bulk upright, she managed a tremulous smile.

At last the lord found his voice. "M-m-my dear lady. Y-y-you're more beautiful than I remembered. I am your humble servant from this day forward."

"How kind," she said above a whisper, then let her eyes stray to Braden.

He gazed at her in painful silence. God, what a fool he'd been. He had expected her to acquiesce like other women he'd known; accept his domination along with his affection. He had assumed she would make no objection to including Tamara in the household once he had told her that was his wish. She loved him. He could see it in her face, written plainly in her haunting eyes. But she would not bend to his will. He was going to lose her to this . . . this duck-of-a-man who was drooling in delight. And the irony was he himself had arranged the match from the beginning.

A servant announced tea and Hugh pulled out a chair for Amanda. After they were seated at the elegant table, tea was served along with elaborate sandwiches, candied fruits and tiny iced cakes. No English drawing room had ever offered a more refined refreshment than that served in Braden Hamilton's great-room, before wide doors open to receive the breezes wafting from the nearby sea.

Conversation was formal and strained. The marquess stuttered his way through endless compliments and ongoing descriptions of his own estates and his accomplishments in the House of Lords.

Amanda offered only polite responses and did not smile again.

Hugh looked completely uncomfortable and concentrated on his food and wine goblet.

Braden couldn't eat a morsel. He drank the excellent tea imported from China, tasted the wine and wished all the while for a strong brandy. Amanda would not again meet his eyes, and he couldn't tear his from her face.

After what seemed hours, the final coffee was served and Amanda asked to be excused.

Instantly the marquess popped to his feet, reached into the folds of his coat and withdrew a box. When he opened the lid, an emerald and diamond ring of enormous size glittered in the late afternoon sun. "For you, my dear, dear lady. It is part of a grand set which will be y-y-yours on our wedding day."

She accepted the ring in stony silence.

"Mistress Sheffield, may we set the date right away? I-I'm most eager to take you back to England as my wife. At my age," he said, chuckling nervously, "one mustn't dawdle, must one?"

Amanda seemed in a trance. Her eyes stared at some invisible point above Lord Pickering's head.

Braden stepped forward. "Amanda . . . ah . . . Mistress Sheffield, I beg you to . . . to allow yourself ample time to—"

Her voice was brittle as ice. "No need for time, Captain Hamilton. The ceremony can be quite simple and take place tomorrow if a minister can be found."

He took a deep breath. "Are . . . are you quite certain?" he asked between clenched teeth. "If you'd allow me . . ."

"*Quite* certain," she said harshly. "Do me this one last favor. Hold the ceremony tomorrow."

He gazed down at her, wondering where she found such will and self-control. She was sacrificing herself like a lamb on the altar to this impossible old man. Why? She knew *he* loved her. How could she go to the marquess after . . . the thought turned his stomach. Was it to save Briarfield? Was it duty to her brother and the Sheffields? Or did she truly covet the marquess's titles and estates? Whatever her reasons, he could see she was determined to go through with it.

"Very well," he said flatly. "Tomorrow it will be. Arrangements for the wedding and a feast to follow have already been made. The ceremony will take place at the Anglican Church in the village, and the nuptial feast will be here at the plantation. A few of my neighbors will attend. It will be a small gathering."

The marquess wiggled in jellylike glee. "Excellent. And you, Mister Sheffield, will give the bride away."

"Aye," mumbled Hugh.

"And you, Captain Hamilton, as a member of the noble house of Wentworth, will attend to the wedding chamber as tradition dictates."

Braden was thunderstruck. "The wedding chamber! But that old tradition is rarely used except for kings and princes and the monarch's childbirth."

"But the Pickering family has continued to observe it. We can veil the bridal bed, of course." He grinned at Amanda's pale face. "Out of respect for maidenly modesty. Only you, her uncle, and her lady's maid will attend. Oh yes, my own lord chamberlain will stand by. Four witnesses will be sufficient. Then when a child is born . . ." he said as he winked, "in nine months or so, there'll be no question I'm the father."

Braden saw Amanda sway and rushed to slip an arm around her waist.

A pale-faced Hugh took her other arm.

Lord Dudley Pickering clucked his tongue and offered a sweet smile of understanding.

Braden paced his room all night like a caged tiger. He couldn't go through with it. It would be impossible for him to stand beside Amanda's wedding bed while that . . . that fat, gloating bastard . . . He considered everything from kidnapping the girl and sailing away on his ship, to throttling the marquess in his sleep and damn the consequences. But Amanda was determined to follow the path of self-destruction. Even as he had assisted her back to her room, she had informed him her decision was irrevocable. She insisted she knew exactly what she was doing and actually found the marquess pleasant and amusing. Upon arriving at her room, she had faced him squarely, stiffened her spine and explained that "doing her duty in bed" was a small price to pay for all she would gain. She had flashed the ring and a mirthless smile. "I'll be fine, Braden Hamilton. And you may continue your life and your previous liaisons undisturbed."

Hell, he had wanted to shake her till she rattled. Force some sense, some human emotion, back into her beautiful head. But she'd ordered him to leave her room, with eyes blazing like liquid fire. She'd beaten him—a thing he'd never allowed before in his life. And he'd live out his days searching for someone, or something, to ease his pain. It was just before dawn when he made his decision. He would play one last card before he lost the woman he loved.

Shortly past nine, Braden walked unannounced into the marquess's sitting room. Lord Pickering was seated at his table in his purple dressing gown, enjoying his first coffee of the morning. Startled, he put down his cup.

"Forgive me, my lord," began Braden, "but there is a matter that must be settled before we proceed with a wedding."

"W-well, I do say," blustered the marquess. "I thought 'twas settled long ago. I sent a large sum to her brother in Virginia; I came here the m-minute you sent word. The lady is more than a-ac-acceptable."

Braden put his hands on his hips. He wore a loose-fitting cotton shirt, American-style buckskin pants and boots, and carried a glove in his pocket. "I must inform you I've fallen in love with the lady myself. I asked her to be my wife, but she refused since she'd given her word to you."

The marquess rose, bumping the table with his belly and shaking the dishes. "But this is outrageous. How dare you interfere after all that's been done. Th-the lady is my betrothed, and I am the Marquess of Staffordshire."

"I know that. And I agree I'm the villain in the matter. But the fact remains I *am* in love with Amanda Sheffield. And I have reason to believe she's in love with me. I'm asking you to release her from her pledge—as a gentleman and a lord of England."

"Damned if I will!" shouted the marquess. "You've only turned her head with your youth and handsome face. She accepted me yesterday and today we will wed. I'll make her forget you soon enough, sir."

"Then you leave me no other choice. I had hoped that behind your kind smile there was an understanding heart." He pulled out the glove and threw it at Pickering's feet. "There is my challenge. I'll meet you— or any man jack of your choice—beneath the cedars by the shore in one hour."

The marquess paled and sank heavily into his chair. "A duel? At my age? Over a woman? Impossible! Besides, I've not been well lately. Something wrong with my innards."

For a moment, Braden thought his ploy had worked. He had never intended to cross swords with this plump partridge. He had prayed it wouldn't be necessary.

But then, "Done!" snapped Pickering. "You said any man jack, and I have just the one. My second mate is as fine a swordsman as ever fought Turk or pirate. He'll be at the cedars and will gladly fight for my lady's hand and honor."

"So be it," said Braden and he strode from the room.

Word of the duel swept rapidly through the household. Within minutes, Coco was dashing from the kitchen to warn Amanda, who was just rousing from another miserable night. Before Amanda could even react to the terrible news, a knock came at the door.

"Who is it?" asked Coco.

"Tamara," came the startling reply.

Amanda froze. "Come . . . come in," she said reluctantly.

Tamara entered and looked at Amanda with furious, tear-filled eyes. "You caused this," she said hotly. "Now he may die because of you."

"I know you hate me," Amanda answered. "I understand why. But I do love . . . care deeply for Braden, despite everything."

Tamara shook her finger near Amanda's face. "Then do something," she cried. "If you don't stop this duel, I'll curse you into your grave, Englishwoman."

Amanda stepped back, half expecting fire to leap from Tamara's fingers.

Coco stepped between the two. "Don't you threaten my mistress, you devil woman. I know a curse that can send you burnin' to hell afore you can blink your eyes."

"Wait, Coco. I can handle this." Amanda eased her maid aside. "I'm going now to try to stop the duel. Let me dress, then show me the way, Tamara."

With Tamara rushing her Amanda didn't have time to complete the buttoning of her dress or even put on her shoes and stockings. With Coco in her wake, she pursued Tamara along the halls and rooms of the house, then out into the garden and down the path toward the beach.

Arriving at the spot beneath the tall cedars, she found Braden with his sword drawn and attended by a swarthy Spaniard. At the opposite side of the clearing stood a burly red-headed seaman, his chest bare and his muscled arms bulging as he slashed his sword through the air. Behind him at a safe distance stood the rotund marquess, his wig slightly askew.

She rushed to Braden. "What are you doing?" she demanded breathlessly.

"If I win, the wedding is off," he answered. "Pickering was forced to agree to the terms."

She stared at him, feeling her own heartbeat throbbing in her throat. She couldn't allow the duel to take place—not because of Tamara's curse, but because Braden might actually be killed. If he died, she would gladly take her own life and follow him to Hell. She slapped him as hard as she could across his cheek.

He blinked in surprise. Blood seeped from his cut lip. "Amanda—damnation!"

"End this nonsense at once, Captain. This *is* my wedding day." She wheeled and crossed to Lord Pickering. "Call off this duel, my lord. I will marry you at four today—*if* you stop the fight at once. You must forgive

Captain Hamilton for assuming I could love him. 'Tis absurd, of course, when I can marry a man such as you."

Pickering strutted forward like a banty cock. "So it's settled, Ha-Ha-Hamilton." He took the sword from his seaman and stabbed it into the ground at Braden's feet. "I'm satisfied if you are. It appears the lady intends to be my bride whether you approve or not."

Slowly Braden lowered his sword. His eyes were as bleak as if he faced the gallows.

Amanda felt her heart break at the sight of him. His head was high, his lips firm, but defeat and pain were vivid in his face. For one brief moment, she fought the powerful desire to rush to him and embrace him, to tell him how she adored him, but she knew his life might be forfeit. She couldn't take that chance.

She looked at Tamara, who was watching from the fringe of trees. Almost imperceptively, she nodded to the girl. It was as if she were making a gift to her—a gift of immeasurable price.

She walked back toward the house between the marquess and Coco, who was dazed and shaking. She took no notice of the crowd of curious now gathering, nor did she feel the pebbles biting into the tender soles of her feet.

CHAPTER
14

Coco buried her face in her hands and sobbed.

"Don't cry, Coco. It's all my fault and I must pull myself together and face whatever will be."

"But, mistress, you don't love him. You don't even *like* him," Coco said between sniffles. "And you . . . you do look so lovely." She wiped her eyes.

Her head high, her chin set in fierce determination, Amanda stood in the middle of her sitting room. She was gowned in yards of creamy satin decorated with hundreds of tiny pearls and delicate glass beads. "I'll put on the veil now, Coco. The carriage will arrive any minute."

Coco lifted a pearl and sapphire studded corona from which drifted a floor-length veil of Venetian lace, and placed it carefully atop Amanda's golden coiffure. Her tears continued unabated. "'Tisn't fair. I jus' know you'll be sorry before dawn tomorrow."

Amanda pulled the veil over her face and let it drape around her shoulders. Before dawn tomorrow? Dear heaven, she was sorry already. She'd been desperately sorry since yesterday. She'd let her stubborn pride carry her on an invisible journey into a future without hope, without love—without Braden. Only a few short days ago she'd had a choice. Now she had none. It had happened so quickly. All her life she must live with her mistake. Could she go through with it—survive this day—and the coming night? She had prayed through the night for strength, for the courage of the Sheffields. If she could live until tomorrow, until the marquess's ship carried her away from this island, perhaps she would eventually find contentment. She had no hope of true happiness, or of ever completely forgetting her love for Braden Hamilton. He would forget her soon, she was sure. Oh, he was hurting now, probably both his heart and his pride. But he had his plantation and his ships—and he had Tamara to comfort him.

But there was another worry. "Coco, I must tell you something . . . something terrible. If I don't speak about it, I shall die."

"Yes'm, what is it?" Coco looked up from where she knelt to secure a loose bead to the skirt's hem.

"Coco . . . I'm not a virgin."

Coco gasped audibly. Her eyes widened like pools of spilled milk on a dark floor. "Oh dear Jesus—but how come . . ."

"I'd rather not explain. The important thing is I must go to my marriage bed and face possible disgrace. If my virginity is very important to the marquess, he may create a horrible scene. He may demand to know who has . . . has already possessed me. And if I reveal the man's name, the marquess will have the right to kill him with impunity—nor will he need to give him any chance to defend himself."

"Oh lordy, lordy. What can we do?"

"We?" Amanda touched Coco's glossy curls. "There's nothing anyone can do. Except I'll never betray the man I first loved."

"Why, it's the captain!" Coco jumped up. "Don't be foolish, Mistress Amanda. The marquess would know right away 'twas the captain. Anybody would."

She swallowed hard. "He might guess that, but he won't have proof unless . . . unless Braden claims to be the one. If he is present in the room, he might say or do anything."

Coco straightened the veil. "Surely he won't. Any man would be crazy to claim such a thing. The captain would have nothin' to gain and a heap to lose."

"I hope . . . I pray, Coco, that he will bear that in mind if Lord Pickering creates a fuss."

The door opened and Hugh poked his head inside. "'Tis time, my dear. Ah, what a vision you are. Are you ready, lass?"

"Yes, I'm ready," she answered as if the chopping block awaited rather than her wedding. With Coco carrying her train, she took Hugh's arm and started on her way.

Braden sat in his study staring at the hands of the clock above the swinging pendulum. Despite his heavy imbibing over the past twenty-four hours, he felt as sober as when he'd begun.

Nearly three o'clock. Time to ride to the church in St. George Towne. A few minutes from now the carriage he'd ordered would arrive at the door to carry the bride and her uncle along the nine-mile road paralleling the sea. By riding his stallion and taking shortcuts, he would arrive at St. Peter's Church in time for the service. He planned to put in his required appearance, then return swiftly to the plantation, where he would hopefully drink himself into oblivion.

Manuel Rodriquez came through the open door. "Pardon, Señor Hamilton. I've brought your horse to the door as you requested."

"Yes, *gracias,* Manuel." Stiffly Braden rose and reluctantly put down his brandy glass. He picked up the black satin jacket from his chair.

Manuel stepped forward to assist him. "Pardon again, señor, but I must tell you I haven't yet located Tamara— though a stable hand reported she rode toward the south beach after daybreak."

Braden clamped on his black wide-brimmed hat. His voice was hollow. "I sent for her twice yesterday, to no avail. I was assured she was busy overseeing the wedding feast and would see me later. I wanted her to know I didn't blame her for any of this. It's my doing—mine alone."

"Forgive me, Captain. I did speak to her for a moment last night. She was upset—weeping, in fact."

Braden took a deep breath. "Women—hell, they're never satisfied. You would think she'd be happy with the way things have turned out."

"She said she believed you hated her for interfering."

"No, of course I don't hate her. But if she's miserable, she's got plenty of company. I'm relieved to know she confided in you. I'm counting on you to comfort her if you can. But we'll talk more about that later. The important thing now is that the wedding and the feast will be to Amanda Sheffield's liking. I suppose Priscilla can oversee the banquet if Tamara chooses to abandon us."

"All is in readiness, Captain Hamilton."

Braden strode toward the door. Yes, all was in readiness. He'd botched everything to a fare-thee-well and now there was nothing else to do but go forward. It was apparent Amanda placed land and titles above all else. Though how she could have given him her body so willingly was something he'd never understand.

What's more, the marquess was sure to be more than disappointed to discover his lovely young bride was not the virgin he expected. What would the grinning old lecher do when his witnesses gathered near the marriage bed to see proof of their lord's potency? The very thought made him clench his teeth and fling himself in a fury onto the back of his mount. If Lord Pickering had half a wit, he'd keep his mouth shut and count himself the most fortunate of men to have Amanda as his bride— regardless of her previous experience—to have her carry his name, to have her loveliness at his beck and call, to have her as the mother of his children. God, the man should spend the rest of his days on his knees giving thanks.

Braden gave his horse its head in a steady gallop, oblivious to the spectacular scenery of seacoast and hamlet through which he rode. His thoughts were black and swirling. If he insults her, I'll kill him, he vowed in a thunderous rage. No matter what pain it costs me to attend her wedding chamber, at least I'll be there to make certain that oaf doesn't harm her. I may be drunk tonight, but not too drunk to run the son-of-a-bitch through if he insults her or hurts her in any way whatever. If I hang, I hang.

Braden skirted Castle Harbour and crossed the wooden bridge to St. George's Island. Arriving at the simple frame church on York Street, he saw the open carriage approaching the entrance.

So this was the moment he dreaded. He swung out of the saddle and left the horse standing near several others. There would be few guests at the ceremony, but a much larger group at the feast afterward.

He entered the candlelit sanctuary and stood at the back against the wall. A harpsichord played soft hymns; the aisle leading to the altar was draped in myriads of morning glory vines interspersed with pink multiflora roses. At the front facing a white satin prie-dieu stood the minister. Near the aisle was a solemn-faced Lord Dudley Pickering flanked by his lord of the chamber.

How could she go through with it? Braden wondered, staring at the paunchy, periwigged marquess, who was perspiring profusely in his elaborate satin suit. But his last hope disappeared when Amanda entered the church on Hugh's arm and rustled past him. The handful of observers whispered and sighed as she walked by.

He stared at her back—the petite waist, the yards of satin, the floating lace falling from her swirl of golden hair. He could have been the man waiting at the altar, he thought bitterly. And now he must stand here silently while his future happiness—and hers, he'd vow—were forever taken from them.

He watched and listened in stoic agony as the reverend called upon the congregation to witness the sacred marriage vows of the Anglican Church. He couldn't hear Amanda's soft responses, but when Pickering gave her a wide smile and assisted her to kneel, he knew she had spoken the words sealing her future to the marquess.

Hell—bloody hell—goddamned bloody hell—curses swam through his brain. Until that moment he'd prayed some miracle might prevent the union. But now 'twas done. And that was that.

Before he could move, the music soared and the newlyweds turned to stroll arm-in-arm down the aisle. Amanda had lifted her veil and Braden knew he couldn't avoid looking at her.

The marquess smiled and nodded at the guests as he led his wife slowly toward the door.

Amanda was so angelically beautiful—her face like the porcelain statue of a goddess—that Braden thought his heart must be bleeding for all to see. He tortured himself by watching her approach, gazing at her unsmiling face like a man looking at his beloved from his deathbed. Using the wall behind him as support, he straightened as she passed, tensing as her full skirts brushed against his knee.

For one moment, he captured her eyes. They were soft and golden in the candle glow—and they glittered with unshed tears. He saw neither remorse, nor anxiety, nor recrimination, only a resigned sadness like a maiden on the sacrificial altar of some pagan god. Pain burned through him like a heated knife.

Then she was gone.

Using every ounce of courage he could muster and muttering every pirate's curse he'd ever learned, Braden made his way outside into the late afternoon sunlight and found his stallion. He rode to a nearby deserted grove of cedars, dismounted and paced in the quiet shadowed bower until he once more regained control of his mind and emotions. The whiskey had been a mistake, he decided. He would not touch a drop until the feast and the marriage bed ceremony were over. A cool head was what he needed now. Amanda was another man's wife, but she might still need help before this business was ended once and for all. One thing he could do was delay the sailing of the lord's ship for at least a week. That would give everyone time to calm their nerves and for him to make sure Amanda was safe and content with her new status. She would now occupy the marquess's apartments at the plantation house. Braden pledged to keep his distance, but he would know if anything was amiss. Amanda wouldn't come to him, he was sure, but he would know just the same. As long as Amanda Sheffield, now Lady Pickering, the Marchioness of Staffordshire, occupied his home, she would receive every courtesy and every protection, up to and including his very life.

When Braden entered the dining hall of Hamilton Plantation, he was completely sober and totally in control. The guests had already assembled at the rows of beautifully decorated tables. Going from person to person, he greeted each guest with a welcoming word and smile. He played the congenial host with great skill and not one person present suspected the incredible effort he was making.

When he reached the place of honor prepared for him and for the bride and groom, he bowed low and kissed Amanda's hand without once meeting her eyes. He spoke formally to the marquess, who stared at him coolly, then he offered a charming toast to the couple, commenting on his long affiliation with the Sheffield family and his brotherly affection for the bride.

He didn't take his rightful place beside Amanda, however, but continued to move around the hall chatting with friends and neighbors. He gave Tamara all the credit for the lovely arrangements: the flowers, the menu, even the musicians who made up a string ensemble of some skill. In his hand, he carried a silver goblet, but he had filled it with a mild peach cider and no one knew he passed up the vintage wine and spirits.

He joked, he laughed, he discussed topics critical to the island. Somehow he got through most of the evening without once taking a close look at the new Lady Pickering. That her eyes often followed him, he was sure. But he would not dare risk meeting them. Not tonight. Not when he knew what he still must endure.

Just before eleven, with the party at its zenith, Hugh Sheffield rose and motioned him into a quiet alcove near the open windows.

"I don't like it, Hamilton, not one bit, do you hear me!"

"What's that? I think it's rather a success."

"I'll tell you what," fumed Hugh. "I understand there's to be some sort of marriage bed ceremony. That old medieval custom of witnessing the bridegroom taking his wife. This is one time I agree with my Puritan brethren. Why, 'tis an outrage. I won't permit it."

"I agree with you completely. But the marquess is absolutely insistent and Amanda has not refused. At least the bed will be shrouded with curtains. It seems the old stag wants to prove to his entourage he is still capable of the rut."

"It's a scandal. If my wife or Philip Sheffield hear of it, heads will roll."

"I doubt it. Neither of those good souls have the power to chastise a marquess who is a member of the House of Lords. And frankly I don't think Philip would care, if his price is met."

"Then *you* must do something. It's your house, after all."

"I tried to do something, as you probably know. I tried to stop the whole damned wedding and got myself into a duel and my face slapped in public by your niece."

"But dammit, Hamilton . . ."

Braden clapped his hand on Hugh's shoulder. "I

understand, sir, believe me I do. But all I can do is make sure you and I and Amanda's girl, Coco, are the only people in the room except for the lord's chamberlain. I'll allow one candle and make sure a heavy cloth surrounds the bed. Amanda should be all right. Maybe she'll even feel safer if we're there."

"Safer? Good God, man, what do you think that fat toad might do?"

"Nothing. Of that, I assure you. He'll do what all bridegrooms do and then take his leave. Then we'll *all* leave, except Coco, and get roaring, stinking drunk."

Hugh shook his head. His temper cooled. "If . . . if you're sure that's all. But it seems downright pagan to me."

Braden steered him back to his seat. "Try not to worry. Have another drink. I'll call my steward."

With that settled, Braden busied himself with his guests, trying not to think about the hell he would soon have to endure, when a bell was sounded near the door. It was time for the happy newlyweds to excuse themselves.

As host, Braden knew he must lead the bride and groom to their chamber. He had been preparing his nerves all evening, but now his courage weakened.

The crowd began to applaud and call out their good wishes. Several threw flowers at Amanda and Lord Pickering as the two stood and waited for Braden to approach and act as escort.

The marquess crooked his finger at his chamberlain and the dignitary rose to join the group.

Braden collected himself and for the first time, addressed Amanda directly. He had to look at her, no matter how much agony it caused him. "My dear lady, may I have the honor of escorting you?"

Her face was extraordinarily pale, her eyes bleak and sunken. Her lips trembled when she took his arm, but she bit her lower lip and regained control.

Braden found it impossible to smile at the cheerful assemblage. He covered Amanda's hand with his and led her from the room. Hugh Sheffield followed at a distance and from somewhere close by Coco suddenly emerged. Her face was stark with concern, but she bravely took Amanda's other hand.

The marquess and his colleague turned away and disappeared into a room adjoining the bridal chamber.

Braden noticed Pickering sway and wondered if the man had been fool enough to overindulge in spirits. It could inhibit his performance—especially at his age.

"Wait," requested Amanda in a choked whisper. "Wait outside, Uncle Hugh—and Captain Hamilton. Coco will help me prepare. When I'm . . . in bed . . . she'll come for you." She looked up at Braden. "Thank you for the wedding and the dinner. It . . . was lovely," she managed before her eyes swam with tears. Quickly she turned away.

Her brave speech was his undoing. "Amanda," he said hoarsely, "I ask only one moment alone . . . please, my lady."

She nodded and allowed him to enter the bedroom, then closed the door. Turning, she gazed at him with a look he would never in his life forget. She was beyond speech.

Finally he said, "I'm only allowing this ceremony for one reason, Amanda. I want to be near in case he makes any complaint. You know what I mean."

She nodded and the tears spilled down her cheeks.

He pulled her gently into his arms. "If . . . if he hurts you . . . or you need help, I'll be close by, my dear. I won't leave until he's safely out of here and Coco tells me you're all right."

She dabbed at her tears and moved out of his embrace. "I'll be fine," she whispered. "Swear to me you'll not confront him . . . unless . . . unless I call for you."

He rested his hand on the short-sword attached to his belt. "If you ask it of me, I so swear."

"Thank you, my friend and—as so often before—my protector. Now go wait outside. We must get through this."

He left the room and motioned Coco inside. For a

time, he stood silently near Hugh in the dark hallway. Why? his mind asked over and over. By all that was holy, he believed Amanda still loved him. Surely there wasn't enough money in the king's treasury for her to put herself through this hell.

At last Coco opened the door and signaled for them to enter.

The room was nearly lost in darkness; the only light was from one flickering taper opposite the elaborately swagged bed.

"She's ready," whispered Coco. "Should I summon Lord Pickering?"

"Yes," answered Braden, though the word was bitter in his mouth.

She crossed the room and tapped on the far door. After a moment it opened and two men entered.

Lord Pickering's pudgy frame could not be mistaken. He wore his purple satin dressing gown and was supported by the lord chamberlain.

Hugh, who had taken seriously his host's invitation to drink, leaned close to Braden and muttered, "He looks drunk to me; he'll never do it—not in that condition."

Braden didn't reply.

Coco drew back the bed curtain just enough for the marquess to climb in, then lowered it and scurried to sit on a stool in the farthest corner.

The bed creaked once. Then followed total silence.

Braden felt sweat trickle down his back. The seconds, then minutes crept by and still there was no sound. Could he stand it? He fingered his sword and wished . . .

"I can't stand it," grunted Hugh and hastily left the room.

Braden sucked in his breath. God almighty, what was happening? Never could a seduction be so noiseless.

Breaking through the stifling atmosphere came Amanda's soft voice. "Coco . . . Coco, are you there?"

He stiffened and half unsheathed his sword as the girl hurried back to the bed. How little it would take for him to plunge the blade into that hulk in Amanda's bed.

Coco approached him, her eyes wide with fright. "Captain," she croaked. "She . . . you better come see."

Brushing aside the chamberlain, he strode forward and pulled back the curtain.

He could just make out Amanda sitting up in bed, her nightgown buttoned to the throat, the silk sheet resting over her knees. Beside her on his face lay the marquess.

"Braden, he didn't even touch me. He's been lying there, and he's radiating as much heat as a yule log."

Braden turned the marquess over to see his face. The man's eyes were closed and his mouth slack, though he breathed heavily.

"Is he . . . drunk?" she asked.

"Possibly. But it could be something more. He *is* hot—unnaturally, I think."

"What can we do?" she asked in the voice of a frightened child.

"You and Coco go at once to your old rooms. No one will see you. I'll send the lord's man for a doctor. There's one still in the dining room." He reached out to touch one golden strand curling over her shoulder. "Get some rest, lass. You've been through enough for one day. I'll take care of things here."

She slipped out of bed and left arm-in-arm with Coco.

Braden sent the chamberlain to fetch the doctor, then walked to the window and threw open the shutters. Breathing deeply, his relief was so enormous he felt light-headed. Perhaps this was only a brief reprieve, but at least, for this night, his darling would not have the marquess violating her lovely body.

CHAPTER

15

For three days and nights, the staff of the manor house moved through the halls like specters, with padded footsteps and whispered conversation. In the east wing, the Marquess of Staffordshire lay extremely ill in a state of semiconsciousness; in the west wing, Amanda remained in seclusion with Coco in attendance.

Braden rode during the cool morning hours to inspect the plantation's tobacco and onion fields. The tobacco fared poorly in the shallow island soil, but the onions were an increasingly popular and lucrative export. He spent the remainder of his day at his fledgling shipyards, where the *Wind Rose* was under construction, the great native red cedar crafted into a sloop of remarkable design. Offshore the marquess's merchantman rode at anchor in the calm bay waters. Braden would not initiate provisioning until there was some definite report on Pickering's health.

The morning of the fourth day after the wedding, he waited for Coco to make her usual foray to the kitchen, then knocked on Amanda's door.

"Who is it?" came the surprisingly vigorous reply.

"It's Braden. I've brought fresh-brewed coffee and grapes I just gathered from the vine. May I enter?"

It was a moment Amanda had longed for and dreaded. Though her strength had returned after a day of rest, she had purposely stayed in her rooms to avoid meeting Braden. It had not been necessary for her to visit her husband since his physician had kept her apprised of his condition. In fact the doctor had insisted she stay away from the desperately ill marquess.

Not that she had truly wanted to visit the sickroom. She had only offered because she knew it was the proper thing to do; he was, after all, her husband. She still found it hard to think of him as her husband, or indeed to think of him very much at all. Though she was humanely concerned with his suffering, she felt quite detached from him personally and guiltily admitted that the delay in fulfilling her wifely duties was more than welcome.

This morning she had been enjoying a quiet romp with Persephone. She smiled at the kitten rolling on its back, its front paws tangled in a fractious ball of yarn. At the sound of Braden's voice, she scooped up the pet and sat in the nearest chair.

Smoothing back her hair, she breathed deeply. "Aye, come in, my lord," she said as casually as possible.

He entered carrying a porcelain pot and a basket of grapes. His face expressed polite concern—nothing more.

"May I serve you?"

"Yes, thank you. The coffee smells delicious. There are cups on the table."

After pouring the fragrant dark liquid, he sat across from her and took a long look. "You appear rested," he commented after a few moments. "Thank God you show no signs of Pickering's illness."

"What do you think is wrong with him?"

"I don't know, but it does appear serious. The doctor hinted it could even be a fatal disease."

"I'm truly sorry for him. He didn't seem a bad sort,

though rather short of temper where you're concerned," she observed wryly.

"Natural enough. Can't blame him for that. Your beauty can drive a man to do some desperate deeds, if I may say so."

"Like challenging the man I planned to marry to a nonsensical duel?"

"The man *I* chose for you to marry, if you'll recall. I selected the marquess to be your husband, and I felt I had to make a serious attempt to undo that damage."

"So you did. I thank you for your concern, but sometimes damage cannot be repaired."

His eyes narrowed. If he thought she referred to his seducing her in the cave, he chose not to make a comment. He put down his cup with a clatter. "Amanda, the marriage was not consummated. Everyone knows that. It could be easily annulled if Pickering survives his illness."

"I've thought of that," she answered frankly. "But then I would lose all claim to the financial settlement arranged for Briarfield. My reputation as a desirable catch would be questioned. It might be difficult for me to find another husband, especially one of such wealth and prominence." Her words were as brittle as breaking glass.

"Good lord, Amanda," he erupted. "I've asked you more than once to marry *me*. You'll never make me believe you want to marry for money. Plenty of women do, but not you."

"I suppose I should be complimented. But your proposal lost some of its appeal after I learned of your *other* love—the current *mistress* of your house—the woman for whom you named your most prized possession— your ship, *The Tamara.*"

"I won't deny Tamara has been dear to me—always will be. But I don't love her, and I'm doing my best to divert her affection in another direction. In fact, she's moved from the house into the old slave quarters. I haven't seen her since the day before the wedding. My overseer, Manuel, is keeping an eye on her and, with luck and time, I hope will do more than that."

"I hear your words, but your actions indicate otherwise," she said, stroking Persephone.

"What are you talking about?" he demanded.

"I watched you and Tamara together the night of the picnic. You share this . . . this magic. Frankly, I don't understand it. You and she appear . . . possessed."

"Possessed?" He laughed heartily.

She arched one brow. "You could be a sorcerer for all I know, Lord Hamilton."

Grinning, he shook his head. "Let me assure you, I'm neither a sorcerer nor possessed." His smile changed. "At least I'm not possessed by little Tamara. Now . . . *you* . . . well . . . perhaps."

"Then how do you explain the fire? Or is that a secret only you and she can share?"

"Not at all. Swallowing fire is an old trick." He leaned forward and whispered, "I'll gladly reveal it to you, but you must keep the secret. It's an illusion easily done using sugar and soap as a protector. Careful timing is the key to eating the flames. As soon as the fire passes the lips, an exhaled breath blows it out."

It appeared he was being honest with her, and his laughter was quite irresistible. For the first time since she arrived in Bermuda, a glimmer of hope seeped into her innermost heart. "I see. Then I plead ignorance. Perhaps I should apologize for condemning you so quickly."

"I demand more than an apology."

"Oh?" she asked crisply.

"I demand a few hours of your time. You've been caged in here for days. The weather is perfect and the sea cool and inviting. Do you know how to swim?"

"I may be ignorant of some matters, but I do have a few basic skills. I learned to swim as a child in Virginia. But it's not considered a particularly ladylike pursuit."

"It is on Bermuda. Children, gents, ladies, one and all love the refreshing waters of the coast. I know a secluded cove where the sand slopes gently toward a reef of incredible beauty. One of my favorite pastimes is diving near the reef, where a sunken Spanish galleon still holds treasure—similar to the cross I gave you."

She remembered how she had thrust the magnificent jeweled necklace to the bottom of her jewel box. "How do you find the treasure?" she asked with interest.

"It's simple. I have some special diving equipment. Why not come with me this afternoon and I'll show you how it works."

How wonderful it sounded. But still she hesitated. "What about the marquess? What if he should ask for me . . . or die while we were away? Why, it would be scandalous if anyone knew I frolicked with you while my husband lay on his deathbed."

"His doctor told me a few minutes ago that Pickering's condition is unchanged. He could lie there for days before his illness turns one way or the other. Only the doctor and a servant are allowed in the chamber. Surely no one could expect you to stay confined for such a long time. Besides, it takes a great amount of scandal to shock anyone on Bermuda. Our citizens are much too preoccupied to bother with trivial behavior."

"Very well," she agreed brightly, "if we don't go too far from the plantation, and if, Captain Hamilton, you remember at all times that I'm a married woman—a marchioness, in fact."

He stood and bowed deeply. "God strike me dead if I forget, my lady," he quipped.

"What does one wear in Bermuda for public swimming?"

"A cotton shift will do. Wear it under your regular clothing. This will make changing very simple. We'll swim, then dry in the sun before we return."

She laughed happily—her first laughter in days. "Oh, I'm certain this adventure is completely outrageous. But as usual, Captain, you tempt me beyond my power to resist. Are you sure you're not the Devil in disguise?"

Smiling, he took her hand. "Today I will behave like a

saint. I give you my word—Marchioness. If I am the Devil, you'll see no sign of my wicked soul."

Braden was true to his promise—at least for a while. He escorted Amanda to a secluded sandy beach at the far tip of the plantation and treated her as if she were a member of the royal family and he was her obedient subject.

When she shyly removed her dress and waded into the curling surf, he acted as if this were nothing out of the ordinary and encouraged her to relax and enjoy herself while she had the chance.

His swimming garb consisted of cotton breeches cut off at the knees, bound at the waist native style with a cord of hemp.

Without touching her, he guided her away from the shore until they bobbed in the gently rolling waves like two children, laughing and sputtering and treading water to stay afloat.

Yes, she could swim, but her skill hardly compared to the powerful strokes and expert surface dives that he enjoyed demonstrating.

After he executed one particularly long dive, she called to him, "You were gone so long I thought you'd found treasure."

"I'm working on it," he answered across the water. "But wait. I must get something on the shore."

She planted her toes in the sand and held her position while he swam to the beach with strong, graceful strokes. When he returned, he was towing a large floating metal pot attached to a long rope. He pushed a wooden plank in front of him. His progress was slow and awkward, but finally he reached her side.

"What's all this?" she asked.

"'Tis what I wanted to show you. I made this to use in my search for shipwrecks. Float the plank in front of you and look down through the glass that's inserted in the middle."

She followed his directions. The sudden clarity of everything beneath the surface was a breathtaking sight. There were her toes and Braden's feet plainly visible. She saw shells and bits of coral and rainbow-colored fish darting about the hem of her shift.

"It's absolutely beautiful," she gasped. "More of your magic, I presume."

"Hold on to the board and kick out to that first protruding boulder. I'll be diving there."

As he swam beside her, pulling the odd kettle behind him, she did as he instructed. Peering at intervals through the glass, she was intrigued to see the deepening sandy bottom become strewn with half-buried timbers partially concealed by waving green fern.

"This is the spot," he called. "I'm going down. There's a reef below where a Spanish galleon perished three years ago. I come here often. Rarely do I fail to find a coin or an artifact from the wreck. Watch me through the glass."

"But what is that bowl you're pulling?"

"It's a breathing pot. I turn it upside down—like this. Then I pull it down as I go. When I can no longer hold my breath, I'll pop up inside and find a bubble of air at the top. I'll take a deep breath, then continue my search for treasure. It doubles the time I can stay on the bottom."

"My, how clever."

"Here I go," he said and winked.

"Good luck," she cried as he inhaled and sliced downward.

Quickly she put her face to the glass and watched in fascination as he moved gracefully amid bubbles and churning sand along the bottom. The sight was perfectly clear. Again she marveled at Braden's lithe body. She saw him put his head into the breathing pot, then return to his exploration. From among shifting sand and waving greenery, he drew an object, then looked up to signal her. In moments he emerged at her shoulder, sputtering and shaking water from his thick hair. Wiping his hand across his eyes, he grinned proudly.

"You found something!" she said in excitement.

"Aye. Not as valuable as the cross, but a treasure nonetheless." He held up a woman's earring made of delicate gold filigree set with a small pearl in the center.

"It's exquisite," she breathed, then held it up to her ear.

"Yes," he agreed, his voice becoming low and intimate. "Exquisite is a good description."

Looking into his intense indigo eyes, she felt the familiar thrill course through her body. "I don't suppose you could find the mate," she asked lightly to mask her surge of emotion.

"Aha, I thought you'd ask." His eyes twinkled as he produced the second earring and handed it to her.

They laughed simultaneously and when their laughter ended, she moved into his arms.

With their heads just above the surface he kissed her, a kiss of unleashed passion flavored with the salty moisture of the sea.

"Take a deep breath," he murmured.

She did and with arms entwined they slipped beneath the surface and drifted downward, downward, revolving slowly, her hair floating around their heads like a veil of dark gold. He covered her lips with his, holding her locked in an embrace like an ancient god of the sea descending with his captive maiden. The moment his feet touched bottom, he gathered his legs and pushed upward, rising swiftly with one arm extended, the other drawing her along at his side.

They surfaced beside the boulder. He grasped it, then held her close against his bare chest while kissing her again, letting his breath flow through his lips and fill her needy lungs. He drew the breath back, keeping his arm firmly wrapped around her waist.

She moaned in sensuous delight and ran her hands along the moist, heated flesh of his muscular shoulders.

He lifted her upper body above the water; her shift clung to her, outlining every inch of her figure. Lowering his head, he softly nuzzled her rounded breasts.

"Braden . . . Braden, my love . . ." she whispered and

laid back her head while instinctively wrapping her legs around his hips. She could feel his hardness pressing between her thighs; desire raced through her like a storm-driven deluge. Only his hold on the rock kept them from sinking. Could they make love? she wondered. Here in the sea? She thought so . . . and the thought sent throbbing desire to the deepest recesses of her womanhood.

Suddenly his hands encircled her waist and carefully, but firmly, he moved her away.

Her legs dropped and she put her hands behind his neck to float against him.

"No, Marchioness. I want you, God knows, but I gave you my word."

"I know," she said as another wave lifted her against him. She felt his body heat through the coolness of the water.

"I must respect my promise—and your vows."

"Yes, of course," she murmured, struggling to match his self-control with her own.

"But, at least you have the earrings," he said in an attempt at a lighter tone.

"No, I don't," she said, her voice strained and touched with sadness. "I'm afraid I dropped them."

He kissed her forehead, using his lips to push back damp curls. "Then, Mandy my dear, today's treasures have eluded us both. But perhaps we'll find them tomorrow."

A combination of salt and tears burned into her eyes. "I don't know, Braden. I can't think of tomorrow."

"Captain!" came a shout from the shore. "Captain! Come quickly."

"It's Manuel," said Braden. "We'd better get back. Something must be seriously wrong. I told him to come here only in an emergency."

With the waves assisting them, they soon made the beach. Amanda pulled herself dripping from the water while Braden deposited the plank and the diving kettle safely ashore.

"What is it, Manuel? What's wrong?" he asked, while retrieving his boots.

Manuel politely averted his eyes from the soaked girl. "The doctor told me to find the two of you. He said it was urgent. He wants you both to come at once, señor."

Amanda squeezed water from her length of hair and picked up her dress. "I'm too wet to put this on," she said, starting to shiver despite the sun's warmth.

"Never mind," said Braden. He swept her into his arms and strode up the hill toward the house.

"Amanda, go to your rooms and change, then meet me in my study as soon as possible." His grim tone matched her own feelings.

Over his shoulder she took one last lingering look at the sun-splashed beach and expanse of sparkling blue sea rolling onto the curve of sand. A sense of foreboding gripped her heart.

Withdrawing her arms from his neck, she nodded mutely. Behind them, now only a memory, the cove returned to a state of serene seclusion.

CHAPTER
16

Plague!

The word hung in the air like a portentous clap of thunder.

Amanda gripped the arms of her chair and stared at the doctor in tight-lipped horror.

"I'm sorry, my lady," the physician continued. "There is no longer any doubt. Your husband must have contracted it during the voyage, perhaps from someone on the ship."

"Is . . . is he dying?"

"Quite likely, I'm afraid. He is not young, and he shows no signs of rallying. I assure you, I've done all I can," he added wearily.

Braden moved from where he leaned against his desk and put his hand on the doctor's shoulder. "We're most appreciative, Roger. I told the marchioness that you're as fine a physician as any to be had—trained in Boston with the best. Has my staff been helpful enough?"

"Excellent, thank you. The African women are utterly fearless and quite good with the patient. But smallpox is not easily defeated even by the young and vigorous."

"Get some rest, sir. I'll do what has to be done,"

Braden said. "I'll give orders at once to transfer the ship's crew to Gates Fort and keep them isolated. After necessary valuables are removed, the ship will be sailed off the coast and burned. I'll take it out myself. Naturally everyone here at the plantation is quarantined—as of now. I'll send a messenger to the servants' quarters. The important thing is to prevent the spread of the disease, if it isn't too late."

Rubbing his head in fatigue, the doctor left the room.

Braden turned to Amanda. "I wouldn't have wished him the pox. Not even to set you free."

"I know. It's terrible news. And of course we're all at risk. Must you sail his ship yourself?"

"I know the tides and currents. I can scuttle it with the help of his first mate and one other. I don't want to risk any more lives than necessary."

She sighed deeply. "I understand. It's just so unfair. Bermuda is an unspoiled paradise. But now evil intrudes from afar and brings this nightmare. I feel much to blame."

He dropped to one knee beside her and took her hand. "Don't say that, Mandy. Ships from ports around the world call here year-round. It could have come anytime from anywhere. Besides, I'm the one who invited the marquess—much to my regret, for more reasons than one."

She was about to offer a kiss when the door abruptly swung open and Coco rushed in. "Mistress Amanda, I jus' heard the news!"

Braden rose. "So quickly? From whom did you hear it, Coco? I'd like to keep panic from spreading."

"In the kitchen. Your . . . ah . . . friend, Mistress Tamara, was there. She had jus' heard and went flyin' to the quarters."

"Tamara? I haven't seen her in days." He glanced at Amanda.

Coco continued, "She said she was comin' right back, soon as she warned all the others. She said she will see you then, Captain Hamilton."

"Well, I won't be here—not until tonight. I'm headed for the marquess's merchantman. Amanda, I must ask for your understanding, no matter what happens during this crisis. Do I have it?"

"Of course," she assured him.

"When I return tonight, we'll have a small gathering here in my library. I need complete cooperation from everyone. I want you and Coco and your uncle Hugh, the doctor, Manuel and Tamara—all of you here or on the veranda if it's warm." He touched her arm. "Will you attend?" he asked more gently.

"I'll do whatever you say." Standing, she placed her hands on his shoulders. "Just please be careful," she murmured.

He smiled down at her, then kissed her forehead. "Go now and have Coco do something with your hair. 'Tis rather in disarray and dappled with salt." His gentle teasing won him a smile in return.

With determined steps she left the room, followed closely by Coco.

Braden and the six people he had invited gathered quietly on the veranda overlooking the sea. The night was clear and unusually still as the others pulled up cane chairs facing their host. Hugh sat next to Amanda, holding her hand protectively. At her other side sat Coco. Beside Coco was Manuel Rodriquez and next to him, Tamara. Completing the group was the physician.

A kerosene torch threw a soft light over their solemn faces. At this dark hour, everyone's attention was drawn to a distant flame. To the northwest, several miles from the coast, the death pyre of the English merchantman made an ominous glow in the velvet tropical night.

Amanda squeezed her uncle's hand. Her emotions were ragged, almost numb after all that had happened since her arrival in Bermuda. She had no further animosity toward Tamara. The pretty, sad-faced girl might even be her friend someday, she thought. This was no time for feelings of jealousy and childish plotting. She thought also of her husband on his deathbed not far away. The man was a total stranger, but one who had changed her life dramatically. And he might inadvertently cause her death. It was all so tragically ironic.

Braden leaned back in his fan-shaped straw chair and addressed the group. Though freshly bathed and wearing an immaculate white cotton shirt and linen breeches, his eyes were sunken and deeply troubled. "As you can see, the marquess's vessel will soon be on the bottom of the bay. The crew is at the fort, by now well into their cups. And why not? Would any of you care for a drink?"

Not even Hugh accepted the offer as everyone murmured in the negative.

"I won't keep you long. But what I have to say is extremely important. After I'm finished, you may go, but I would ask Lady Pickering to remain for a few minutes. I've some items from the ship you should have, my lady."

She nodded her agreement.

"I have an order and an extremely important recommendation for each of you. The order is that no one leaves the vicinity of this house for at least one week. No one will be allowed to enter. We have ample stores for everyone's comfort. When the marquess dies, his body will be cremated and his ashes buried in the Anglican cemetery at St. George. At some future time an appropriate state funeral will be held and news of his passing sent to England on the first ship traveling east.

"Now for my recommendation. My ward, Tamara, approached me a short time ago with a startling idea. Not a new idea—only new to me—and no doubt to most of you. Bear with me and I will explain. In Turkey for many years, a simple process has been used to protect people from the plague—smallpox as we call it. It is widely used and quite successful, she says. I know it's hard for Christian communities to imagine anything of a medically advanced nature coming from a non-Christian part of the world, but nonetheless, the process has been used there and many lives saved as a result. I'm not a man with medical knowledge, but I have named the method *transplantation.* It consists of making an incision in the flesh of a healthy person and placing into it tissue from an infected person. The well person then suffers a very mild case of smallpox, followed by complete recovery. That person will remain immune to the disease for quite some time—months or years, though more study is necessary to determine the time period."

"My God!" the doctor interrupted. "It's completely insane. No one would submit to such a process."

"I agree," Hugh barked. "It's blasphemous as well as absurd. Who would take the word of . . . of a simple Turkish slave girl? We're talking life and death here."

"Wait," Coco said, jumping to her feet and bravely facing the group. "May I speak, Captain?"

"Of course, Coco."

"Mistress Tamara is not the only person who knows of this process. In fact, I've had it done to me years ago in Virginia. It worked jus' fine."

"In Virginia?" Amanda asked.

"Yes, ma'am. Once when the sickness started in the quarters. I had the treatment and all the other slaves did too. We had a fever for a time, then we was all well. Some white people died, but none of us did. The old woman who gave us the treatment was from Africa. She say it's done there but sometimes with the . . . ah . . . tissue of a sick cow, if one is found."

"Sick cow!" shouted Hugh. "Now that *is* ridiculous. I'll have no part of it. Sounds like witches' tales to me."

"Nor will I," said the physician. "If the best doctors in England and Massachusetts can't cure the plague, I doubt the Turks or Africans can do it. In fact I'm shocked, Captain Hamilton, to hear you support this nonsense."

"I'm sorry you don't agree, Roger. I had hoped you would help perform the transplantation on all who are willing to have it—here and in other parts of the island. I'm convinced it will save lives."

"Well, I won't and that's final. It could spread the

disease to everyone in Bermuda. You can be certain I'll advise everyone I know to abstain from such folly."

Braden shook his head. "I'm disappointed. But naturally I can't force anyone to do it. Tamara knows the proper procedure and the proper amount, so she says. It could be too late for me, but I intend to have the transplantation and I strongly urge everyone else to do so, especially those of us at Hamilton Plantation."

Amanda moved to kneel in a billow of skirts at Braden's side. "Captain . . . Braden, are you determined to do this?"

He looked at her for a long moment, then answered, "I've been on the plague ship. Without the treatment, I would surely face death. Aye, I'll have it done within the hour."

"Do you also insist I have it?"

His look was heavy with concern. "I pray you will. Even though there is risk. It will certainly cause illness, maybe even death. But yes, I hope you will trust me in this, my dear girl." He finished in a voice low with feeling.

She nodded. "Then I will." She rose and faced Coco. "You also think it's wise?"

"Yes, ma'am. And I will have it too. I had it so long ago I might not be safe now."

Amanda turned to Hugh. "I pray you to reconsider, Uncle."

"No," he said firmly. "It's the Devil's work. If I could, I would take a ship at once for Boston and take you with me, like it or not. I took responsibility for you, Amanda Sheffield. If you do this unholy thing, I wash my hands of you—niece or no!" He stomped from the veranda into the house.

The doctor also headed for the door. "I'm going to check on my patient. I won't leave his quarters again, and I will stay here for a week after he dies. As for this . . . this transplantation business—I'll have none of it."

Amanda reached for Tamara's hand. "We haven't had

a chance to become acquainted, Tamara. I hope we can become friends, after all."

Tamara took the outstretched hand, but only for a moment, then withdrew it and said sharply, "We have work to do. Earlier today the lady caring for your husband scraped tissue from his body. The doctor didn't know, of course. I have it with me. All the servants in the quarters have been treated. So have I." She looked at Manuel. "Will you agree to it, señor?"

"I . . . I don't know," he said, frowning. "I'd like to consult the priest."

Braden stood. "Everyone who is willing come into my study. I'll have Tamara administer the treatment to me at once. The rest of you can choose to wait a few hours to see the results." He gave a half smile to Amanda. "If a devil such as I can survive, the rest of you should be safe enough."

Within a short time, everything was in readiness in the bright light of the library. Braden sat on the edge of his desk with his sleeve rolled high along his upper arm.

Amanda watched closely as Tamara lifted the small scalded knife blade. For an instant she met Tamara's cool, deep brown eyes. Her smile of encouragement received no answering response.

Then Tamara turned to her work. She made a small cut in the flesh of Braden's arm and dabbed several drops of fluid from a vial into the wound. There was only a trace of blood and he made no complaint. Afterward she wrapped the arm tightly with clean cotton. The procedure was very simple and very quick.

He smiled. "Done. And no goblins or lightning have appeared as yet to punish me."

"I'll do it too," Manuel now said bravely. "You saved my life more than once, Captain. And if Tamara believes in it, I'd like to try."

Tamara gave Manuel a pleased smile and again prepared the knife while he rolled up his sleeve.

Amanda pursed her lips, then said, "Well, I don't see any reason to wait until tomorrow. After Señor Rodriquez, I'll be next—if Tamara will oblige. Coco can follow me, if she likes."

"Yes, ma'am." Coco heaved a sigh of relief. "We'll all be sickly tomorrow and another day or two. But then we'll be jus' fine. At least I'm pretty sure we'll be so," she added hopefully.

After the treatments were completed, Braden excused Coco and asked Manuel to escort Tamara back to the servants' quarters, where she was determined to stay.

Alone now, Amanda and Braden gazed at each other for a long, poignant moment.

Finally Braden extended his hand. Amanda walked around the desk and eased into his lap. Resting her head on his shoulder, she said softly, "Your Tamara may have saved our lives. I'll never forget that."

"I'm sorry she insists on staying at the quarters. I've always treated her more like a daughter than a servant, and she's lived in the main house with rooms of her own. She can be a bit tempestuous, but she's still very young."

"Braden, I do apologize. She's more than welcome in the house. I had no right to suggest otherwise."

"Your apology is accepted, but I didn't ask her to leave. I suppose she disliked sharing a roof with you as much as you did with her. All female nonsense as far as I'm concerned."

"Then your understanding of women is incomplete," she quipped.

"I'm learning," he said, caressing her arm. "But Tamara is such a headstrong, inexperienced little soul. I told Manuel to keep watch over her, but . . ."

She stirred in his arms. "Maybe you should go see about her. Don't let me detain you."

He slipped an arm around her waist. "Damnation, woman, I see green sparks in those golden eyes. One minute you're above jealousy and the next, your temper's on the rise again."

She relaxed a bit. "You're right. I suppose I'm just being difficult. I promise to do better." Her eyes clouded. "If only we all survive this awful disease."

"We will. I'm sure of it. All except poor old Pickering. Oh yes, that reminds me . . ." Reaching across her, he opened the drawer to his desk and pulled out a sizeable iron box. "This came from the safe on the merchantman. It had your name on it. All the other papers and valuables are at the fort."

She stood to inspect the box. *Amanda Sheffield Pickering* was plainly etched on its surface.

"Should I open it?"

"Certainly. It's yours."

"It's just that I don't feel right about claiming anything of the marquess's."

"Listen to me, Amanda. He came all this way to make you his wife. You married him and made him happy on his last healthy day on earth. In truth, had he lived, I'd have pleaded for an annulment, even though you would have lost everything. But he's dying. He has no heirs. You're his legal wife. If nothing else, you're entitled to this box and its contents."

Carefully she opened the box. A large folded parchment lay inside atop two velvet pouches. She opened the parchment, read it, then handed it to him.

"Hmm. Extremely generous. This assigns a substantial sum to you to be used for Briarfield Plantation in Virginia. It's far and above the original amount promised. Your brother will be delighted if he gets his hands on this. What about the pouches?"

She emptied one sack onto his desk. Exquisite gems of various types and sizes, all unmounted, glittered before them. Several of the diamonds were large enough to be of great value.

"Dear heaven," she gasped. "Why would he give me so much?"

"He was a very rich man and close to King Charles when the monarchy was restored. And you, my dear, were to bear his only offspring, if you remember. What's in the other sack?"

The second pouch contained a heavy golden coronet

set with several dozen diamonds and rubies of extraordinary size. Even Braden was momentarily awed.

"It's incredible," Amanda finally murmured. "Fit for a
queen. Oh, Braden, I don't think I should keep it."

"There's no one else more deserving. Certainly not
some distant cousin in England who probably meant
nothing to him." He took the crown and placed it atop
her head. "Yes," he said, "it suits you, my princess.
Though 'tis outshone by your own fair beauty."

She took it off and put it back into the pouch. "I'm
sorry, I just don't feel right wearing it. Maybe I could sell
it. Just think how much good could be done for Briarfield
—or for the sick and the poor—in exchange for that one
gaudy bauble for a woman's hair."

"Your generosity shames me, Mandy. I fear I've always
been more a bandit than a benefactor."

She smiled up at him. "But a bandit with a good heart
and much courage. With such qualities, wealth is not so
important."

"Still, one must be practical. As the wife—or as the
widow—of the Marquess of Staffordshire, you're a very
wealthy woman, a woman of independent means. It was
thoughtful of him to provide for you. His estates, of
course, will go to his blood kin—or to the Crown, if the
king so desires."

She shook her head. "It's confusing and quite sad. And
I'm so tired." She placed her hand over the bandage on
her arm.

"Are you in pain?" he asked gently.

"A bit. No more than you, I'm sure."

He pulled her into his arms and kissed her forehead. "You do feel feverish. It could be the treatment,
or heat from today's outing in the sun." He smoothed
back her hair and held her close for a long moment.
"Go to bed now, my brave little Mandy. Let your body
rest and fight the disease. I pray to God that Tamara
and Coco are right. If . . . if anything happened to
you . . ."

"Shh." She touched one finger to his lips. "All will be well. We'll meet again in a few days. Then we'll discuss the future."

He grasped her hand and kissed the palm.

"Take care, my love," she whispered. Then she turned away before she could be tempted to linger.

CHAPTER
17

Carrying a tray with a teapot and cup, Manuel entered the bedroom of his lord. He smiled broadly at Braden and placed the tray on the bedside table. "*Buenos días,* señor. I took this from Lucy and promised to see to it you drank every drop of her concoction. She swears it will put you on your feet in no time."

Braden pushed up on his pillows. "Hell, the stuff tastes like boiled frog tits laced with water from the mangrove swamp."

"You're looking better, Captain. You've been sleeping like a dead man. We were worried . . ."

"Sleep was all I could do with any gusto. I'm feeling much better today. One thing's certain, I've been abed far too long."

"Only two days longer than I, señor. All of us have been sick with fever and chills. But it appears we'll all recover, thanks be to God."

"How is Lady Pickering?"

"She appears well now. In fact, she has stopped by your room several times this morning. I caught her stealing a look inside more than once—much to Mistress Tamara's annoyance."

177

"Tamara . . . and Amanda? Good lord." He chuckled at the thought. "You mean those two ladies have been taking turns at my sickbed? If I'd known, I'd have recovered sooner just to see the sight."

Manuel grinned. "They have gone about their duties quietly—united by a common concern, I suppose."

"And what about the marquess?"

Manuel's face grew solemn. He announced, "On August fourth, at two-fifteen in the morning, Lord Dudley Pickering, Marquess of Staffordshire, departed this earth due to smallpox." He made the sign of the cross.

"Um. August fourth. When was that?"

"Four days past, señor."

"Anyone else?"

"Three of his crew are dead. Three more gravely ill. All are confined at the fort . . . with proper care, of course."

"No one in Bermuda?"

"None."

"Thank God." Braden threw aside the sheet and started to rise. "Damnation." He sank back on the pillow.

"You must eat, Captain. It will help the weakness pass."

"You're damned right it will pass. I have much to do. Among the first is my marriage to Lady Pickering." He rubbed the stubble on his chin. "Get the razor, Manuel. And my pants. And feed that gruel to the potted plant. On second thought, you'd better not. I'd hate to kill the thing."

"But, señor . . ."

"Do as I say. I must receive the lady in proper fashion."

"But, señor . . . she may not see you."

"What do you mean?" he said, swinging his legs from the bed. "See here, I'm feeling much better already. Hungry enough to eat a snake."

"I'm pleased, señor. But the lady may not come."

"And why not? She's been here while I was sleeping, you said. Why not now?"

"As soon as I told her you were awake, she hurried away."

"Well, help me bathe, then go get the girl," he fairly shouted. "I want to set a date for our wedding."

Manuel was gone less than ten minutes when he returned and bowed Amanda into the room, then quickly made his exit.

Braden was dressed and clean-shaven, pale but smiling, when she walked in. He looked at her for some time before speaking. At last he said, "We survived, Marchioness. Please remove your veil and come into my arms."

To his surprise, she remained steadfastly by the door. She did, however, lift her veil. With head high, she answered coolly, "I am relieved you are near recovery, Braden. But as you can plainly see, I'm in mourning. I hardly think your arms are the proper place for a widow to express her grief."

"Your *grief!* Amanda, the door is closed behind you. We're entirely alone. Whatever appropriate behavior you have adopted since the marquess's death, you are now here with me. You have no need to speak of *grief.*"

Garbed in heavy black, her veil flowing behind her, she lifted her head regally. "The marquess was my husband. Not for long, I admit. But he left me with prestige and wealth. As his widow, I owe him the respect of a proper period of mourning."

"All right. How long has he been dead?"

"Four days."

"Long enough." He bridged the distance and pulled her into his arms.

She allowed the embrace, but stiffened perceptively.

Keeping an arm around her, he cupped her chin in his hand and forced her to look at him. Her face was pale as alabaster, and blue circles shadowed her eyes. "Darling girl," he murmured. "Forgive me. In the satisfaction of my returning strength, I failed to consider all you've endured. I want you to become my wife, but not until you're ready. We can delay awhile if you prefer." He touched his lips to her forehead. "But I hope not too long," he whispered.

Her eyes were distant and lifeless. "I'm exhausted, Braden, to the center of my bones. I've had much time to think while lying in bed with the fever. My husband's ashes are still unburied. The money he left to Briarfield is not yet delivered. My uncle is deeply annoyed with me and wants to return home immediately. I do love you, of course, but so much has happened. I . . . I feel I've aged a dozen years in a single week."

Gently he stroked her cheek. "No doubt, little one. Again I apologize for my lack of consideration. Why don't you rest a few days. Bathe in the sea. I want to see your cheeks bloom again and hear your laughter. At least the fear of plague is behind us."

"Braden," she said firmly, moving from his embrace. "I want to go to Boston with Uncle Hugh and then home to Briarfield. I'd like you to take me, if you will."

"Home?" He stared at her in disbelief. "But, Amanda, I want this to be your home. As soon as the *Wind Rose* is ready, I'll send Hugh to Boston. He can deliver the funds to your brother following your directions. Certainly there's no need for you . . ." His voice trailed when he saw her determined look. He was still weak and his fatigue shortened his temper. "You . . . you do intend to go, then?"

"As soon as possible. If you will take me to Boston, we can rest there briefly, then sail to Jamestown. Naturally I'll pay all expenses."

"Hell, Amanda," he snapped in frustration, "forget the money! If you want to go—we'll go. I'll start provisioning the frigate at once. We could sail in three days, if that's your wish."

"That would be fine." She turned to go, but hesitated. "Oh, yes, I'd like to bury my husband's ashes before leaving. Could that be arranged?"

"Yes—Marchioness," he said icily. "Your *husband* will receive all due respect."

After she closed the door, Braden sank into the nearest

chair. His knees felt like water and his hands were shaking. He must get some nourishment, he thought, or he'd end up back in his sickbed. God's blood, he didn't understand women. He rested his head in his hands. Well, he had a long journey ahead. Somewhere along the way, he'd convince Amanda Sheffield to become his wife.

By the following day, Amanda's gloomy mood had indeed begun to lift. She slept a solid twelve hours and woke with an appetite. After a hearty breakfast eaten on her patio while Persephone played in the shafts of sun at her feet, she was feeling quite invigorated. Things weren't so bad after all. She was happy Braden had been so accommodating about taking her to the mainland. The trip would give her time to make serious plans for the future. Naturally she would marry Braden at some appropriate time—perhaps at Jamestown in the little church on the Commons—followed by a reception in the grand dining room at Briarfield.

Sipping the strong coffee, she contemplated the scene: Old Reverend Trask could conduct the ceremony; Philip would give her away, like it or not, and play host to a sumptuous meal elegantly served to guests from town. How different it would be from the dreadful experience of her wedding to the marquess.

What would she wear? she wondered, smiling now in anticipation, imagining the ceremony and her walk down the aisle with Braden waiting by the altar. Could she wear her mother's wedding dress? White would be unseemly, she supposed. And how long should she observe mourning? A year would be proper, but not at all convenient. Perhaps four months would do. In fact, Christmas would be a delightful time for the wedding.

Lost in thought, she put down her cup. She would have to speak to Braden about building a home at Briarfield. Though, of course, they would spend some of the year here in Bermuda. She stretched her arms above her head, luxuriating in the balmy air. Yes, Bermuda was a wonderful place and Braden would make her happy all of her days. She would accept Tamara for his sake. Surely the girl would find a husband of her own before long— maybe that good-looking Spaniard, Manuel, who so obviously adored her.

She left the table and went indoors. "Coco," she called, but her maid was absent. Never mind, she could begin packing without her. She felt ever so much better today. The only unpleasant chore that remained was to take Lord Pickering's ashes to the churchyard. She'd don heavy mourning once more this afternoon, then put her weeds away till she reached Boston. She pulled open a drawer and began tossing items to the bed. Tomorrow— tomorrow danced in her head. Tomorrow Braden would take her home.

Braden's frigate, *The Tamara,* was provisioned and ready to receive passengers by noon, August 11.

Hugh had boarded early and was busy aiding in the last-minute inspection of the ship. He made it quite clear he wanted little to do with his niece and her maid—or Captain Hamilton for that matter. He had not forgiven any of them for their slide into heresy. He felt fine, so they had no cause to gloat over their own escape from the pox.

Amanda arrived with her belongings just after noon. Her trunks and boxes were stored aboard and Coco began organizing their quarters. The maid had laughingly told her that all she did these days was "pack and unpack, hang and fold, press and polish." She'd be glad when they "settled in one place or t'other."

Amanda took a spot at the rail with Persephone tucked under her arm. The cat had grown since they left Boston and was plump and content, no longer likely to scamper away to find a hiding place.

An hour passed, then two. Everything was in readiness, but Braden hadn't been seen since midmorning, when he had returned home after a final check of the ship. The breeze was up and the tide right for sailing. As more time passed, Amanda began to feel uneasy. She prowled around her cabin, ate a small snack, then returned to her place by the rail.

The sun was starting to dip toward the west when Braden strode up the gangplank and engaged his first mate in a lengthy conversation. He then turned and shouted to the waiting crew, "Prepare to weigh anchor." Then he hurried up the steps and faced her, his look heavy with concern.

"What's wrong?" she asked, easing Persephone to the deck.

"It's Tamara. She's missing."

"But I saw her this morning. Maybe she didn't want to tell you good-bye."

"'Tis more than that. She's been . . . well, depressed of late. I knew she was upset, in a sort of childish fit of jealousy . . . or so I thought."

"She does adore you, you know."

"She depends on me, and she fancies herself in love. As I've told you before, I expect her to switch her affection before long to Manuel Rodriquez, who is certainly in love with her."

"You say she's missing?"

"Yes. And worse than that, she has threatened to take her life."

Amanda gasped. "Suicide?"

Braden shook his head. "I don't know. She left a scribbled note pinned to Manuel's door about an hour ago. He searched the estate high and low, then brought me the note. I'm afraid he's taking this very seriously."

She studied his face. "But *you* are not?" she ventured.

"Hellfire, I don't understand women," he snapped. "The little scamp could be playing a trick to keep me from sailing, or she could be foolish enough to think she can't live without me. Whatever the case, I can't leave Bermuda until she's found."

"I see," she said, not quite sure how she should respond. Naturally he must help Tamara if the girl was in trouble, but perhaps there was more to it than that. She tried to read his expression. The Braden standing before her with his hands on his hips was a man she hardly recognized. It was as if he were daring her to argue with him. He was looking at her, taking time to explain, but his thoughts were obviously elsewhere.

"What am I supposed to say, Braden? The ship is about to sail. I heard you give the order."

"It sails without me."

So that was it. He was sending her away while he went in search of Tamara, and he wanted her to know he had no time for argument.

"You must find her, by all means. But I won't leave without you. We can wait—delay the voyage."

His look mellowed. He put his hands on her shoulders. "Listen, my darling. I know you want to go to Boston, and your uncle is determined to leave at once."

"But . . . what about you . . . our plans?"

"I'll follow as soon as possible. The *Wind Rose* is ready for launching. Actually, I'm eager to test her. With luck, I might overtake you in midocean." He attempted a reassuring smile.

Her heart was in her throat. Was he telling her the truth? Had he changed his mind about marrying her? Could he be using Tamara's disappearance as an excuse to end their relationship? She admitted to herself she had been less than charming these past days.

"I can see you have no choice," she said with effort. She couldn't resist adding, "You were right, Braden, when you described your island as a wind rose. The forces surrounding Bermuda, and you yourself, are like that—tumultuous and unpredictable."

A gruff voice interrupted the moment. "What's the delay, Captain?"

She turned to see Hugh approaching, his scowl revealing his impatience.

"Tamara's missing," Braden said. "She's threatened suicide. I can't leave until she's found and placed in safe hands."

"Then stay. I built this ship, and I can make certain it reaches Boston in good order."

"Uncle, please, I know you're angry with us over the treatment, but I don't think we should leave without Braden."

"Nonsense. I absolutely refuse to stay on this plague-infested, ungodly island one more hour. We'll sail at once with the tide and the ship can return after we've been safely deposited in New England. I suppose, Hamilton, your Mister Stiles knows how to captain the ship in your absence."

"He does. Your leaving presents no real problem. I'll follow as soon as possible in the new sloop. Is that agreeable, Amanda?" he asked, his impatience all too evident.

"All right, Braden," she managed. "I can't win against the two of you—and naturally, I want you to help Tamara." She prayed her voice didn't betray her inner doubts and deep disappointment.

He leaned near and gave her a quick kiss. "Don't worry, Mandy. I'll see you soon." Without a backward glance, he hurried down the steps and across the gang-plank to the dock.

She waved and called after him, "Braden, be careful. I love you." If he heard, he didn't respond. Her uncle quickly left her side.

The plank was pulled in and the sails hauled into the wind, which blew seaward out of a distant thunderhead.

She gripped the rail as Persephone meowed and curled around her ankles beneath the hem of her skirts. Picking the animal up and cuddling her, she stared longingly at Braden's disappearing figure. "He's gone, Perci," she whispered. "I thought we'd be together always, and he's gone so suddenly. I didn't have time to tell him . . . oh, Perci, I pray he'll come back to me." Running her fingers through the soft fur, she tried to convince herself all would be well.

Braden hurried to the stable, where Manuel waited with two saddled horses. He would have preferred to linger at Amanda's side, but the ship needed to catch the wind and the tide. For the moment, he would have to deal with this problem, just in case Tamara was serious in her thinly veiled threat. At least Amanda was safe; soon he would be with her. Tamara could be in serious danger, though he couldn't conceive of the girl becoming so desperate she would actually kill herself. Her note to Manuel had said, "Farewell, my friend—I am empty and the depths will receive me. Tell Braden . . ." It was incomplete and unsigned, but Braden recognized the careful lettering he had taught Tamara years ago. It was also plain that the note was intended more for him than for Manuel, to whom it had been delivered. He would wager a sizeable bet the note was nothing more than a ploy to keep him from leaving with Amanda. Manuel was so smitten with her, he may have overreacted to the situation, but still, she must be found.

"Do you have any idea where she's gone?" he asked Manuel as he swung into the saddle.

"She isn't on the estate; I've looked everywhere."

"Did you question the servants?"

"A few. But most left at midafternoon for the mangrove swamp. They've planned a picnic and bonfire for the evening."

"Umm, I suppose to celebrate my exodus."

"Just an innocent gathering."

"'Tis fair enough," Braden observed. "Why in hell didn't Tamara go along and join the fun instead of creating this mess?" he added under his breath. More loudly he asked, "What do you think she meant by 'the depths will receive me'? Does she intend to drown herself?"

"Possibly—if she's really serious. She has occasionally confided in me, you know, but she never talked about death."

"We'll go to Spanish Point. 'Tis a favorite spot of hers, and the tides are often strong." Braden put his mount into a gallop along the path cutting across the island. Maintaining a swift pace kept him from thinking about the possibility that Tamara might simply disappear, slip away into the cool depths of the tropical sea, and leave him with a load of guilt, whether deserved or not.

Within the hour, they arrived at the deserted beach. The twilight gave the lovely spot an ethereal serenity.

"Tamara!" Braden shouted. "Tamara, if you're here, come out at once. I demand you show yourself." His demand was met by the sound of the waves and the cry of seabirds.

The two took opposite directions and began a thorough search of the shoreline. An hour later when they again met, neither had found a trace of the girl.

Manuel's mouth was grimly set. "If she's done it, we'll never find her. She'll wash out to sea and that's the end of it."

"Take heart, friend. I refuse to believe she's dead. At any rate, it's too dark now to continue the search alone. We'll ride to the swamp and get help from the servants. We'll fire torches and comb every inch of the island."

They rode briskly side by side until they reached the beginning of the swamp at the western tip of the island. Here the sea reclaimed the land, leaving two small islands connected to the mainland by a mile-long swamp filled with towering mangroves.

"Your people will be surprised," Manuel observed, dismounting. "They think you're on the ship sailing to Boston."

"Wish to God I were," responded Braden under his breath.

It took a quarter of an hour for them to hack and slosh their way to the interior of the swamp. Their last efforts were guided by the glow of a bonfire.

"Wait a moment," Braden whispered. "I just have a hunch. Let's do a bit of spying."

Squatting amid the gnarled roots of an ancient mangrove, they peered into the dry clearing. The sight they saw shocked them both into momentary silence.

"I'll be damned . . ." Braden finally muttered.

"Por Dios," said Manuel. "You were right all along."

The scene before them in the light of the roaring fire

was a riotous gathering in full swing. Fifteen or twenty revelers were snaking, hands-to-waists, around the fire to the low-throated beat of native drums. And Tamara led the dance.

"I don't understand," Manuel muttered. "What is she doing?"

Braden thought for a moment. "I understand—all too well. The little fox planned it all and led us on a fool's errand."

"She guessed you'd not leave with Lady Pickering until you found her?"

"I'm certain of it."

Manuel shook his head sadly. "She must be very much in love with you, señor. I have no chance with her."

The rhythm increased as the snake dancers formed a circle and Tamara whirled into the center, spreading her arms, her skirts swirling, her raven-black hair flowing about her head and shoulders. Someone began a counterrhythm on a wailing guitar.

"Look, that's Paco," said Braden. "And there are your friends, Emilio and Maria. Half the Spanish settlement is here, and all my African house staff, including Simpe, my cook."

"They think you've gone, Señor Hamilton. They're making the most of their master's absence."

"I have no quarrel with that. But Tamara's plotting is unforgivable. All that business with the note and talk of sinking into the depths. She thought only of her own desires. She knew I would be alarmed and begin a search. You call that love, Manuel? Nay, I call it jealousy. She wants what she cannot have. It's not an uncommon failing among women—and men, as well."

Manuel stood. "Then we can return home. I apologize for my part in all this."

"Don't blame yourself. You were right to warn me. But wait a minute. Let's not rush off just yet. The frigate has sailed and in two or three days, I'll leave on the sloop. The important thing now is to settle the score with Tamara, once and for all. She needs a good spanking, and

she must be made to realize I love Amanda Sheffield and intend to marry her. Return to the horses. I'll get the lady."

The party in the clearing became increasingly unrestrained as flasks and botas were passed from hand to hand. The fiery Maria took center stage after Tamara's performance and broke into the staccato movement of gypsy flamenco. Never had its Moorish origins been more evident and appreciated. A gleaming African woman swayed into the firelight and accepted wild applause. Twisting and arching, her ample breasts swaying beneath her bright cotton shift, she wailed a primitive cry from the land of her ancestors.

A gunshot shattered the night.

The music was instantly silent and the dancers froze in place.

Braden strode into the firelight, his face dark with anger, a smoking pistol in his hand.

"Braden!" cried Tamara. She ran across the clearing and threw herself against him. "Braden—I knew you'd come," she said wildly. "I knew you'd look for me. Were you worried?"

"Your conniving was both cruel and childish, Tamara. You should be severely punished."

"But . . . I *might* have killed myself . . . if you hadn't come back."

"Don't lie. I've been watching from the swamp. You're enjoying yourself thoroughly. You have no intention of dying over me or any other man, isn't that right?"

She stared at her slippers. "No. I'm sorry." Looking up, she gave him a winning smile. "But you're here now. We have food and drink. You can join us."

He shook his head in frustration. "My God, Tamara! You still don't understand. I should be on my ship, sailing to Boston. The woman I intend to marry is on that ship traveling without my guidance on a dark sea because of you. You wrote that ridiculous note not caring about anyone's feelings but your own."

"Yes, but . . . I thought if you didn't go with her, you'd change your mind. I thought—"

"I know now why the sheik was having you whipped when I found you. The man was as exasperated as I am." His angry voice echoed around the clearing. He gripped her arm. "Come with me. We'll get back to the house and leave these good people to their revelry. Enjoy yourself, friends," he invited. "You've earned your night of fun."

He marched her out of the firelight and into the moon-splashed swamp. As they slogged through the ooze, her sniffles turned to sobs.

He stopped walking and faced her. "Your tears are wasted. Do you want me to carry you?" he asked sharply.

She yanked away her arm. "No," she yelled, her eyes suddenly blazing. "Don't touch me. I don't care if you *do* marry that simpering milkweed. You're a liar. You never loved me . . . you . . . you cursed son of a half-eaten lizard, you jackal . . . you filthy maggot-filled corpse of a pig!" She ended her verbal attack by slapping his face with all her strength.

He grabbed her wrist to fend off a second blow. "What a hellion you are, woman. I don't know what Manuel Rodriquez sees in you."

"Rodriquez!" she cried. "Why, he's ten times the man you are . . . ten times as handsome . . . as brave . . . as . . . as kind."

"I expect he'd like to hear that."

"I did hear it," came Manuel's voice from just beyond their vision. He pushed aside some vines and plodded over to them. "Excuse me, señor, but now that this lady has spoken her mind, I will take charge of the matter. I'm Spanish, after all. We Spaniards know how to capture such wildcats . . . and tame them." With that, he scooped up Tamara, leaving her slippers stuck in the mud.

Her red-brimmed eyes were wide with amazement as Manuel carried her a few yards to solid ground where the horses were waiting. With her hands securely locked around his neck, she gazed up at him with an entirely new expression.

Trailing behind, his face stinging and his boots weighted with ooze, Braden found himself smiling. He'd missed his ship's sailing, had his teeth rattled in his head, and lost a beautiful woman to another man. But he was extraordinarily pleased with the outcome.

Manuel mounted and held Tamara in front of him on his saddle.

Silently observing, Braden swung atop his stallion.

"I left my horse beyond the swamp," Tamara said meekly, wrapping her arms around Manuel's neck.

"Never mind, the others will bring it home. Besides, you'll have a new pony any day now."

"I will?"

"*Sí,* my pet. I sent for one of the pretty little jennets from the Indies. I requested a gold one with white mane and tail."

"Oh, Manuel," she cried. "How wonderful! But it must be very expensive." She threw Braden a scalding glance. "Braden has been promising me a horse, but he's been too busy with *other* matters to remember his promises."

"The horse is purchased. I made the arrangements myself weeks ago," Manuel explained proudly.

"Oh, thank you," she crooned and lightly kissed the tip of his chin. "You're a wonderful horseman—the *best* in Bermuda. I'll work hard on my lessons so we can ride together."

"That's exactly what I had in mind, *chica.*" Above Tamara's bouncing locks, Manuel's eyes met Braden's.

Braden nodded his approval. Yes, Manuel knew the way to a woman's heart. And it was certain his Latin blood had found a match in Tamara's spicy Turkoman spirit.

CHAPTER
18

Amanda told herself over and over that Braden *would* come. She watched for him constantly, staring hour after hour at the empty expanse of ocean while idly stitching on her embroidery.

Each morning and before retiring at night, she knelt on the gently swaying floor of her cabin and prayed fervently for his safety and for his return to her arms. She resolutely buried any thought that he might have abandoned her for Tamara. It was necessary and right for him to do everything in his power to help this girl who depended on him. She must have faith in his love. Surely he would come as he'd promised.

But as one bright blue day passed into another and the winds held strong, her spirits drooped and she had an increasing sense of despair. Coco was mildly seasick once more and poor company. And Hugh was apparently still angry with her and kept strictly to his quarters. Either that or he was treating his tendency toward seasickness with his favorite strong beverage.

On the fifth day out of Bermuda she lay reading, propped up on her bed with Persephone curled at her feet, when a heavy knock came at the door.

Coco moaned and turned her head to the wall.

Amanda opened the door to a grim-faced Mister Stiles.

"Excuse me, Lady Pickering. I hate to disturb ye, but I fear I've a problem I must inform ye about."

"Certainly. Come in, please."

"Nay, I think ye best come with me, your ladyship."

"Very well. I'll just get my wrap. We seem to be picking up a bit of a squall."

She followed Stiles down the companionway to the door of Hugh's cabin. The seaman turned to her and with furrowed brow announced, "The gentleman's mighty sick. The cabin boy found him at noon and reported to me right away. But the lad didn't go near him—nor has anyone else." He pushed open the door, but kept his arm across the opening, preventing her from entering.

"Let me by, if you please. I'll see to him."

"I must warn ye, my lady. It could be—"

"The plague?" she asked sharply.

"Yes, ma'am."

"I've been afraid of this," she said. "But one can't tell what's wrong at this distance, Mister Stiles. Please let me pass."

"But, ma'am, if 'tis the plague, we could all be in danger. Especially anyone entering the room."

"You needn't enter. And no one else should be allowed inside. I'll stay with him until we know for sure. After all, the poor man is my uncle and he needs care."

His scowl deepened. "Captain Hamilton made me promise to look after ye. If ye should catch the pox, he'd tear off my hide."

"I appreciate the captain's concern, but he isn't here and this is an emergency. Besides, I've had a special treatment that should keep me safe. So has my maid, though she's too ill from mal de mer to be of much help. Now please step aside. Who knows, maybe he's just suffering from a bit too much spirits."

Stiles moved back and allowed her to enter the room.

She took a close look at Hugh, felt his brow, and knew at once it was not a hangover that had brought him to this condition. She opened his shirt and studied his throat and armpits. Yes, the telltale eruptions were in evidence. At least the poor man was unconscious and not suffering.

She looked up at Stiles, who remained just beyond the door. "I doubt it's plague," she lied. "But he's extremely ill and we'll take no chance. Bring me a supply of clean linens and several buckets of hot water. Also a cot, if you will. I'll stay here until the fever breaks or . . . or he dies. Please bring an abundance of hot tea and coffee and have three simple meals left outside the door each day."

Hugh moaned and moved restlessly on his bed.

She stroked his head and fought back tears. What a terrible thing to happen. Poor dear Uncle Hugh. If only he'd done what Braden asked.

"My lady?"

"Yes, Mister Stiles?"

"I just wanted to say ye're the . . . the bravest, most beautiful lady I've ever known. God keep ye. I'll see ye have everything ye need. And no one will disturb ye."

"Thank you. Shut the door now, please."

Twenty-four hours later, as she dozed in the chair beside Hugh's bed, she heard the death rattle in his throat. She held his hand and prayed that his tortured body would find release.

"I'm so sorry, Uncle," she whispered in a voice hoarse with weariness and sorrow. "You won my heart from the beginning. We could have been great friends, you and I. But now you're in Heaven with your brother James. I'll always remember your kindness to me." She folded his hands and pulled the sheet over his colorless face.

She walked to the small window and threw it open to the day. The sun shone in the blaze of noon and the air was fresh and sweet. Taking comfort and mustering her strength, she filled her lungs and thanked God for the blessing of vigorous health.

Turning back, she surveyed the small cabin. Everything Hugh had touched would have to be disposed of, and *she* would have to do it: linens, eating utensils, clothing, including her own—everything. She would arrange a funeral for Hugh and commit his body to the sea. She hoped she could convince the crew he had died of some cause besides plague. Otherwise the ship might not be allowed to dock in Boston.

Her thoughts leaped forward as she cleaned the room. They should reach Boston in a week or less. If no one else became ill, it should be safe to bring the ship into the harbor. And she would have to break the news to Aunt Sara.

When Amanda had stripped the room bare and aired it well, she pulled off her soiled clothing and pushed it through the window—including her undergarments and slippers.

She had saved one clean linen sheet and now wrapped it around her and slipped out the door.

She dashed furtively up the steps and hurried into her cabin.

"Ayee!" screeched Coco from her place on her bed. "Oh, mistress, you scared me half to death."

But Persephone strolled over to greet her with a happy meow.

Amanda picked up the cat with her free hand. "Uncle Hugh is dead, Coco," she said, nestling the pet under her chin.

"Oh my. I thought he must be bad when you didn't come back. I tried to talk to Mister Stiles, but he just say go back to bed, missy, your lady will come back when she's ready. Was it the pox? And where are your clothes?"

"Yes, and they've gone out the window along with everything else from his room. Promise not to tell, Coco. I'm going to blame it on his heart. He wasn't young, after all. There's no use frightening the crew half to death."

"I'm surely sorry. I jus' wish I could have been down there helpin' you. You look plenty tired, Miss Amanda."

"I am truly." She sighed as she sat on her bed. Tears welled into her eyes.

"Why don't you lie down and sleep awhile. I'll go to the kitchen and bring hot water for a nice bath. And soup too."

"Are you sure you feel like it?" she asked sleepily.

"I feel well enough to tend a brave lady like you. Rest now. I'll be back soon."

After Coco left, Amanda fell back to the pillows heavily. The sheet slipped to the floor as she covered her face with her arms and let the cool afternoon breeze wash over her. She reminded herself that death was part of life, though never easy to accept. As she drifted into sleep, she let a few stray tears roll along her cheeks to her pillow. Uncle Hugh was dead. She was a widow at nineteen. And Braden wasn't coming . . . if indeed, he wasn't injured or dead. She should never have left Bermuda without him, no matter how much he insisted. It was agony not knowing his fate or whether he had ever truly loved her. As exhaustion and despair overcame her, she fell into a dreamless sleep.

It was thus that Braden found her. He flung open the door and entered the cabin, only to stop short and let her name die on his lips.

He gazed at the reclining figure dappled by sunlight, one foot tucked under her knee, her arms resting above her head, her wrists intertwined with her froth of honey-colored hair. Her breasts, her small waist and rounded hips, the pale golden softness between her thighs, all were revealed like a Renaissance master's work of art.

He started to leave, but then she moaned and shifted to her side. Minutes ago, after he had boarded *The Tamara*, he had heard from Mister Stiles the story of her dedicated attendance at her uncle's last hours. Stiles explained the fellow had died of "some heart ailment." Braden knew after one look at the body exactly what had killed Sheffield. He also knew Amanda must have gone through hell and taken considerable risk to see the old fellow into eternity. He prayed the Turkish transplantation would protect her.

She had been intelligent as well as courageous. She had wisely done everything correctly to protect the crew of *The Tamara* and make certain the ship could enter the port at Boston. What a lady she was: smart, brave—and so exquisitely lovely. He couldn't help feasting his eyes once more, though it caused him no little frustration to do so.

He picked up the sheet and laid it over her. She didn't stir. Her thick brown lashes didn't even tremble on her cheeks and it tore at his heart to see traces of tears on their softness.

Quietly he pulled up a chair and sat beside her, stretching his booted legs outward and relaxing. There was no real harm in spending a few minutes in this peaceful ambience, though he was certain to get a tongue-lashing from both Amanda and Coco when he was discovered.

A sudden meowing broke the stillness and Persephone crept from under the bed. Sitting on her haunches, she fixed him with a cat-look of slant-eyed, haughty questioning.

"Perci," he whispered. "Guarding your mistress, eh? Good girl." He picked up the cat, who offered no resistance. Holding it rather awkwardly before him, he returned the look. "Fat and well-furred," he murmured. "That black diagonal mask, those golden eyes do give you a sinister look. But we know better, don't we, Perci. Unless of course, I happened to be a mouse. Perhaps we'll find you a husband in Salem Town. Would you like to be a mother? I suspect Amanda would love a basketful of your offspring."

The door creaked open and Persephone squirmed out of his grasp and scooted back under the bed. A round-eyed Coco stood framed in the doorway, her mouth gaping in shocked disbelief while she balanced a tray of steaming pots.

Putting one finger over his lips, Braden silently rose and went outside to speak to her. "She's sleeping soundly, Coco. I wouldn't disturb her for a while."

"I suppose. I don't think it's seemly for you to be there yourself, Captain—if I may speak my mind. But, I do know she'd be glad to see you. She's been mighty worried."

"Please reassure her when she awakens. I'm quite all right and Tamara is safe and in good hands."

"But . . . won't you do the reassuring in person? I mean, she'll be awake soon . . . and have her bath."

"I'm sorry, I can't stay on board, Coco. I took a chance as it was leaving the sloop to come over in the longboat. The seas are rough and the winds rising. More rough weather ahead, I think. I just wanted to see her—to know she's safe—and to tell her . . . well, it can wait till Boston."

"Then you're going right back to your ship?"

"Aye. As soon as I confer once more with Stiles. Just tell her I'm sorry about her uncle, that *The Tamara* will dock in Boston and I'll sail the *Wind Rose* into Salem Harbor about the same time, or maybe a day sooner. Tell her I'll see her in Boston soon after we dock—and Coco . . ."

"Yes, Captain?"

"Tell her I think she's the most incredible woman I've ever known. Will you do that?"

"Incredible. Yes, Lord Hamilton, I'll be jus' real pleased to tell her what you said. But she'll raise a terrible tantrum when she finds out you was here and didn't wake her."

He patted Coco's shoulder. "You can handle that, I'm sure. Take good care of her; make her rest and eat well. I'll see you in Boston."

With the wind whipping his coattail, he climbed down to the wheel, where Mister Stiles awaited his orders.

CHAPTER
19

"Oh, how dreadful!" Amanda stared in dismay at Mister Stiles, who stood before her with his cap in his hand.

The Tamara rode with sails furled at the mouth of Boston Bay. A chill fog swirled across the deck, creating a fitting atmosphere for the news Stiles had just delivered.

"We cannot dock here," Stiles continued. "We'll have to go north or south in search of a safe port."

Amanda nibbled on her lip. "Are you certain, sir?"

"The port authority said plague was spreading in the city and that no ships were being allowed to dock."

She shook her head. How ironic this should happen after all the care she had taken to safeguard the frigate. "But I must go to Boston. I'm sure you understand that I must carry the news of my uncle's death to his widow. And it is there I will rendezvous with Captain Hamilton." For the past few days, ever since Braden's visit to her bedside, her spirits had soared. Yet part of her remained unsettled. The message he sent to her by way of Coco had been somewhat vague and noncommittal. That he thought she was "incredible" was a lovely compliment, but it did not mean he still wanted to marry her. He had promised to see her soon. She had been counting the hours until they would be together. But now this terrible announcement from Mister Stiles. She shivered despite the heavy black dress and veil she had donned for this difficult day.

Stiles shook his head. "It's not safe, your ladyship. I daren't risk my crew, and ye shouldn't take such a risk either."

What would Stiles say if he knew she had done all the intimate chores for a man dying with smallpox? She spoke firmly. "I've had an inoculation against the pox, sir. 'Tis a new treatment and I highly recommend it to you and your crew. If you'll speak to my maid, she will explain it. Naturally I wouldn't have you dock under the circumstances. But *I* must get to shore. Do you have a longboat and two crewmen to row us in? They can return at once and you can be on your way."

He rubbed his chin. "Well . . . I suppose . . . if ye do insist . . ."

"I do. We're packed and ready. If you'll just put my trunk and the bags in the boat, we'll go at once."

"Very well, Lady Pickering. But I do hope Captain Hamilton will not have me strung up."

"I'll make sure he doesn't. And, Mister Stiles—take my advice on the inoculation. It could save your life and the lives of all on board."

By the time Amanda and Coco were deposited, bag and baggage, on the wharf, the late August sun was burning off the fog. With a tug at her heart, Amanda remembered that bright day not so long ago when her uncle had strode forward, wreathed in smiles, to greet her and offer his affection. How different was this arrival. And how much she dreaded the encounter with Aunt Sara. To make things worse, there was plague in the city. She wondered how many souls had succumbed and how long it would be before everyone had the benefit of the inoculation.

Coco sat on the edge of a trunk. "How we goin' to get to the house? There's no one abroad."

"I suppose we can hire a wagon at the livery. It's only a

block away. Stay with our things, Coco. You're too weak to walk far. I'll go over and see what I can arrange."

When she arrived at the livery, she discovered a burly man hard at work repairing a damaged wagon wheel. His eyes gaped in surprise at her approach.

"I swear, wot ye doing here, lady? Everyone knows Dan the smithy came down with the sickness two days ago. I had it meself in London so I kin tend to the stable. But ye best stay indoors for a time."

"I'm Lady Pickering. I just arrived by longboat from the ship in the bay. I've also had a touch of smallpox, so I feel safe enough to be about. But tell me, how bad is it here?"

"Just a few cases so far. Lots of folks have gone inland, to the villages."

"But they shouldn't—oh, never mind. It's too late if they've already gone. Now, sir, I must get myself, my maid and my baggage to my aunt's house—Goodwife Sara Sheffield."

He rubbed his hands on his work apron. "Aye. I know the house on Milk Street. Know the Sheffields too. Fine man, Mister Hugh. I'm glad to help any relative of his'n."

"I'm sorry to tell you that Hugh Sheffield has recently died at sea. I carry this sad news to his wife."

"I say, that is bad news. Sure, lady, I'll oblige ye right away. Just let me hitch up the horse and wagon."

In less than half an hour, Amanda knocked on her aunt's door. One of the housemaids admitted her to the parlor while Coco made her way to the kitchen entrance. Amanda was sure that considering today's circumstances, Coco was happy to stay well out of the way.

The dour Sara greeted Amanda with a stiff embrace. "You surprise me, Niece" she said without a word of welcome. "I had thought by now you'd be on your way to England with the marquess."

Amanda lifted her veil. No matter what the temperature, this room and her aunt always made her feel stifled and exceedingly uncomfortable. "Unfortunately the marquess became ill and died soon after our wedding. I return to you a widow, though I carry the title of marchioness—dowager, I suppose."

"Well, well. So much lost—and so much gained, in so brief a time." Her eyes glittered knowingly. "Yes, most unfortunate. I see you wear mourning, and I'm certain you're quite stricken with grief at your loss."

She could have strangled the self-righteous biddy. The implication that Amanda was happy to be a rich widow was cruel and insulting. "I *am* in mourning, in my husband's memory, though he was a stranger to me, but also for someone I cared about deeply—someone who passed away a week ago during the voyage to Boston."

Icy silence lay between them as Sara's eyes narrowed. As the idea struck her, her hand moved to her throat. "Not . . . not Mister Sheffield . . . not *my* husband."

"I'm afraid so, Aunt Sara. I'm terribly sorry to be the one to bring you the news. I was extremely fond of my uncle, and I nursed him during his illness until he passed. I can tell you he was unconscious most of the time, and suffered little."

Sara drew herself up and clasped hands before her. Though she had paled at the announcement, her eyes were dry and her lips tight. The only visible emotion was something resembling hatred in the look she gave her niece. "Of what cause did my husband die?"

Amanda hesitated, but Hugh was Sara's husband, and she deserved the truth. "He died of smallpox. I was careful not to let anyone else on the ship come in contact with him."

Sara visibly shrunk backward. "You . . . you nursed him?"

"I did—for several reasons. One because he was my father's brother and I had already begun to love him. Also I didn't want the crew to panic or the ship refused entry into Boston Harbor. Unfortunately it was denied anyway. Luckily I have had a treatment called transplantation, or inoculation, which I believe will prevent me from getting the disease . . . at least for a while."

"Treatment? Wha-what is this?"

"It's a new method of preventing the plague. It's used in Turkey and in Africa. My servant knew all about—"

"How dare you!" Sara's jaw worked; her face flushed with rage. "So you and that Negress woman brought black magic to my husband's deathbed."

"Not at all. Quite the contrary. Uncle Hugh refused the treatment or he might have lived. And it has nothing to do with black magic."

"Thank God he didn't sink into such blasphemy. Where was the illustrious Captain Hamilton during this time?"

"As a matter of fact, Captain Hamilton was sailing his new sloop in our wake. He visited *The Tamara* once to issue orders, then sailed on to Salem. I might add that a proper Christian burial was conducted at sea for your husband."

Sara pulled a handkerchief from her pocket and covered her mouth, though there was still no sign of tears. She spoke through the cloth. "Ungodly. The lot of you. I warned Mister Sheffield not to go to that decadent island of heathens and . . . and Anglican ne'er-do-wells. Did anyone else contract the disease?"

"As far as I know, only my own husband and some of his crew. The marquess was the first to become ill. As I said earlier, he died the week following our wedding."

Slowly Sara lowered the handkerchief. "This is extremely shocking. I will retire to my room now to pray and meditate. And I will notify Reverend Mather. He will comfort me as he has so many others who have lost loved ones from the black death."

"Yes, a good idea," Amanda said, feeling suddenly fatigued and despondent. Remembering Mather's earlier kindness toward her, she added, "I'm sure the reverend's presence would be helpful to both of us."

"To *me*—not to you," Sara spat. "How dare you—an Anglican and a believer in black magic—how could you think of asking the reverend for help! For now you may stay in your old room upstairs. As soon as possible, I want you out of my house and out of Boston!" She marched from the room in rustling stiffness.

Amanda sat in the nearest chair. She still had on her cloak and her gloves, which she began pulling angrily from her fingers. She had expected Sara to be shocked, but she had also expected some hint of sorrow and regret, perhaps even appreciation for her efforts to ease Hugh's last hours. Instead, the terrible woman had practically accused her of contributing to his death. Black magic, indeed. But at least Sara had made one good suggestion in calling for Cotton Mather. She had been thinking of him during her wagon ride through the Boston streets. He was just the man to talk to about the transplantation. He had great influence among the people in Boston. And he was obviously more sophisticated than many of the Puritans she encountered. If his religion didn't close his mind to the idea, perhaps he could be instrumental in saving many lives.

Never had Amanda felt so surrounded by gloom. Mornings were dark and gray with fog, afternoons brighter but heavy with oppressive heat. The household retired immediately after the simple evening meal had been served to her and her aunt, a meal seasoned with silent hostility.

A few friends and neighbors came to extend their sympathy to Sara, but no formal memorial was held because of fear of plague. There seemed to be only two subjects of conversation in Boston these days: the black death and the witchcraft trials under way in Salem.

Amanda found no escape from misery, but at least she discovered a way to be useful. A few inquiries revealed the homes where plague victims lay abed in need of medical attention or simple care. Over the most stringent objections of her aunt, she spent much of her day going from house to house, preparing meals and offering what comfort she could to a dozen sick women and children. She was not allowed in a man's sickroom, but she could offer a word of comfort to the man's family. In the beginning, she described the new transplantation she had received, but when her advice was received with everything from shock to horror, she discontinued her efforts to promote the treatment. Often she just missed crossing paths with Cotton Mather. His ministrations to his flock was equaled only by his more highly publicized involvement at the Salem trials.

At the end of a week, she was not only exhausted from her work and the unbearable tension in the Sheffield home, but increasingly concerned over the whereabouts of Braden. He should have arrived by now. Surely he had completed his business in Salem. Was there any chance his ship had encountered problems?

On Sunday, her seventh day in Boston, Cotton Mather at last came to call.

"My sincere condolences," he said, bowing first to Sara, then to Amanda. Both ladies sat in the parlor with folded hands and solemn expressions.

"May I offer a prayer?" he asked.

"Please do," said Sara.

The reverend took a seat near the ladies, closed his eyes and raised his hands in supplication.

Amanda thought the prayer exceedingly long. Not only was Hugh Sheffield remembered at great length, but each plague victim, each sick person, every sinner in Boston, and the poor tortured souls in Salem were placed in God's hands after a detailed explanation of their suffering.

She couldn't resist stealing a glance beneath lowered lashes at Mather's grim visage. Why, the man had aged ten years since she'd last seen him. Did he alone have to tend to all the needs of the Puritan faithful of the area? Between seeing burdened souls to Heaven and guarding the innocent from the evils of witchcraft, he must be nearing the end of human endurance.

Amanda wanted to speak to him about the transplantation, but it must be a private conversation. That opportunity presented itself with surprising ease. Before an hour was up, Sara rose and asked to be excused. Her grief was overwhelming, she explained.

Reverend Mather also rose to leave, but Amanda asked for a brief word. "Reverend, I hesitate to speak of this, but the possible saving of lives forces me to take courage."

She received the first smile of the afternoon; though not joyful, it held a hint of his previous warmth toward her. "Lady Pickering, the last thing I would question in your character is courage. Everywhere I go among the sick, I hear praise of your brave efforts on their behalf. I would have contacted you before now, but I've been in Salem for several days." Leaning forward, he covered her hand. "You prove that Christian spirit exists in pure hearts, regardless of the church one attends on the Sabbath."

"Reverend Mather, it's the plague that I wish to speak to you about. You see, it requires no great courage for me to tend the sick. I have received a treatment that renders one safe from the disease for a time, and I believe many lives could be saved by extensive use of it."

"Treatment? As you know, my lady, medicine is my second calling. There is an angelic conjunction between the study of medicine and divinity."

"Yes. That's why I dare to tell you about the transplantation. A small surgical implant of diseased tissue causes a light case of smallpox. The patient recovers and cannot become ill with the disease for quite some time."

"Um." He eyed her with furrowed brow. "You've had this transplantation yourself?"

"Yes. In Bermuda. My maid had it too, along with several others. In fact, Coco had knowledge of the procedure from her early days in Jamaica. It came originally from Turkey and from Africa. She swears all the slaves had it at our home in Virginia—unbeknownst to us—and not one contracted smallpox while many white people died."

His grip on her hand tightened. "My dear girl, if this is true, it could be the medical discovery of the ages. But I must warn you that most people, even physicians, will call it insane . . . or magic. I would like to speak to your maid, then consult the books in my library, though I doubt this is mentioned. To be honest, my deepest fear is not for myself, but for my darling wife and children."

"I believe it works, sir. I tended my dying uncle and many sick people in Boston. As you can see, I show no signs of illness."

"Dear Heavenly Father, I pray guidance in this matter. Lady Pickering, could you summon your servant?"

Amanda brought Coco from the kitchen and within the hour, Cotton Mather left the house in a state of high exultation, vowing to try the procedure on himself, then on his children. He pledged both Amanda and Coco to absolute secrecy. "It smacks of magic," he said. "Considering my present efforts in Salem, I must be doubly cautious. If it is successful, however, I will make it my personal crusade to publicize and promote the treatment."

Sara reappeared in time for the evening meal. Instead of her usual pale visage, her cheeks held spots of color and her mood was slightly agitated. They ate their soup in silence. During the fish and potato course, she remained silent. But following the bread pudding, she put down her spoon and gazed directly at Amanda. Unquestionably an important announcement was about to be made, one which pleased Sara despite her efforts at self-control.

After a dramatic pause she spoke. "I've sent for your brother, Philip. He will take you home to Virginia."

Amanda was stunned. "But . . . but you should have consulted me. I'm expecting Captain Hamilton any day. He promised to meet me here and escort me home. As I told you, he rendezvoused at sea with our frigate a week out of Boston. He must be in Salem at this very moment."

"Oh, yes," she said with narrow, frosty eyes. "He is indeed in Salem."

"You . . . you've had word from him?"

"Not directly. But I received a written message late today from a clerk in my husband's office. It informed me that the frigate, *Tamara*, was returning to Bermuda after provisioning in Gloucestershire. It also stated that Captain Hamilton's sloop is docked at the Salem wharf."

"Oh, he's here! He's safe."

"Not entirely, my dear girl." Sara's lip curled. "It seems your friend, Braden Hamilton, is under arrest."

"What?"

"He's incarcerated at Salem prison."

"But why?"

"It's very interesting, *Marchioness*. It seems that he is accused of being a sorcerer. He's under examination for the practice of black magic. Fascinating, don't you think, my dear niece?"

CHAPTER
20

Braden had just finished exchanging ribald pleasantries with Flint the bartender when two stout men burst into the pub and without a word, pinioned his arms behind him. One placed a pistol to his temple and the other rattled a set of leg irons in front of his nose. It all happened so quickly, he had no chance to resist.

"What in bloody hell—" he started to protest.

"What's going on here?" Flint interceded as he hurried from behind the bar. "I say, Gardner, this gent's an old friend—from Bermuda, he is."

Gardner, who held the pistol, replied, "This man is accused of sorcery—that's what. Be glad he took a liking to you, Flint, or you'd be in sore trouble, I kin promise."

Braden laughed with the same hearty mirth he'd given Flint's joke. "A sorcerer, eh? Now that's the most intriguing name I've ever been called—by friend or foe. I'd like a chat with my accuser. He must have some knowledge of me of which I'm unaware."

"Ye'll laugh through a noose if ye're not careful," Gardner said. "Bind him, Rob. Then put on the leg irons. If he twitches an eyelash, I'll put his brains on Flint's counter."

Flint took a step backward. "A sorcerer," he muttered. "Who'd of thought it."

"Sounds like you believe them, Flint," Braden observed while his ankles were being locked into the heavy irons. "I guess I've made a worse impression than I thought during my visits to your charming inn."

"Don't know, Captain. There's plenty of strange goings-on these days. Saw five witches hung in July right out there on the hill. Another five last week. Why, the place is crawling with witches, and I never suspected a thing."

"Ten hanged? Damnation. First Boston is infested with plague, now Salem's full of devils. I'd sure as hell have stayed in Bermuda if I'd known."

"See there?" crowed Gardner. "He sounds guilty already. It'd be right satisfying to see this high-and-mighty Anglican knee-bender dancing on the gallows. Course if he confesses, the judge will set him free, I reckon."

"Is that so?" Braden questioned, as he was guided noisily toward the door.

"Aye. The judges believe if a witch confesses, there's hope for its soul to be saved. If a witch don't confess, 'tis better off hung."

Feeling considerable relief, Braden shuffled along the street toward the center of town. Flanked by the two men, he saw no chance of immediate escape. But if a confession of devilment would set him free, he'd give it gladly and head for Boston. He had no fear of plague and was eager to see Amanda. With any luck, he'd have her on his ship headed for Virginia by day after tomorrow.

With his two escorts gripping his arms, he was marched into Essex County Courthouse, where a large crowd had assembled to watch the proceedings. His appearance caused an outbreak of excited conversation.

He was halted before a white-wigged judge who seemed to have spent his life waiting for just this moment.

"Ah, Captain Braden Hamilton of Bermuda. We've been hoping for your return."

"You don't say. Well, I'm here, so let's get on with it."

With a heavy scowl, the judge rose and motioned two young girls to approach.

Braden was surprised to see Mary Walcott and Elizabeth Hubbard creep forward, their arms intertwined, their feet dragging, their faces gaunt and eyes wildly staring.

"Why, hello, Mary . . . Elizabeth. I'd hoped you two would be through with this nonsense by now."

To his complete amazement, Mary screeched and tore at her hair. Her eyes rolled back in her head and she sank to the floor, crossing her legs stiffly as she sprawled on her back.

Elizabeth began to scream obscenities no Puritan lady should ever have heard. Then she too fell to the floor, kicking and waving her arms and rocking from side to side.

The girls' screams were echoed by several spectators and it took the judge's gavel to quiet the crowd.

"Get him out of here!" shouted the judge. "His specter's loose on the girls like they warned it would be. Put him in a cell. We'll examine him later."

Stunned, Braden was hurried from the courtroom. Never had he seen such a sight as those two young women rolling in a frenzy on the floor. Why, the last he'd seen of Mary, she had been a shy, sweet girl bringing him a kitten in a basket. What had happened to her? And Elizabeth was barely known to him.

Before he gathered his senses, he was pushed into an airless cell and the heavy wooden door slammed behind him. "Wait," he shouted. "I must talk to someone— someone with authority." For the first time, a sense of real foreboding crept along his spine. This business in Salem was no laughing matter and he could be in a hell of a fix. He considered Mary's terrible display when she'd seen him. It made no sense, unless she was finding revenge for his rejection of her. There was simply no other explanation. But didn't the chit realize her childish revenge could actually lead to his death?

"Damnit to hell," he muttered and turned to survey his cell. As his eyes adjusted to the dim light seeping through a slit near the bottom of the door, he realized he was not alone. A man sat cross-legged on putrid straw in the corner. "What in God's name is going on here, sir?" Braden asked harshly.

For a moment there was no response, then the man said in a croaky voice, "You might as well sit down, whoever you be. If you're accused of witchcraft, you're in for a long visit in this cheerful place. Examination first, then a hearing, then a trial. Maybe a little extra persuasion now and then so you'll admit some heresy."

Braden squatted to get a closer look at his companion. "So who are you? Have you been here long?"

"Name's Giles Corey. I've been here weeks—months—I don't know, lost track of time. But I won't testify. Wife's accused too. I can't speak for her, but I swear before God, I'll not open my mouth one way or t'other."

Braden stood and leaned against the stone wall. The man must be a half-wit or addled from his confinement. For several seconds he struggled with his bonds, but to no avail. It appeared he had no choice but to wait for events to turn his way. One thing was certain—he'd been trapped in a spider's web of evil.

The rented carriage bumped southward along the well-traveled road between Boston and Salem. Inside, Amanda, dressed in widow's weeds with a black veil shielding her face, sat tensely rigid. She rehearsed in her mind exactly what she would say to the authorities at Salem prison. In a pouch attached to her belt, she carried two dozen gold pieces to be used if necessary to buy Braden's freedom. Puritan or not, most men would exchange a favor for a price. Across from her sat an equally disturbed Coco.

"If only they will let me talk to him," Amanda said. "The accusation is so absurd, I'd think it was a cruel joke except for those poor people already hung."

"I know about old Tituba. She's an Indian slave woman from the islands. When we come last spring, the Sheffields' kitchen servants said Tituba could bake a powerful witch cake. Some say she started the whole thing in Salem."

"Has she been executed?"

"Nay. She confessed to witchcraft so she was spared."

"But . . . if she was a witch, why didn't they hang her?"

"'Cause if a witch confesses, it's a sign the Devil's lettin' go of her. She must confess and say the Lord's Prayer without a slip or stammer. Now Bridget Bishop was found with dolls with pins stuck in them." She lowered her voice. "Like . . . like . . . you remember."

"Hush, Coco. Don't even whisper about that terrible thing. Why, if anyone knew you'd made one, you could be accused as well."

"I know, mistress. I been scared to death ever since. They surely hung Bridget Bishop."

"Oh, dear." Amanda sighed. "If only I can free Braden from this horror. I would even be glad for him to return home to Tamara if he wishes. If he loves her, I'll have to give him up. But at least he will be alive and happy."

"And you, missy? What will you do?"

She stared unseeing at the passing scenery. "I will . . . I'll go to Briarfield, I suppose. I have no interest in the marquess's property in England. It will go to his legal heirs. I'll sell the jewels in Boston. In fact, they're already in the hands of a merchant who has given me an advance in gold. He promises to get me a fair price."

Just after noon, the carriage halted before the Salem Meeting House.

"Wait at the livery stable," Amanda instructed Coco. "Make sure the carriage is available for our return trip. I'll come or send word as soon as I've made arrangements for Braden's release."

To her surprise, the Meeting House was packed with most of the citizenry of Salem—men, women and children. The heat, combined with the silent tension of the room, engulfed her as she entered, as if she'd just stepped into the anteroom of Hell. Inhaling deeply, she found a spot at the back where she could view the proceedings unobtrusively.

Two robed justices were seated behind the bench on a raised dais. Before them stood a pair of young women in their middle teens.

"Bring forth the accused," called out one of the judges.

Along with everyone present, Amanda watched as an ordinary-looking man was led down the center aisle to face the bench and the two girls.

"I am Judge Hathorne," announced the magistrate on the right.

"I know that," answered the accused. "My family has been in Salem as long as yours, Hathorne."

"State your name," Hathorne said, ignoring the gibe.

"Giles Corey."

"You're accused of practicing specter witchcraft. How do you plead, Mister Corey?"

"Not guilty."

A murmur arose from the onlookers.

"And how will you be tried?"

"By God alone," he answered.

The murmur in the courtroom became a roar.

Judge Hathorne pounded his gavel on the bench. When order was restored, he continued. "Now, Mister Corey, are you denying the authority of this court?"

Corey remained silent.

"Giles Corey, you must say, 'By God *and this court.*' Do you hear me?"

"I hear you."

"Then say it so we can proceed with the examination."

For an entire minute, not a sound was heard in the oppressive courtroom.

Hathorne again pounded his gavel and shouted, "Take him away. He cannot be examined until he agrees. 'Tis the law."

Giles Corey was summarily marched down the aisle and out the door.

The onlookers erupted. Opinion appeared divided on what could be done about this unprecedented action by Giles Corey.

Amanda saw her chance to approach the bench. She elbowed her way forward until she stood directly in front of an agitated Judge Hathorne. "Pardon me, your honor. I must have a word with you." As she called to him, she lifted the veil from her face.

At once he gave her his attention. "Who are you, woman? Do you have business in this court?"

"I do, sir. I am Lady Amanda Sheffield Pickering, Marchioness of Staffordshire—newly widowed, I might add."

His eyebrows raised almost to the edges of his powdered wig. "Marchioness? We're honored, my lady. What is your interest in the proceedings here?"

"I've come to speak on behalf of an innocent man— Captain Braden Hamilton—who has been falsely accused of witchcraft. I have known Captain Hamilton for many years and can attest to his innocence and devotion to God."

Hathorne scowled. "The man's an Anglican. Are you one as well?"

"Yes. But does that mean we are guilty of witchcraft?"

"No, of course not, but—"

Abruptly one of the young girls who stood nearby began to scream. Pointing at Amanda, she sank to her knees. Her eyes reflected unspeakable terror. She then fell to her back and twisted from side to side while crying in hysterical agony.

The judge came to his feet. "Pick Mary up," he commanded. "Lift her at once and make her touch the woman in black."

Two men raised the flailing girl and forced her hand to touch Amanda's sleeve. Instantly the girl stopped her gyrations and sagged weakly in the men's arms.

"It's gone now," Mary gasped. "The evil woman's specter left me when I touched her."

Wild commotion broke across the room. Someone

shouted, "She's a witch! She's in league with the sorcerer Hamilton! Arrest her!" Others took up the cry as details about the girl were passed throughout the crowd. "She must be examined. Did you see how she affected Mary? An Anglican—no better than a Papist, they be. Question her. Question her."

This time the audience was in complete agreement. After the disappointment over Giles Corey, they now had a new suspect, a woman garbed in heavy black and as beautiful as an enchantress. Not only was she of questionable faith, but she was a member of the English nobility who lorded it over the colonials in a most hated fashion.

"Arrest her! Imprison her!" they shouted with one voice.

Amanda was completely stunned. She started to protest, but was gripped by two strong men and virtually carried outside.

"Let me go!" she screamed. "How dare you! I've come from Boston to see Captain Hamilton; I *must* see him."

Her pleas were ignored. The men walked her across the Commons to the prison and unlocked the iron door.

"Put her in the empty cell at the end," said one.

"'Tis next to Hamilton and Corey. Suppose they work some mischief."

"Not likely. The walls are well-built and will keep them apart."

"But if they're witches, their specters might go right through—you know, like it done with the girls."

"Wait," pleaded Amanda. "I'll go to my cell without protest—for now at least—if you'll grant me one minute with Captain Hamilton." She raised her hands with her wrists touching. "Bind me, if you like. I only wish to see him for a moment to know if he's well. I . . . I have gold to pay you."

"Gold!" the men said simultaneously.

"Yes. I'll tell you where if you grant this one request."

The men looked at each other. Then one said, "Let's have the gold first. Then we'll bring Hamilton into the hall—but only for a moment. Lock the outside door, Gardner."

Amanda's hands were shaking as she withdrew the pouch. Behind her, Gardner slammed shut the door, then hurried back to see what she would offer. She emptied the shining contents into four waiting hands.

Delighted, the two stuffed away their treasure. "Get him out while I bind her wrists," ordered the man in charge. "We'll let them talk, but keep close watch."

Standing in the half-light, Amanda allowed her wrists to be tied. From down the corridor, she heard the grate of a key, then saw a door swing open. A tall man ducked under the lintel and made his way toward her. His hands were free, but his legs were chained in irons.

Unkempt and unshaven, Braden squinted in the gloom, then his eyes widened in disbelief. "Amanda . . ." he said hoarsely, "My God, what are you doing here?"

The tightness in her throat made immediate speech impossible. Finally she murmured, "I came to free you, but . . . I fear I've only made things worse."

"But they've tied you . . ." He took her hands in his. "You're trembling. Jesus, what have they done to you?"

"Stand back, Hamilton," ordered the guard.

Instead, Braden pulled her into his arms and embraced her fiercely.

Lifting her face to his, she received his kiss, heated and surging with unleashed emotion.

When the kiss ended, he kept his arms around her. "I've longed to see you—to hold you once again—but I'm dismayed to see you here and I'm afraid to ask how you came to be bound."

"I came here to declare your innocence or to buy your freedom, whichever was required."

He lifted her palms to his lips and kissed each tenderly. "My darling girl, I love you to distraction. I will love you till I close my eyes in death and God willing, I will love you throughout eternity."

"Here now," interjected the guard. "Enough of that shameful talk."

Amanda couldn't stop her tears. She pressed against him, offering him her lips once more in a kiss fired with latent desire and bittersweet longing.

"I said get back!" the guard roared. He thrust himself between them and motioned for Gardner to assist him.

Braden put his hands willingly behind his back. "Very well. We'll not touch again. But let us speak for a moment."

She thought her heart would explode with the overpowering emotions coursing through her. He loved her after all. It was she, not Tamara, whom he wanted. But to see him like this—cruelly treated, accepting humiliation to buy precious time with her, to see the pain in his eyes—it was almost more than she could bear.

His look penetrated her soul. "Tell me the truth, Amanda. Why have you been brought here like this?"

Swallowing the lump in her throat, she answered softly, "I'm under arrest, I assume. Just now in the courtroom, a young girl acted as if I had possessed her—with specter witchcraft, they said. I'm frightened. I don't understand."

He shook his head, then attempted a smile. "Don't be afraid, little one. The girl who accused you was Mary Walcott, no doubt. I fear her anger at my rejection of her has brought us both into this absurd mess."

"She loved you?"

"So she thought. A childish infatuation, I suppose. Specter witchcraft means she is accusing you of possessing her body with your evil spirit. It is the Devil working through you to torment her. Much of the evidence of these trials is based on such drivel, though the girls are convinced of the truth of it."

"But . . . what will we do?"

"Simple enough. When we're examined, we'll confess to witchcraft. It's the surest way to be released, so I've been told."

"Confess? To witchcraft? Never!" she said emphatically. "I'll do anything else, Braden. But I will never speak such a lie and truly lose my soul to Satan."

"But, my darling, 'tis the only way. You *must* do it or you could hang."

"Then I suppose I will hang." She faced him defiantly. "Confess if you like. That is your decision. I love you with all my heart but my soul must belong to God."

"That's enough conversation," snapped their guard. "You can argue through your walls if you like. Into the cells now."

She wouldn't look back at Braden as they guided her to the last cell in the building and pulled open the door. As much as she adored him, she felt he was asking the impossible.

"No, Amanda," he called from behind her. "Listen to reason. Damnation, woman! If you won't confess, how the hell can I? Holy saints, I'll have to think of some other way," he added lamely.

It was just after two in the afternoon of September 2 when the neighboring cell doors were slammed shut against Amanda and Braden.

Amanda spent a sleepless night in the dank enclosure. It appeared she'd been put there and forgotten. Straw and a chamber pot were the only amenities. She passed the hours by tugging on her bonds until her wrists were raw and bleeding. But gradually her fear subsided. The circumstances were so strange, so nightmarish, as to seem unreal like some trick of her imagination. Her anguish was tempered by the knowledge that Braden was just beyond her vision on the opposite side of the wall and that he loved her after all.

Sometime the next morning, the door swung open to admit a nearly frantic Coco.

"Only a minute now," came the familiar voice of the guard before he locked the door.

With a cry, Coco started to embrace her, then saw her bound wrists. While tears streamed from her eyes, she untied the ropes. "It's an awful thing, mistress. They wouldn't let me in till now. I didn't know what was happening."

"How did you manage it, Coco?"

"I told the guards I'm the servant of Mrs. Hugh Sheffield . . . that she had sent me to speak with you since you was her niece. I . . . I told them you had some of Mrs. Sheffield's jewelry she wanted and finally they let me in for jus' a minute. The carriage is waitin' outside." She began to sob. "Oh, missy, I didn't know what else to do."

"You did fine, Coco. I'm sure all the Puritans know the Sheffields of Boston. Your story got you inside and that's the important thing. Here, take these." She removed delicate gold and onyx earrings from her ears. "I gave my gold to the guards yesterday, but I have two coins left. Take them as well."

"But why?"

"They're for you. You've been a dear friend and loyal servant. You're in great danger here, Coco. These witchcraft trials have turned into mass hysteria. Take the earrings and sell them. With that and the coins, you can leave Massachusetts."

"Leave? Without you? No, ma'am," she said emphatically.

"Listen to me. Your presence here endangers both of us. If they arrested me, they could also arrest you. And if they ever found out about the voodoo doll . . . well, you'd very likely hang."

"Oh my, I never thought of that."

"I don't know what will happen to me or to Captain Hamilton. He's in the next cell, but we have no way to communicate. I can only pray Aunt Sara will do something to help me. Also, she said my brother, Philip, had been summoned. Surely he can help prove my innocence as well as Braden's."

"Oh, Lordy, I pray so," cried Coco.

"Promise to leave here at once. You should make your

way to Briarfield if you can—by land or sea. You have friends there in the quarters."

"I . . . I suppose so. I could go there and wait and pray."

"There is one other thing. Do you know where Persephone is?"

"Yes'm. Right outside. She's under the wagon seat where she hopped in before we left Boston. I found her yesterday at suppertime."

"Fine. Perhaps you can take her with you. I'd like her to have a good home . . . just in case . . ."

Coco began to cry again. "Of course I'll take care of the kitty. You can count on that."

A fist hammered on the door. "Come along now. Time's up."

Amanda gave Coco a tight hug. "Do be careful, Coco. Leave here in the carriage, but slip away south as soon as you can."

"Yes, mistress." She sniffled.

"And, Coco, I have one very important bit of *good* news."

"Whatever could it be?" the girl asked, wiping her eyes.

"Braden Hamilton loves me. I know it now for sure."

CHAPTER
21

With an uncharacteristic show of warmth, Sara Sheffield greeted the man who had just entered her parlor. "It's good of you to come so far, Philip. Heaven knows the times are dreadful."

"I came as soon as I received your message. Luckily there was a ship sailing north from Jamestown within the week. Naturally I was most eager to help you—under the circumstances."

"Draw up a chair. You might prefer to be seated when I tell you what has happened since I summoned you."

Still dressed in traveling clothes, Philip Sheffield accepted his aunt's offer to be seated. Despite his protestations of concern, his face was relaxed and his manner almost nonchalant.

"We'll soon have tea," said Sara. "I'll have your luggage placed in my husband's room. It's yours as long as you're in Boston."

"Kind of you, Aunt Sara." He patted her arm. "Naturally you have my deepest sympathy on my uncle's untimely demise."

"Thank you, dear. My husband and I had not been close for years. Still, his death was unfortunate. He worked hard at the shipyards. I fear the business will suffer. I dislike his manager and cannot be sure he's trustworthy. To put it bluntly, I'm concerned about my future income, though of course I prefer to live modestly as our Lord directed us."

"Um," he said, making a steeple with his fingers. "I have money concerns as well. I received enough funds from the Marquess of Staffordshire prior to Amanda's marriage to cover my debts. But I expected more once it was a fait accompli—a great deal more. Your letter telling me of the man's death threw my plans into disarray. I thought it would be wise to hasten here at once—to offer Amanda a brother's comfort—and to investigate the matter of a will."

Tea was delivered and conversation briefly interrupted. Then Sara continued. "I must be honest, Philip," she said while resting her cup and saucer in her lap. "I don't care for Amanda. Your father's first wife, your mother, was a lady of breeding, though I never met her. I'm guessing Amanda's mother was an opportunist, with more gumption than education—a woman who failed to stay in her place. I see these traits in her daughter and what's worse, I see a dark and dangerous side to her nature."

"Dangerous? I agree with you about her willfulness, but I never considered the chit dangerous."

Sara placed her cup on the table. "Her pretty face and figure are deceiving. The truth is, I suspected her and her black servant to be inherently evil the moment I laid eyes on them. My instincts have now been proven tragically correct."

"What do you mean?"

"I must tell you that even as we speak Amanda resides in jail at Salem, charged with witchcraft. The maid has disappeared and taken evidence of Amanda's guilt with her—a dreadful-looking cat which I'm certain was her familiar."

"Wha-what? My God—this is most shocking." Philip ran his hand through his shoulder-length dark blond hair. "Amanda a witch? But this is terrible news. It could mean all is lost."

"Perhaps. Perhaps not," said Sara. One eyebrow quirked upward. "I've done some investigating myself. While it's true, as the *widow* of the Marquess of Staffordshire, she'll receive none of the English estates, I've learned that she was given a fortune in jewels, including a tiara worth a king's ransom. She's given these to a jeweler in Boston to be sold. The jeweler was a friend of my husband and he is most sympathetic with my plight."

"Is that so? Then there's hope. When Amanda is released—and I'll do all I can to see that she is—she'll be greatly indebted to me. I will see to it that my sister is most generous to me and also to you."

"My dear nephew, there may be another way."

"Oh? What's that?"

"If Amanda is proven guilty of witchcraft—and I have every reason to believe she *is* guilty—she will be executed. The jewels in their entirety will then be yours. Naturally, if I find it my spiritual duty to testify against her, you could afford to show your concern for your widowed aunt with a nice gift from the proceeds."

"Executed!" He shook his head. "Hanged, I suppose. I never thought . . . um." He studied her as her suggestion took root.

"Philip, pay attention to what I'm saying. Your sister's husband, the marquess, survived his wedding by only one week. He fell unconscious behind the curtains of their wedding bed and never awakened. She alone attended my ailing husband while they were at sea; he died within twenty-four hours after she began her vigil. Since her arrival in Boston, she has moved among plague-ridden homes with immunity, though several of her patients have died."

"You think she killed her husband? And . . . and Uncle Hugh?"

"I have no proof, but it's quite possible."

"But why?"

"Because of Captain Braden Hamilton."

"What's this? Where *is* the captain?"

Her lips curled slightly. "In Salem Town jail awaiting trial. He's accused of practicing sorcery and witchcraft."

Philip's cup clattered to the table. "My word! This is stunning news. I've known the captain for years. He's been a rake at times, but seems honest and industrious— hardly how I'd picture a sorcerer."

"Who knows what's in a man's soul? All I know is he followed Amanda here from Bermuda; he was seen embracing her at the Salem jail, and two innocent young girls have declared he is the source of the devil's specter possessing their tortured bodies."

For a long moment, Philip was speechless. "Incredible," he finally muttered. "My own sister, a witch. But I often had the same feelings as you, Aunt Sara. She was always headstrong and full of mischief—defiant too. Now that I think of it, she always liked to ride abroad at night. Said she liked the moonlight and fresh air. And she was friends with the slaves—too friendly by far. Aye. It could be true, though it would break my father's heart to know it."

"Think of it, Philip. First her mother died, then her father. Next her husband, then *my* husband. No doubt Hamilton became her lover. And he appears to be a sorcerer. We have no choice, dear boy, no choice at all. As a devout and God-fearing Puritan lady, I must see justice done. And you must be the instrument of that justice. For, of course, I'm in deepest mourning and must not go abroad."

Shaking his head, Philip sank back in his chair. "Amanda and Hamilton—what shocking news. But I can see you're right. If she is executed, we'll be devastated, of course. Naturally, if she dies, she would want us to have the money from the sale of the jewels. After all, no one else would have a rightful claim, now would they?"

* * *

Things improved considerably for Amanda soon after Coco's visit. She was moved to a cell which she would share with another woman accused of trafficking with the Devil, a larger cell which not only had a small window allowing light and a bit of fresh air, but two cots and a square oaken table. Her hands were left unbound, and a Puritan lady with the face of a saint brought her a canister of porridge and water for washing.

Her companion was a pudgy, fair-haired woman in the middle months of pregnancy.

"Elizabeth Proctor," the woman announced. "I'm already condemned, so I'm through with their poking and prodding. My husband, John, was hung three weeks ago. I'll die after the birth of my babe," she added without emotion.

"Oh, but this is terrible," Amanda said, taking a seat next to Elizabeth on the cot. "Can't something be done?"

"Not as long as the dreadful citizens of this community stand against ye. My poor husband was judged guilty before he ever came to trail and nothing he could say or do could save him."

"How did this happen?"

Elizabeth dabbed at her eyes. "They used torture, they did, though torture is not sanctioned by English law."

"They tortured your husband?"

"No, but they did others, including our son. They tied him heel to neck till blood gushed out his nose—oh, 'twas most horrible—then made him swear he had been to a witches' Sabbath and seen his father perform evil rites. Lies! Lies! Who wouldn't lie after hours of such treatment?"

Amanda was aghast. How could she and Braden have become enmeshed in so horrible a scene? It was the fault of those wicked young girls, she thought. If anyone was conniving with the Devil, it was they.

Exhausted and with the first real tongues of fear licking at her heart, she lay down on her cot and closed her aching eyes. Braden. Braden. His image rose before her.

That he loved her gave her great joy, but what good was it if they were soon to die? Should she do as he wanted and admit to being a witch? The thought was more repugnant than the thought of hanging.

"Why don't you eat, lady," suggested Elizabeth. "It's all you'll get till supper."

"I'm not hungry. You're welcome to it, if you like."

Elizabeth raised off the cot and picked up the bowl and spoon. "Suppose I will. I must keep body and soul together till the babe is delivered. At least the wee one will have a future, though I pray it will be somewhere a long, long way from Salem."

Down the hall from Amanda, Braden sat cross-legged on the floor and stared at the slit of light beneath the wooden door. Giles Corey had told him a stub of a candle would be provided at mealtime; the rest of the time they would sit on the floor in the dark until they became more cooperative. That would be never as far as Corey was concerned. But Braden had no desire to be a dead hero. He had everything to live for, especially since he'd found love with Amanda. If only he could talk to her, persuade her to say or do anything to escape. She was so stubborn. Didn't she realize she was dealing with hysterical fanatics? Why, a year or two from now, these same folks might look back on all this with horror and regret. But by then, it would be much too late for the innocent victims of the noose. If he didn't think of something quickly, he and Amanda could be among that unfortunate group.

For several agonizing days in the black, airless room, Braden struggled with various plots and ploys. He found Giles Corey poor company. The man had little to say even to help pass the time. Corey remained convinced he would be set free when the judges realized he was not going to recognize their authority.

Almost a week after his incarceration, Braden was chained once more with leg irons and directed down the hall into a room at the back of the prison. The sight he beheld was like a vision from hell itself.

Amanda was standing in the middle of the room, her outstretched arms held by two guards. Her head was bare, her hair disheveled and curling loosely around her shoulders; her eyes held a look of sheer terror. She was surrounded by several men and women in Puritan dress, and the only light was the flicker of torches set in sconces along the stone walls. Worst of all, her dress was unbuttoned to the waist and one side pulled away to reveal one bare breast.

"What in hell . . . Let her go!" he demanded. He started forward, but the chains jerked against his ankles, causing him to stumble.

"You'd better tie his hands," ordered the man holding Amanda. "And hold a knife to his throat. If he admits he's a sorcerer and this woman's a witch, we'll set him free."

"Amanda . . . my God, what are they doing to you?" he asked as they secured his arms behind him.

She was obviously too stricken to speak. Her cheeks flamed as she averted her eyes.

"We're searching for a witch's mark on her body. Could be an extra tit or just a place like this," said the man while pointing to her exposed breast.

"Holy Christ! You bastards!"

A knife was placed against his Adam's apple, but he took little notice.

"We found the mark," spat one of the women present. "Plain as day. Right next to her left nipple. That's where her familiar suckled. If we could find the creature, we'd have more proof."

Braden jerked forward, but the knife cut his skin. "Leave her alone," he growled. "She's innocent. Innocent, I tell you."

"Braden," Amanda gasped. "It's no use. They won't believe me . . . or you. The mark is just a small brown spot I've had since birth."

"Enough talk," said the man. "We intend to prick the devil's mark. If it doesn't bleed, that will prove she's a witch."

Braden's jaw clenched in helpless rage. "Goddamn you," he cursed under his breath.

One of the matrons pointed to the small mark on Amanda's full, beautifully formed breast. "There it is. Right there. Prick it and see what happens."

Amanda started to sag, but the men gripped her arms tightly. She closed her eyes and bit her lip.

Braden struggled despite the trickle of blood along his throat.

The male examiner stepped forward and confronted Braden. "Do you admit to bewitching this woman? Or can you swear she is truly a witch? If you tell us the truth, it will go easier on both of you."

"No, Braden, no," cried Amanda, her eyes opening wide. "Let them prick me. It will bleed and my innocence will be proven."

He swallowed the fury rising in his throat. It appeared he had no choice. Physically he could do nothing to help her. And he wasn't about to declare her a witch—not as long as her piercing eyes forced him not to say it.

A small bodkin or prick knife was produced by the examiner.

Amanda looked down as it was pointed at her breast.

The slender point pressed against her pale flesh and began to disappear. She stared at it without flinching. There was no sign of blood.

"What in hell?" Braden snapped. "It's impossible. 'Tis a trick knife. I've seen the like before."

The matron raised her hands and cried, "She doesn't bleed. I knew it. That's certain proof."

The bodkin was held up, its point clean and gleaming in the firelight.

"No," Amanda rasped. "It didn't penetrate my skin. I felt nothing."

Above the uproar now erupting among the dozen

onlookers, Braden shouted, "I demand you let me see the knife. The magicians in England use such a bodkin—the magicians and the unscrupulous witch finders. The blade retracts into the handle."

He was totally ignored.

"Take him back," ordered the examiner.

In white-hot fury, he rammed his body against the man on his left, knocking him sideways to the floor. Springing to the right, he threw his entire weight against his other captor.

In a flash, three other men grabbed him and pounded him with their fists on his face and shoulders. Someone kicked him from behind and another reached down and yanked the connecting chain holding his ankles. He crashed to his knees and a booted foot slammed into his jaw. It was the last thing he remembered until he awoke in his cell.

He was stretched out on his cot. His hands were free, but his legs shackled. He ached from head to toe and the slightest movement sent waves of pain to half a dozen points on his body. He felt his jaw and found it swollen and his lip encrusted with dried blood. He coughed to clear the mucus from his throat.

"Had a bad time, didn't ya, friend?" came Giles's voice through the gloom. "No use fighting, I can guarantee. Follow my example and keep your mouth shut. Tell your lady to do the same. If the court can't try you, what can they do but set you free? May take a while, but at least you'll live . . . and not endanger your soul by confessing to witchcraft."

"If hatred damns the soul, mine is doomed today. There's a few citizens of Salem I'd like to open with a musket ball. God, if they torture Amanda . . ." He ground his teeth in anger and frustration.

"Doubt if they'll do more than search for the witch's tits. That will give them proof enough, along with the falling-down fits of the girls."

"Mary and Elizabeth?"

"Oh, there's more. Once the thing got started, it spread like the plague. Cotton Mather tried to heal the girls with prayer and fasting, but did no good a'tall."

Braden groaned and lay his arm across his burning forehead. "My God," he muttered, "where will this madness end?"

CHAPTER

22

Amanda's trial took place on a pristinely beautiful autumn day the third week in September. As she walked between two guards across the Commons to the Meeting House, she breathed deeply of the sweet air, warm at midday and scented with woodsmoke from hearth fires in the village. Birds flittered and sang in the tree branches; late summer vegetables lay ripe and ready for picking in surrounding gardens; a young family of geese quacked and waddled toward the millpond, and children in white bonnets gathered apples in the nearby orchard. It was like a lovely stitched quilt resting lightly over a bed filled with scorpions and snakes. She shuddered when she walked into the crowded courtroom.

As before, two judges sat behind the bench facing the accused. As she was led forward, her eyes fell on Braden, who stood in chains at one side of the platform. He was clean-shaven and well dressed, but his face was gaunt and his eyes shadowed with concern.

She managed to give him a slight smile, then she looked up at the judges.

"I am Judge Hathorne, madam. I will preside with the assistance of Judge Corwin. We are honored to have

Reverend Cotton Mather here today. I've asked him to offer an opening prayer."

Surprised, she looked around, then bowed her head as Mather's rolling bass voice called on guidance from the Almighty. She felt a tiny sparkle of hope. Cotton Mather was her friend—or as close a friend as anyone she knew in Massachusetts.

At the end of the long and passionate prayer, she located him near the dais. His look was dark and troubled. She remembered how she had told him in confidence about the transplantation. And she also remembered how he had pledged her to secrecy for fear he would be accused of practicing black magic. With a sinking heart, she realized he could be here to testify against her, to offer even more proof that she was indeed a witch.

The judge began by reading a few facts from Amanda's background which he said were compiled from firsthand reports from members of her family: that she had grown up in Virginia as a plantation owner's daughter; that she had traveled in England and was a declared Anglican; that her parents had died tragic deaths, followed in time by her husband of a few hours; that her uncle, a highly regarded Puritan shipbuilder of Boston, had died in her presence. She was known to travel with a woman from the island of Jamaica. She also owned a cat which was given to her by Braden Hamilton, a suspected sorcerer who was an English privateer from Bermuda with a reputation as a blackguard and occasional pirate.

After this description of her questionable past, the judge said he had three witnesses who would testify against the marchioness. Following that, he would ask for witnesses on her behalf. At the close of the trial, the two young girls who claimed they were possessed by her specter would be brought to the courtroom.

The first witness was the saintly appearing woman who had delivered to Amanda her daily meals and brought clean linens and items of clothing. In a pleasant manner, the woman said she had witnessed the test on Amanda's witchmark and she could swear on the Bible the mark did not bleed when punctured.

The next witness was a member of Sara Sheffield's household staff who had often driven her and the black servant to houses of the ill in Boston. Often their excursions had been late at night and he testified that very strange things occurred behind those doors. He also confirmed that Amanda's familiar was a cat named Persephone. Mrs. Sheffield told him "Persephone" was the name of a pagan goddess of the underworld; he knew the accused put great store in that cat. But perhaps most damning was his testimony that with his own eyes he had seen a voodoo doll owned by her maid. He had seen her conceal it in her pocket one day when she went upstairs to visit the marchioness. And he never saw it again, though he snuck a look in the girl's pocket later that day.

The courtroom was abuzz. No other suspect had had such blatant evidence revealed. This woman, this outsider, this hoity-toity bearer of a noble title, must surely be as guilty as sin.

Through it all, Amanda remained calm and steadfast. None of this came as a surprise. Occasionally her eyes strayed to Braden and she longed to linger there. But if she was convicted as a witch, her relationship with him would do him little good. Still, his look of absolute love and admiration gave her enormous comfort.

Then came the most shocking surprise of all. The judge called forth the final witness—none other than Philip Sheffield, the brother of the accused.

"Philip," Amanda breathed as if in prayer. At last she had help. But . . . the judge had called him a witness against her. He must have been mistaken or she had not heard correctly.

Dressed in black linen, a high white collar, black hose and slippers and a white powdered periwig, Philip stood before the court. He looked directly at her and for a fleeting moment, she saw pure hatred pass over his face. Then he took on a benign and sorrowful pose and began to speak. His words tore every shred of hope from her mind and heart. "I am shocked and heartbroken to discover my half sister has apparently been transformed into the Devil's handmaiden," he said as if reading from a prepared text. "We were never close as I was some years older and busy overseeing my father's farm. She was always a strange child, often attending the gatherings in the servants' quarters. She claimed to like the field hands' singing. Naturally I assumed it was innocent amusement. Later I learned one of the African women was a voodoo priestess called a mamba. When the mamba was arrested, we found in her possession the remains of a coat known to belong to Captain Braden Hamilton." He lifted his eyes upward. "In my naive innocence, I still did not connect any evil with Amanda or the captain."

While the judge calmed the room by pounding his gavel, Amanda gazed at Braden. His look was directed at Philip and there was murder in his eyes. She wanted so desperately to reach out, to hold him, to stroke away his anger. All was lost; they were doomed, so what did it matter? Nothing mattered really. If only for one moment she could feel his arms around her, shutting out the clamor and cruelty she felt closing in from all sides.

Judge Hathorne questioned Philip. "Do you believe then, that your half sister, the Marchioness of Staffordshire, is indeed a witch?"

After a long pause, Philip answered in a low voice. "Though I am devastated to say so—yes, I believe it is true."

Again the judge called for order. "Step down, sir. We appreciate your coming so far to testify. And we do understand what courage it took to reveal the truth. Now, bring in Mary and Elizabeth."

Amanda covered her eyes. She was past the point of tears, but it was the only way she had of shutting out the horror, both that which had just occurred and that which was certain to come next.

Sure enough, both young women arrived at the bench

looking pale and distraught. The moment their eyes fell on her, they began to scream and tear their hair and clothes, and finally fall to the floor and roll from side to side.

"Enough! Enough!" shouted the judge. "'Tis plain the woman's specter, her powerful evil spirit, has possessed the girls. I command you, madam, to withdraw your specter at once."

She stared blankly at the judge.

"Then take the girls away," he ordered.

After Mary and Elizabeth had been half carried from the courtroom, Judge Hathorne said almost as an afterthought, "Oh, yes, we must ask if anyone present will speak in favor of the accused."

The spectators quieted. It was no surprise when no one came forth.

Amanda dared to look at Cotton Mather. Whatever else he might believe, he knew why she had been able to assist the ill in Boston. He knew the medical reasons for the transplantation. And surely he knew she was not as evil as everyone believed.

But he said nothing. Though he briefly held her eyes, he quickly looked away. She felt bitterness and disappointment rise in her throat.

Then suddenly, Braden stepped forward. "I claim my right to speak," he said in commanding tones. "I speak on behalf of the accused, though I make it clear I do not recognize this court's authority over my own case."

The assemblage fell silent.

"You may witness," Judge Hathorne stated.

"I knew the lady as a child in Virginia. She was as sweet as any young girl could be—entirely innocent of any evil in thought or deed. Her parents adored her, though her older half brother was extremely jealous of their affection. Today I have seen that jealousy come to full fruition. I can only say to Philip Sheffield—you are a blackguard, sir, with the vilest heart I've ever seen. I hereby challenge you to a duel to the death, if that can be arranged."

It took Judge Hathorne a full four minutes to restore order in the court. When at last he resumed control, he faced Braden. "What you suggest is out of the question. You haven't improved your plight in the least by your offer. Now, do you have anything else to say?"

Braden turned to look at Amanda. Despite the chains on his wrists and ankles, he radiated power and enormous personal magnetism. His lips formed the words *trust me* before he gave her a smile which carried a hint of his old devilment.

"I do, sir," he said firmly. "Knowing that this court has no jurisdiction over me, I will now reveal the truth. I have great unearthly power; for the past four months, my spirit has possessed the body and the soul of this vulnerable and innocent lady."

Later when Amanda was back in her cell, she tried to recall clearly what had happened after Braden's stunning announcement. Cries and gasps of shock and amazement had been followed by the loudest uproar of the day. Guards had taken hold of both Braden and her, and no amount of gavel pounding had been able to calm the riotous onlookers. The courtroom was cleared and the trial scheduled to resume the following day.

Amanda sat now in the growing dusk, oblivious of the Proctor woman slumped against the opposite wall, oblivious of the dish of cold porridge and brown bread, and numb to any emotion except the pulsing knot of fear that served as her heart.

She couldn't think why he would do it. It was such an absurdly obvious, boyishly flamboyant attempt to save her; she wondered why any reasonable person couldn't see through the sham. Admittedly these people were not entirely reasonable, but they were not stupid either. Many were well educated, most were hardworking and peaceful, and all were most certainly pious. Naturally they wanted to expel witches from their midst. Every community throughout recent history had done the same. Witchcraft just couldn't be tolerated. But to find herself so accused was beyond her comprehension.

And Philip. How could he do such a thing? Her own flesh and blood. They had the same father who had loved them both. Did Philip hate her so much that he would travel this distance and speak lies that could end in her hanging? Why? What had he to gain besides satisfying his jealous nature? Money? But she knew the marquess had already paid him a princely sum. And she had been on her way to Virginia with more funds to help Briarfield —money she would obtain by selling the jewels which were a gift from her husband.

She considered a moment. Of course if she were hanged, as her next of kin he would get the money without any restrictions. Perhaps that was the reason. But as little as she respected his moral integrity, she couldn't believe he'd have thought up such a diabolical plot on his own.

Sara. Now there was one who might be the perpetrator of such a scheme. Amanda recalled Sara's threats, how the woman had screamed at her, accusing her of evildoings. Yes, the more she thought of it, she'd wager Sara had put Philip up to this.

She cupped her chin in her hands. There was still a chance she could escape with her life if she would admit she was a witch. But to say the words these dreadful people wanted her to say was unthinkable. Not only that, but she could be putting her immortal soul at risk.

In addition to these matters tumbling through her mind, there was Braden's shocking statement. How could he possibly prove he had possessed her and used her for his own evil deeds? She was absolutely certain he had condemned himself to hang. He hadn't exactly confessed to being a sorcerer, but everyone knew the power of specter possession came from the Devil. Before the trial began, his guilt had been assumed. Now he had no chance at all to establish his innocence. What tore at her heart was that he had sacrificed himself to save her.

If Braden was put to death, she wanted to die at his side. She had no interest in living in a world where he didn't exist. Not long ago, she had been prepared to give him up, but at least he would have been alive and happy. Knowing that he loved her to the point of dying to save her changed everything. She would gladly go with him, through the brief pain of death to live forever with him in the life hereafter. Her only wish was that they were husband and wife.

Feeling better with her decision made, she rested on the cot. Whatever tomorrow would bring, she would be ready.

She had barely closed her eyes when the door opened and the Puritan matron entered carrying a package.

"This was just delivered for ye, girl. A nice loaf of bread; it's still warm," said the woman.

She sat up and reached for the bundle. Who in this community of strangers would make such a thoughtful gesture? It couldn't be from Sara. That *dear* lady had proved treacherous beyond belief.

"Thank you," she said coolly. After all, this kindly-looking lady had testified against her a few hours ago.

"I'll watch while ye open it."

Amanda knew the woman's offer held more suspicion than simple curiosity. She unwrapped the cloth and held up a crusty, sweet-smelling loaf of freshly baked bread. "There. Isn't that nice?" She glanced at Elizabeth Proctor, but the lady was heavily asleep. "Could you tell me who baked it for me?"

"Don't know who baked it," the matron said with a trace of disappointment over the simple gift. "I was in the front room talking to Mister Gardner when a man I'd never seen before brought it into the prison."

"What did he look like?"

"Oh, 'twas a bit scruffy—full beard and knit cap over long, straight locks. Clothing unkempt, scuffed bottle-boots. Could have been a waterfront rapscallion by the look of him. Surely no one from Salem Town."

"I'm sure you're right about that," she agreed, thinking of the spotless and carefully groomed Puritans she'd seen.

"I'm going now," said the woman, no longer interested in the bread loaf. "But I'll bring breakfast in the morning —early."

After the door was closed and bolted, Amanda inspected the bread. It was certainly a mysterious gift. Maybe some caring soul among the villagers wanted her to know she wasn't totally alone and abandoned.

The fragrance did tempt her lagging appetite. She had no knife, so she tore a piece off one end. There, stuffed inside the fluffy warm interior, was something metallic. She almost laughed at the success of the old trick. Thank goodness the matron had left the room.

She probed with her fingers and pulled out her cross— the lovely jeweled cross Braden had rescued from the sea. But who on earth had taken it from her bureau drawer in Boston? And who would know of its significance or how comforting it was for her to have it at this terrible time?

She found her answer when she held up the cross to the light. Wrapped around the center stone were a few golden hairs and a few black ones as well.

"Persephone," she breathed. Coco. She pressed the cross to her breast. Coco had somehow returned to Sara's house and retrieved the cross, then smuggled it to her. What a daring act for the simple girl to perform. She was deeply touched by the gesture. Not only was the cross a comfort to her, but it was also a message. It told her Coco was somewhere in the vicinity of Salem. The girl hadn't run away, after all. How clever it was of her to include strands of Perci's hair. It was a clear indication of the sender's identity, and it also told her Perci was safe as well.

She put the cross around her neck. While pressing it close against her breast, she popped a morsel of bread into her mouth. It tasted delicious. She smiled to herself through the first tears she'd shed in days.

CHAPTER
23

The Meeting House was packed to overflowing. The aisles were full, and youngsters perched in every window. Anticipation sparked through the room from corner to corner.

The guard accompanying Amanda had to shout and shove to clear a path to the bench. The judges looked over the assemblage with stone-faced aloofness. On the dais to the left of the magistrates stood Braden.

Amanda caught his eye, but he gave no sign of greeting. Again he was neatly turned out, though today he wore no coat, only a smock-type cotton shirt with flowing sleeves and neckline slashed open almost to his waist. His ankles were locked in irons, but his hands were free. She thought he looked absolutely magnificent. He appeared disdainful of the gathering and its proceedings—not only unafraid, but actually a bit amused. His courageous demeanor and calm self-assurance helped her to control the nervous fluttering in her stomach.

Judge Hathorne called the court to order. A hush fell over the crowded room.

"Ladies and gentlemen, I insist respect be maintained at today's hearing. There are lives at stake, as you know.

241

If there is any disorderly conduct, I will clear the court and conduct the remainder of Lady Amanda Pickering's trial in private.

"Now," the judge continued, "when we adjourned yesterday, we had just received a request from Captain Braden Hamilton, himself one of the accused, to speak on behalf of Lady Pickering. There is overwhelming evidence that the lady has some connection with Satan's power. Damaging evidence was presented by Mary Walcott and Elizabeth Hubbard. The lady's own brother gave courageous testimony to assist our search for the truth of this matter. But Captain Hamilton has suggested *he* is the actual source of the evil possessing the accused. I will now direct my questions to the captain."

Braden faced the judge.

"Captain, you have refused to acknowledge the authority of this court, yet you offer testimony. How can you explain this contradiction?"

"What I deny is the power of this court over *me,* an English citizen residing in the Crown Colony of Bermuda. The accused lady is a citizen of the English colony of Virginia. She may decide for herself what authority you have over *her.* The point I intend to prove before this assemblage is that Amanda Sheffield Pickering is innocent of any wrongdoing or collaboration with the Devil. It is I who possess Lady Pickering. I possess her—and I can set her free."

"What proof do you have, sir?" the judge asked.

Braden turned toward the audience. "In July of this year, I came to Boston to take the then Mistress Sheffield, daughter of old friends, to her wedding in Bermuda. During the voyage, I myself fell in love with the lady and decided to make her my wife."

The room was quiet as a sealed tomb. No child snickered, no one coughed, not a breath was heard. Even the birds outside the windows seemed to have stopped their chatter to listen.

"I obtained a kitten in Salem and gave it to Mistress Sheffield. The kitten came from a litter belonging to

Mary Walcott so this can easily be confirmed. The cat acted as my familiar as they often do, serving as a go-between as I penetrated the lady's spiritual being. I soon felt my spectral force seducing her, but still she resisted and finally married the marquess. It was that same night, before the lady's marriage could be consummated, that her husband fell ill and eventually died. I might add he died under my roof at the plantation I own on the island."

When Braden paused, the releasing of the collective breath of the onlookers sounded like a rush of sea breeze preceding an approaching storm.

Listening to Braden tell his bizarre tale had hypnotized Amanda just like everyone else present. She slowly shook her head in amazement and denial. How could he invent such an absurd and dangerous story? Would anyone believe he was capable of doing all he described? While many had been accused and found guilty of spectral powers, no one had actually admitted to doing it, much less supplied the details as if it were a matter of following a simple procedure.

Judge Hathorne appeared nonplussed as well. "Are you saying you took control of this woman, murdered her husband, then followed her back to Boston—all in the name of love?"

"Love is the greatest power of all," said Braden. "Through the years, I've used it in one form or another to enhance my other powers—the dark forces which often travel in invisible juxtaposition within man. It creates a two-edged sword—one which I can use to turn life in any direction or end life altogether—if that is my desire."

For a long moment, the judge was speechless. Then he said, "You make outrageous claims, Captain. Words are easily spoken. The only evidence I've seen so far is your creating hysteria in Mary and Elizabeth. Lady Pickering does not appear hysterical. Quite the contrary, in fact. And today I see she wears a cross—no doubt as an attempt to protect her against evil."

Braden looked at her for the first time.

She moved her hand away so he could see the necklace that carried special meaning for both of them.

One corner of his mouth crooked upward in private acknowledgment.

She responded with a shake of her head. Somehow she must get him to stop saying these dreadful things. Didn't he know he was dealing with deeply religious people who would like nothing better than to destroy the Devil wherever he appeared—and in whatever guise? By now they must be seeing horns growing from Braden's forehead.

"I agree," Braden said, turning back to the judge. "She appears serene and as lovely as an angel. But I can provide proof of what I say. Absolute proof. First I will demonstrate my own power. Then I will show you—visibly—how I possess Amanda Sheffield and how I can release her."

At this revelation, no amount of threats from the bench could stop the commotion.

Judge Hathorne left his seat and spoke privately with Hamilton. He shouted and crooked one finger, summoning the illustrious Cotton Mather from the crowd to join in his conversation. The three men conferred while pandemonium reigned around them.

Spellbound, Amanda watched the scene. It held a strange sense of unreality. It reminded her of her descent through opaque waters to the sunken Spanish galleon off Bermuda. She felt light-headed and quite overwhelmed by the unfolding events. Fingering the cross, she forced herself to think clearly. Whatever Braden was doing, it was meant to save her life. The least she could do was match his courage with strength of her own.

The judge returned to the bench and lifted both arms. He was rewarded with instant silence and absolute attention.

"I have agreed to Captain Hamilton's demonstration of proof. He has assured me there will be no danger to anyone present. Reverend Mather will stand close by and give his comments at the closing. It is hoped a decision will be quickly forthcoming regarding the guilt or innocence of Lady Amanda Pickering. You may proceed, Captain."

Braden stripped off his shirt and tossed it aside. Several ladies tittered at the sight of his coppery, well-muscled torso.

Amanda stood transfixed. While his leg irons were being removed, he gave her an intimate and reassuring smile. Every eye in the room turned to look at her. Some of those looks verged on envy.

He walked to the edge of the dais and from his belt removed two foot-long sticks tipped with cloth balls.

Then she knew. Dear heaven, it was the fire trick. He was going to perform the fire trick here in the courtroom. Certainly none of these simple, God-fearing people had ever seen such a thing. Why, she herself had almost believed him a devil when she'd first seen it. She had to stop him. "Braden! No!" she cried. "You'll damn yourself."

He grinned at her and called back, "My darling Amanda, I long ago gave up my hope of eternal paradise. Allow me, my love, to do this last performance for you." He then made a bow to the awestruck spectators.

"Let 'im do it," shouted a man standing near.

"Let's see his power," called a woman.

"Continue, Captain," instructed the judge.

Braden lighted both tows and held then aloft. Several children screamed. With great flair, he arched his back and lowered first one, then the other flaming ball into his open mouth. More screams were joined by pleas for God's mercy.

The flames were snuffed. He faced the crowd with a haughty look and bowed low.

There was no applause, only shocked gasps, and a commotion near the back of the room where a woman had fainted.

He pulled a chair from behind the bench and climbed

on it. While staring solemnly across the crowd, he stretched his arms outright. In each hand he now held a small candle. Bending forward, he lighted these from the lantern on the bench.

Heart-stopping anticipation gripped the spectators.

He moved his hands above his bare shoulders and tipped the candles till drops of wax fell to his skin.

Amanda clenched her teeth. What was he doing? This was going much too far.

In a quick movement, he touched the candles to his shoulders, then flung his arms outward. Orange and blue flames coursed along his arms, arched across his chest, and sprayed outward more than a foot from his fingertips.

Screams broke out all around the room. Some people at the back scrambled for the door. Both judges were standing and shouting for him to stop this display.

The fire disappeared as quickly as it had erupted.

The crowd grew silent as Braden stepped down from the chair, smiling and none the worse for his incredible performance.

"He's the Devil himself," came a shout.

"He's a sorcerer all right. He's Merlin come to life," cried another.

Braden looked directly at Amanda, his eyes alive with merriment.

Her relief was enormous. She remembered what he'd said about the fire trick he'd learned in England, how sugar and soap protected him. Why, this display would put Satan to shame, she thought wryly. Her earlier fears were replaced by a peace she hadn't felt in days. With such a man to fight at her side, she couldn't possibly come to harm. Whatever happened after this, this was a moment of absolute victory. He had won. Never had she felt such adoration for anyone. She returned his smile and nodded her approval. If she had glanced at Cotton Mather at that moment, she would have seen he was also giving Braden an amused, admiring look.

Judge Hathorne's wig had gone awry, but he took no notice as he hammered for order. "Stay calm," he yelled, showing little control himself. "I order you to remain calm and pay attention. This court is not adjourned."

When quiet was restored, Hathorne turned to Hamilton. "Captain, you are a dangerous man, of that we have no doubt. We'll have more to do with you later. You've proved your unholy power, but you have yet to prove your control over the lady."

"Oh, I intend to do that now, if she'll come forward."

A path cleared at once; Amanda walked forward and stepped onto the platform. She was enchanted by him; she almost worshipped him. As she looked into his eyes, she loved him with a heart completely possessed.

He stood so near, his look holding hers, his eyes no longer smiling, but steeped with emotion. His words were for her alone. "I must do something now which will surprise you. Are you afraid?" he asked softly.

"No, my love. My will is yours," she whispered.

He glanced once at the breathless audience, then gave her his complete attention. He cupped her face with both hands. They were damp with perspiration. She saw drops of sweat on his face, rolling down his temples, curling his hair moistly along his forehead and temples. Aware only of his gleaming body close to hers, the strength of his fingers moving along her temples and down her cheeks, she lost herself in the hypnotic depths of his eyes.

He moved his hands along her upper arms, then across her shoulders, then up until they encircled her neck just above her collar.

"Braden," she murmured and took hold of his wrists.

"It's all right, little one. This will soon be over. Tip your head back, love, like you do when you defy some demand I've made." His presence was overwhelming. His fingers caressed her throat—searching, moving along her neck—pausing.

His thumbs pressed the tender flesh beneath her ears. Suddenly her mind whirled; she began falling uncontrollably toward him. She drifted into soft black velvet. She felt nothing, saw nothing, heard nothing. She slept deeply, without dreams and without remembrance.

When she awoke she was lying on her cot in her cell. Cotton Mather was sitting beside her.

"What . . . what happened?" she asked, waiting for the fuzziness to clear from her mind.

The reverend interrupted his prayer and smiled at her. "Your captain is a very clever man. He accomplished by daring and trickery what my prayers have been unable to do. Or perhaps my prayers did some good after all. As we know, the Lord works in mysterious ways."

"I don't understand," she said, sitting up on the cot.

"You're free, Amanda. The judges took just five minutes to decide your case. They called it indisputable spectral possession on the part of the captain. I also spoke on your behalf. It was obvious to everyone you were the victim of the captain's evil spirit. He explained to the court—while holding your unconscious body in his arms—that he had seduced your will and hypnotized you into believing you loved him. He announced he had released you. He put you into my care for a spiritual cleansing."

"You mean he took my guilt onto himself? And now I am free?"

"Exactly."

She put her face in her hands. It was too much to absorb in one moment. She couldn't help being relieved she was no longer charged with witchcraft. But what about Braden? She had been prepared to die at his side. Now it appeared he would go alone to the gallows. She looked again at Mather. "Reverend, do you accept the court's decision? Do you believe I was possessed by Captain Hamilton and that he is a sorcerer, an instrument of the Devil?"

Mather pulled up a chair. "Captain Hamilton most certainly has a bit of the devil in his spirit. But he is not a sorcerer. Of that I'm sure."

"Oh, I'm so glad to hear you say so. I know he's

innocent of such charges, but after today, I thought no one else would believe it. What convinced you?"

"Listen to me, young lady. I have prayed and meditated over the matter of witchcraft for years. I can easily tell an authentically evil person from one merely performing a bag of tricks. As you know, I have traveled abroad. That trick with the fire is well-known in England and performed often at fairs and circuses. As a medical man, I know how the proper application of pressure on the neck can induce an unconscious state. It comes as no surprise, however, that my flock here is awed by the magic. I will enlighten them soon in a Sunday sermon. But for today their lack of knowledge served Hamilton's purpose."

"Then you always believed in my innocence?"

He took hold of her hand. "My dear girl, I've never met a more truly kind and courageous woman. Your goodness and strength of spirit shine from your eyes, though I'm sorry you're not of my faith. I've talked to the families of the people you cared for. They had nothing but praise for your gentle manner and tireless devotion. Some of the people died, it's true, but through no fault of yours. And perhaps most important, I—and my family —probably owe our lives to you and the treatment you and your servant shared with me."

"Then you had the transplantation?"

"After great soul-searching, I did indeed. When I recovered from the brief illness, I inoculated my children. It was the most difficult decision of my life and Sammy was quite ill. I was afraid he would die and I would never know if . . . well, if I had caused his death."

"A terrible ordeal, I'm sure," she agreed gently.

"But we all recovered. I intend to thoroughly investigate this treatment in the months and years to come. What a great blessing for mankind to discover a way to save future generations from the scourge of the black death."

"But why didn't you testify on my behalf at the trial?"

"It was my intention to do so, no matter how shocked

my friends might be that I had experimented with the treatment. I came today for that express purpose. But when Hamilton took the blame upon himself and you were exonerated, that was no longer necessary."

"But, Reverend, what about Braden? We both know he's no sorcerer, but everyone else is convinced otherwise. We must do something—at once." She rose from the cot. "If I'm free to go, I must insist on seeing him now. He'll have to prove his innocence."

"He cannot," said Mather. "Don't you see, to do so would put you once again in jeopardy."

"I don't care!" she stormed. "I refuse to let him hang. You must help me!"

"Be calm, lady. I have some ideas, but we must take one step at a time. He has gone to great lengths to save you. I'm sure he knew I would make certain you used caution."

"The devil take caution," she snapped, "if you'll forgive my rudeness, sir. I'm going to see him at once."

"That shouldn't be too difficult. He's two cells away, heavily chained, though the judges had a hard time finding anyone with courage enough to lock him up."

Leaving Mather, she hurried down the hall, but faced a solid locked door. She was standing before it, hands on hips, when two guards approached.

"Unlock this immediately," she demanded. "I must speak to Captain Hamilton."

"Well, Lady Pickering, ye're mighty bossy for a woman who just escaped the noose," said one of the men.

"How do we know he won't possess you again?" asked the other.

"I'm quite myself, thank you. I have no fear of the man. Now open this door. Since he has been good enough to . . . ah . . . set me free, I must make certain he is not mistreated."

"Mistreated?" the guard guffawed. "He'll be treated just fine. Strung up like the others. Why, in any other place he'd be burned alive." Grinning, he inserted a key in the lock and pulled open the door. "We've come for

Corey," he announced. "Come on, Giles. Your turn to face the judges."

She entered the dim cell, ignoring the commotion made by the guards' removal of Giles Corey. Her heart in her throat, she looked at Braden.

Behind her the guard said, "We're closing the door, lady, but we won't lock ye in. That fellow's not going anywhere just now."

She could see that would be impossible. Braden was still shirtless, but his leg irons were back in place. In addition, both wrists were now chained to iron hooks fastened to the wall. And worse, a heavy metal collar had been fastened around his neck and attached to a hook behind him. He had no choice but to stand with his back against the stone. She was appalled at the cruelty and wondered how long he would have to endure such treatment.

She moved to him and gazed up at his face, barely lighted by the one flickering candle sitting on the floor. "Braden . . . dear heaven . . ." Her voice caught.

He gave her a slow smile. "Don't blame the Puritans. People always fear what they don't understand. And I did my best to scare them half out of their wits. It worked too."

Reaching up, she ran her hands across his shoulders, along his forearms, then closed them over the irons confining his wrists. She leaned against his chest, her cheek resting against the curling mat of hair. She could hear the beating of his heart. What could she say to him? What words were there to express what she felt at this moment? She knew it was a sin to love anyone or anything more than God, but at this moment, she would have laid her soul at Braden Hamilton's feet.

She felt his lips touch the top of her head. A choked sob escaped her lips.

"Come, little one, no tears. I've won, don't you see? Worked like—well, like magic." His words were light, but there was an undertone of tension. "Look at me, Amanda."

Her eyes brimming, she looked up to meet his tender blue gaze.

"Go to the *Wind Rose*. Wait there until you hear I'm . . . dead. You've fancied yourself a sea captain. Take charge of the sloop—with Mister Jones's help, of course. He's a fine seaman and will take you to Bermuda . . . or England . . . wherever you want to go. I wouldn't advise you to go to Boston or Jamestown. At least not while your scheming, cowardly brother is still abroad." He paused. "Amanda? Do you hear me?"

"Yes, I hear you," she said. "And I will go to your ship on the day that you go with me and not before."

"God, woman, you're stubborn as a stump. Don't tell me I've wasted all my talent on such an unappreciative chit."

"Braden, I'm not leaving you. I've spoken to Cotton Mather. He has great power and influence—more than anyone in Massachusetts. He doesn't believe you're a sorcerer. I'm sure he'll help us."

"He's a decent man, all right. Has more brains than any local I've met so far. That's why I put you in his charge. He admires you, I've noticed. I counted on him to get you safely away."

"I'm not going and that's that."

He leaned his head against the wall. She could see his pulse throbbing along his throat above the cruel collar.

"Braden," she whispered, "you're in pain and I stand here arguing. I'm fetching Mather at once."

Straightening, he shifted in his irons. "No. Not yet. I can stand it awhile. A day or so, if that must be. My trial is scheduled after Giles Corey, so I've been told. And he's just been taken."

"But that could last days. Surely they won't leave you like . . . like this," her voice rose shrilly.

"Corey is a clever fellow. He'll not plead guilty or innocent. He believes the judges cannot pass sentence as long as he remains silent. I've decided to adopt that same tack. And there's something else."

"What? What?"

"He's discovered an English law which states the Crown can claim any property belonging to a person convicted of witchcraft. He has lands and property he intends to leave to his children. He made a will a few days ago."

"I don't care about Corey or his will," she cried. "I just want to get you out of here."

"Shh," he soothed. "Let's see how Giles fares. Then we'll decide what's best."

Moving away, she clenched her fists and paced around the room. "I must think . . . think," she said half to herself.

The door opened to admit Cotton Mather. "They told me to take you away now, Amanda," he explained apologetically. "But I have permission to offer a prayer for the two of you."

"Thank God, Reverend," Braden said. "Say a quick one and get her out of here before someone reports she is still trafficking with the Devil."

She was obligated to bow her head, but she heard nothing of the prayer. When "Amen" was spoken, she again stood before Braden. "Don't despair, my love," she said softly. "We'll see what happens to Giles Corey today. If his plan works then maybe you also will be set free. If not, I'm taking action. Hopefully with Reverend Mather's help."

Cocking an eyebrow, Braden said, "Beware, Amanda. Remember what happened in the courtroom. Must I be forced to repeat my display of power over you to get you away from Salem?"

His teasing words at such a time were most exasperating. "While you're trussed up like a slaughtered carcass, I'll do as I please." She gave him a plucky smile. Then leaning near, she stood on tiptoe to kiss his lips. "Tomorrow, Braden," she said in hushed tones. "Tomorrow I will get you out of this terrible place."

CHAPTER
24

The hearth fire crackled merrily beneath a kettle of simmering water. Daniel Hobbs and his wife, Mercy, had retired early, leaving their two boarders to tend the fire and serve themselves one last cup of tea before going to their respective rooms.

Amanda sat on the cushioned rocker and waited politely for Reverend Mather to finish stoking his long-stemmed pipe. For the first time in weeks, she felt real hope that things would end all right.

The Hobbses' cottage was just down the lane from Salem Commons. It was the reverend's favorite lodging when he arrived late or was too weary to ride back to his home in Boston. The rented rooms would be simple, but quiet and comfortable, he had explained to Amanda. And Mercy's apple brown Betty was second to none in Massachusetts, he added.

Amanda had eaten well and was already feeling relaxed and drowsy. She forced herself not to dwell too much on Braden's present condition. There was nothing she could do for him until tomorrow. Then he would be set free and they could make plans for their future.

Many things had changed because of the events of the

past days. One enormous disappointment was Philip's betrayal. As a result of that, she had no further interest in helping him at Briarfield. As painful as it would be, she would have to give up all claim to the home of her childhood. Let Philip have it. She would never go there again. She had her jewels and she and Braden would find a way to benefit from their value.

"Excuse me, Reverend. You are very meditative this evening, but I had hoped we could visit before retiring."

"Certainly, Amanda. Forgive me, but many things weigh heavily on my mind."

"The witch trials, I'm sure."

"Yes. I've prayed endlessly for the Lord's guidance. The magistrates at the trials have used my words and my writings to condemn the guilty. I pleaded with them to spare the lives of all but the worst offenders. That most of the executed were truly guilty I have no doubt. And certainly those practicing witchcraft not only sin in the eyes of the Church, but they endanger the lives of innocent people in the community. The courts must try the accused. But proving without doubt that a man or a woman is a witch—that is not a simple matter."

"Did you know I was accused of having a witch's mark on my breast? A prick was used and no blood came forth."

His look was somber. "I heard you endured the usual search and questioning. I heard the testimony at your trial."

"Braden said the piercing bodkin was fake—a false blade, he said."

"'Tis possible, unfortunately. Tomorrow if you'll show me who did this to you, I'll investigate it personally."

"What do you think will happen to Giles Corey?"

"It's out of my hands. He's not been a popular man in this town. And his wife has been found guilty and will hang in a few days. The afflicted girls are certain he is tormenting them. But if he won't acknowledge the court's authority, it cannot legally pass a sentence of hanging. Still, there are other ways."

"Other ways?"

"Let's wait until tomorrow. Then God's will be done."

She nodded, thinking that as soon as Corey was released, she and Mather could petition for Braden's release for the same reason. She stifled a yawn. "I fear I cannot keep my eyes open another minute. Mercy has promised to wake me early so I can go to the Meeting House with you."

He stood and held his hand over her head. "Bow for an evening's benediction then," he suggested.

Following his heartfelt prayer for strength and wisdom, she started for her room. Pausing long enough to take one last look at the famous clergyman, she saw him on his knees on the rag rug before the dying embers. He had lain aside his pipe and his hands were folded in prayer. She didn't envy him the heavy burden he carried. Actually she pitied him. She would always remember him as her friend and as a man of courage and conviction.

Amanda was up before dawn and took breakfast in the kitchen with Mercy Hobbs.

Reverend Mather soon appeared and by eight o'clock, the two were walking toward the Commons in the fresh dew of the September morning. The path was strewn with red and gold leaves from the forest of oak and maple, and there was a slight chill in the breeze carrying aloft land- and seabirds in their first food search of the day.

She had expected the Commons to be deserted, but instead a sizeable crowd had gathered outside the Meeting House.

"What is it, Reverend? I can't see what's happening."

"Corey, I believe. They're bringing him out again from the prison. Dragging him, in fact."

"Do you see Braden anywhere? I'll go to his cell if he's not here."

Mather craned his neck. Several men at the back of the gathering saw him and began to clear a path. "Stay close,

Amanda. And keep Mercy's hood and cape around you. Your captain's fear for you could still be justified."

With lowered head, she moved along behind him. When he suddenly halted, she nearly bumped against him. "What is it?" she asked, still unable to see.

He revolved slowly to look down at her. "Go back. I was afraid of this. Go to Mercy's and wait there."

"But why?"

"There's a sight here that you mustn't see. Not you or any woman."

"Is Braden here?" she persisted.

"Yes. He's still in chains and flanked by prison guards."

"Then I'm staying. When Mister Corey's trial is ended, I intend to see that Braden is also freed."

Mather placed his hands on her shoulders. "You must be strong, my dear. In the matter of Giles Corey, he is being forced to acknowledge the court's authority. He will not be allowed to remain silent, after all."

"What? But how . . ." The look in Mather's eyes sent renewed fear racing to her heart. "Let me pass," she insisted. "I *will* see Braden."

She pushed past him to the front of the crowd. People were streaming now from all corners of the village. Men, women, children and the two afflicted girls stood nearby. Braden was at the front of the clearing. She looked at him, but he didn't see her in her hooded cloak. His gaze was fixed to his right. Giles Corey was being laid on his back on a narrow platform.

Then she too looked. It was several moments before she realized what was going on. When she did, she felt the shock like a physical blow to her body. Her throat tightened and her hands clenched beneath her cloak.

Giles was stretched on the platform while his hands were bound tightly to stakes hammered into the ground at his sides. He groaned slightly, but appeared too weak to struggle.

A man beside her muttered, "Yesterday and again today. He'll speak now, I'll wager."

She felt sick at her stomach but couldn't take her eyes from the scene. Looking again at Braden, she wondered if somehow she could make her way to him, manage a few words.

As she and the crowd watched in silence, two hefty men lifted an oaken plank and placed it on top of Giles's body, leaving only his face above its edge. His lips formed an O, but no sound emerged. His eyes were open and staring at some point in the sky.

One of the magistrates leaned over him and said so all could hear, "Giles Corey, you are now subjected to *peine forte et dure*—until you answer your indictment or until you die. Speak and you will be spared to stand trial. Otherwise what was begun yesterday will be finished today."

Corey's head raised slightly. In a voice amazingly strong, he cried, "Put on the weights—I'll have no judgment but God's."

The onlookers gasped. They had seen many dramatic sights these past months, but nothing to compare with this.

"Begin," ordered the judge, stepping back.

Amanda looked at Braden. He had told her he could expect the same fate as Giles. The thought sent horror catapulting through her body. No doubt that was why he alone of the accused had been brought to witness the gruesome proceedings.

"Ah—ah—" Corey groaned as a large slab of rock was placed over his chest.

She bit her lip to keep from screaming.

Two additional men were put to work bringing boulders to pile atop Corey's body. His head lolled from side to side and the sound of cracking ribs was plainly heard. He moaned, he gagged—but he did not speak.

Minute followed agonizing minute. An hour passed. Amanda stood with the others, knowing the man being gradually pressed could not possibly live much longer. The entire atmosphere was more of a wake than an execution. Everyone prayed, women cried, children were ordered home. Still Giles Corey clung to life.

Dear Lord, let him die, she began praying to herself. No one should ever endure such suffering.

"More—hurry—more weight," he was heard to plead hoarsely.

She covered her mouth with her hand. Hanging was a terrible end, but this . . . why, he would have been better off to be hanged or even burned at the stake.

The judge bent over him. "Very well, Mister Corey," he said. "More rocks—bring the biggest. This man is determined to meet his maker. This has gone on long enough."

Another huge boulder was piled on top of the others.

She buried her face in her hands as the crowd groaned along with the dying man. When she looked again, it was over.

The people around her shook their heads in disbelief. No one thought he would go through with it. What amount of anger and determination did it take to die in such torment? While the crowd was distracted, she made her way to stand by Braden.

He looked down at her for a moment, as if not quite able to accept the reality of what he'd just witnessed.

"Braden, we must do something. Now, before it's too late," she whispered. "I'll go to your ship—arrange a rescue."

"No," he snapped. "Impossible. I don't want you involved any further—nor any of my crew endangered."

"But then you must acknowledge the court, go to trial, anything. But not this," she choked in desperation.

His eyes were stark and disbelieving. "That man was innocent. He chose his own way to die. In my opinion, Giles Corey is a good example to follow."

"No—no," she cried. "Don't say that."

Braden's guards turned at the sound and took his arms. "Oh, no ye don't," one snorted. "Back ye go—and remember what ye saw here. Tomorrow's your turn, sorcerer," he said with a sneer.

Amanda had no choice but to watch him being led away toward prison. For a moment she felt faint, but then an arm went around her shoulders.

"Have faith, Amanda," said Cotton Mather. "I'll do what I can at his trial."

Her knees felt like newly churned butter. But she was already forming a plan. She motioned Mather to follow her to the trees where they could speak privately.

She removed her hood and fixed him with a determined look. "Captain Hamilton may die tomorrow. If he does, I will also die—not so quickly, but a little each day of my life. I must confess to you that I not only love this man with all my heart, but I have bedded with him in a sinful union. We had planned to wed. If we do not, our souls could be forever lost."

"Oh, dear Lord," he murmured. "I had no idea . . ."

"Only you know, and only you can save our souls. Marry us, Reverend Mather. Today. In the church or in the prison—I care not which. I want us to go to our Lord united in soul as well as body." She gripped his sleeve. "I beg you on the lives of your children—do this for me."

He drew her into his arms. She was wracked with sobs, clinging to him, using his strength to keep from falling.

"Sh . . . sh, child." He patted her. "I will arrange it. I'll get the documents and say the words at the prison. Ye are Anglican. The church therefore would not be appropriate."

"Thank you," she choked through her tears. "How long will it take to get the papers?"

"An hour, considering the confusion today."

"I'm going to Braden's ship. My maid is there, I believe, and someone to witness for the captain."

He tipped up her chin. "Are you sure this is what you want, Amanda? You could again be a widow the day following your wedding."

"This is not the same, not at all. I'll meet you at the prison in one hour. And thank you, sir, from the depths of my heart."

CHAPTER
25

Lieutenant Jones was admitted to Braden's cell shortly before three in the afternoon. He carried a jug of water, soap, towels, a razor and a bundle of clothing.

With considerable trepidation, the guard unlocked the accused sorcerer's wrist, neck and leg irons. "I'm keeping an eye on both of you," he snorted. "Clean him up and be quick about it."

Braden moved as if in a trance. Sleepless nights and pain for hours on end had taken their toll on his mental alertness. Only for brief periods had he been allowed to rest from his ordeal of the chains. Rubbing his wrists, he stared at Jones in confusion. "What . . . what are you doing here?"

"Cotton Mather and the lady arranged it. They'll be here at three o'clock or thereabouts. Ye'd better wash up a bit and get into these clean clothes. I picked out one of your silk shirts."

"What's going on? My execution?"

"Not today, though perhaps tomorrow, I regret to say. Let me help ye, sir."

Aching in every joint, Braden removed his filthy

clothing and washed and dressed in silence. His head was beginning to clear and his eyes to focus when Cotton Mather entered, followed closely by Amanda and Coco.

Tucking his shirttail into his leather belt, he looked at his unexpected guests. "What the hell's going on?" he asked as if just waking from a deep sleep.

Amanda had done her best to make the occasion resemble a proper wedding, if for no other reason than to bolster all their spirits. She had gone to Braden's sloop, despite his orders to the contrary, and arranged for Coco and Jones to appear at the ceremony. While there, she had borrowed Coco's best dress: a pink cotton frock trimmed with blue ribbon around the neck and elbow-length sleeves. On the walk back from the waterfront, she had picked a late-blooming aster to place in her freshly washed hair, which was tied at her nape with a matching blue ribbon. It was hardly the wedding gown of her dreams, but at least she had discarded the dreary black garment she'd been wearing during her confinement these past days.

She looked up at Braden, then used one finger to brush an errant lock from his forehead. "My darling, we're going to be married."

His eyebrows lifted. "Married? I must say, Widow Pickering, you have a penchant for short marriages."

She was able to match his light tone. "True. But I do choose the most fascinating husbands, don't you agree?"

"I suppose I must. I seem to have little choice in most matters these days."

She cocked her head. "I assume, Captain Hamilton, your offer to make me your wife is still in effect."

His teasing look evaporated. He took both her hands in his and lifted them to his lips. They were warm against her fingertips. Then he pulled her gently into his arms. With controlled emotion, he spoke to her and to the others watching. "I proposed to this lady some time ago. I accepted her rejection, though it tore at my heart. I can honestly tell all of you gathered here, that regardless of the circumstances—and whatever the future holds—

this is the happiest moment of my life and I consider myself the most fortunate man on earth."

Coco burst into tears, then buried her nose in a large kerchief.

"Come then," said Cotton Mather, visibly moved, "we'll say the words, sign the papers, then move the newlyweds out of these most unpleasant surroundings."

"You mean we can leave here?" asked Braden.

"Leave *this* cell," Mather answered. "Not the prison, I'm afraid. I arranged for you to spend the night in the cell Amanda previously occupied. At least there's a bed and a table and washbasin."

Braden turned to Mather. "I appreciate your efforts, Reverend. But after the ceremony, I must insist you take Amanda away from here. I'll not have her spending one second longer than necessary in this foul place. I told you before I want her out of here—out of prison—out of Salem—out of New England," he said heatedly. "She can leave on my ship right after the ceremony."

"Braden." Amanda took his arm. "I'm not leaving you while there's hope. Reverend Mather will appear at your trial tomorrow to speak on your behalf. He will spend the remainder of this afternoon preparing your defense. Please, my love. The magistrates have given me permission to stay with you—thanks to the reverend's influence. In return, I agreed to leave immediately after your trial no matter what the judges decide."

He slipped his arm around her waist. "The judges won't decide. I've made my own decision, as I told you yesterday. I will go the way of Giles Corey. Though of course I greatly appreciate Reverend Mather's efforts."

She threw her arms around his shoulders. "You must wait until tomorrow and in the meantime, I'm not leaving."

Gently he moved her arms away. "Amanda Sheffield, of all the women who ever drew breath, you are the most stubborn, the most beautiful and far and away the most amazing." He leaned to kiss her as passionately as if they were not being stared at by four witnesses.

Mather cleared his throat. "Excuse me—may we begin."

Braden released her, but his eyes consumed her with absolute adoration. Taking her hand, he led her forward to face the clergyman.

Reverend Mather conducted the simple ceremony. After he pronounced Amanda and Braden man and wife, he closed his book and waited while Braden tenderly kissed the bride.

Lieutenant Jones stepped forth wearing a shy smile. "Er . . . 'scuse me, Captain. I brought this for ye . . . for her." He handed Braden a gold and pearl ring.

A smiling Braden slipped it onto her finger. "Good of you, Jones," he said, keeping his eyes on Amanda's face.

"It's done," interjected the almost forgotten guard. "Let's move along," he said impatiently.

After the signing of the documents, Amanda hugged a sniffling Coco while Braden again expressed his thanks to Mather and Lieutenant Jones. The atmosphere was laced with tension despite everyone's effort to achieve the semblance of a happy occasion.

"Enough, enough," snapped the guard.

The wedding party trailed through the bleak hallway until arriving at the cell previously occupied by Amanda and Elizabeth Proctor. Elizabeth had been moved elsewhere and now Cotton Mather took his leave with a promise to reappear at the trial the next morning. Coco handed Amanda a pouch, then hurried away beside Mister Jones. Without a word, the guard slammed the door and bolted it.

Amanda stood awkwardly before Braden, wondering if ever a bride had experienced such a whirlwind of conflicting emotions.

He took her hand. "Good of Jones to think of bringing the ring. I showed it to him after we left Bermuda. Told him it was for my bride, whom I hoped to attain before returning home. I hadn't expected it to be quite like this."

"It's a lovely ring, Braden. It fits nicely." She held it up to catch the light of the afternoon sun filtering through the small window.

"It belonged to my mother's mother, the Countess of Wentworth. I'm glad you like it, little one."

She gazed up at him. "I will treasure it till the day I die—pass it on . . ."

"To our child?" he said, reaching out to stroke her hair. "The child we'll conceive tonight—God willing."

"I pray so," she murmured, then turned to light the lamp on the table. The sun's rays were fast fading from the cell, leaving deep shadows covering the blank walls. She picked up the pouch Coco had left on the table. "What do you suppose is in here?"

The contents were pleasantly appropriate. First she removed a folded satin sheet. When it was opened, a delicate gown of lavender silk was revealed. Also in the pouch was a flask of fine Burgundy wine from the ship's store.

She gave Braden a brave smile. "See? We have everything we need for a perfect wedding night."

He responded with a teasing grin. "Maybe too much. The gown is perhaps . . . not entirely necessary."

"What a shocking thing to say, Lord Hamilton," she quipped.

"You have a scandalous husband, Lady Hamilton, or hadn't you noticed?"

The awkwardness they had felt evaporated in their mutual laughter.

"Lady Hamilton," she said happily as she circled the room with mincing steps. "Yes, I do like the sound of it."

He followed her and pulled her into his arms. "There are some advantages to having a lady locked inside one's bedroom. Escape is quite impossible, my dear girl."

"Hmm." She raised her eyes to his. Her heart caught, but before she could succumb to the tragic reality of their surroundings, she forced a smile and tossed her head. "First you must provide refreshment. 'Tis only proper."

"Oh, yes—the wine. I doubt if the lavish feast I ordered will arrive anytime soon. We shall begin without it."

She moved to the table and put a finger to her cheek. "My goodness. We have but one chair at our table and no goblets at all. I must speak to the servants."

He picked up the satin sheet and with a flourish, wafted it onto the thin mattress. "Have a seat, my lady, on the chaise."

She sat primly and waited for him to open the flask.

He sat beside her. "You may drink first," he offered. "By taking turns, we will have our first sharing as man and wife."

She took a long drink from the lip of the container, then handed it to him.

He drank deeply, then passed it back. Her eyes held his while she sipped.

He took the flask from her hand, placed it on the floor, and eased her into his arms.

His lips, warmly searching and tasting of wine, covered hers. She answered his search with the tip of her own tongue, then closed her eyes and let the kiss explore and tease, igniting passions deep within her.

When he began loosening her bodice, she covered his hand. "Nay, love. I will do it. After all, this is our wedding night. We must observe some propriety."

"Whatever you say, my lady wife," he answered lightly. "I want it to be perfect for you."

At his words, her eyes misted and she quickly turned away. No matter what, she must keep up the pretense that nothing was amiss on this night of nights. "You know, of course, I'm not entirely inexperienced," she said turning back, her emotions once again under control.

"Ah, is that a fact? If I should meet the gent who first partook of your charms, I shall . . . congratulate him on his enormous good fortune."

"But since this is our wedding night, you must pretend . . . well, close your eyes. I will surprise you."

With an amused smile, he obeyed.

Quickly she turned away and took off the borrowed dress and undergarments. She slid into the gossamer gown and tied its satin ribbon beneath her breasts. She removed the pins from her hair and allowed it to fall in silken waves along her back and shoulders and tucked the aster behind one ear.

When she turned, Braden was lying on his side on the narrow cot, his head resting on one hand. His eyes were closed as she'd requested.

"Now," she said as she moved toward him from behind the table.

His eyes opened and his smile deepened.

"Don't speak yet." She held up her arms and revolved, letting the delicately sheer fabric drift and flow around her. Her slender body was silhouetted by the lantern's glow. When again she faced him where he lay in the shadows, she saw his smile was replaced by a look of unconcealed desire.

"You tempt the devil, my lady," he said in low tones. "Bride or not, you're a temptress without equal. Come here at once."

Happily she moved near, but hesitated when he continued to lie prone on the bed.

"The cot requires some . . . imagination," he said. "If you'll allow me to lead you, I believe you'll be pleased."

She sank to her knees on the floor beside him. He was bare to the waist and still darkly tanned despite his confinement. She caressed his shoulders, pausing to wince at the feel of the badly chafed flesh along his throat and wrists. She instantly reminded herself she must not think of any terrible experiences, at least not for this one enchanted night.

Leaning toward her, he slipped his hands around her slender waist and placed her astride him as if she were a plaything. The silk gown fell open below the ribbons. Her inner thighs were parted and her triangle of softness rested on the bare flesh of his waist. Tossing her hair, she arched against him, moving her hands behind her till she gripped his knees. The feeling of dominating his hard masculine body sent shivers of excitement to her very core.

His hands found the ribbons; the gown drifted away. Moistening his fingertips, he circled each of her taut nipples, then gently massaged the perfectly shaped young breasts.

Sighing with pleasure, she rocked against him. His calloused hands moved along her hips, then one claimed the area between her thighs.

"Braden . . . oh . . ." She stretched out along his body. Her hair tumbled around their faces like sunlight shimmering through a summer shower.

While holding her tight against him, he kissed her deeply and hungrily. Then shifting to one side, he removed the remainder of his clothing.

She lay facing him. Entwining her fingers in his thickly curling hair, she kissed him with increasing fervor.

He pulled her buttocks against his hips. Feeling his aroused hardness, the heat smoldering within her blazed into a searing fire.

"I need you," she pleaded.

"I know. As I need you, my own sweet love." He lifted her again to sit across his body.

She looked down at the sculptured lines of his face. He was solemn now, intense, his eyes promising fulfillment if she would follow his lead.

"Like this?" she asked softly.

"Aye. If you like—if you're comfortable."

"Yes, but I never thought—"

"With you above me? Of course, my darling." With his knees, he parted her legs, then positioned himself directly beneath her softest area.

She felt him, strong and vital, throbbing against her.

He placed both hands along her rib cage and lifted her upward, while at the same moment, pressing himself into her hidden sweetness.

"Ah." She sighed, throwing back her head as she received him. As he moved beneath her, she felt wave after moist wave of spiraling desire. "Oh . . . yes," she said, echoing the happy cry of a thousand generations of fortunate women.

He raised up to nuzzle each breast in turn. His lips found her extended nipples; he suckled them and encircled them with his tongue. Then with a groan, he lay down to more deeply possess her.

She planted her hands on his stomach as he gripped her hips and rocked her gently, then with quicker rhythm. Every movement sent showers of heat and uncontrollable need through her inner recesses.

Moaning with delight, she allowed her body to become one with his. Her whole being surged and plunged until her savage need for him was almost unbearable. Still he thrust, his breath coming fast, his flesh damp now, his muttered half words of love drifting to her as if from far away.

"Love me . . . love me," she gasped in desperation.

Once more he rocked into her while pressing her downward, then again—exploding—together their bodies a torrent of unleashed passion.

Her cry of pleasure mingled with his low-throated moan. Only as the tide slowly subsided did she realize her cheeks were wet with tears.

With extreme tenderness, he lowered her to his damp chest, withdrawing carefully, stroking her, pushing her moist hair away from her temples. "Are . . . are you all right, Mandy? I didn't hurt you?"

She lay her head against him and cried brokenly, embarrassed that she couldn't stop, wanting to explain her joy and her heartbreak, but unable to speak.

"It's all right, little one. I understand." His voice was soothing and achingly sad. "You've endured so much— and your strength has just now been drained away. Rest, my sweet girl . . . my darling wife. Later, before dawn, we'll love once more—to ensure a babe."

She felt his deep sigh. Her heart and her throat were too full to allow her to respond. She merely ran her lips across his chest and softly stroked his shoulders. She no longer held his masculinity, but it would return, she knew. And she would welcome him with all the love of which a woman was capable. Whether or not a baby was the result, this night would blaze forever in her memory, like the sunshine of a thousand tomorrows, tomorrows they might never share.

She dozed for a time, lying beside him, held secure in the crook of his arm. Sometime in the darkest hours, long after the candle had expired, he placed her on her back and took her again—again with sweet and filling passion.

After that she didn't sleep, but lay still, listening to his even breathing. Despite herself, a snake of fear began to coil in the pit of her stomach. Daylight would bring separation, terror, perhaps even death. What would she do if he were pressed like Giles Corey? Could she survive the sight? Would it cost her her mind, if not her life? Could she run away, abandon him at his darkest hour? He wouldn't want her there, she was sure. But how could she not show as much courage as he?

She laid her hand over his heart. Let him live, dear God, help me today in my mission. Let me say and do the right things. Guide my actions and my words. Please, God—oh, please, I pray Thee.

CHAPTER
26

Purple tentacles of light seeped into the prison cell, warning Amanda that the night of love was over, and she must face the terrible challenge of the coming day.

She suspected Braden had also been lying awake for some time. She snuggled against him and moved her hand lightly across his chest. Sometime following their last lovemaking, he had pulled the edge of the sheet over her to protect her from the cool dampness of the cell. Was this to be their only night to share such small joys? Would she never again lie so close beside his body—safe, sheltered, loved—even in sleep? Before tears could start, she removed the sheet and swung her toes to the frigid floor. She jumped when a varmint scurried away into some hidden hole.

From behind, Braden slipped his arm around her, holding her gently, not suggesting passion, but allowing them one final moment of bittersweet togetherness. His forearm encircled her breasts; his lips sought the back of her neck between tangled curls. It was plain in the growing light that he would soon be painfully in need of her. And there was no more time. The guard would arrive any minute to take her away.

She took his hand and lifted his scarred wrist to her lips.

He caressed her back, lingering, his desire to prolong the poignant moment an unspoken wish.

"You must get ready," he said. "I only wanted . . . a few minutes more . . ."

Leaning back, she nuzzled against his chest and placed a feathery kiss at the hollow of his neck. Then quickly, she left the bed and began to dress.

With teeth clenched against heartbreak and anxiety, she pulled on the rumpled dress and searched for her stockings and shoes. Shivering with more than the chill air, she performed the task hurriedly and mindlessly.

When she dared look back at him, he had on his breeches and was putting the sheet into Coco's pouch. "Thank her again," he said. "'Twas a thoughtful thing indeed."

She couldn't stand it. She rushed to throw her arms about his waist, bury her cheek in the raspy hair of his chest.

"No—no, Mandy," he said hoarsely. "We must get through this, and you've made a brave beginning."

She could barely choke out her words between chattering teeth. "Don't let them do . . . that to you. It's horrible—unendurable. It would kill me too."

He held her close; his words were firm and final. "You must live. You hold the future inside you, I pray. It's more important . . . no, 'tis mandatory that the court not condemn me as a criminal. Briarfield will be lost to you as long as Philip is in control there. You have no further claim to the marquess's estates in England. But you *are* Lady Braden Hamilton. You are the mistress of Hamilton Plantation of Bermuda. If I should be found guilty of witchcraft, the Crown could claim all my property. Mandy"—he tipped her chin upward—"whatever happens, you will go to the plantation, take care of it in my memory, raise our child there . . . if indeed we are blessed. You have great courage, my darling. Promise me you'll leave as soon as the decision is made. Don't stay. Swear to me—now."

She stepped back and stiffened her spine. "I will swear to go to Bermuda if you die. If I bear a child, it will be raised to honor your memory always. But I still have hope we may yet win your freedom with Cotton Mather's help. As for leaving Salem while you still breathe, I will not. And that is absolutely final."

Approaching footsteps broke into the tension. Placing her hands on his shoulders, she halted his protest with a swift kiss. When the door opened, she rushed outside without looking back.

She walked rapidly through the village. Early morning cookfires were beginning to perfume the morning air as she hurried to the wharf and went aboard Braden's sloop. She roused Coco, who was occupying the small cabin next to the captain's, and changed into the black frock of yesterday. With a straw basket tucked under her arm, she rushed back across the Commons toward the Hobbses' cottage. As prearranged with Cotton Mather, her last desperate effort to save Braden would begin there.

Mercy Hobbs opened the door. "They're already here," she said in a conspiratorial tone. "In the parlor. The reverend's been praying over them for nigh half an hour."

"How do they seem?"

"Very upset. Crying a lot. I couldn't help overhearing, you understand. Whatever Mary Walcott says, Elizabeth Hubbard echoes her. I never did like those smarty young girls. Why, they act more like spoiled children than nearly grown women."

"Maybe they're just terribly overprotected, Mercy," Amanda observed while returning Mercy's cape. "Thank you for the wrap. I won't need it today. It's warming rapidly. Besides, I don't care who recognizes me."

"Excuse me . . ." Mercy began with a shy smile, her rosy cheeks flushing, "I heard you were married yester-

273

day. I know things look bad, but Reverend Mather has assured Daniel and me that he believes both of you are innocent. His word is all I need. I do hope things come out all right, ma'am."

Amanda gave her a sad smile. "You're very kind to say so, Mercy. It takes courage to stand against others' opinions. I only pray the reverend can convince the judges."

"If anyone can, he will," she said pertly.

"I'll go in now. Do say a prayer for me, Mercy."

"Yes, ma'am. I certainly will."

Amanda said one herself as she knocked, then opened the door to Mercy's parlor. "Reverend Mather, may I come in?"

"Of course, dear. We were just speaking of you." Cotton Mather was sitting beside the hearth fire. On the floor in front of him sat two girls in their late teens, both wearing traditional Puritan dresses and crisp white bonnets, both pale with dark blue circles under deeply sunken and tragedy-filled eyes. They visibly shrunk toward the minister as she entered the room.

"Mary . . . Elizabeth . . . may I introduce Amanda Hamilton. Yesterday I had the pleasure of joining Amanda and Captain Hamilton in holy matrimony." His voice was remarkably cheerful under the circumstances.

Rather than taking a chair, Amanda sank down to the floor to face the girls. After all, she was only a year or two older than they.

She smiled with as much warmth and sympathy as she could muster. Regardless of what she thought of them, Mary and Elizabeth held the key to Braden's life.

"I asked the reverend to arrange this meeting," she said. "I'm so glad you both came. You're Mary, I presume. My husband told me you were a most attractive and sensitive girl." She knew Mary was the one to win over. She hoped Elizabeth would then follow along.

"He . . . he did?"

Amanda put the straw basket on the floor. "When I

told him I planned to see you this morning, he suggested I bring along an old friend of yours. Look in the basket."

Mary looked up at Mather. He nodded his approval. Carefully she opened the basket, then closed it with a squeak of fear.

Amanda spoke soothingly. "Now, Mary, you remember the darling kitty you gave Braden a few months ago. You *know* she's quite harmless. You own her sisters and brothers . . . her mother, do you not?"

"Well . . . yes . . . but at the trial . . . your brother said . . ."

"Nonsense." Amanda grinned. "My jealous brother is such a sissy to be afraid of your sweet little kitten. Don't you think that's just plain silly?" She opened the basket and Persephone hopped out. To her private joy, the cat went at once to Mary and began to meow as if she remembered her.

"Oh," Mary exclaimed, unable to hide her pleasure. She stroked the cat and held her atop her apron. "You're so big. My goodness, bigger than the others."

Amanda smiled again. "I'll tell you a secret, Mary. She's going to be a mother."

"Really? Oh, I knew she was a good cat. I wanted Captain Hamilton to keep her always to remem—" She stopped; her eyes narrowed. "But the captain hates me now. He was trying to hurt me."

Reverend Mather spoke up. "Now, Mary, we've talked about that. In the case of the captain, there's no real proof he's a sorcerer. His tricks were done to save the lady he loves, the woman who is now his wife. He upset you because he was a stranger and an Englishman— maybe even a privateer. The deeds he's done while a soldier made him seem evil, but they were done for the good of England. You're a sensitive lass and only felt his adventurous spirit, not any true devil inside him. He's really harmless and would like to leave Massachusetts and continue building ships to help in protecting us from Spanish pirates."

Mary continued to pet Persephone while saying in a

childlike voice, "I thought he should hang like the others. I thought he made me believe I loved him, but I don't anymore. He was too scary—with the fire and all. No, I don't love him, but I don't hate him either."

Amanda's hopes soared. "Of course you don't, Mary. I'm sure you and Elizabeth don't hate anyone."

"No, ma'am," said Mary.

"No, ma'am," said Elizabeth.

Mather said, "The girls have been terribly disturbed over Giles Corey's manner of dying. Though he was guilty of causing them terrible suffering, they have said to me they hope no one else will die like that."

Amanda searched Mary's face. There was indeed suffering there, geniune misery—and perhaps a touch of dementia. "I'm so deeply sorry for you . . . for both of you. As you know, my husband is a citizen of the colony of Bermuda. He has a beautiful home there and wonderful birds and flowers. He told me he hoped you could sail there for a visit one day. He can dive to a sunken galleon and bring you a gift like this cross he found for me. Would you like that?"

Mary nodded.

Elizabeth nodded.

"But if he is executed as a witch, he will lose his home. The king will take it for himself. You wouldn't want that, would you?"

Mary and Elizabeth shook their heads.

"So . . . he will have to be pressed to death just like Giles Corey. He will have to remain mute and die under the boulders."

"Oh, no," Mary said, wide-eyed. "I don't think that will happen, if Reverend Mather tells everyone he is innocent—that whatever evil he held over Elizabeth and me has now disappeared."

Amanda's heart was in her throat. Careful, she told herself. Choose every word with care. "Maybe, but it's not certain they'll believe him. Of course, if you and Elizabeth would appear and say you agree with the reverend . . ."

Mary sat in silence while continuing to pet the cat.

Amanda was certain her heartbeat could be heard by everyone present.

Finally Mary said, "I don't feel very well today. My mother said I should stay in bed."

"Mary dear," Mather said, putting his hand on her head, "you have endured much, but you don't want Braden Hamilton to be pressed to death. Do me this favor and accompany me briefly to the trial. You too, Elizabeth. As soon as each of you has spoken, I'll take you home. Then the judges will make their decision, and you will have no further concern in the matter."

Mary lifted her face to Mather. "I'm so tired . . . sometimes I want to die."

"I know, child, but the Lord will give you strength. Will you do it? Already the trial has begun. We should go at once if we wish to save the captain."

Amanda gnawed her lip to keep from screaming. Why, the girl had seen so much death, so much tragedy, she appeared immune to feeling. How could Mary use the excuse of fatigue to keep her from saving an innocent man's life? But she held her tongue.

"All right—if you want me to." Mary stood and handed the cat to Amanda. It was said as casually as if she had accepted an invitation to go for a walk in the woods.

Amanda took the first real breath she'd had in an hour. With a trembling smile, the best she could manage, she put Persephone in the basket and said, "If you'd like one of Perci's kittens, I'll see you have one."

"No, thank you," Mary answered listlessly. "I have enough cats."

Reverend Mather preceded the three girls in their walk toward the Meeting House.

For Amanda, every step was agonizingly slow. Having left Persephone in the care of Mercy Hobbs, she draped her arms comfortingly around the girls' shoulders and marched them along the leafy path.

To her horror, she saw a crowd gathered outside in the same spot as Giles Corey's execution—a pretty clearing dappled with sunlight and shade by the huge oak trees surrounding it.

The reverend's appearance caused a stir. Amanda followed him through the gathering, aware now of both girls' sudden trembling. Dear heaven, if the two had fits of hysteria at this point, all would be lost.

When she reached the clearing, she stopped to watch Mather approach Judge Hathorne. The judge and his assistant had completed their meeting inside and brought their English sorcerer to this pleasant setting in the fresh morning air to complete his trial—one which was headed for a dreadful conclusion.

Her eyes fell on Braden and her heart turned over inside her. Never had she seen him look more handsome. Apparently Lieutenant Jones had delivered his royal-blue captain's uniform of King Charles's Royal Battalion. The rich color of the coat accented his eyes and the fit across his broad shoulders and tapered hips emphasized his fine physique. The white pants were snug-fitting above knee-high boots. He carried no weapons, but he was indisputably a man of authority and pride. His expression was one of calm resignation with not a trace of fear or bitterness. It was the look of a man who had chosen his course, and no matter how difficult, he would see it through to the end.

As Amanda looked at him, a seed of memory pushed its way into her mind. It intruded while she tried to rehearse her speech to the judge. It was more a vision than a lucid thought. It rose before her like a grotesque, long-forgotten nightmare, forcing its way from a black inner prison into the reality of this moment of life and death.

A blue coat, a brass button, a masculine figure—once whole, now crushed and broken on the ground.

She swayed under the awful realization of her memory. The voodoo doll, the figure Braden himself had willingly smashed under his boot. No. No, her mind screamed in denial. But fear raced through her body like a raging flood.

Mary looked at her. "What's the matter?" she asked through colorless lips. "You nearly fell. We can leave . . . yes, I'd like to go home."

Amanda knew she must regain control at once. Her weakness could ruin everything. "I'm fine now. I'm just so anxious about my husband. We were almost too late."

Judge Hathorne lifted his hand for silence. "I've just been speaking with Reverend Mather. Before the accused is strapped to the board, the reverend wishes to speak."

Mather offered a brief prayer, then announced he had great doubts regarding the captain's guilt. "I know he demonstrated unusual powers," he said, "but it was to convince you of the innocence of his beloved, whom I gave to him in marriage yesterday."

"You said holy words over those two witches?" a man shouted.

"Blasphemy," yelled another.

"My dear friends," Mather continued, "I have never misled you. Indeed it is my own writings on which you've based some of your conclusions as to the power of witchcraft. I ask for your trust now and I assure you I have talked to Our Father at great length. The only thing this man is guilty of is performing simple magic tricks to save the woman he loves."

"No, Mather," interrupted Braden. "She's innocent. Don't suggest otherwise."

"I wouldn't. First, I will explain your tricks. In fact, I've prepared my own demonstration." He faced the crowd, then stepped gingerly onto the plank used for pressing. He took a bottle and poured some sticky liquid over the fingers of his right hand. "Watch closely," he shouted. "I learned this magic in the captain's homeland, from a street entertainer in the west end of London." From some hidden source, fire blazed along his fingers and leaped from their tips.

The crowd gasped as they watched this great man of

their church raise an arm with flames erupting and throw back his head in laughter.

Then the fire died as quickly as it had appeared. Mather pulled a cloth from his pocket and wiped his hand, then held it up for all to see. "Just a mummer's trick," he said, grinning. "Instead of a sorcerer, the captain is only a fake."

The audience had fallen under Mather's spell. They laughed at their own gullibility and clapped in appreciation of his bravado.

"Better give up the cloth, Reverend," a gentleman shouted. "Ye'd make a fortune as a trickster."

With a flourish, Cotton Mather bowed. But then he raised his arms, demanding silence. "My dear friends of Salem. You've been entertained, but this is a serious occasion, after all. I have another announcement and witnesses to corroborate what I'm about to tell you."

The spectators hushed.

"At Lady Amanda Pickering's trial, you saw evidence of spectral possession involving Mary Walcott and Elizabeth Hubbard. I've warned you not to rely on this type of evidence, have I not?" He shook his finger at them like they were naughty schoolchildren. "This very day I met with the girls and with the former Lady Pickering, now Lady Hamilton. The three young women are here today and you'll see there is no evil in their relationship. Come forward, if you will, my dears."

Astonished gasps came from the onlookers.

Amanda held the girls' hands and the three emerged from the crowd, looking for all the world like three young friends on their way to some pleasant outing.

"What's the meaning of this?" shouted Hathorne.

Mather confronted the judge. "Give the girls a chance," he insisted. "You may be surprised."

Judge Hathorne approached them. "Is this true, Mary . . . Elizabeth? You have no further qualms about this lady?"

"No, Judge," murmured Mary.

"She does not possess you or cause you harm?"

"No, Judge," Mary answered.

"You feel she poses no threat—nor does the captain?"

"Yes, it's quite all right," Mary said as Elizabeth nodded in mute agreement.

The crowd erupted in excited conversation.

Amanda dared not breathe, nor even glance at Braden. She waited, her thoughts in desperate prayer, while keeping a serene expression on her face as the judges conferred. It seemed an eternity.

At last Judge Hathorne turned and raised his hands to quiet the gathering. "Since Captain Braden Hamilton has not agreed to recognize this court, and since there are no further accusations against him, he will be freed at once. And since Reverend Cotton Mather and Mary Walcott and Elizabeth Hubbard support the innocence of Lady Amanda Hamilton, she is also no longer accused. The two of you are free to go."

Amanda sank to her knees in the grass. The relief was so sudden and so overwhelming, it sent her senses reeling. She heard little of the commotion around her; it was like the buzzing of a dozen bumblebees. Her hands were touching the wooden plank, the plank on which Braden had expected to die in agony as a price for her future security. Her lips formed a prayer; tears blurred her vision. She had won. Braden had won. They had defeated the court, the voodoo doll, and the witch hunters of Salem. With Cotton Mather as an unlikely ally, they had triumphed over lies and sin and death. Whatever debt Mather owed her had been more than repaid.

She was lifted by strong arms. She couldn't quite focus her eyes or settle the spinning of her head.

"My darling girl," came Braden's voice near her ear. "Hold on to me and we'll soon be out of here."

She clung to him, resting her head against his coat as

he strode briskly for several minutes. The noise of the crowd faded.

"Is she all right?" sounded a woman's familiar voice.

"I think so, Coco," Braden answered. "Did Jones get the carriage?"

"He's bringing it now. He ran to fetch it the minute he heard the judges' verdict."

Amanda opened her eyes. "I'm fine now, Braden. I can stand."

"Relax, my love. It pleases me to hold you."

She was pleased to obey him.

A coach arrived on the road and Jones leaped down from the seat. "Are you sure about this, Captain? We're ready to sail."

"Yes, I'm sure. I'm not leaving until it's settled. Take the sloop to the Boston dock right away. We'll leave from there before nightfall."

She looked up at him. "But, Braden, where are we going? We can leave on the sloop."

He placed her on the cushions inside the coach. "Not quite yet."

"But why not?"

He closed the door and spoke through the window. "I have unfinished business in Boston—with your relatives."

"But, Braden . . . wait . . . Coco . . ."

"Yes, ma'am?"

"It appears my husband is taking us to Boston. Please go to Mercy Hobbs's and retrieve Persephone. If you see Cotton Mather, tell him I'm eternally grateful . . . and Coco—don't linger in Salem Town."

The jolt of the carriage threw her back against the seat. She'd forgotten all about her brother and her aunt—and the jewels. The jewels she cared little about, and she knew Braden felt the same. But Philip and Aunt Sara— no doubt Braden was furious with the two. As the coach bumped briskly along the road leading south, she leaned back and closed her eyes. From the seat above, Braden urged on the horses. She wished Braden would forget thoughts of revenge and go directly to the ship. Of course she understood his fury with the two; why, they'd plotted the deaths of both of them. Naturally his hot-blooded masculine nature demanded satisfaction. As for her, she had never been happier in her life.

CHAPTER
27

Braden drove the carriage at a breakneck clip from Salem to Boston. He vented all his pent-up fury and the unrelenting tension of the past weeks in reckless speed as he maneuvered the coach along the narrow road by the shore and through primal woodland. He couldn't direct his anger at the two milksop teenage girls, who were obviously in a true state of mental unbalance. But he sure as hell could confront that pompous, cowardly, disloyal twit-of-a-brother of Amanda's. How dare the man stand up in court and declare his own sister to be a witch! Why, Amanda had given herself in marriage to the marquess to save Briarfield and Philip from financial disaster. If anyone deserved death by pressing, it was Philip Sheffield.

He halted the carriage in front of the Sheffield house and jumped from the seat.

Opening the door, he snapped at a frazzled Amanda, "If you'll hand me the box that Jones put under the seat, I'll soon be done with this and we can be on our way."

"Just one minute," she flashed. "You have rattled my teeth for the past hour and driven that horse to exhaustion—all in your haste to take revenge on my brother and aunt. Now you order me about like . . . well, like an officious commanding officer. Perhaps it's your handsome uniform that inspires you or the thought that since I'm now your wife, I must jump to do your bidding."

He reached up to assist her from the coach.

"Well, Lord Hamilton, let me hasten to assure—"

He stopped her words by kissing her soundly.

"A shrew," he said when he released her. "I've married a fishwife who is prone to argue even when I'm on my way to avenge her honor and reputation as a Christian lady."

She ran her hands across his shoulders. "Braden, forget your anger. I never want to see Philip again. And I certainly don't want any more to do with Aunt Sara."

"I'm of the opinion your aunt is much to blame for what happened. Do Puritans have nunneries? I'll have her placed in one."

"No, I don't think so. But it doesn't matter. She's done her worst and has lost the battle. Let her stew in her own miserable concoction."

"I don't suppose I can do more than put the fear of God into her—which I intend to do. Let her face hellfire for lying about her innocent niece. But Philip is a different matter. Never mind, I'll find the box myself."

He reached under the seat and removed a flat mahogany box. He opened it to reveal two ornately etched French dueling pistols.

"No, Braden—no!" Amanda stared horrified at the weapons. "I never realized how . . . how serious you are about this."

"Deadly serious."

"But he's my own flesh and blood. No matter what he's done, I beg you not to kill him. And besides, there's risk for you too. Haven't you faced death enough these past days?"

He studied her for a long moment, his blue eyes darkly contemplative. "I'll keep your request in mind. But only because I love you and don't want this conflict to come between us. Still, I must confront him and see where it leads. Wait here, Mandy. I don't want you in the middle of whatever happens."

Without responding, she climbed into the driver's seat and picked up the reins. "I'll soon be back," she said coolly. "I do hope you'll control your devilish temper until I return."

"Come down from there, Amanda. Where are you going?"

She urged the tired horse forward and left Braden standing in the middle of the street.

Chagrined, he watched the carriage turn the corner and disappear from sight. Would he ever understand women? he asked himself. Probably not. Tucking the box under his arm, he mounted the steps and pounded on the door.

The houseboy opened it a crack.

Braden pushed past him. "I'm here to see Philip Sheffield or Madam Sheffield," he demanded.

"Who is it?" a woman's voice called from the parlor. "I'm receiving no one."

"You're receiving *me*," Braden said sharply and strode into the room.

Sara's face turned white at the sight of him. Her fingers fluttered at her throat. "Captain, what . . . what are you doing here?"

"Actually, Madam Sheffield, I've come looking for your nephew."

"But we thought you . . . and Amanda—"

"Were dead—executed by now—making Philip and you the heirs to her modest fortune? It took me no more than a few minutes to figure out what he had to gain by her death. But there's something you didn't know. If she had been hanged, her inheritance would have been claimed by the Crown. You're shocked, I see."

"But . . . she didn't hang? But that's . . . ah . . . wonderful. Where is the dear girl? I'll welcome her home."

"She's out of your reach, you bigoted bag of deceit."

"But . . . how did she survive?" Sara managed to croak.

"Your friend Cotton Mather personally came to her defense—and to mine. We owe him our lives."

"What?" She half rose from her chair. "Cotton Mather? Defending a witch? I don't believe it."

He resisted the urge to shake her. Between tight lips, he said coldly, "Don't ever again refer to my *wife* as a witch. If anyone deserves that title, 'tis *you,* madam."

"Your . . . wife?"

"We were married yesterday by Reverend Mather. Whatever else he's done, the reverend has been a blessing to us. I hope history judges him fairly. Now, if you'll direct me to your nephew, I'll leave you to contemplate your corrupt, lecherous nature. Be grateful you have time to repent. If you were a man, I'd send you to meet your Creator before teatime today."

Her hands were shaking. She appeared about to swoon. "Philip . . . has . . . gone to the mill," she stammered. "He was going back to Virginia as soon as—"

"As soon as he got the money from the sale of the jewels?"

"Well . . . I don't know. We hadn't discussed . . ."

"The hell you hadn't!" he stormed. "There's another lie to add to your confession. I'm taking one of your horses and riding to the mill. Farewell, Madam Sheffield. I consider it my good fortune to take my leave of you—forever." He wheeled toward the door, then looked back to say, "I suggest you not delay tea waiting for Philip to return. In all likelihood, you'll next see him at the morgue."

As he left, he heard Sara Sheffield crumple into her chair and begin a frantic prayer. Her discomfort was well deserved, he thought without regret.

In minutes he saddled a startled carriage horse and galloped toward the mill at the end of the pond. He passed along cobbled streets lined with stately residences, then a few scattered farm tracts before he saw the mill, with its massive wheel churning the Charles River into power for grist. He also saw a dapper Philip Sheffield tying his horse to the hitching rail outside.

He reined up in a swirl of dust and called to Philip, "I say, Mister Sheffield, I'd like a word with you."

Philip turned and froze in his tracks. "My God, Jesus . . . Christ . . ." he sputtered.

Braden swung down from his mount and grasped Philip by his snowy linen collar. "I understand your surprise. I've already explained the circumstances of my survival to Goodwife Sara; I don't intend to waste my breath on you. Let it suffice that I am here as a free man, and Amanda is free as well. We were both found innocent—no thanks to you."

"But . . . but . . . I only did what I thought was right. Why, Aunt Sara told me—"

"Goddamn you, Sheffield, I'm sick of unholy accusations." He released his hold and held up the box he carried in his left hand. "I have pistols here. You can thank your sister's pleas and my honor as a gentleman and an officer of the Royals that I didn't shoot you on the spot and leave the country. But I'll give you a chance to defend yourself." He opened the box and held it under Philip's gaping eyes.

"But . . . *now?*" Philip choked. "No seconds . . . no witnesses?"

"That is correct. The pistols are perfectly matched and there is the load. Take your choice and we'll stand away ten paces. Hurry now, I've got a ship waiting for me in the harbor."

"My God, Hamilton, please. This isn't a duel. It's . . . it's . . ."

"An execution? Then you *do* remember my marksmanship from the old days. Good. Let me just mention that Amanda would have hanged by her fair slender neck, while I, Mister Sheffield, was about to spend my last days with a ton of stone on my chest. Consider yourself lucky, dear fellow. A pistol ball in the heart is quick and easy."

"Dammit, Hamilton, please don't do this. I'll . . . do whatever you say. She can have Briarfield—anything. I'll go to the Indies. I have friends there. Just please, please don't kill me." He was blubbering by the time he finished.

Braden stared at him in utter disgust. "Hmm. Perhaps there's some merit in your suggestion. Mandy loves Briarfield. She would enjoy restoring the place, I'd wager. She might even—"

"She can have it. I'll sign it over to her right now." He fumbled in his satin waistcoat and produced a scrap of paper. "They'll have a pen in the mill house—and someone to witness my signature. I beg you, Hamilton. I really hate farming. Always have. I swear I'll never bother her again."

They were interrupted by the arrival of a sweating horse pulling a carriage—driven by a stern-faced Amanda.

She dropped the reins and hopped down from the seat. Ignoring Braden, she held up a pouch, then tossed it to Philip.

Startled, he failed to make the catch. The pouch fell to the ground and spilled open. Out tumbled dozens of sparkling jewels, some mounted, some loose and rolling in the dust. "What's this?" he asked, shifting his puzzled look between Amanda and the treasure.

"The fortune you've dreamed of for so long, dear Brother. A fortune I obtained for you by marrying the Marquess of Staffordshire—God rest his soul. It's to be used to salvage Briarfield. And I hope it will settle the matter between you and Lord Hamilton. It's yours, Philip, but only if you decline to duel with Braden."

Braden laughed. He guffawed. He held his sides and roared.

Amanda's eyebrows lifted. When she could be heard, she asked, "What's so amusing, my lord?"

"You're about to waste your fortune on this coward, my dear girl. Not only has he already declined to duel, but he agreed to sign over Briarfield to you."

"He did?" she said, amazed. "He gave up the plantation—the finest in Virginia?"

"It seemed fair to him," said Braden, "in exchange for his life."

She put her hands on her hips. "Well, I declare. Philip, you're disgusting. I claim no kin to you at all."

"Suits me," he said sharply. "I'll take the jewels, since you've been so kind to offer them, and sign the place over to you right now. Then I'm off to the Indies."

"Wait a minute," interjected Braden. "Amanda, you don't have to give him anything. Our bargain was to trade his life for the plantation."

"Oh, let him have the jewels. After all, he is my brother, and he did help our father in the early days. Then I'll have no feelings of guilt over possessing Briarfield, and the marquess's agreement with Philip will be honored."

"If you like, my love," Braden agreed, giving her an admiring look. He closed the box containing the pistols. "All right, Sheffield—into the mill. You can sign and we'll go our separate ways. Your sister and I are eager to be off on our wedding trip."

The subtle announcement of his sister's marriage was lost on Philip as he marched solemnly into the mill house.

Amanda perched on the downy coverlet of Braden's bunk in the diminutive but comfortably furnished captain's cabin. She would have a few more minutes to wait while he skillfully sailed the sloop past the jutting cape, with its beacon marking land's end and the open sea beyond.

A short time ago, she had bathed and washed her hair with help from Coco. Now she watched the disappearing Massachusetts coastline, twinkling with myriads of tiny lights against the soft lavender of the coming night. Her emotions tumbled one after the other as she thought of all she'd experienced there—the friends and enemies she'd made, how close she had come to death, the bittersweet wedding, and the poignant and passionate night in Braden's arms.

She put her hands on her bare stomach, exposed by the open front of her silk negligee. Did they create a baby last night? Possibly—but if not, there would be all the nights of love yet to come. Never had she known such supreme peace and joy.

The door opened and Braden entered. He had shed his blue coat and wore his customary seaman's shirt and rugged breeches.

Through the gathering dusk, he paused to look at her. "If I'd known you were waiting in such alluring attire, my love, I'd have relinquished the wheel sooner."

Lying back in the softness, she curled her arms into the pillow over her head. The seductive movement dislodged Persephone, who had just settled down for a nap. The cat flipped its tail and left the pillow it had claimed as its own, meandered along the bed and snuggled against Amanda's side.

She stroked the delicate fur head and chuckled along with Braden. "How fortunate you are, Captain. You have two girls in your bed. One for certain is an expectant mother—the other, just perhaps."

Smiling, his shirt removed, he stretched out beside her and propped his head on his palm. With his free hand, he caressed her stomach and her breasts. "There is certainly some question, Lady Hamilton. I feel nothing new there beneath your flesh. I think we'd be wise to give it another try."

"Braden . . ."

"Yes, my dear," he murmured while his lips touched her ear.

"You're certain Tamara is happy with the Spaniard?"

"I guarantee it."

"I'm glad." She gently stroked his shoulder. "And I must thank you again for changing the name of the sloop from *Wind Rose* to *Amanda Joy*. This is the loveliest ship I've ever seen."

"It gave me great pleasure to do so, little one."

"You must have ordered the name change done while you were in prison."

"Yes."

"But you didn't know if you would live or if we would be here together."

"I knew I would be here with you, if only in spirit. And I was sure you'd like the name—no more storms, with my heart in the safe harbor of our love."

She rolled over to look at him, once again disrupting Persephone. With a resigned meow, the cat left the bed to find comfort on its own cushion nearby.

With a sigh of contentment, she slowly traced one finger along his finely chiseled cheek and across his chin. "I'm sorry I was jealous. I caused a great deal of trouble. It seems so foolish now, after all we've been through."

"I was also at fault, little one. I will try to be more understanding of your fiery nature. Of course, if you're completely unreasonable . . ."

She chuckled and poked him in the ribs.

With a playful snarl, he pinned back her arms and nuzzled the hollow of her throat with his day's growth of beard.

Laughing, she twisted in mock resistance.

Beyond the stern windows, the azure twilight of evening flowed into the swells of the jade-green Atlantic. The only sounds in the gently swaying cabin were the soft purring of Persephone and the rhythmic splash and throb of the water against the hull of the sleek vessel. Wrapped in each other's arms, Lord and Lady Hamilton were aware only of each other.

With her sails billowing in the brisk winds of evening, the *Amanda Joy* headed south toward the Chesapeake of Virginia, her only port of call before turning east— toward Bermuda—and home.

Perplext no more with Human or Divine,
To-morrow's tangle to the winds resign. . . .

—*Rubaiyat* by Omar Khayyám

Dear Readers,

Many thanks to each of you who gave my first novel, *Ride the Wind,* such a warm reception. I appreciated hearing from you, and will continue to respond personally to your letters. By coincidence, *Wind Rose* takes place in the same eventful year, though in the New World instead of the Old. I have done my best to portray the life and times of this period as accurately as possible, the romance as well as the hardships and prejudices. I hope you will enjoy traveling back with me to this dramatic era.

Krista Janssen

Please write to Krista at:
223 N. Guadalupe,
Suite 237
Santa Fe, NM 87501